ACCLAIM FOR ANDREW VACHSS AND

PAIN MANAGEMENT

"The Burke books make the noir-film genre look practically pastel. . . . The plot-driven stories churn with energy and a memorable gallery of the walking wounded." —*The Philadelphia Inquirer*

"Vachss is in the first rank of American crime writers." —*The Plain Dealer*

"A terrific book. . . . This is a series unlike any other, by a writer who has never lost his commitment to the innocent." —Martha Grimes

"There's no way to put a [Vachss book] down once you've begun. . . . The plot hooks are engaging and the one-liners pierce like bullets." —*Detroit Free Press*

"The world Andrew Vachss has created—Burke's world—is inimitably dark, feverish, nightmarish, and righteous. *Pain Management* is a compulsively page-turning journey into the hellish outer regions of the human psyche. Read it and be changed." —Jonathan Kellerman

"Vachss's voice, as always, is one of the most distinctive in crime fiction—lean and tough." —*Publishers Weekly*

"Andrew Vachss has become a cult favorite, and for good reason." —*Cosmopolitan*

"Vachss's writing is like a dark roller coaster ride of fear, love and hate." —*The Times-Picayune*

"When the history of crime fiction in the twentieth century comes to be written, if there is any justice, the name of Andrew Vachss will be up front, up-close and flagged up as very dangerous. . . . His writing is raw, jagged-edged and staccato and also spookily sexy." —*The Telegraph*

"I've always been a great fan of Andrew Vachss's work, but I'm an even bigger fan now. *Pain Management* is wonderful! He's taken the series in sharp new directions that amaze, entertain, and dazzle us with his genius." —Joe R. Lansdale

"Vachss seems bottomlessly knowledgeable about the depth and variety of human twistedness." —*The New York Times*

"Many writers try to cover the same ground as Vachss. A handful are as good. None are better." —*People*

ANDREW VACHSS

PAIN MANAGEMENT

Andrew Vachss has been a federal investigator in sexually transmitted diseases, a social caseworker, a labor organizer, and has directed a maximum-security prison for youthful offenders. Now a lawyer in private practice, he represents children and youths exclusively. He is the author of numerous novels, including the Burke series, two collections of short stories, and wide variety of other material including song lyrics, poetry, graphic novels, and a "children's book for adults." His books have been translated into twenty different languages and his work has appeared in *Parade*, *Antaeus*, *Esquire*, *The New York Times*, and numerous other forums. He lives and works in New York City and the Pacific Northwest.

The dedicated Web site for Vachss and his work is www.vachss.com.

ALSO BY ANDREW VACHSS

Flood

Strega

Blue Belle

Hard Candy

Blossom

Sacrifice

Shella

Down in the Zero

Born Bad

Footsteps of the Hawk

False Allegations

Safe House

Choice of Evil

Everybody Pays

Dead and Gone

Only Child

PAIN MAN

AGEMENT▶

ANDREW
VACHSS

VINTAGE CRIME/BLACK LIZARD
VINTAGE BOOKS
A [illegible]N OF RANDOM HOUSE, INC.

FIRST VINTAGE CRIME/BLACK LIZARD EDITION, OCTOBER 2002

 Published in the United States by Vintage Books, a division of Random House, Inc., New York, and simultaneously in Canada by Random House of Canada Limited, Toronto. Originally published in hardcover in the United States by Alfred A. Knopf, a division of Random House, Inc., New York, in 2001.

The Library of Congress has cataloged the Knopf edition as follows:
Vachss, Andrew H.
Pain management / Andrew Vachss.—1st ed.
p. cm.
ISBN: 0-375-41322-7
1. Burke (Fictitious character)—Fiction. 2. Private investigators—Oregon—Portland—Fiction. 3. Pain—Treatment—Fiction. 4. Missing children—Fiction. 5. Portland (Or.)—Fiction. 6. Drug traffic—Fiction. I. Title.
PS3572.A33 P35 2001
813'.54—dc21 2001029868

Vintage ISBN: 0-375-72647-0

Book design by Virginia Tan

www.vintagebooks.com

Printed in the United States of America
10 9 8 7 6 5 4 3

for Skot Travis <Burke111>

defender of every child but himself. manager of everyone's pain but his own. a warrior who finally fell. down in the Zero, still searching.

give Pansy a marrow bone for me, partner.

PAIN

MANAGEMENT

The first time you end up Inside, you think serving your sentence is going to take forever. But soon you learn: no matter how much time you have to do, some parts of it never take long.

The Aryan clenched his fists, glancing down at his cartoon-huge forearms as if to reassure himself all that cable-tendoned muscle was real. He was on the downside of steroid burnout, dazed and dangerous.

The Latino wouldn't know a kata from the Koran, but he was an idiot savant of violence, with the kinetic intelligence of a pit bull.

They faced each other in a far corner of the prison yard, screened off from the ground-level guards by the never-intersecting streams of cons flowing around them.

Any experienced gun-tower hack could read the swirls below him, see something was up. But the convicts knew the duty roster better than the warden. They knew the tower closest to the action was manned by a tired old guy with thirty years on the job and a good supply of gash magazines. All they had to do was keep the noise down.

"Only play is to stay away." The Prof spoke low to me.

"Yeah," I said. "Larsen's not built for distance. If Jester gets him tired, he can—"

"*Our* play, fool!" the Prof hissed at me. "The fuse is lit; it's time to split."

We faded, working our way back through the crowd sneaking glances at the duel. By the time the whistle blew and the first shots sounded from the tower, we were standing on either side of the sally port as the Goon Squad rushed through, hammering wildly at every con within reach.

Larsen didn't run. He was facedown on the filthy asphalt, Jester's shank protruding from the back of his neck. The matador had gone in over the horns.

They locked the whole joint down, tore up everyone's house looking for weapons. But all that did was simmer the pot more, as plots and counterplots festered into a Big House brew of pus and poison. Usually it was black against white, with brown trying to stay out of the crossfire. But this one had rolled out different.

Larsen rode with a motorcycle gang; there were a lot of bikers Inside then. And Jester had been flying colors at sixteen, when he'd taken the life that had bought him a life sentence. The kid he'd killed was another PR, from a rival club, but that didn't matter anymore.

Back then, when it came to prison war, race trumped tribe every time.

You never got a choice about that. The cons had all kinds of names for areas of the prison—Times Square, Blues Alley, D Street—but I never heard of one named Switzerland.

"On the bricks, niggers do the paper-bag trick," the Prof told me. "But Inside, you can't hide."

"What's the paper-bag trick?" I asked him. The Prof had been schooling me for a while, so I didn't even blink at a black man saying "nigger." I knew words were clay—they took their real meaning from the sculptor.

"I ain't talking about passing, now," the Prof cautioned me. "It's a class thing. Motherfuckers'll hold a paper bag next to they faces and look in the mirror, okay? If they darker than the bag, there ain't but so far up the ladder they can climb, understand?"

"I . . . guess."

"Nah, you *don't* get it, son. I'm talking about the *colored* ladder, see? Mothers want they daughters to marry light. They know high-society niggers don't want no darkies at their parties."

I just nodded, waiting for mine, knowing it was coming.

"Yeah," he said, softly. "It's different with white folks. Color ain't the thing. Boy like you, you was *born* trash. You could be light as one of them albinos; wouldn't make no difference."

I knew it was true.

By the time they ended the lockdown and we could mix again, the clay had hardened. Larsen's crew called it for personal, put out the word. They weren't going race-hunting. They only wanted Jester.

I guess the hacks wanted him, too. They never bing-ed him for the killing, and they knew Jester would never take a voluntary PC. That section of solitary was marked "Protective Custody," but the road sign was just there to fool the tourists. Cons called it Punk City. Jester, he'd rather swan-dive into hell wearing gasoline swim trunks.

For a lot of the Latin gang kids I knew coming up, it wasn't whether you died that counted, it was *how* you died.

When Jester hit the yard, he wasn't alone. There was a fan of Latinos behind him, unfurling from his shoulders like a cape in the wind.

"Jester don't mind dying, but he sure mind motherfuckers *trying,*" the Prof said out of the side of his mouth.

The motorcycle guys stood off to one side, watching. Everyone gave the two crews room, measuring the odds. There were a few more of the Latins, but they all looked like they'd come from the same cookie-cutter—short and slim to the point of being feline. The motorcycle guys were carrying a lot more beef. Question was: What *else* were they carrying?

"Only steel is real," the Prof said, summing it up.

The yard buzzed with its life-force: rumor. Was it true that the hacks had looked the other way, let the whites re-arm? Had the search squad really found a few live .22 rounds during the shakedown? What about the word that they were going to transfer a new bunch of bikers in from Attica and Dannemora to swell the ranks?

Jester turned and faced his crew, deliberately offering his back to the whites. One of them started forward; stopped when their leader held up his hand.

It wasn't going to be today.

And the next three weeks went by quiet.

The motorcycle guys trapped me in a corridor near the license plate shop. My fault—I should have been race-war alert, but I'd let the quiet lull me.

"How much?" their leader, a guy named Vestry, asked me.

"How much for what?" I said, stalling, but honestly puzzled, too.

"For the piece, man. Don't be playing dumb with us. You're all alone here."

"I don't know what you're—"

"Your boy, Oz, he's the guy what makes all the best shanks. So we figure he's got—"

"The Man shut him down. You know that. Oz don't keep a stash. Makes them to order and hands them over soon as they're done."

"We're not talking about no fucking pig-stickers, Burke. We want the piece. If the hacks found bullets, there's got to be a gun. And, word is, it's yours."

"The word is bullshit."

"Look, man, we're willing to pay. Or did the spics get to you first?"

"I'm not in this," I told him. "If I had a piece, I'd sell it to you. You know I'm short—you think I'd bag my go-home behind getting caught with a fucking *gun*?"

"We know you got it," Vestry said, stubborn-stupid, stepping closer. A sound came from the men behind him—the trilling of a pod of orcas who'd spotted a sea-lion pup far from the herd.

One of them said "Oh!" just as I heard a sound like a popgun and saw his hands go to his face. He stumbled to one knee, said, "I'm . . . ," and fell over.

Another popgun sound. Vestry grabbed at his neck like a bee stung him. But blood spurted out between his fingers.

Everybody ran. Everybody that could.

"It just came out of the shadows," I told them. "Like it was a ghost or something."

"At least two ghosts, then," Oz said. "Vestry made it to the hospital in time; the other guy didn't. But there were two shots."

"So—not a zip," the Prof said, thoughtfully. "Ain't no way to reload one of those suckers that fast."

"Or two zips. And two shooters," Darryl said.

Everyone went quiet for a while. Then the Prof said, "I think Schoolboy nailed it the first time."

We all looked at him.

"It was a ghost," the little man said. "And we all know his name."

The Prof was on the money. So, by the time Vestry came up to me on the yard—alone, with his hands held away from his body—to ask his question, I had the answer ready.

"Five hundred dollars?" he said, stunned. He patted the yellowing tape around his neck that held the stitches in place, as if that would make his ears work better.

"Soft money," I told him. "No smokes, no trades, no favors. Folding cash."

"There ain't that much soft in this whole—"

"You got chapters on the bricks," I said quietly. "Take up a collection."

I guess they raised the money. When they racked the bars for the morning count a couple of weeks later, Jester didn't move. Died in his sleep, word was. Maybe something he ate.

"I already paid half," Vestry said the next day. "In front. How do I know he did that spic? I heard the docs don't know *what* killed him."

"You know who you're dealing with," I told him. "You don't come up with the other half, that's what they'll be saying about you."

The prison library was always full of guys working on their own appeals. And jailhouse lawyers working for cigarettes, or dope, or the use of some wolf's punk. It was the DMZ, neutral turf, off-limits for violence. Any problems there, the Man would be only too happy to close it down. So it stayed peaceful.

I spent a lot of time there, reading with my thick little pocketbook-sized dictionary next to me. You could make steady scores writing letters for guys, especially to pen-pal women they were trying to pull. I was known to be pretty good at it, even as young as I was.

I never saw him coming. Nobody ever did. One minute I was all alone. The next it was as if a cold wind had blown past, and then Wesley was sitting beside me.

"They paid," is all he said.

And then he was gone.

I was cut loose before Wesley was. I went back to thieving. When Wesley got out, he went back to what he did.

One time, they didn't pay him.

Wesley settled accounts with them all, and then he was gone again.

Dead and gone, people said.

But the whisper-stream still vibrated at the sound of his name. Odds on dead? Pretty good. On gone? No takers.

Homicides still happened. And when they happened to certain people, in certain ways, when no one ever got popped for them . . .

I wondered what they whispered about me now. I'd been dead and gone myself for a couple of years. Gunned down in the abandoned flatlands of Hunts Point, dumped in front of the ER unconscious, in a coma for . . . a long time. When I'd finally come around, the cops were there. My prints had marked me. They knew who I was. Only problem was, *I* didn't know who I was.

One of the bullets had scored my brain when I took one in the head—the one that broke the binocular connection between my eyes—and my memory was gone. I kept telling them that, anyway.

I'll never know if they believed me. Whether they thought I'd finally escaped that hospital, or had just wandered off in a brain-damaged sleepwalk one night.

Later on, a Russian gangster got himself blown away right in his own restaurant. Maybe the police knew something then, provided they knew he was the same guy who'd hired me to middleman a swap: a bag of cash for a kidnapped kid.

The swap had turned out to be an ambush. The only thing exchanged was gunfire. I took some of it. My partner Pansy took the rest of it. Died with our enemy's blood in her mouth.

As soon as I got myself into good enough shape to get around, I met Dmitri in his restaurant. I told him I needed the names of the people who'd hired him. He told me that would be bad for business. Took a professional's stance—he'd been paid; he did a job. Had no idea the whole thing was a hit. He was sorry about it; but, after all, I'd survived, so what was the beef?

"They killed my dog," I told him.

"Your . . . *dog*?" he said.

I didn't—couldn't—try to explain Pansy to him. Just told him

I was ready to kill him, right then and there, if he didn't give me the names. He told me I was bluffing. His last words.

But, considering the power struggle going on in that section of Little Odessa back then, the cops could never be sure.

Even later, they found a severed hand at the bottom of a Dumpster. Just the bones, actually, not the flesh. And, in the same place, a pistol with my thumbprint on it. That was enough for the cops. They figured my string had run out and I'd ended up the same place I'd started from.

By that time, I was on the move. Somebody had wanted me dead. Went to a lot of trouble, spent a lot of coin. Maybe they thought they'd gotten the job done, maybe not. I only had two choices: hide or hunt.

If it hadn't been for what they'd done to Pansy, I might have stayed invisible.

When the hunt was finished, so was I. Even Mama wasn't pressing me to come back . . . not for a while. My face wasn't the same—bullets and the surgery it takes to save you from them will do that—but my prints were.

Maybe NYPD bought the severed-hand story. They should—it was one of their own who had pulled my thumbprint from inside Mama's, transferred it to the pistol. But that didn't matter, really. I wasn't a fugitive. My people checked. No wants, no warrants, no BOLOs, federal or state.

Probably safe to go back, they told me. But maybe better to stay where I was for a while. Rest and rebuild.

Sure.

Oregon's a good place to hide. People don't *expect* you to be born local. None of that "You ain't from around here" stuff you get in some other places.

In Oregon, they bitch about the California money vamping north and buying up all the good real estate, but they come all over themselves when they think about how much their houses are worth *now.* They correct you when you pronounce their state "Are-a-gon." They want you to say "Origun," or something like that. But the city—Portland—is just like New York. Or Chicago, or L.A., or Atlanta. It rains a little more . . . although they have a lot more weather reports than they have weather. The people are a touch more polite, the buildings don't climb quite as high. There's plenty of traffic, but a whole lot less rage in the drivers.

Still, they got gangbangers, dope fiends, skinheads, homeless, hookers, and hustlers right alongside all the upscale restaurants and cultural opportunities. And probably more strip joints per square mile than any place outside of Bangkok.

The city even has outer boroughs. Vancouver is to Portland what Brooklyn is to Manhattan—even has a bridge you have to cross to get there. And they feature plenty of those licensed-to-steal "title loan" shops.

South of Portland, the coastline is an ever-shifting blend of retirees from other states and tourists rolling through in waves of RVs.

Eastern Oregon has a lot of mountains, a lot of small towns. A lot of pots brewing, from Christian Identity to crank.

Disappearing is easy. Connecting is what's hard.

Gem's key clacked in the front door's heavy deadbolt. I didn't move from where I'd been sitting, staring out the top-floor back window at a thin slice of empty sky.

She walked across the wood-planking floor of the loft, tossing her purse onto the futon, unbuttoning her blouse.

"I thought you were going shopping," I said, looking at her empty hands.

"I did. For many hours."

"They were—what—all out or something?"

"Ah," she said, doing something to the waist of her skirt. It fell to the floor. She stepped out of it, came closer to me. "The word is different for men and women."

"What word?"

"Shopping. When you say 'shopping,' you mean to go out to buy something. A specific thing, yes?"

"Sure."

"When *I* say 'shopping,' I mean to go and look."

"You mean for bargains and stuff?"

"No. I like the looking. I like to know I *could* buy things. I do not *have* to buy them."

"Oh."

"Yes, you are so *very* interested in this, Burke."

"What difference?"

"I do not understand," she said, kneeling next to where I was sitting.

I ran my hand through her thick black hair. "What would it matter if I faked like I was interested?"

"You asked me the question."

"I did. I was just . . . I don't know . . . maybe being polite. You're right. That's not me. I won't do it again."

"Huh!" she said, bending forward and nipping at the web of flesh between my thumb and forefinger. Harder than she usually does.

While I was waiting, I looked around for a score. There's a couple of casinos south of Portland. I borrowed a black Corvette from Flacco and Gordo—Gem's partners—got into some halfass-flash clothes, kept my sunglasses on inside, playing a two-bit high roller, dropped some random cash. Every con who came up when I did dreamed of knocking over a racetrack or a casino. All that absolutely untraceable cash. I owed it to them to scope it out.

But it turned out to be like most convict's dreams. Right there . . . but out of reach. I'd been hearing that "It's not for you" song my whole life.

When I graduated from gunpoint hijacking to stinging and scamming, I realized you need the same things to be successful in either game—a complicated mix of anonymity and rep. In Portland, I was even farther under the radar than I'd been in New York—I didn't exist. And my name on the street wasn't worth the quarter any skell would drop in a pay-phone slot if he thought I was worth something to the cops.

I didn't have Max the Silent at my back. I didn't have the Prof and Clarence by my side. I didn't have the Mole mixing his potions in his underground bunker. I didn't have Michelle, didn't have Mama.

But even if I risked it and went back to them, I wouldn't have Wolfe.

And I wouldn't have Pansy, ever again.

When you're away—Inside, I mean—your people don't visit you. Not if they all have priors. That's not how it's done. I took a fall for Max and the Mole a long time ago. Well, not in place of them—I was going down anyway. But I held off the other side until they could get gone.

It had been a perfect hijacking. A big fat stash of dope, quick and clean. We didn't want the dope; we wanted to sell it back to the same mob family we stole it from. Everybody wins. Nobody gets hurt.

I set up the meet in an abandoned subway tunnel. Only, instead of silk suits, the men who showed up were all dressed in blue.

No, the cops hadn't cracked the case. The mob had sold me to a few of their friends, that was all. Maybe they thought they could get their heroin back from the police evidence locker. Wouldn't have been the first time.

A bouncing grenade with the pin still in it was enough to convince the law that a frontal assault was out of the question. They knew they had a heavily armed lunatic on their hands, so they decided to do the smart thing and negotiate.

But they only had one end of the tunnel blocked, and the longer we talked, the safer my people got. Everybody made it out. Everybody but me.

I did the time without visitors. But never without backup. Between people on the street who would do anything—*anything*—for me, and a steady stream of money on the books, I was golden.

Besides, I was young then. Going back to prison was like an alumni reunion. If it was some college, I guess they'd be checking the parking lot, see what kind of car you drove up in. Inside, you got your status from the crime that brought you there. That, and from coming back by yourself.

That was me, back then. I wanted to be a con's con. High-status. Good crime, good time.

I remembered some of those good times. The manic rush of high-risk scheming for a little more territory, the gambling coups, making home-brew, handball, story-swapping, boxing, lie-telling, concocting elaborate escape plots that you were never going to try . . .

When you start getting nostalgic for prison, you're never far from going back.

"I can't stay here," I told Gem the next morning.

"I know."

"Then why didn't you—?"

She gave me one of her eloquent shrugs.

I expected her to say she'd follow me anywhere, like she had before. Tried to beat her to the punch by telling her I'd send for her when I found a place that was safe.

"No," she said, soft but flat. "There is no place for me where you are going."

"Not yet, maybe. But when I'm—"

"Ah, you will never be at peace, Burke. You're not just restless and bored, you are depressed."

"Sad. Not depressed. Sad."

"As you say."

"Gem . . . I just can't . . . work here."

"You did those . . . jobs I found for you."

"There isn't enough of it. I need a score. A big one. And I couldn't even put a string together here. I don't know anyone."

She opened her mouth to say something, but I put two fingers across her lips, said: "No, I couldn't bring my own people out here. They'd be as lost as I am."

"A bank is a bank," she said, a deep vein of stubbornness inside her precise voice.

"A bank? Little girl, bank jobs are for dope fiends and morons. There's no money in them anymore. Not in the tellers' drawers, anyway. Anything else takes an inside man. And out here, I could never—"

"You went down to the casino . . ."

"And crapped out. There is no way you could hit a place like that. It's way out in the sticks. It'd have to be a goddamn commando raid—helicopter on the roof, a dozen men, all that. Cost a fortune just to put it together, and the take wouldn't be worth it. It's a nice little operation, but it's not carrying the kind of action worth that investment."

"Where is the money, then?"

"Armored cars are the best, if you're talking pure rough-off. But the deal with them is, you've got to be ready to kill a couple of people, minimum."

"Oh," is all Gem said. But I knew what she was thinking.

"Not for nothing," I told her.

She just nodded.

"What I've got to do is put together a scam. A big one. Or go back to grifting, a little piece at a time."

"You could do that here."

"I could. Maybe. What's wrong with that little-piece-at-a-time thing is that you're going to be dropped, sooner or later. I'm a two-time loser, both for what they call 'armed-violent' felonies today. I get tapped for even some little nonsense, I'd pull the same time I'd get for homicide. They'd bitch me for sure."

"Bitch you?"

"Ha*bitch*ual offender. That's a life-top in most states. Even without that, it's double figures, guaranteed. Time I got out, I'd be ready for Social Security—"

"—only you are not eligible," she finished for me.

She didn't drop it easy. Never thought she would; that's not Gem.

"I have a goal," she said. "A certain sum of money. When I have it, I will stop what . . . I do. Is it the same for you?"

I caught her depth-charge eyes on me, didn't even make the effort to lie. "No, child. I've *had* money. Not now, but once." Thinking of the fortune I'd spent tracking the humans who'd killed Pansy. Down here, where I live, people don't save their money for a rainy day. They save it for revenge. "And it didn't make any difference," I told her.

Days passed. I felt like I'd spent the night on a bench in a Greyhound terminal . . . and woke up without the cash for a ticket to anyplace else.

Gem found some occasional work for me. You'd think you have to know a city real well to do what I do, but that's not true. Take New York—you can't ever really know it. Sure, some of the old-time cabbies can find addresses City Hall doesn't even know exist—although most of the new ones can't find any street above Ninety-sixth or below Fourteenth. But that's not the same as going *into* the buildings. Or, worse, into their basements.

New York's a shape-shifting demon, never letting you get your bearings before it morphs again. A slum block turns into six-figure co-ops overnight. A neighborhood vanishes like a migrant laborer moving on to the next harvest. A mini-city rises out of the river, built on landfill. Times Square still sucks tourist dollars, but now they come to *take* pictures, not to buy them.

Don't get me wrong. New York is still one place where you can buy or sell anything that exists on this planet. But the trading posts keep moving around, and the maps are useless before their ink dries. You're always starting from scratch.

And always scratching.

I had tracked the Russian couple whose kid had been kidnapped—the one I was supposed to exchange the cash for—from Chicago to a mail drop in Vancouver. But I needed a note written in Russian to spook them into the open. And someone fluent enough to dialogue with them if the trick worked.

I found Gem through Mama's network. She signed on. Did the job. But instead of walking away, she'd stayed with me all the way to the end . . . out past the twelve-mile limit.

Somewhere along the trail, Gem decided she was my wife. I'd never heard that word from a woman before. Love, yes. Two women had died for my love, and another had taken it with her when she went back to Japan. Even babies, women I'd been with had talked about. But I can't make babies. Had myself fixed a long time ago.

Gem knew I wasn't going anywhere near *any* license. I'd been registered since birth. Born a suspect, then tracked by the fucking State until I learned how to live under its radar. Gem didn't care. Sometimes she called me Burke, sometimes "husband."

The ID I have says I'm Wayne Askew. I've got a full set—passport, driver's license, Social Security, credit cards . . . all perfect. I've never used them around here. Got them from Wolfe, the beautiful ex-prosecutor with white wings in her long dark hair and gray gunfighter's eyes. She'd gone outlaw when her ethics got in the way of the DA's ass-kissing. Now she was an info-trafficker, with some of the best contacts in the business.

What she'd never been was mine. I'd had my chance there. And, being myself, killed it.

Another reason not to go back to New York.

Gem had her own business, and I stayed out of it. I never worried about her. She'd survived the Khmer Rouge when she was a little girl, learning Russian from the strange men visiting the opium warlord, who'd kept her alive because she was so good at math. Making her plans, waiting. When the window opened a crack, Gem slid through like smoke, made her way here, and did . . . whatever she did . . . ever since.

I don't know where Gem found customers for the kind of stuff I got hired for. Like Kitty, the stripper whose boyfriend wanted her to work a different circuit. Harder work. More money. Kitty wasn't a genius, but she was smart enough to be scared.

Gem was the cutout. The stripper never met me. And the

boyfriend probably thought it was a random mugging that hospitalized him—if he could think at all; those head injuries are tricky things.

The cops wouldn't spend a lot of time on the case. The victim was such a nothing, who'd hire muscle just to fuck him up? Besides, the guy *was* black. With a white girlfriend. And with those roving gangs of skinheads in certain parts of town . . .

By the time the hospital kicked him loose, his property was long gone.

Gem found other work for me, and I did it. But when she first told me about the runaway, I pulled up short. They're a different game, runaways. One of the things I did—a thousand years ago, when I still believed I could be something more than what I am—was find people. When someone pays you to do that kind of work, you have a lot of choices. You can take the money and never look—just make up some nice stories for your "progress reports" until the mark calls it off. Or you can find the target, ask him what it's worth for you to go Stevie Wonder on whoever asked you to look.

Hell, you can even do the job, straight.

With kids, I always looked for real. I was young myself—still didn't get it, how things worked. People who hired me, they had nice homes, nice cars, nice lives. I knew why I'd run away myself when I was a kid. It's a POW's duty to escape. And to keep trying when they recapture you.

But, the way I figured it at first, kids from the nice homes, they ran away for the adventure. Their parents were worried about them. The streets were ugly. Things could happen. So I really looked.

When I found the kids, some were happy to see me. Relieved. They'd made their statement. Things would be different when I brought them back, they told me. But other kids, they told me different things.

Those kids I didn't bring back.

I found other places I could bring them. Some of the kids stayed. Some of them testified. And some of them went back to The Life.

After a while, I stopped doing that kind of stuff.

But I still knew how to do it. And I needed the work. So, when Gem told me about the money these people were putting up, I said okay.

Most of the clients who hired me for tracker jobs had no illusions. They knew what they were buying, and me not having a PI license was part of what they paid for. This thing Gem had set up was a different game—the clients had started at the other end of the tunnel.

Their kid was missing. A teenager. Soon as they figured out she was gone, they'd played it by the numbers. The cops had marked the case as a runaway, not a career-making abduction. Said they'd keep looking, but more than likely she'd already left town. . . .

When the parents took that bait, the detectives recommended a high-tech investigative firm, heavily staffed with ex-cops. Not a kickback, you understand. A "referral." Just another way the Man protects and serves. And some citizens are more grateful than others for the service.

But, despite all their licenses and contacts and computers, the firm drew a blank. Then the parents tried looking themselves. The father, anyway. The way it came back to me, he thought he had some special rapport with street kids. Never picked up his daughter's trail, but he got close enough to the whisper-stream that Gem picked up his.

So, when she told him I didn't have a license and had to be paid in cash, he not only didn't balk, he snapped at it.

People with money love the idea of men with shady connections and no particular aversion to violence working for them.

Telling their golf buddies that they "know a guy" raises their status a lot higher than a new luxo SUV. But citizens can't tell a working pro from a two-bit loudmouth, and *Consumer Reports* doesn't rate working criminals. So the buyers rely on the one standard of truth they've come to trust over the years—the movies.

Some chumps are more sophisticated than others. Gem gave me the readout on the father, said he was educated *and* intelligent. In our world, we know those are separate things—so we figured he wouldn't be looking for something out of *The Sopranos*.

Besides, Gem let him think he was hiring an ex-mercenary, not an ex-con. For some reason, citizens think mercs are an honorable breed of outlaw. White citizens, anyway.

I pulled to the curb in front of their house in a two-year-old dark-gray Crown Vic sedan. I was wearing an off-the-rack navy-blue suit and generic tie, clean-shaven, with my hair cut military-short. I couldn't do anything about my face, but it went nicely with the shoulder holster I'd make sure they got a good look at—it would help them convince themselves they were getting what they were paying for.

I gave the door a light two-knuckle rap. It opened so quickly I was sure my sense of having been watched from the window was on the money. The woman looked to be in her mid-forties, too thin for her age and frame, ash-blond hair carefully arranged to look casual, a salmon-colored dress belted at the waist with a silver chain, a matching set of links around her neck. Business pumps, sheer stockings, salon-level makeup. She had chemical eyes, but I couldn't tell what was on her prescription pad.

"Are you—?" she said.

"Yes, ma'am. Our appointment was for—"

"I know, but my husband won't be home for a couple of hours," the woman said. "He had to work late, and he didn't know how to reach you. . . ."

"That's all right," I said, stepping past her into a narrow hall. "I can get background from you, talk to him when he gets here."

"Background? We already told the police everything."

Didn't her husband tell her me and the cops weren't exactly colleagues? I kept my face expressionless, said, "Nobody ever does that," and moved toward the living room, bringing her along in my wake.

"Does . . . what?" she asked me, her hands tightly clasped at her waist, as if she was afraid of wringing them.

"Tells anyone 'everything.' There's no such thing."

"What are you saying?"

"Not what you think," I told her. "This isn't about you 'cooperating.' You're not a suspect. But one thing I learned from doing this for so long—until you really take them through it, people don't know *what* they know."

"I don't under—"

"Here's what that means," I interrupted her, helping myself to a seat in a Danish-modern chair opulently padded in black leather. "You have information. You might not *see* it as information, but I would. It's never the fault of the . . . source. It always comes down to the investigator not asking the right questions."

"And that's what you do?" she said, seating herself delicately on a love seat upholstered in what looked like tapestry cloth. If my chair suggested money, hers bludgeoned you with it.

Behind her was a giant blowup of the famous photograph of a young woman kneeling next to the body of a demonstrator gunned down by the National Guard at Kent State.

"It's part of what I do," I told her, more convinced than ever that her husband had told her I was some kind of "alternative" to the police, not the working thug he'd known he was hiring. "Because I don't have the same handicaps as the police, I can work differently."

"What . . . handicaps?"

"Cops have bosses. They have to answer for their stats. But, mostly, they're prisoners of their minds."

"Prisoners of their—?"

"Cops don't believe anyone actually runs away, ma'am. In their mind, the bodies are always in the basement."

Two sharp dots of brutal red burst out on her cheeks. She made a swallowing sound, reached out with one hand as if she'd lost her balance. I didn't move. Her hand found the arm of the love seat. She gathered herself slowly, eyes on the carpet.

"How could they—?"

"It's nothing personal," I said gently. "That's what I mean by them being prisoners of their minds. You can't expect them to overcome their conditioning."

"But they didn't act like that at *all,*" she said, an undercurrent of something like resentment in her voice. "They were almost . . . I don't know . . . dismissive, perhaps. The only thing they seemed really interested in was that damn computer."

"You mean your daughter's . . . ?"

"Yes. As soon as they found out she was online, they got very excited. They even got some specialist to examine it. He did a . . . 'hard-drive sweep,' I think they called it."

"Sure. Thinking maybe she got lured away by someone she met in a chat room."

"That's exactly what they said. But after they got done with the computer, they said there was nothing. They asked us about her friends, her teachers . . . but you could see their hearts weren't in it."

"How did they leave it, then?"

"They have Rose listed as a runaway. No evidence of foul play, that's what they said. One of them told us she'd probably turn up. The other didn't even seem to care *that* much."

"You expected . . . ?"

"More," she said, somewhere between bitter and disappointed. "I expected . . . more." She took a shallow breath, switched to a singsong voice, as if she were answering stupid questions: "No, our daughter was not a Goth, not a drug addict, not an alcoholic. No, our daughter was not involved with someone we didn't approve of. No, our daughter was not adopted . . . although why they thought that was important, I'll never know."

"Kids . . . teenagers—they're natural seekers. Adopted children sometimes get this romantic notion about their 'real' parents, especially when they hit puberty and start to have social problems. They get the idea that DNA can explain things happening in their lives. If they ask their adoptive parents questions, and don't get the answers they're looking for, sometimes they go looking for themselves. That's all they meant."

"Oh. Well, they *said* all the right things. They just didn't seem truly . . . concerned, I guess."

"Concern's just window dressing," I said. "It might make you feel better, but it wouldn't make them do a better job."

"My husband didn't trust them."

"Because . . . ?"

"Kevin doesn't trust the police," she said, making an apologetic noise in her throat.

"Any special reason?"

"He was almost forty when Rose was born," she said, as if that explained everything. When my expression told her it didn't, she went on: "Kevin was an antiwar activist."

"Ah. And now?"

"Now he's an architect," she said, pride rich in her voice. "A very fine one. With a very prestigious firm. But I wish he'd go out on his own."

"You sound as if that's something you've discussed more than a couple of times."

This time her laugh came from her chest. "Only about once a night for ten years. But Kevin makes so much money where he is. . . ."

"Did your daughter ever get involved in those arguments?"

"Rose? Don't be silly. And they weren't arguments. I just think Kevin could do better for himself professionally. Be more creative, choose his own projects. But he's more comfortable where he is."

"All right," I said, deliberately moving her away from any domestic unhappiness. "Could I have a look at Rose's room?"

"I . . . Kevin *hated* that."

"Letting the police search her room?"

"Yes. He said it was an invasion of Rose's privacy. *We* would never do such a thing ourselves. So it seemed . . . bizarre . . . that we would let anyone else do it."

"Well, given the circumstances . . ."

"I know. Kevin agreed, finally. But he just wasn't comfortable with the whole thing. He insisted on being there every second. Not to look at anything himself," she assured me, "to make certain the police were . . . respectful."

"He's a very protective father?"

"Oh, I wouldn't say *that*. I think I'm more . . . strict with Rose than he could ever be. Kevin believes too much parental control stifles a child."

"Do you want me to wait until your husband comes home to check Rose's room?" I asked her bluntly.

"No . . . I don't think so. I mean, Kevin knows you're coming. And, anyway, you're working for us, not the police, isn't that correct?"

"I've got nothing to do with the police," I said, making sure she got it. I knew better than to try and hold her eyes to emphasize the point. My eyes don't track together ever since I took that *coup de grâce* bullet that hadn't worked out like the shooter intended. People who try and stare me down get disconcerted pretty easy.

"All right, then. You can—"

She clamped her mouth shut suddenly as a little girl exploded into the room. The kid was maybe ten, wearing a red-and-white barber-pole-striped T-shirt and blue jeans. "Mom! Can I—?"

"Daisy, we have company. Do you think you can wait until I have—?"

The kid spotted me, whirled to bring me into focus. "What's your name?" she demanded.

"B.B.," I told her, pulling it out of the air.

"Like a BB gun?"

"Yep," I said, going along.

"What happened to your face?"

"Daisy! What kind of question is that to ask our guest?"

The kid ignored her mother, watching me like she damn well expected an answer.

"I was in an accident," I said, keeping my voice level and polite.

"Oh. A car accident?"

I nodded agreement, trying for gravity.

"How come your eyes are two different colors?" she demanded.

"That is *it,* young lady," her mother said sharply.

"You're here about Rose, aren't you?" the kid asked me, hitting the mute to her mother's station on some private remote.

"I am."

"You're the private detective!"

"That's right."

"And you think *you're* going to find her?"

"I'm going to try."

"The cops will never find her," the child said solemnly.

"Why do you say that?"

"Because they don't know her."

"That makes sense, Daisy. And *you* know her, right?"

"Yes. We are very close," the child said, smug and sad simultaneously. Proud of her adult phraseology . . . and terrified that she'd slip and use the past tense when she was referring to her sister.

"Then, later, you and me, we'll talk, okay?"

"Okay," she said, coming closer and sticking out her hand for me to shake. I did it, sealing the bargain. She whirled and charged out of the living room on full boil.

"I must apologize for—"

"She just wants to help," I said to her mother. "And—who knows?—maybe she can."

"I'm . . . not sure. She absolutely *worships* her sister, but I don't think she could possibly know anything about . . . this."

"It can't hurt," I assured the woman. "And it would make her feel better to be helping."

"Do you want to see Rose's room now?" she replied, moving me away from something that made her uncomfortable.

The girl's room was on the second floor. Bigger than most Manhattan apartments, with its own attached bath. Between the skylight in the sloping ceiling and the triple-pane bay window, the room was flooded with natural light.

The furniture was a polyglot mixture of different woods and fabrics. The only linking theme was that it was all old. Looked like reconditioned flea-market stuff to me . . . except for a magnificent rolltop desk that stood in one corner, closed. As soon as I slid it open, I knew it was some kind of priceless antique: a maze of tiny, perfectly aligned drawers, each with a separate inlay, intricately rendered in contrasting woods, and miniature handles so small you'd need a toothpick to pull them open. The pigeonholes were widely varied in size. Reminded me of the California Job Case I was trained to work with in the institutional print shop when I was a kid. I couldn't see the slightest trace of a nail. The whole piece was hand-finished to an artistic perfection beyond what any machine could hope to duplicate.

I'd heard that artists always sign their work, but I couldn't see any evidence of that until I noticed the brass plate surrounding the keyhole had "Erwin Darrow" engraved on it. I'd heard that name before. Michelle once told me he was an American master, explaining why she'd laid out a couple of grand for a jewelry box he'd made. The desk probably cost enough to buy a nice car. But it fit right in with all the recycled stuff, somehow.

The double bed was covered with a bright patchwork quilt that showed more enthusiasm than expertise. One wall was papered with concert posters—Joni Mitchell, Tracy Chapman, Sinead O'Connor. Against the facing wall was a bookcase made of long bare planks laid over cinder blocks. The shelves were filled—mostly serious-looking trade paperbacks. Each rack was bookended with half of a large purple-and-white geode.

On the bottom shelf I saw a set of thick black books, about the size of airport paperbacks, but bound like hardbacks. The spines were blank. I picked one up, opened it. A notebook, the pages as empty as the spines had been. There were another half-dozen of them. All the same, the pages as unused as a pawn-broker's heart.

The computer stood on one of those two-tiered workstations, an incongruously modern purple-and-white iMac . . . maybe to match the geodes? Above it was a pen-and-ink rendering mounted on some kind of artist's board. A pair of crows perched on a high wire. It looked as if they were deep in conversation. The detail was incredible; you could see every feather. And the light-of-life in the birds' eyes. In the lower right-hand corner it said: "Maida and Zia, 39/250, Geof Darrow."

Darrow again. Was there any connection? Could the girl know their family or something? I filed it away, went back to work.

The phone was a relic—black Bakelite, with a large rotary dial. It perched on a thick pad of music composition paper. Blank. I moved the phone aside to take a closer look. Under the pad was a stack of comics. All issues of something called *Cuckoo.* Didn't ring a bell with me.

"Is this the way Rose kept her room?" I asked the mother.

"What do you mean?"

"It's incredibly neat; everything in its place. Looks like it's ready for military inspection."

"Oh," she said, making a sound I didn't recognize. "I see what you mean. Yes, Rose always kept her room immaculate. But that was her choice. Her father . . ."

It took me a few seconds to realize that the woman wasn't going to say anything more. I stepped back to the desk, took a closer look. Inside, some of the pigeonhole slots were filled—envelopes, stamps, paper clips, a stapler—but most of them were empty. On the writing surface sat an old-fashioned green blotter with worn brown leather corners. Centered on the blotter was a pad of typewriter-sized paper, horizontally ruled in sets of five lines separated by white spaces. A square-cut glass inkwell stood guard to the side.

"Did Rose use a dip pen?" I asked the woman.

"I . . . don't know."

"Has anyone been in here since she left?"

"The police . . ."

"Sure. I mean, has anyone straightened up the room? A maid, maybe?"

"A maid? Kevin would never allow us to have a maid. That would be exploitation of—"

"A housekeeper, then? Someone who comes in once a week to help you with the heavy cleaning?"

"No. I do everything myself."

"Must be a lot of work."

She clasped her hands across her stomach. "Well, I don't want you to get the wrong impression. The girls are very helpful. And Kevin does his share, too."

I got it. This Kevin was Alan-fucking-Alda to the third power.

The closet doors were wood slats; they opened accordion-style. Inside, it looked like a sixties revival—long dresses in flower prints, platform shoes and clunky boots, dozens of pullovers, even an old army jacket with the peace sign hand-drawn on its back in black Magic Marker.

A guitar case stood alone in a corner, propped wide open to display its torn purple plush lining, as if to mock the searchers it knew would be coming.

The bureau was so old it had glass pulls on the drawers. It was nearly full, all neatly arranged—underwear, pajamas, T-shirts, socks.

I moved over to the bay window, checked it out. The large center portion was fixed in place, but the smaller panes of glass on either side could be opened by a little crank. I turned one experimentally. The opening was big enough to let someone in. Or out. I looked down. It was maybe a fifteen-foot drop into a lush pad of grass surrounded by trees. The backyard had no fence.

"The garage is on the other side of the house from here?" I asked.

"Yes. It's attached. With an apartment over it."

"Apartment? You have a tenant?"

"Oh no," she said, as if I had asked her if they kept space aliens in the attic. "Kevin uses it for a studio. Like a home office."

"Hmmm . . ." I muttered, to give her the impression that I was working on a thread. I walked out of Rose's room, got down on one knee, took a sight line to the bay window, nodding to myself.

"What are you—?"

"What's down the hall?" I interrupted her.

"That way? Just Daisy's room and a guest room. Our room, our bedroom, I mean, and Kevin's den, and . . . well, there's a whole separate section, but it's on the other side of the stairs as you go up."

"Is there a side door off this floor?" I asked, moving down the hall, trailing my conversation behind me.

"No. There's only the staircase. The way we came up," she said, not quite catching up to me, but staying pretty close. By then, I'd reached the end of the hall and gotten what I wanted—a glance into Daisy's room. It looked like someone had been searching for a lost coin, using a backhoe. I made my way back to Rose's room, rubbing my chin like I was contemplating something.

"Would you mind leaving me alone up here for a while?" I asked the woman. She opened her mouth, but no sound came out. "It's going to sound silly," I said, apologetically, "but I like to get a . . . sense of the place where the . . . person involved lived. I'm no psychic or anything, but, sometimes, I can pick up a clue to the person's essence."

"I don't see why I can't—"

"Oh, you're welcome to stay," I lied. "You just have to keep perfectly still, all right?"

I turned my back on her, sat down on the woven-rag rug in the middle of the room, threw my legs into a reasonable approximation of the lotus position, and closed my eyes.

It took her less than five minutes to clear out. I kept my eyes closed, waiting. I didn't know how much time I'd have until her husband showed up. Or even if my hunch would play out.

"What are you doing?" the voice said.

"I'm looking for Rose," I told Daisy.

"How can you look for anything with your eyes closed?"

"I think you know," I told her.

"You're weird," she said.

I sat quietly, counting to a hundred in my head. Then I asked, "Do you write songs, too, Daisy?"

I felt the disruption of air as she ran out of the room.

When I was sure Daisy wouldn't be coming back, I got up and went over to the telephone. On first inspection, it had looked old, but the wiring turned out to be modern. And the modular jack housed a splitter, so Rose could choose between the Internet and a regular call off a single line. The line itself was at least a dozen feet long, neatly folded over and held together by a plastic twist-tie. I measured with my eye. Yeah, it could reach the bed, easily.

I picked up the phone, pulled one of the comics out of the middle of the pile underneath it, and stuffed it into my jacket.

Rose's bathroom was as immaculately organized as her bedroom. And sparkling clean. But it was a beat off—something . . . dishonest about it. I prowled the medicine cabinet and the flush-mounted linen closet. Slowly, the way you do when you're looking for what *isn't* there.

I didn't expect Luvox and Lithium, or lamb-placenta rejuvenation face cream, any more than I expected a plastic-wrapped pistol in the toilet tank. But no anti-acne stuff? No aspirin? No shampoo or conditioner in the shower, either. The sink was ancient white enamel, heavily chipped. It was set into the top of a wood cabinet. I knelt, opened the cabinet. Lots of cleaning supplies, but no toilet paper.

And no matter where I looked, I couldn't find a single box of napkins, pads, tampons . . . nothing.

I went back into the bedroom, looking for two things. When I couldn't find the backpack, I figured I knew where the other thing was, too.

I came downstairs and spent the next hour or so listening to the woman ramble on about not much of anything. Her chemical eyes were a little more toxic than before, but her speech was as flat and unemotional as it had been from the beginning.

Daisy stuck her head around the corner twice, but darted away each time I shifted position.

I was glancing out the front window when a burgundy Volvo P1800 pulled up. It must have been thirty years old, but it sparkled like a new jewel, even in the evening's soft light. As the driver waited for the garage door to open, I could see the little Volvo had the squared-off, mostly glass back that turned the close-coupled coupe into a mini–station wagon. Maybe the husband liked his toys practical.

He was inside the living room in a minute, reaching down to shake hands with me. Tall and thin, with a thick mop of shaggy brown hair and a heavy mustache. Not one thing about his appearance disappointed me until he turned his head to say something to his wife and I noticed he wasn't sporting an earring.

"She told us she was sleeping over at her friend Jennifer Dryslan's house," he told me. "That was a Friday night, the first weekend after school let out for the summer. We didn't expect to see her until sometime Sunday evening."

"Did she call or anything during the weekend?"

"No. But that wasn't unusual."

"Are you sure she didn't call? Or that you just didn't speak to her?"

"There was nothing from her on the answering machine," he said, choosing his words like he was in court.

I didn't ask him where Daisy had been that weekend, or whether they'd ever questioned her about a message. Instead, I said, "Did it turn out that Rose spent *any* time at Jennifer's that weekend?"

"Jennifer's parents say no."

"What about Jennifer herself? Did she say Rose asked her to cover in case anyone called?"

"She said Rose never said a word to her about any of it."

"Okay. What about the note?"

"We already told your . . . associate," the husband said. "We figured if the police saw what Buddy wrote they wouldn't even look for her."

"Buddy?"

"That's my husband's name for her," the woman said. "Her name is Rosebud. It was kind of half for each of us. I call her Rose; Kevin calls her Buddy."

"What does Daisy call her?"

They looked at each other. Neither one answered me.

"You still have the note?" I asked the wafer of space between where the husband and wife sat on the love seat.

The husband got up without a word. I watched him walk away. Toward the garage . . . or maybe his studio above it.

He was back in a couple of minutes. Walked over to where I was sitting and handed it to me.

It was on one of those blank music sheets, written in perfect calligraphy, the words fitted neatly between the ruled lines. I tilted it against the light. Ink-on-paper, sure, but it was a computer font, not handwriting:

> I went to find the Borderlands. I'll be back when I learn enough.

It was signed R❤B.

"Nothing else?" I asked them.

They both shook their heads.

"You don't like the police being involved, right?" I put it to the husband.

"No, I don't. I *never* liked the idea. If it wasn't for . . . my wife," he said, nodding in her direction, "I wouldn't have notified them at all, to be honest."

When people make a point of telling you they're being honest, pat your pocket to make sure your wallet's still where it should be.

"Then why—?"

"The authorities," the woman said. "If we *didn't* let them know, we could end up . . . suspects or something. Isn't that true?"

"It is," I confirmed for her, watching the self-satisfaction briefly gleam in her eyes. "But if the cops saw that note, they'd make you report her missing, maybe even file a petition against her in court."

"Court?" the husband said sharply. "What the hell is *that* all about?"

"Your daughter's a minor. About sixteen, yes?"

"She'll be seventeen in September," the wife said.

"Sure. Anyway, if she's running around unsupervised somewhere with your permission, that could look like neglect to the law. Unless you're in contact with her, sending her money . . ."

"No," they both said in unison.

"But if she's gone with*out* your permission, and if you want the law to bring her back, you'd have to file a petition so she could be brought back against her will, understand?"

"I would never go to court against my own—"

I held up my hand like a traffic cop. I was there to get some leads, not listen to a discourse on the philosophical perspectives of the privileged. "What else do you have that might help?" I asked them.

The husband showed me a dollhouse he'd built for his daughters. "Well, it was originally for Buddy, but by the time Daisy was old enough to be interested, Buddy had pretty much outgrown it anyway."

The dollhouse was ultra-modern, almost futuristic. It was as precise and substantial as a miniature of the real thing, but it didn't have the warmth of Rosebud's rolltop desk. Didn't look as if anyone had ever played with it, either.

I stayed for dinner, some quasi-Oriental dish, heavy on the presentation. Afterwards, the husband offered me a joint.

"I'll pass," I told him.

"You have problems with marijuana?" he asked, a faint trace of belligerence in his voice.

"By me, it's just an overpriced herb, a hell of a lot less dangerous than booze."

"Exactly right," he approved. "But even in an 'enlightened' state like Oregon, it's still a crime to possess it, except for medical reasons."

"Yeah, well—"

"We've been smoking for . . . how many years, Mo?"

"*You've* been smoking for decades," his wife said. "And I have asked you a million times not to call me that."

"Excuse me, Mau*reen*," he said.

Apparently, the secondhand ganja hadn't mellowed out their relationship. From the way Daisy *didn't* react, the exchange was nothing new to her.

"Did Rosebud . . . Buddy . . . smoke?" I asked.

"No," said the mother.

"Once in a while," said the father.

"She didn't like it," Daisy added.

I took notes—I don't need to write things down, but it always makes clients feel better—while the father filled me in on his missing daughter's life. If she'd had a boyfriend, either it escaped his attention or he didn't see fit to share the info with me.

By then, I knew who would know, but I could see I wasn't going to be alone with her again on that visit.

I didn't leave until almost ten at night. Felt like I had been vacuuming for hours, but without a lot of suction.

Before I left, they gave me a couple of photos of their daughter. She was a medium-built girl with long straight hair and a crowd face. Not a single scar, tattoo, blemish, or disfigurement to set her apart. The shots weren't candids; she looked at the camera stiffly—not unhappy, not even bored; just . . . composed. Maybe it was the bland expression that made her look so generic.

I got up, carefully slid the photos into my jacket.

"I'll walk you out," the husband said. His wife was looking straight ahead. Not at me. Neither of us said goodbye.

Outside, in the night, I cupped my hands around a wooden match, fired up a cigarette, giving him time to say whatever he wanted to. I don't smoke anymore, but I never go out without a pack. They cost so much today, because of the piety taxes, that they're good for mini-bribes. And it's always smart to let people think you have habits that you don't.

"Buddy is a good girl," he said quietly, as if he'd thought about it carefully before pronouncing his opinion.

"Okay."

"I mean it."

"Sure. What difference?"

"I don't understand. I was just trying to—"

"You don't know where she is, right?"

"No. Of course not."

"So I have to look *around,* understand? There's no special place where good girls *wouldn't* go. You're not narrowing down my search any with that."

"Well . . . I just meant, I mean, Buddy doesn't use drugs. Wouldn't that be a help for you to know, for example?"

"You know why she took off?"

"No. We told you—"

"So how can you be so sure about the drugs?"

"I . . . All right, I get your meaning."

"Okay. I'm on the job."

"You don't sound very optimistic."

"I don't want to get your hopes up. Your daughter seems like a very intelligent, very organized young woman. She could be a hundred places by now."

"She's around here," he said, certainty in his voice. "I'm sure of it."

"Up to you. Me, I'm on the clock. You know the rate, you decide when I've been out there enough."

"Can I have one of those?" he asked, nodding his head at my cigarette.

I gave him one, handed him my little box of matches. His hands were steady.

"Mr. . . . ?"

"Hazard. B. B. Hazard. That's the name I gave your daughter."

"My . . . Oh! You mean Daisy."

"Yeah. She's a little pistol, that one."

"She is that. Buddy spoiled us. No notes from her teachers, no disciplinary problems at school . . ."

"Daisy and her are different personalities?"

"Night and day," he assured me. "Uh, what I wanted to . . . discuss with you . . . when you find her, what do you do?"

"There's a few options."

"Such as . . . ?"

"I could try and get an address, turn it over to you. I could brace her, try and talk her into coming home. Or at least into giving you a call, let *you* try the persuasion. . . ." I let my voice trail off, giving him the opening if he wanted it.

"Suppose she . . . refuses to come back. Is there anything you could do then?"

"I could bring her back," I said flatly, no emphasis anywhere.

"You wouldn't hurt—?"

"No. Is she on any medication?"

"Medication?" he said, on the thin edge of hostility. "What are you talking about?"

"Medication. Like you get from a doctor. Anti-depressants, stuff for allergies, insulin . . ."

"Oh. No. No, she isn't. But what diff—"

"Some medications don't mix."

"Look, Mr. . . . Hazard, I'm not following you here."

"You want her brought back, whether she wants to come or not, right?"

"I . . . yes."

"One way is physical force; one way is with . . . medicine."

"You mean like a Mickey Finn?"

"Something like that," I said, watching his eyes. "And if she was taking other stuff, the combination could be dangerous. Even chloroform could—"

"Maybe you'd better not . . . I mean, isn't there some way you could just . . . hold her wherever you find her? I've got a cell phone. You could ring me any time, day or—"

"I couldn't hold her in a public place."

"But you could follow her and—"

"Sure. And if she's staying somewhere permanent, that might work out. But if she's crashing different places, or sleeping outside, or with a crew, or . . . well, thing is, I may only get the one shot. And if she knows she's been located, she might bolt. There's a lot of roads out of Portland."

"I don't like this," he said bitterly, throwing his cigarette down, grinding it dead with his heel.

"Look, I'm not promising anything," I told him. "Only a crook would do that. It's long odds any way you look at it. But what I can do, I can see if I can pick up her trail but keep in the background, all right? If anyone's going to make a pitch, it shouldn't be me, it should be you or her mother."

"It should be me," he said.

I didn't say anything.

"Look, this is complicated," he said into the silence. But that was all he had to say.

"You paid me for ten days," I told him. "If I turn her up in that time, I'll call you. Then you decide how you want to play it."

"And if you don't?"

"It's still your call. If you want me to keep looking past that, it's the same rate."

"What are you saying? If you don't find Buddy in ten days, you won't be able to at all?"

"I'm not saying anything until I start looking. I don't know if the trail is cold, or even if there *is* a trail. I'll have a better idea after I've poked around."

He told me the number of his cell phone. "Don't you want to write it down?" he asked.

"I'll remember it," I promised him. "Writing certain things down, it's bad for business."

"I . . . All right," he said, sounding more depressed than convinced.

He walked back to his architecturally unique house. I started up my commonplace car and took off.

Driving back, I ran through it in my mind. Even adding up everything I'd seen and been told, there was a lot I didn't know. Nothing so strange about that. But I guess what bothered me the most was why they had all lied to me. Every one of them.

"She wrote music," I told Gem the next morning. "I'm dead sure of it, especially since her little sister ran out of the room when I brought it up."

"But why would her parents—?"

"I don't know. But that's not all of it. No way a girl her age, living in that kind of room, wouldn't have a backpack, but I couldn't find one. I couldn't tell if any of her clothes were missing; there were too many of them. But . . . no guitar, no backpack, no menstrual . . . stuff. The notebooks, you could tell they were part of a series, but the only ones she left behind were blank. Like the music-composition paper. This was no snatch. Wherever the girl was going, she planned it. And she figured on staying, too."

"That 'Borderlands' reference . . ."

"*If* she wrote that note herself, yeah. It was just a computer printout—anyone could have done it."

"Why would anyone—?"

"Pro snatch artists would have something like that prepared in advance—it can buy them a lot of time. And the parents could have written it themselves, after . . ."

"After she left?"

"After they killed her. Wouldn't be the first time."

"That doesn't make any sense, Burke. If they killed their own daughter, they would hardly be hiring private assistance to find her."

"You mean O.J.'s *not* spending his NFL pension on private investigators to find the Colombian drug dealers who killed his ex-wife?"

"Sometimes your sense of humor is offensive," she said, eyes level.

"And sometimes," I told her, "you just don't get the joke."

Hours later, she came into the room where I'd been sitting with my eyes closed.

"Have you learned anything?" she asked in a neutral voice. Gem knew where I went when I searched with my eyes closed, but she didn't like to talk about it.

"I thought the comics might have a clue," I said, "but they're all about a girl dealing with MPD."

"MPD?"

"Multiple Personality Disorder. Only now they call it DID—Dissociative Identity Disorder. Madison Clell—the one who writes and draws the comic—she has it herself. This *Cuckoo* is kind of . . . harsh. Right on the nerve endings. Powerful stuff. But I think Rosebud was just interested in it . . . artistically . . . not because she herself had the same thing."

"Perhaps one of her friends?"

"I don't think so. If that was it, she might've had *one* of the comics, but not the whole set. Some kids collect comics, but these were the only ones in her room, so I don't think that was it, either."

"Did this . . . *Cuckoo* person run away, too?"

"Damn! I didn't think of that. Not in this issue, anyway. Doesn't say anything about her writing music, either. But I just don't think that's it."

"Because . . . ?"

"Because she left the comics behind, Gem. And it looked like she took along everything that was precious to her when she ran."

"What will you do, then?"

"Everybody's lying," I told her. "Those people, they never showed the girl's note to the cops. Probably just handed them a pile of bullshit. A lot of rich people, they think the cops work for them *personally*. Like servants."

"Truly?"

"Sure. Say their kid wants nothing to do with them, okay? But the kid's of age, so the parents can't turn her in as a runaway. What they do, they call the cops, tell them the kid has been really depressed lately, they haven't heard from her . . . and she *always* calls regularly, so they think she may have done something to herself.

"The cops go pound on the kid's door, probably scare the hell out of her. Just what the parents want: they prove to the kid that they've got the power; the law will do what they tell it to."

"That is disgusting."

"Sure. Sometimes the kid *doesn't* panic. She proves to the cops that she's an adult, and that her parents were just playing them because she wants the parents out of her life and they don't know how to take no for an answer. And sometimes the cops get angry about being used.

"But, most of the time, they just play the role—tell the kid she really should sit down and talk with her parents, all that crap. It's none of their business, they shouldn't be doing it; but, the way they figure, a little gratitude from people who have money never hurts."

"Do you believe that is what these people are doing?"

"Well, aren't they? Let's say the note's for real—the kid's a runaway, then, and they know it. Why would they keep that from the cops?"

"But if the police locate—"

"The parents will just say they never saw the note, sorry to have troubled you . . . but thank God our precious baby is back home, and we'll be sure to write a nice letter for your personnel file."

"Oh."

"Yeah, only it's not just the parents who are gaming. The cops might have the kid's photo posted; she might even make a milk carton or a few Internet sites. But no way they're bringing out any of their big guns on this."

"Big guns?"

"Extra officers, heavy overtime authorized, squeezing informants, putting out the word that they're offering a felony walk-away for a solid lead . . . like that."

"Why do you believe the parents told you the truth, then?"

"They didn't. I already said—"

"No, no. I don't mean the truth about the . . . things you said. But why did they tell *you* the truth about her running away?"

"People like that, they see the cops as public servants, but not necessarily *their* servants. Me, they're sure of—I'm bought and paid for.

"Besides, they know I'm not exactly comparing notes with the law. That's what they hired me for. Most PIs are ex-cops. That's what people pay them for; they can get information by just walking down to the precinct and spreading a little goodwill. That's great if you're a defendant, or even a suspect. But if you're coming across as a victim, you don't need all that. And the firm they hired—the ones the cops touted them on—you can bet it's full of ex-cops, too. So they could never trust them, either. Me, I'm an outlaw. No question about my loyalty . . . at least in their minds."

"You sound as if you despise them."

"I don't know what I feel about them—yet. I guess I'd have to find the girl to know for sure. But I don't *like* them; that part's true enough."

I parked behind the strip club, in the vacant spot Gem said would be waiting for me. It was the kind of joint where every button on the speed-dial is set to 911. Gem was at a little table in the back, as far from the action as you could get and still be hit with the cover charge.

"Anything?" I asked her. Before I went out into the street, it was worth seeing if the girl had made headlines in the underground newspaper—the one that isn't printed. Gem had a subscription.

"Nothing. Not by her name, anyway. And the description is almost . . . meaningless. It could fit so many."

"About what I figured," I told her, not disappointed.

One of the house features swivel-hipped her way over to us, asked Gem if she wanted to buy a lap dance for me. Even standing still, the woman was in motion, packing enough silicone to grease a battleship through a car wash.

Gem looked a question at me. I shook my head no. The woman licked her lips at Gem. "No, thank you," Gem told her, politely.

"What's your problem?" I asked Gem as soon as the handjob hooker took off.

"My problem?"

"Yeah, your problem. You have to ask me if I want some fucking slot machine to sit on my lap?"

"Oh. So sorry."

"Cut it the fuck out, all right, Gem? You're about as Japanese as I am. And you're too bossy to be a geisha, anyway."

"She was just—"

"Never mind. You ready to go?"

"You didn't like her . . . looks?" Gem asked me that night in bed.

"Who are you talking about?"

"The dancer. With the big chest."

"I didn't pay any attention."

"How could you miss them?"

"What?"

"Her breasts. Do you like such big ones?"

"Ahhh . . . they're like . . . I don't know, red silk sheaths."

"Because you can buy them?"

"No. Because they look good on some people, and not on others. I don't like red silk sheaths all by themselves. If I saw one on a hanger, it wouldn't race my motor, okay? On some women, they look perfect. Really gorgeous. On others, they look . . . ridiculous. You don't look at the trimming, you look at the tree, understand?"

"Oh yes. Certainly. Would you like me in such big breasts, then?"

"No."

"Why not? Do you not think I would—?"

"They'd look all out of proportion. Like they were stuck on with glue."

"That is the way they looked on her, too."

"Maybe."

"Oh? You do not agree?"

"I didn't pay any attention."

"Huh!" is all she said. For the rest of the night.

I tried it in daylight first. Invested a lot of cigarettes and a few dollars, but I didn't come up with anything other than a few numb attempts at shining me on. I collected some stale info, a few bad addresses, a couple of street names. I didn't push it; why squeeze when there's no juice?

Pioneer Square was the downtown see-and-be-seen place, preening and posturing the order of the day. There were a few skateboard artists, a juggler, a threesome doing a little close-up Frisbee, music blasting from a dozen boom boxes, some "Look at me!" dancing. A guy made the rounds, flexing an upper body that must have looked a lot better in his own mirror. Anarchists handed out leaflets about some demonstration coming the next day. They seemed pretty organized about it. I watched people watching people for a while, getting nowhere.

It wasn't a particularly good spot for buskers, but a few tried. None that looked remotely like Rosebud.

A young, pretty, nicely put-together girl walked by, slowly. The black Lab at her side sported a set of saddlebags—a working partner, not a pet. I flashed on Pansy and *drove* the thoughts away before they hurt me. The girl had a toolbelt of some kind around her waist, and a backpack that looked homemade. She wasn't panhandling, she was scavenging, carefully checking the ground for anything of value, occasionally putting something she picked up into the Lab's saddlebags.

There's plenty of street kids in Portland, but no single street culture. And I was way too old to try fitting in, so I went looking for a guide. I finally ran across one of their halfass gurus in a coffeehouse, but all he wanted to do was rant about the Internet.

"If you deconstruct it, the whole thing is a sham. A fake. The Internet is supposed to be all about personal freedom, but, if you think it through, you see that the whole Net culture is about invasion of privacy. It's just a ruse to register us all, man."

I was running into this all the time, that intersection thing—where the extremists on both ends of the political continuum looped back onto each other until you couldn't tell them apart. This guy wasn't any great distance from the gun loons who'll tell you that banning private ownership of armor-piercing bullets or rocket launchers is just the opening salvo in ZOG's plan to disarm all American citizens.

The guru may have been a little slow in the synapses, but he had his finger on the pulse—if there's one common cause between the hyper-right and the ultra-left, it's that they hate the very *idea* of Registration.

"This girl I'm looking for . . . ?" I opened, trying to get him off his topic and onto mine.

"She has to find *you,* man. It can't go the other way," he intoned, as the two stick-figure kids at his table nodded sagely.

"Fair enough. But she can't find me unless she knows where to look, right?" I said, handing him a business card with my name and cell-phone number on it, wrapped around a twenty.

"Right, man," the guru said, pocketing the offering. "The Internet is all bullshit, you know. I mean, even the fucking *anarchist* Web sites send you cookies!"

I don't think he noticed me leaving.

The black guy couldn't have been out of the joint long. The prison weight-room muscles were still chiseled, the eye-lock was race-war hostile, and my color still made him glance behind me to make sure I was alone. "Who asking about Odom, slick?"

"Cash."

"Like Johnny Cash?"

"Like Benjamin Cash."

"What the fuck kind of name that be, slick?"

"It's a Muslim name," I told him. "Benjamin 5X Cash."

"You must think I be someone to fuck with, slick," he said, closing the distance between us.

"No, he thinks you're someone who understands English, dumbass," said a voice from behind him. "You're putting up five yards to . . . what, man?" he asked me, stepping forward out of the gloom in the back of the bar. Much smaller than the body-builder, with a yellowish cast to his skin. I'd have about the same luck guessing his age as I would an alligator's.

"Odom's the one I need to talk to."

"And you never met this 'Odom' dude, is that it?" the smaller man said, telling me who he was.

"Not by face. Only by status."

"Status?" the bodybuilder snarled. "Motherfucker, you talk some strange—"

"He means *rep,*" Odom told his pupil. "Listen and learn. Now," he said, turning to me, "where'd you get word on me?"

"Inside."

"You was in the SHU? Where? Pelican Bay?"

"No. I did all my bits on the other coast. But word travels; you know how that works."

"Yeah, I know. You got friends still in, then?"

"Might have."

"Might be AB, too, right?"

"Some of them."

"You going to give up some of those names?"

"I never give up names," I said.

He smiled at that. Thought for a moment. Then said, "They got some mighty strange-looking undercovers these days."

"I heard that, too," I agreed. "But, see, an undercover, he'd be looking to score some dope. Or a piece. Or . . . well, you know how it goes. Me, I got five hundred dollars for you to tell me something. If you know it. And, if you don't, to find it out."

"Ain't no crime to listen."

"Right. Okay to sit down?"

"Glad you asked, man. Slide into that booth over there."

I wasn't exactly blown over from shock when the bodybuilder slid in right next to me, with Odom across the table. No way for me to move. Just the way I wanted it.

"I'm looking for a girl," I said. "A runaway. Her parents are worried."

"I got nothing to do with girls," Odom said.

"I know you don't. That's why I came here. If the girl was merchandise to you, then I'd be messing in your business, and I wouldn't do that. She's on the street, somewhere. You've got people out there. Here's what she looks like," I said, handing him one of the copies of Rosebud's photo I'd had made.

He glanced at the photo, his face expressionless.

"Here's how to find me," I said, handing over the card.

"That be two out of three, my man."

"The five is if you turn her up."

"No, man. The five is for my people to be on the eyeball. I know there's got to be a nice reward for this little girl. People *had* to have money to hire you and all."

"The reward's only for people working on commission."

"Yeah. Brutus, you had his white ass pegged, brother. This motherfucker *is* slick, all right." He swiveled his head toward me. "How much?"

"Another five, only not centuries. Five large."

"That ain't enough to pay for a tuneup on my Rolls, man."

"You want to raise, you got to have chips," I told him.

He nodded slowly. When the boulder who'd been blocking my exit finally understood what the nod meant, he stood up to let me out.

By the time the ten days was up, all I'd accomplished was to make sure the whisper-stream knew a man was looking for Rosebud. It was like betting on a horse without looking at the form. Hell, without even knowing if your horse was in the goddamned race.

So, when the father renewed my contract, I went back inside myself, looking there. I had one card I thought I could play, but it was too early to be sure. And if I moved too soon, it could backfire. In the meantime, that *Cuckoo* comic still nagged at me, so I went looking for a way in.

Took me only about an hour to find a little comics shop. It was devoid of customers, and the proprietor, a fat, balding guy with a face that had once been jolly, was glad to shoot the breeze with me. He recognized my copy of *Cuckoo* right away.

"Oh sure. That's Madison's."

"Madison, the guy who wrote this?"

"Yep. Only she's not a guy. She lives around here, you know."

"No, I didn't."

"Portland's really a big town for graphic artists," he said in a confidential tone, like he was disclosing secrets. "Dark Horse Comics, that's one of the *major* independents, they're right over in Milwaukie."

"Is that right?"

"Sure."

"And they publish this one?" I asked, holding up my one copy of *Cuckoo*.

"Nah. That's from a *real* indie operation. There isn't much money in comics anymore, not like the old days."

"The old days?"

"Yeah, like, oh, ten years ago, there were all kinds of comics selling hundreds of thousands of copies. *Big* collector's market, too."

"But not anymore?"

"Right. The bottom's dropped out for everything but the super-primo stuff. But you know what? Comics are coming back, my friend. Those of us who stay the course, we're the ones going to clean *up* when it turns around."

"Uh-huh. So this *Cuckoo,* is it a good investment?"

"Could be," he said, stroking his chin, considering. "The early editions, especially the first one, they could be worth a nice piece of change. The later ones . . . I don't think so. It's gotten real popular now. Won some awards. Not as collectible."

"But it would be better to have the whole set, right?"

"*Always* better," he assured me. "A mint set, from number one on, well, I'm not promising anything, but that'd be a good play, I think."

"Okay, I'm sold," I told him, wondering what I was letting myself in for. "How much for a whole set?"

"Well, see, I don't *have* a whole set here. We don't keep back issues much anymore; it just doesn't pay. I've got . . . let me see . . . okay, I've got numbers five through nine."

"But you could get the others, right?"

"Sure. Might take a while, but . . ."

"You think Madison would have back issues?"

"Oh sure, man. Every creator keeps copies of their own stuff."

"Creator?"

"Yeah!" He chuckled. "That's what comics folk call the people who *create* comics, like the people who draw them, you see what I'm saying?"

"Yeah. Well, could you give her a call, ask her?"

"Uh . . . I guess so."

When he saw I wasn't going to move, he fumbled around with some papers behind the counter. Finally he said, "I don't see her number here, man. Tell you what, okay? I'll ask around, find it out easy enough. You want to check back in a few days?"

"That's a little hit-or-miss for me," I said. "Are these comics like books? I mean, are they worth more if the author signs them?"

"Absolutely," he said, reverently.

"So, okay, here's the deal. How about five hundred for a complete set, but all *signed,* okay?"

His eyes flickered, so I guessed I'd bid a little high.

"I can get that for you," he said quickly.

"Fair enough. You track her down, give me a call, and we'll set up a meet."

"A meet? What for?"

"Well, look—friend—no offense. I don't know anything about comics, but I know how things work. She's got to sign them in front of me, so I know it's legit; fair enough?"

"I can authenticate—"

"That's the only way I want to do it. Look, I'll leave you my number, you reach out, find out if it's okay with her. It is, you give me a call. It's not, no harm done."

He was dubious, but he took my number. When I left, the place was still as empty as a senator's conscience.

It didn't take him long. My cellular buzzed the next afternoon.

"What?"

"Uh, this is Smilin' Jack, man. From Turbocomix. Remember, you wanted to buy—"

"Sure, I remember. Madison going to sign them for me?"

"Well, man, here's the thing. She's willing to sign them, sure; but—I got to tell you—Madison, she's a real nice person, we all like her a lot."

"So?"

"So I told her you don't look like no comics collector to me, man. And I think I might have made her nervous."

"So tell her to bring a few friends."

"Well, she wants to do it a little different, man."

"Tell me."

"She wants to meet you at the federal courthouse. Outside, on the steps."

"Okay."

"Just like that? You know that address, man?"

"Sure," I lied, figuring it couldn't be that hard to find.

"Always a lot of cops around there," he said, obliquely. "But so what, right? I mean, it's only going to take a couple of minutes for her to sign your books."

"Sure. Fair enough."

"You don't care?"

"No. I figure, she's an artist, right? They're all weird."

"Tomorrow." He chuckled. "Eleven a.m."

I could have sent Gem, but I figured this Madison would be less likely to spook if the person waiting for her matched the comic-shop guy's description. At 10:52, I strolled up Southwest Third Avenue to the courthouse. I was wearing a charcoal suit with a faint chalk stripe over a white shirt and port-wine tie, carrying a black belting-leather briefcase. Lawyer-look; corporate, not criminal . . . although, if the Portland cops were anything like their New York brothers, they wouldn't acknowledge a difference.

The courthouse was nothing like the Roman Colosseum monster they have in Manhattan. It was simple and kind of elegant, with a short flight of steps flanked on the left by a slab of black marble, complete with the obligatory quote from some historically significant person. I leaned against the marble slab, put the briefcase between my feet. Then I opened my copy of *Cuckoo* and scanned it like it was a court decision.

People streamed by on the sidewalk. Hard to imagine a more public spot. Whoever this Madison was, she knew something about self-defense.

Directly across the street was a small public park—just wide enough for a few trees, a couple of benches, and a statue. I saw a guy with long dark hair sitting on a bench, a pair of binoculars to his eyes. Bird-watchers can be some pretty dedicated people, but I'd never heard of one interested in pigeons.

She approached from my left, moving slowly . . . wary and alert, a bright-colored comic book in her right hand. A slender woman with long, wild white-blond hair, scarlet lipstick harsh against a never-seen-sun complexion. She wore black pants, a black thigh-length jacket, and a white blouse, with a big red purse on a strap over one shoulder. I tucked my comic under my arm, spread my hands a little, caught her eye. I knew better than to try a smile.

"Are you—?"

"Yes. I'm the man who wants to buy a complete set of your series," I finished her sentence for her. "Signed," I said, to keep it consistent.

"I . . . have them right here," she said. "There have been only fifteen issues so far. . . ."

"Fair enough," I told her. "Is there something special you sign comics with? I mean, the covers are so slick, it looks like ink would just slide off."

"We use these," she said, taking a gold-colored tube from the breast pocket of her jacket. "It's called a paint pen. Only thing is, you have to be sure to let each one dry before you bag them."

"Bag them?"

"You don't . . . ? Well, it doesn't matter; I already have them set up."

"Great," I said, deliberately turning my back on her and walking up the steps. I pointed to the top of the black marble slab. "How's this? For signing them, I mean?"

"It should be fine. . . ."

"Oh yeah. I'm sorry," I told her, reaching into my inside

pocket. I brought out ten new fifty-dollar bills, handed them to her.

"This is a lot of money for the comics," she said earnestly. "You understand that there's no guarantee they'll ever be worth so much, don't you?"

"I'm a gambler," I told her.

"Well . . . all right, then." She opened her purse, took out a stack of comics, each one inside a clear plastic sleeve with white cardboard backing. She opened the first bag, carefully slid out the comic, positioned it until she was satisfied, then shook the paint pen vigorously and tested it on her thumb. She nodded to herself, then signed her name with a sharp, fluid motion. "It's good it's not raining today," she said, setting the signed comic on the flat surface to dry. She opened another bag. Her movements were practiced, professional. Maybe she wasn't used to scoring five hundred bucks for a single deal, but she'd signed a lot of comics before.

While she was concentrating, I said, "Can I ask you a question?"

"Sure," she answered, her tone a lot more guarded than the word.

"I was looking through the one issue I already had. People write you letters, right?"

"Sure," she said again. I could hear the barriers dropping into place.

"You can't print all of them that you get . . . ?"

"Well, I don't get *that* many."

"But more with each issue, isn't that so?"

"Yes. But how would you—?"

"It just makes sense. As the series gets more popular, picks up word-of-mouth, more people get to read it. So there's a bigger pool of people who might write to you."

"Uh-huh."

"Anyway, I was thinking, you couldn't possibly print all the letters. Besides, there are probably some you wouldn't *want* to print."

"I don't understand. You mean the idiots who—"

"No, I didn't mean anything negative. I was thinking . . . people might write to you because they'd know you'd understand what they were going through. So maybe they'd want advice or whatever. And you'd keep their names confidential if they asked, wouldn't you?"

"That's right," she said, her voice as pointed as the pen she was using.

"I'm trying to help someone," I said abruptly, sensing she wasn't going to hang around after she finished signing her books. "And I was hoping maybe you could help me do that."

"I don't understand."

"I'm a private investigator," I said. "And I'm looking for a girl who's run away from her home. Or, at least, people *think* she has. It's my job to make sure she's okay."

"What does that have to do with me?"

"Well, I know she was a big fan of yours."

"And how do you know that?"

"She had a whole stack of *Cuckoo* in her room. And those were the only comics she had."

"That doesn't mean—"

"Ms. Clell, I'm not saying it means anything. I just thought that maybe, *maybe,* she wrote to you. If she did, then it might be possible that you could—"

"I don't know you," the woman said. "And I'm not telling you—"

"I don't want you to tell me anything," I said softly. "Her name is Rosebud. Some people call her Rose, others call her Buddy. *If* she wrote to you, and *if* she left an address where you could write back, I think you would have done that."

"I—"

"I don't *want* the address. All I want is to give you this note," I told her, handing her an envelope. "It's unsealed; you can read it for yourself. It explains who I am and why I'm trying to make sure she's okay. It's got a phone number she can call. This one right here," I said, pulling my jacket back to show her the cell phone I carried in a shoulder holster under my left armpit. "I just want to know that she left of her own free will, and that she's not in any kind of trouble."

"I'm not—"

"You do what you want," I said. "I'm playing a hunch, that's all."

"A hunch that this girl wrote to me?"

"A hunch that you'll do the right thing," I said.

She turned to face me. "What makes you think that?" she asked.

"That one copy of *Cuckoo* I had," I told her. "I read it."

She didn't say anything. But she didn't walk away, either.

I put my signed and bagged comics into my briefcase, made my eyes a soldering iron between the woman and the truth of what I'd told her, bowed slightly, and moved off.

"Why do you need all this information about their neighbors?" Gem asked me that night.

"Too many times, a missing kid, you find the body under the bed of some other kid right close by. Or buried in a backyard, rotting in a shed, chopped up in a shower . . ."

"But—"

"Yeah, I know. She's a little old for that. When a kid's the perpetrator, you expect the victim to be younger. Smaller and weaker, anyway. Unless there's a gun involved. But the stealth jobs, it's usually a *little* kid that's targeted."

"I was not going to say that," Gem said, tapping her child-sized foot the way she does when she's impatient. "There was a note."

"A computer note, remember? Not in her handwriting. Anyone could have written it."

"Do you believe that is why the parents did not show it to the police?"

"I don't know what to believe. This whole thing reeks. Gem, listen to me for a second, okay? What exactly did you tell them about me when you pitched the job?"

"I told him nothing specific. Just that you were a man accustomed to difficult, dangerous jobs, and that you expected to be paid well to do them."

"You tell them I was a—"

"Not 'them,' Burke. I never met anyone but the father."

"Okay, *where* did you meet him?"

"At the club. The same place where the girl Kitty worked. The one with the boyfriend who—"

"I remember. He was looking *there* for his kid?"

"Not looking for her. Looking for someone who might help him find her. One of the dancers told him she might know somebody. Then she called me. And then I met him."

"I should have asked you this before, I'm sorry. Tell me everything you can remember, okay?"

"Yes. He thought I was Vietnamese. I did not disabuse him. He told me he had been against the war. I did not say anything, but I encouraged him to speak more."

"How could you—?"

"Like this," she said. She cocked her head slightly, widened her ocean eyes, and oh-so-innocently used the tip of her tongue to part her lips.

"Ah . . . all right, little girl. What did *that* get you?"

"He . . . implied that he had done many things to stop the war. Illegal, even violent things. I did not press him for details. He also told me he studied what he called 'the arts' for many years, and that he did not trust himself to confront those who might have lured his daughter away, because he could very easily kill a man with his hands."

" 'The arts'?"

"That is what he said. He asked me if I had a relationship with you. I told him that I was a businesswoman; I did not associate with those I worked with. He apologized. He said he wasn't trying to get nosy, that he knew the value of confidentiality. He said he only asked me about my relationship with you because I was a fascinating woman. That he would like to know me better, but he didn't want to . . . intrude, I believe he said."

"This is after telling you he's married?"

"Oh yes. I told him that he, too, was a person I was doing business with, so it was not possible."

"He bought that?"

"I do not think he did. He is like most Americans you meet in places like that—all their images of Asian women are as sex toys. Between the stories servicemen tell of Vietnamese whores and Bangkok bar babies, the 'Asian Flower' services that advertise in the magazines, and the strippers they see in clubs, they find all they care to know. He acted as if we were playing an elaborate game but the outcome was not in doubt."

"Where did he get the idea I was a mercenary?"

"Well, in the dictionary sense of the word, I suppose I told him. You are a man for hire; that is what I said. But he thought I was referring to war, I am certain."

"Why?"

"He asked if I was familiar with your résumé—that is the specific word he used. I told him, yes, I was. He asked if you'd ever served in Africa. At first, I felt a little shock—like a warning jolt. I had not told him your name—I *still* have not—nor did I describe you. But you *were* in Biafra, and I didn't see how he could have . . . But he kept talking, and I realized that he was just asking questions out of some movie."

"You mean, he was a buff?"

"A . . . buff?"

"A . . . fan, sort of. Cops get them all the time. Some people get turned on by the whole police thing. They collect badges, keep a scanner in their house, volunteer to be auxiliaries. They hang out in cop bars, *talk* like cops. Some cops're flattered by all that, specially if the buff is a broad. But the more experienced ones, they're smart enough to keep them at a distance.

"There's mercenary buffs, too. They buy the magazines, collect the paraphernalia, talk the talk . . . usually on the Internet.

The more extreme ones just fake it, spend a lot of time in bars dropping names and places. He come across like that?"

"I . . . am not sure. Every time I did *not* answer one of his questions about you, he would nod as if I just had. As if we were sharing secrets. It was very strange."

"I can't make it fit," I told her. "But you'll get me the stuff on the neighbors?"

"I am here to serve you," Gem said, bringing her hands together and bowing.

When she turned to go, I smacked her bottom hard enough to propel her into the next room. My reward was a very unsubservient giggle.

"Do you have something?" he said, his voice feathery around the edges.

"I'm not sure," I lied. "I may have found a connect to her. I can't be sure until I go a little deeper. And I need a couple of things to do that."

"What?"

"You take a lunch hour?" I asked him.

"Yes. But most of the time, it's with clients. Lunch is when we get to—"

"Today?"

"I don't—"

"Are you having lunch with clients today?" I cornered him.

"Well, no."

"Okay. Tell me where you want to meet. And what time. We'll finish this then."

There was cellular silence for half a minute. Then he asked me if I knew my way around the waterfront.

"You said you needed two things," he greeted me abruptly.

"Yeah. The first is from your lawyer."

"My . . . lawyer?"

"Sure. You've got a lawyer, don't you?"

"No. Not really. I mean, I *know* lawyers, of course. But—"

"You've got a lawyer you're close with," I said confidently. "Doesn't have to be one you *use,* okay? Just someone who'd do a little favor for you."

"How little?"

"Very little. I don't have a PI license. That's no big deal; it's not against the law to be asking questions on the street. But you know how the fucking cops are," I said, taking the cues from my conversation with his wife and what Gem had told me about him, "they could roust me for nothing, especially if I start getting closer than they are."

He nodded knowingly, but said, "What do you think I could do about that?"

"Not you. The lawyer. See, you hire the lawyer to represent you in this whole matter of your daughter going missing. Maybe you're thinking about suing her school for negligence or whatever. It doesn't matter, that part's all camouflage. What *does* matter—okay—is that anyone working for a lawyer as an investigator doesn't *need* a PI license. That's what I want now: a little more cover."

"I . . . I can do that. I have a friend who does a lot of criminal-defense work, as a matter of fact. I'll ask him, how's that?"

"Good. And what I also need is some money. Not the *actual* money," I said quickly as he opened his mouth to . . . I don't know what. "But there's got to be a bounty put out; a reward, understand? There's people who wouldn't do anything for love, but they'd move quick enough for money."

"I'd thought of that myself. But I didn't want to attract—"

"Sure, that's the whole idea. It would be *me* offering the

money. For information, see? My own idea, not yours. But if someone actually comes up with your daughter, I'd have to pay it off."

"How . . . much are we talking about here?"

"Ten grand should do it, at least for now."

"Ten thousand dollars?"

"Yeah."

He pretended to be thinking it over. People with money always see themselves as consumers, and their road maps through life are always marked by brand names. When they rant about corruption, all you're really hearing is jealousy. They want a friend on the force, an insider contact, a political connection. All that crap about a level playing field always comes from people who'd be happy to stand at the top of the hill if they had the chance. And pour boiling oil down the slope.

"All right," he finally said.

By the time the lawyer agreed to meet with me, I knew a lot more about him than he'd ever know about me. His office was in a big-windowed townhouse. Whitewashed walls lined with posters of Che, Chavez, and other visionaries whose convictions had been stronger than their support. Delta blues growled its way out of giant floor-standing stereo speakers.

The lawyer was a short, chubby man with thinning blond hair that turned into a ponytail past the collar of his blue-jean sports coat. He sat behind a free-form desk with what looked like a bird's-eye maple top under fifty coats of clear varnish. I selected a straight chair from a motley collection arranged against one wall, carried it over so I could sit right across from him.

"Kevin said you were doing something for him?"

"He tell you what that was?"

"You're a cagey man, Mr. . . . ?"

"Hazard. B. B. Hazard."

"Sure," he said, making it clear he wasn't buying it.

"But I'm using different ID for this job," I said, sliding the driver's license Gem had gotten made for me across to him.

"So I'd be hiring Joseph Grange," he said, reading the plastic laminate of my photo, "DOB 10/19/52. Is that right?"

"Not 'hiring,' " I told him. "I'm what you'd call an independent contractor."

"I see," he said, chuckling to let me know he was hip. "But you'll need a . . . document of some kind, to verify that you're on assignment to this office, yes?"

"No. I just need whoever answers the phone here to vouch for that. If anyone should ever call."

"That isn't difficult. But . . . Kevin didn't tell me very much about you. . . ."

"So?"

"Well, I was thinking . . . we might know some people in common."

"I don't run dope," I said, dismissing any chance we had mutual friends.

"I see my reputation precedes me."

"The way I hear it, it comes to weight busts around here, you're the man."

"Lots of people hear that. Where did *you* hear it?"

"Inside," I said. Softly.

"Not many of *my* clients there."

"Exactly."

He laughed. "I like you, Mr. . . . Grange." He leaned back in his chair, lit a long white cigarette. The scent of cloves wafted over me. I looked at a spot behind the middle of his pale eyebrows. "Kevin tells me you did some work overseas," he said, blowing a smoke ring at the ceiling.

"Does he?"

"We don't just defend people who have run afoul of the draconian drug laws here. A lot of our work is . . . political, I suppose would be the best way to describe it."

"Cool."

"Probably not. At least, probably not *your* politics."

"I don't strike you as a liberal?"

"No. No, you don't."

"Your receptionist didn't like me either."

"We don't make judgments here. And we're very good at what we do. You might want to keep that in mind if you run into any trouble while you're working for Kevin."

"I will. You know what that work is, right?"

"You're looking for his daughter."

"Yeah. You ever meet her?"

"Buddy? I've known her practically since she was born."

"She ever work here?"

"Why would you ask that?"

"Well, the kind of office this is, I figure it'd be like heaven to an idealistic kid. Free Huey one generation, Free Willy the next, right?"

"I appreciate your sarcasm. But Buddy isn't *that* kind of idealist."

"What kind is she?"

"She's more . . . introspective, I would say."

"Okay. Any idea where she went?"

"Not a clue."

"Or why?"

"That's an even bigger mystery. She had an . . . I almost said an 'ideal' . . . life. I know that's not possible for a teenager; at least not in *their* minds. But I never knew a happier, more well-adjusted young woman."

"You have kids?" I asked him.

"No. You?"

"Four," I told him, just keeping my skills in practice.

Being a teenager in America is a high-risk occupation. They're the most likely to get shot, stabbed, sexually assaulted, beat up, bullied, turned on to chemicals, turned into zombies—and used and abused by the people who "counsel" them after all that.

And their peer-pressured cynicism makes them the easiest to trick, too.

It wouldn't have shocked me if Rosebud had been driven to a remote area and killed by some other girls who didn't like the way she spoke to one of their boyfriends. Or was snuffed out because some freakish boys wanted the "experience." Or didn't survive a gang rape.

But those kinds of crimes always seem to pop to the surface, like a river-disgorged corpse. Back in the sixties, there was a young guy in Tucson who killed a couple of girls for the fun of it. Buried them out in the desert. If he'd been a nomadic serial killer, the crimes might still be unsolved. But he had to tell some of his groupies about his feats. And when they scoffed, he showed them where the bodies were buried.

When teenagers commit crimes, they tend to talk about it. Today, they even make videos of it.

But the wires were quiet.

Or maybe Rosebud had been in a secret romance with a guy who killed her in a rage when she said she was going to tell his wife.

It never takes much.

But if she'd had a boyfriend, the guy had to have been sneaking into her room at night. Because it turned out that Rosebud had led a tightly scripted life . . . and one that made Mother Teresa look like a slacker. Two nights a week at the hospital's children's ward, visiting kids with cystic fibrosis. Saturdays, she volunteered at a shelter for battered women. That was when she wasn't reading books into a tape recorder for the blind, or collecting signatures to abolish the death penalty, or delivering canned goods for a local food bank.

I thought back to what the father's lawyer had said about Rosebud. Maybe, to him, anything less than overthrowing a government was "introspective."

The high-school principal talked to me readily enough after she got a call from the father. She was surprised, though, that Rosebud was into all those activities—she certainly didn't do any extracurricular stuff at school. Her grades were good but not spectacular.

When I asked about her friends, the principal just shrugged. At her level, she just heard about the extreme kids—the ones bound for the Ivy League, and the ones they were holding a prison cell for. She told me to try the guidance counselor.

He was a black guy in his thirties, dressed casually, with alert eyes. Told me Rosebud had never been in to see him. About anything. He knew of her only in the vaguest terms. A loner, not a joiner. "It was more like she . . . tolerated school."

"Any chance she was more friendly with one of her teachers than she was with the other students?" I asked him.

His eyes went from alert to wary. "What are you saying?"

"I'm not saying anything. Sometimes a kid relates better to adults than to peers. You've seen that yourself, right?"

"Not the way you're implying. Not at this school."

"Whatever you say."

"You don't sound very satisfied, Mr. Grange."

"Yeah. Well, that's not your problem, is it?"

"I'm not sure I'm following you."

"Why should you, when you don't like where I'm going? Look, Mr. Powell, this is a big school. And you've been here a while. You don't seem like the kind of man who spends all his time pushing paper. You've got your ear to the ground. On top of that, the kids trust you. Some of them, anyway."

"And you know all that how, exactly? Instinct?"

"More like experience. I've been doing this for a lot of years."

"That's just another way of spelling 'generalization.' "

"I'm a hunter. It's no generalization to say that lions prefer crippled antelopes. They're easier."

"And you hunt teachers?"

"You know, I did hunt one, once," I told him, keeping my tone conversational. "I knew he was a freak. I knew what he liked. I knew where he'd been, so I figured out where he'd be going."

"I'm not sure I'm following . . ."

"This teacher, he never had a single complaint lodged against him in thirty years. But he quit three jobs. Pretty good jobs, near as I could tell. And moved on. Nobody at any of his old jobs had a bad word to say about him. So I took a look. My kind of look: a hard one. And what all the schools he left had in common was this: each one had banned corporal punishment. You understand what I'm saying, Mr. Powell?"

"I believe so."

"Yeah? Well, let me spell it out for you, just in case. This guy was a child molester, but he never had sex with any of the kids. No, what he did was 'punish' them. That's how he got his rocks off, paddling kids. Nothing illegal about it, in some schools. And every time one of the schools changed their policy, he'd just go someplace else. Where he could have his fun."

"That's sick."

"I'm sure that's what the teachers' union would have said, if he'd ever gotten busted for what he was doing."

"You don't like teachers much, Mr. . . . Grange?"

"I like teachers fine. I don't like freaks who hide behind authority to fuck with kids. Do you?"

"Look! I told you—"

"Hey, that's all right," I reassured him. "I'm sure, no matter who I ask around here, nobody tells me about one single teacher in the whole history of this school who ever had a thing for students. Not even a whisper of a rumor."

"Rumors are pernicious," he huffed, still offended.

"Thanks for your time," I told him, getting to my feet.

"Sit down a minute," he said. He got up, walked over to the door, and closed it. "You want me to level with you, that's a two-way street."

"The girl is missing," I told him, flat out, no preamble. "Not a trace, not a clue. Disappeared. The cops have it marked as a runaway. The parents don't think so. They hired me to see what I could find out."

"Uh-huh. That's what Principal McDuffy told me. That *and* to keep it quiet. There's been nothing in the papers. . . ."

"And there's not going to be, not for a while. The parents don't want to . . . put on any pressure. If she was snatched, they'll hear from the kidnappers. If she ran away of her own accord, they don't want her to think they're . . . hunting her. And if she's already dead . . ."

"*Dead?* Where did *that* come from?"

"She's gone, okay? When you work one of these cases and you've got a blank piece of paper in front of you for possibilities, 'dead' is one of the things you write on it."

He leaned back in his chair, as if to put some distance between us. "What if there *was* the kind of teacher you were talking about here? Not the . . . one who liked to beat children . . . the . . . For the sake of argument, an English teacher who picked out a new girl—a budding poet—every year. Say everybody knew about it, but nobody ever said anything, because it doesn't seem as if he ever got . . . sexual with students."

"Uh-huh."

"I don't want to argue abstractions with you. Especially since we're only speaking theoretically here. But what if, say, you knew about this particular teacher, but you *also* knew he couldn't possibly be connected to Rosebud?"

"And how would I . . . theoretically . . . know that?"

"Because he . . . this hypothetical individual . . . has a pattern. One a year, right through the next summer. And he's still involved with someone. A graduated senior. Over eighteen."

"Yeah. What if?"

"I'm trying to help out here. To the extent I feel comfortable doing so."

"Much appreciated," I said, getting up again. This time, he didn't make any attempt to stop me. Or to shake hands.

"She was more *studious* than she was a *student,* if you understand my meaning," the English teacher told me in the front room of his charming little cottage. I could hear sounds of another person coming from the kitchen, but nothing more specific.

"I'm a little slow, doc. Help me out."

Reference to his Ph.D. seemed to transform him from nervous interviewee to pontificator. "Rosebud was very interested in the *subject* of creative writing, but not always so interested in the individual assignments."

"Typical of a kid her age, right?"

"Not really," he said, condescension hovering just above his voice. "Young people her age are much more mature in their decisions than a layman would expect."

"Uh-huh. Well, is there *anything* you can tell me?"

"I think not," he said, carefully. "I doubt I had a single conversation alone with her during the entire year."

I sat silently, listening to the sounds from the kitchen. A drawer closing, a dish rattling against a counter, refrigerator opening . . . Whoever was in there wanted me to be certain I knew *someone* was.

"I know she was a vegan . . ." he finally said, once he realized I was too thick to know when I'd been dismissed.

"A . . . ?"

"A vegetarian, only more intense about it. And she loved old Jimmy Cagney movies."

"Thanks. That could be a big help."

I stood up to leave, then turned to him and said: "Tell me, who's a friend of hers. Any friend."

"I have no idea."

"Sure you do," I told him. "You never spoke to her, but you spoke to someone who knew her well enough to tell you about that vegan thing and the movies."

"I . . ."

"You know what you said before? About some kids being a lot more mature than people would think? That's especially true for girls, isn't it?"

We both listened to the sounds coming from his kitchen. I looked in that direction, making sure he saw me do it.

Then he told me the friend's name.

"I heard she took off," the tall, rangy girl said, bouncing a basketball absently. We were standing together at the end of her driveway, the hoop on a stanchion nearer the garage.

"That's what it seems like, Charmaine."

"Well, if she did, I'm not going to help you find her."

"If she took off for a good reason, I won't bring her back," I said.

The girl looked at me as if she was thinking about taking me to the hoop off her dribble. "I don't know," she said, thoughtfully.

"I'm not asking you to *tell* me anything," I said softly. "Just to give her a message if"—I held up my hand to stop her from interrupting—"*if* she gets in touch. Okay?" When she didn't say anything, I handed her my card.

She chewed her lip. "You want to play some one-on-one?"

"Do I look like a basketball player to you?"

"Basketball players don't *look* like anything in particular," she said. "People think if you're tall you can play basketball. But that isn't necessarily true."

"You can, right?"

"I had to teach myself," she said quietly. "It didn't come naturally or anything. It was a lot of work."

"I respect that," I said. Telling the truth.

She bounced the ball a couple of times, stepped off, and launched a long jumper, goosenecking her wrist to guide it home.

Nothing but net.

"An easy three," I congratulated her.

"They're never easy," she said. But a smile teased at her lip.

I went quiet, waiting for her decision.

"Rosie is the most . . . moral person I know," she said, finally. "She wouldn't do anything wrong. I don't mean she wouldn't, you know, break the law. If she thought the law was . . . immoral. Like civil disobedience. But she wouldn't do anything . . . unethical. Like cheat on a test. Or even tell lies. She didn't drink and she didn't do drugs. . . ."

"Her father said she smoked pot."

"*I* never saw her do that."

"Maybe he got it wrong."

"He probably did. He doesn't know her."

"Fathers never know their daughters, do they?"

"Mine doesn't," she said, the smile gone from her voice.

The next day, I went back to the school, walked the corridors for a while. But it was pretty much cleared out for the summer. When I came back outside, a girl was perched on the front fender of my Ford. She was auburn-haired, wearing blue-jean shorts with matching suspenders. They were strapped over a white T-shirt as flimsy as the excuses she'd probably been trafficking in since she was thirteen. Her mouth was a wicked slash of dark red, and she was licking a green lollipop like she was auditioning for a porno movie. I couldn't tell if she was sixteen or thirty-three.

"You're the guy, right?" she greeted me.

"What guy would that be?"

"The guy looking for Little Miss I'm-All-That."

"Oh! You thought I was looking for *you*. Sorry, young lady. You've been misinformed."

"That's cute." She shrugged her shoulders against the off-chance I was confused about her not wearing a bra. "You know who I'm talking about."

"I don't know *what* you're talking about," I told her, taking out a cigarette.

"Give me one," she demanded, holding out the hand without the lollipop.

"You're not old enough."

"Get real. People don't have to be as old as *you* to smoke."

"People don't have to be as old as me to be retired."

She gave me a long look. One that apparently required her to arch her back deeply.

I kept my eyes on hers.

She put the lollipop back in her mouth, then bit down on it, hard. I could hear the crunch as the lollipop fragmented. She pulled out the empty stalk, tossed it away.

I lit my cigarette, took a drag. She reached over, plucked it out of my hand, took a drag herself. She didn't return it to me.

"What's it worth to you?" she asked, crossing her meaty thighs to emphasize the ambiguity.

"To stand around in a parking lot and play games with a kid? Nothing."

"I'm not a kid. I'm a girl. A bad girl."

"Congratulations. You look as if you put a lot of effort into it."

"Look, I know you're not a cop."

"Is that right?"

"Yes. I heard you were asking around. About her. I figure someone hired you to do that. So maybe you want to hire me."

"Hire you to do what?"

"Help you. Like, be your assistant. For what you're trying to find out, you're too . . . I don't know . . ."

"Old?"

"Scary. You already scared some people. Nobody's going to talk to you."

"If they don't know anything, what's the difference?"

"They might."

"Sure."

"What's your name?"

"Hazard. B. B. Hazard."

"You didn't ask me mine."

"That's right, I didn't."

"You don't care?"

"No. I don't play with kids."

"My name is Peaches."

"Uh-huh. Is that what it says on the birth certificate? You know, the one that says you're twenty-five."

"Twenty-two. And it's not a phony."

"Right. And you're a schoolmate of the person you think I'm looking for? How many times were you left back, exactly?"

"Why do you have to be like this? Bobby Ray told me you were looking for this Rose girl. I didn't say I knew her or anything. But I could help you find her. If you paid me."

"Who's Bobby Ray?"

"He works for Project Safe. You know, like an outreach worker. He's out there every night."

"Red-haired kid, freckles? About my height, wears a Raiders jacket?"

"That's him!"

"I don't know him."

"But you just said—"

"I ran across him. That's all. He can't vouch for you."

"Ask him, okay? I mean, you can check *him* out, can't you? Where he works and everything? So, if Bobby Ray tells you I'm cool, that would be enough, wouldn't it?"

"Look, kid—"

"I'm not a kid. And I *could* help you."

"Let's cut to it, okay? You know where the girl I'm looking for is, we can do a deal. Name your price, I'll run it past the people who hired me. They go for it, *and* you turn her up, the money's yours."

"How do I know you'd—"

"You tell me you know where she is, I'll let your pal Bobby Ray—you know, the guy *you* trust—I'll let him hold the stake."

"I *don't* know where she is. But I *could* help you find her."

"No sale, kid."

She hopped off the fender like it was a glowing griddle. Denim is a restrictive fabric, but the curve of her rump imposed its will anyway. I watched her walk away . . . just to see what car she got into. But she turned the corner of the building and disappeared.

Just like the girl she said she could lead me to.

"You know a girl named Peaches?" I asked Bobby Ray that night.

We were standing on a corner in the Northwest, a few doors down from a building where kids crashed. It wasn't a South Bronx burnout, not even abandoned, really. The kids had moved in while the owner waited for financing on the renovations he would need to rehab the rental units. The way I heard it, the place had running water, but no electricity. Probably no heat, either, but the weather kept that from being a big deal.

It had taken a couple of more weeks, and another extension on Kevin's money, to get this close to Bobby Ray. We weren't pals, exactly. But he wasn't distancing himself from me by body language anymore, deliberately warning kids off, the way he did when I'd first come up on him.

"I know a lot of people," he said, vaguely.

"Bobby Ray, I asked you if you know her, okay? Not who she hangs out with. Not what she's up to. And not where to find her."

He gave me a measuring kind of look. I knew what that meant. A question he wanted answered. Bobby Ray was a trader. Info for info. He kept his street position by being in the know. You couldn't buy his knowledge for money, and that's why he got so much of it for free.

"Is it true you were a mercenary?" he asked me.

I kept my face blank. *Maybe the girl's father is nosing around again? Name-dropping while he's at it?* No point asking Bobby Ray where he'd heard something like that: the whisper-stream flows through every city in the world.

"What do you mean by a mercenary?" I said. "Like a 'soldier of fortune' in the movies? Someone who gets paid to kill people in a country where the only law *comes* from killing people? What?"

"I don't know, exactly. I never really thought about it. A lot of Vietnam vets you meet out here say they were—"

"I'm not a Vietnam vet," I cut him off. I don't mind lying about who I am or what I've done, but something about posing as a Vietnam vet makes me sick to my stomach. Tens of thousands of kids sacrificed to testosterone politics and business-worship while their better-born counterparts stayed home and partied. Back then, the only sincerity was in the antiwar movement. But that rotted at its core when movie stars started preening for the heroic torturers of the VC.

It was an impossible tightrope to walk—oppose the war, but support the soldiers—and most fell off to one wrong side or the other. A few of the antiwar radicals died, and a few more went to prison. Some of them are still there.

Some of the white members of the "underground" surfaced to yuppiedom. But the blacks couldn't go back to where they'd never been. The profiteers and the cherry-pickers found new targets, the SLA survivors got paroled, and ex-Panthers and former SDS members ran for Congress.

Some revolutionaries of that era stayed true. Leonard Peltier is still buried alive in a federal POW camp. But he gets less media attention than Vanilla Ice. And *much* less fan mail than Charles Manson.

The war itself was as big a lie as the "war on drugs." Politicians announcing a war, sending others to do the actual fighting . . . then fixing it so they couldn't win.

And the kids who died for the lie—all they got was their name on a fancy slab of marble.

It's a whole syndrome now: people pretending to be Vietnam vets. Especially popular among guys in the financial industry, for some reason I don't get . . . probably the same twits who think they grow bigger balls every time some Internet stock runs up. See, it's chic to "support" the people who fought over there, now that it's over. So every guy who tries to glom a handout, he's a Vietnam vet. People who would have had to be three years old when they enlisted, they're Vietnam vets. They're running for office, working a barroom, hustling women . . . all playing that liar's card.

And now we're all buddy-buddy with Vietnam, right? Like it never happened. Hell, business is business, and the slopes over there like McDonald's even better than the niggers do over here. Great market for cigarettes, too. And you can't beat those cheap labor costs with a stick . . . although it's okay to beat the laborers.

MIA. Money Is All.

I turned eighteen while Vietnam was still raging, but I was safe from being called up—they didn't have a draft board in prison. They had one in court, though. Plenty of guys my age went when judges safe from the draft did their patriotic duty by letting young men trade a sentence for an enlistment. That's how Wesley learned to work long-distance—Uncle taught him some new tricks.

I got out of prison while it was still going on, but I never went near the army. I ended up in another jungle, on another continent. A genocidal war fueled by tribalism, but ignited by nondenominational lust for oil.

Years later, a government spook told me I was still listed on the Nigerian registry of war criminals. Good joke. The Nigerian government is a fucking crime cartel, holding whole tribes down by military violence, while their privileged classes spend their time making the country the international scam capital of the world.

I'm a veteran of a lot of things. War is only one of them. But Vietnam's not on that list; and there's something special about it keeps me from adding it to the fabric of lies I roll out for strangers.

"So where'd you learn the military stuff, then?" Bobby Ray asked. A clever kid. Or one who had been interrogated by professionals often enough to learn some of the tricks himself.

"Why is anything like that important?"

"You never know," he said, solemnly. "You never know what something's worth."

"That's true," I said. Thinking I wouldn't have to go through this crap if I was back in New York. My references were all over the street there. And the threads were never so tangled that I couldn't find someone who knew me *and* whoever was asking about me, too. But in Portland, I was nobody and nothing.

There was an upside, sure. Nobody looking for me, either.

"I've been in military conflicts under foreign flags," I finally said. "Good enough?"

"Do you know, like, karate and shit?" he asked, pronouncing the word "cah-rah-dee," not "ka-rah-tay." I liked him for it.

"Nope."

"So you're, like, into weapons?"

"I'm a pacifist."

"You don't look like that was always the case."

"When I was your age, I did a lot of stupid things."

"Yeah? Like what?"

"Going to prison."

"For what?"

"For being stupid."

He waited for me to add something. Finally, he realized I was done.

"What kind of name is B.B.?" he asked.

"Same kind as Bobby Ray."

"You know, I'm thinking it might just be. Bobby Ray, that was the name my mother . . . I mean, my . . . Anyway, that was the name I was born with. Sounds kind of like a hillbilly one, right?"

"If you mean Appalachian, yeah."

"Well, so does B.B. You ever notice how, sometimes, the white people who hate blacks the most, they're the ones most likely to have the same kind of names?"

"It's not so surprising. They come from the same places."

"The South?"

"Poor."

"Oh. Yeah. Does B.B. stand for anything?"

I measured the depth of his eyes. Made the decision. "Baby Boy," I told him.

His face went sad enough for me to know he got it.

We talked for another hour or so; exchanging now, not fencing like before. A woman with one bad leg hobbled past, moving with the aid of a stout stick. A rednose pit bull trotted alongside of her, off-leash, but obviously hers, from the way it was moving. When she stopped to ask Bobby Ray for a smoke, the pit sat beside her. It was wearing a little white T-shirt, with "ICU" written across its broad chest in big red letters. I gave the woman a whole pack, saluted to tell her I got the joke. She gave me a ghosty smile back.

I wonder if she knew that pit bulls were a "forbidden race" of dogs in some countries. Like Germany. Or if she'd get *that* joke.

Finally, Bobby Ray did the mental math and figured I'd brought enough to get some. He said: "I know Peaches."

"Yeah . . . ?"

"She's not a runaway. Maybe she was, once. But she's got to be thirty, at least. Been hooking out here even before I came."

"On the street?"

"Sure," he said. Meaning, "Where else?"

I couldn't picture the girl who'd braced me in the parking lot with a street pimp. She was too brassy-sassy for that. And way too fresh-looking. So I came in sideways. "I guess the johns couldn't miss all that red hair."

"Red hair? Not Peaches, man. She sports a natural. Not many do that anymore—it stands out."

"She's black?"

"Peaches? Does Nike suck?" he said, the Portland street-kid equivalent of "Is the Pope Catholic?"

"Hmmm . . . I must have been confused that night," I told

him, giving a cigarette from a fresh pack to one of the kids who stopped and stood in front of us, wordlessly.

When the kid moved along, I tried to divert Bobby Ray off any trail he might have thought he'd discovered. "How'd you get into this?" I asked him.

"This?"

"Outreach . . . whatever you call it."

"Oh. Well, it's a long story. But I'm sure you could put it together easy enough."

"You were out here yourself, once?"

"No, man. I had a home. A *foster* home. That's what saved my life."

"I've been in a few myself," I said, my voice level, inviting more info. I didn't think it would be a good idea to mention what happened in one of the foster homes I'd done time in. Or that I'd used one of Wesley's credos to get out of it: "Fire works."

"Yeah, I know," he said. "I've heard it all. Foster homes are just warehouses for kids, run by people who do it for the money. Or even abuse the kids themselves. You know what? Maybe that's true for *some* of them. But the one I was in . . . man, they raised *dozens* of kids. And I mean *radically* fucked-up kids. Like I was."

"Drugs?"

"Drugs? Maybe my *mother's* drugs, I don't know. Me, I was two years old when I came there. And I never left."

"I thought they usually bounced foster kids around from place to place."

"Nobody was going to bounce *anybody* out of Mom's place," he said. "She was a tiger, man. Once they dropped you off, you were *hers,* that's all there was."

"Your bio-mother," I said, watching close as he nodded at the term, "she never tried to get you back?"

"When I was around eleven, she did, I think. There were some people coming around, and I had to go to court, talk to the judge, and all. But it was nothing.

"She was . . . I didn't remember her. She was mad about that.

Like it was my fault that I didn't. Anyway, she said she'd give me up if she could have some pictures taken with me. I didn't know what that was all about. But my mom—Mrs. Kznarack was what everybody called her—she said, Sure, go ahead, Bobby Ray. So I did. But as soon as . . . as soon as my 'birth mother' left, the fun started."

"The court wanted you to be freed for adoption, right?"

"Yeah! How'd you . . . ? Ah, never mind, I guess that's the way it always is. *Usually* is, anyway. My mom, she wasn't going for *that*. I can still remember her yelling at the judge. At *all* of them. She said the time for me to be adopted was when I was little, but they kept putzing around, giving my bio-mom one chance after another, and now who was going to adopt me, eleven years old?"

"How come she didn't just—?"

"Oh, she *did,* man. I see where you're going, but Mom was way ahead of you. They told her the plan was adoption, and that's the way it was going to be. So Mom told them, cool, *she'd* adopt me. There wasn't a thing they could say. . . ."

"Had she adopted a lot of—?"

"Look, man," he said, his voice turning hard for the first time since I'd met him, "this is my mom we're talking about, not some Mia Farrow wannabe, all right? Foster mother, adoptive mother, didn't make a damn bit of difference to her. Or to me."

"She sounds like one hell of a woman," I said by way of apology.

"She is. And Pop's no slouch himself, although he lets Mom do all the talking."

"Working guy?"

"*Hard*-working guy. He's a stonecutter. Best around."

"I thought that was a lost art."

"Pop says it'll never be lost, so long as someone's doing it. He taught us all stuff, but we didn't all have the gift for it. My sister Helene, she's the one he picked to carry it on. She's a *genius* at it, man."

"The foster kids those people had, they all turned out so . . . ?"

"You're cute, man. But I'll tell you straight. Some turned out better than others. Like in any big family. But not a motherfucking one of us hurts their kids; you understand what I'm telling you?"

"Yeah. That DNA doesn't mean squat when it comes to how you act."

"On time!" he said, offering me a palm to slap. "Mom and Pop proved that one. Too bad the shitheads running the government never snapped to it."

"Too bad there aren't more like your parents."

"Truth, man. But there's a lot more than there used to be, if you get what I'm saying."

"Sure. Your parents couldn't have *had* that many kids, but they *raised* a whole pack of them. That's what counts."

"That's what counts," he repeated. "And that's why I'm out here. What I do, it counts, too."

I didn't know what the girl's note about finding the "Borderlands" meant, but I knew she wasn't going to be working at Starbucks to save money for the trip.

I'd been trolling for Rosebud mostly on foot, using the Ford to get me to the starting spots. But if I was going to play it like she was out there using her moneymaker, the Ford's plain gray wrapper wouldn't do. It just screamed "unmarked car," and I needed to make my approach from downwind.

When I ran it down at dinner one night, Gordo offered me his ride. I was grateful—I knew how much he had invested in that car. Money was the least of it. But the Metalflake maroon '63 Impala was as distinctive as the Ford was anonymous. And its dual quad 409 had a sound that stayed with you.

I thought of a station wagon, but it wouldn't go with my face. I could use some of that Covermark stuff Michelle got for me on the bullet scar, and the missing top of my right ear wouldn't show.

No one would see the mismatched right eye, either; there has to be some decent light for anyone to notice. But the one eye they'd make contact with would tell them I wasn't a citizen.

Flacco said they had plenty of cars in the garage. People who came to them for custom work expected their rides to be tied up for a while.

I took a look. Finally, settled on a white Cadillac Seville STS. Central Casting for the role I'd be playing.

I started that same night. They don't mark the prostie strolls on tourist maps, but you don't need to be a native to find them. I just nosed the Cadillac in ever-widening figure-8 loops, using a down-market topless bar as a starting point. It didn't take long.

They work it in Portland the same way they do in every city I've been. Brightly colored birds with owner-clipped wings to keep them from flying away, fluttering at every car that cruises by slow. Like Amsterdam, only without the windowboxes.

The more subtle girls worked about half dressed; the rest of them put it all right out there. Lots of blond nylon wigs, torn fishnet stockings, and run-down spike heels. Cheap, stagy makeup around bleached-out eyes. A shabby, tired show that needed the murky darkness to sustain the illusion. Pounds of wiggle, not an ounce of bounce.

If Rosebud had been younger, I'd have looked elsewhere. I didn't know if the local cops swept for underage hookers, or kept tabs on their pimps, but I figured it was like anywhere else—if you're pushing kiddie sex, you do it indoors. In America, anyway.

Sure, Rosebud was underage, but just barely so. She could tart up legal easy enough, if that's the way she was earning. And even gutter-trash pimps know where to get passable ID today.

My own ID was top-shelf. A Beretta 9000S, chambered for .40-caliber S&W. You might think a handgun would be the opposite of a walkaway card if you got stopped by the cops . . . if you didn't know how things work. A passport may be the Rolex of fake documents, but all it will do is trip the cop-alarms if you flash one around anyplace but the airport.

An Oregon carry permit is a better play. Just possessing it tells the law you've already been printed and came up clean: no felony convictions, no NGIs, not even a domestic-violence restraining order to mar your record. Who could be a better citizen than a legally armed man?

Oregon's one of the few states that closed the gun-show loophole; you want to buy a firearm here, you *are* going through a background check. The piece I was carrying had been purchased new from a licensed dealer in a small town in eastern Oregon a couple of years ago. Then the dealer had gone out of business. But a back-check of his records would show that he'd sold the piece to the same Joseph Grange my driver's license said I was.

In some towns, winos sell their votes once a year. In the more progressive jurisdictions, they can sell their prints once a week.

Some of the working girls were more aggressive than others; nothing special there. Nothing special anywhere. I spent a couple of hours, crisscrossing, not making any secret of the prowling, as if I were looking for something a little different. In some cities, the legal-age girls act as steerers for the indoors-only stuff. I didn't know if they did it that way in Portland, but I wasn't going to ask around until I got a better sense of who was hustling.

"You looking for a date, honey?" the high-mileage blonde asked. She leaned into the passenger-side window I'd zipped down when she'd approached. Her partner was dark-haired, but with the same tiny arsenal of seductiveness; she was licking her lips with all the passion of a metronome.

"No thanks, Officer," I told her.

Her giggle was juiceless. "Oh, *please.* Do cops come right out and tell you they'll gobble your cock for twenty-five?"

"Nope. But I've had them promise to look the other way for fifty."

Her laugh was a snort. "You're a funny guy. But I'm not out here to be talking."

"Fair enough," I told her, feeling for the power-window switch with my left hand.

"Wait!" the blonde said. "What makes you think I'm a cop?"

"Cops work in pairs," I said, nodding my head at her partner.

"Oh, man, come on. We're just selling sandwiches. And you look like you got just the right meat. Try some three-way; you'll swear it's the *only* way."

"Some other time," I told her, and pulled away.

I spent a lot of time listening to approaches, alert for the right girl—one who'd been out there for a while, kept her eyes open, wouldn't mind making a few bucks doing something that didn't require penetration. But no matter where I went, the approaches were mostly by pairs.

It rang wrong. Sure, pimps would put a new girl out with a more experienced one. And some hookers—lesbians who knew that most of the action would be them playing with each other while the trick watched—*only* worked three-ways. But this was happening much too widely for those thin blankets to cover.

After four nights, nothing had changed. It wasn't a one-time spook, so I knew what it meant. What it *had* to mean.

There hadn't been anything in the papers or on the news. But down where hookers stroll, the whisper-stream flows especially deep. And if they got scared enough, they'd play it for pure true.

But while I was thinking it through, another couldn't-be coincidence flowed across my path like a shark in shallow water. A big black car with a smooth shape, chromeless, its running lights banked. I'd seen it a dozen times over the past few nights, always in motion, moving unhurried but slippery at right angles to where I was going.

I knew it was the same car—a Subaru SvX—because of its window-in-window mortised side glass, like the DeLorean once sported. The SvX had been a techno-triumph, an all-wheel drive luxury barge that cornered well and ran strong, but it never caught on, and Subaru stopped making them years ago. Couldn't be that many of them still around, even in the Pacific Northwest, where most of them had been sold.

The Subaru was only vaguely menacing. It didn't follow me when I finally left the grids late every night, and it didn't seem to frighten the girls any more than the cops who rolled by on bicycles every once in a while did. A pimp, maybe? Checking his traps? But the car was the opposite of flash, and any pimp big enough to have girls working a half-dozen different spots on the same night wouldn't be driving anything but ultra. Maybe a "documentary"-maker who'd learned how to work his videocam one-handed? Or a screenwriter trying to pick up a little "noir"?

Ah, whatever. Trying to figure out every reason people scope hooker strolls would give a mainframe computer an aneurysm.

"You know a cop?" I asked Gem one morning.

"I know many police officers."

"Any you can trust enough?"

"Enough to . . . what? There are degrees of trust."

"Something's going on. In the street. I think I know what it is, but I can't be sure."

"Does it have anything to do with the girl you are looking for?"

"I . . . don't know. Don't think so, in fact. But it may affect the *way* I look."

"Do you have something to trade?"

"Trade?"

"Yes. Something in exchange for the information you seek."

"I always have the same thing. Just depends on how much of it he wants."

"He?"

"The cop. Or 'she,' I guess. It doesn't matter. And I'm talking about money, Gem. What else?"

"I am not sure. But . . . not money. There is one policeman I know who is a detective. He is not . . . I would not say he is unhappy, perhaps that is wrong. But he could do more than he has been . . . given the opportunity to do. I know what he would want; and it is not money, it is information. I just don't know what kind."

"I'm not a—"

"Burke, what is wrong with you?"

"Nothing."

"That does not seem correct, 'nothing.' You thought I was suggesting you become a police informant?"

"I . . . no, I didn't think that. It's just that . . . you can't speak for this cop you know. It may not be in *your* mind, or in mine, but it could be in *his,* understand?"

"Understand? Yes, I understand. I am not as stupid as you seem to believe, sometimes."

"Gem . . ."

"Never mind. You will meet my police officer, then you will decide for yourself."

By the time I took off that night, Gem still hadn't said another word to me. But she'd been on her phone a lot.

The stroll I tried was one of those streets that always seem wet at night, as if the violence shimmering beneath the surface had popped out like sweat on skin.

I caught the Subaru's chromeless flicker as it came up on my flank like a moving oil slick, then veered off into a side street. By that time, I had enough of a sense of the car to be able to pick it up on my own radar. The Subaru was a streak of light-eating matte against the sheen of the street, running through Hookerville as steady and mysterious as a midnight train.

But I never thought about trying a tail. Gordo had hooked the Caddy up with a set of toggle switches so I could alter the light configuration at the front and rear ends, but anyone who'd gone to the extent of powder-coating his car wheels black would be hip to that trick. Besides, whoever was piloting the Subaru knew the back streets real well, and had the horsepower to run away and hide, if that's what they wanted.

I talked to a few more girls. But the only thing shaking was what they were selling.

I slept late, spent the afternoon killing time. The radio had some homophobic harpy who seemed to believe God had anointed her to rant her sleazy morality at the rest of us. I treated her show like its sponsors should have, then turned on the TV. Local news had a story about some community-spirited woman who apparently devoted her life to harassing hookers out of certain neighborhoods. Seems she built up quite a following . . . until she pepper-sprayed some teenage girl on her way to school. I bet the self-righteous babbler on the radio would have approved.

I gave the hookers the night off, tried my luck in downtown. The weather brought out the flowers. And the humans who live to pluck them. Most predators have a sweet tooth.

Plenty of kids on the street. Some of them cute as candy-stripers, some as ugly as truth. The usual mix—kids who believed they could read crop circles, and kids who snuck out at night to make them.

All trying to manage their own pain, their own way. Thinking of a rich girl from Connecticut who'd named herself Fancy. I can still see her. On a bed. On her hands and knees, facedown, marble bottom thrust high and defiant. "Kiss it or whip it," she harsh-whispered to me. "I don't do vanilla sex."

And the Prof, watching with me as rubber-gloved guards carried past the body-bagged remains of a young con who'd hanged himself late the night before. "The poor dope couldn't cope with hope," the little man said, warning me and keeping me focused at the same time.

I always listened to the Prof. Not just because I loved him; because he *knew*. "You call it, you got to haul it," he'd taught me.

That was the truth, Inside or out. If you took the label, you had to live up to it.

Different labels, different expectations. Watch enough prize-fights, you'll see plenty of heavyweights who aren't tough at all; they're just bullies. They lose their spine quick enough when they have to face an opponent who can really slam. But you'll never see an intimidated bantamweight.

Something wasn't adding up. I had an idea, but that was all. The next morning, I drove over to where Gordo and Flacco were working. When they weren't at sea, they spent all their time in the garage, doing a frame-off on Gordo's '56 Packard Caribbean hardtop. Gordo had spent years working on Flacco's 409; now it was Flacco's turn to make his partner's dream come true.

"¿Qué pasa?" I asked, ritualistically.

"De nada," one of them replied, completing the circuit. The two men liked their games—neither one remotely resembled the name he went by.

"Going to be unreal," I said, sighting down the rear fender of the Packard toward the trademark cathedral taillight. They both made sounds of fervent agreement.

"It was your idea, *hombre,*" Gordo, the mechanic half of the team, reminded me.

"It was," I acknowledged, proudly. "Never thought you'd find one so quick, though."

"Well, it was a total basket case," Flacco said. "No engine or tranny; the torsion bars all busted down below—no way anyone does a numbers-match resto on this bad boy. Good damn thing, too; they wanted too much for it as it was."

"It'll be worth it," I assured him. "You could cruise for years and never see another like it."

"¡Sí!" Gordo confirmed. "And I got the best metal man in the business going for me, too."

"This job's going to be a stone motherfucker," Flacco said, bobbing his head slightly at his partner's praise. "But we get it perfect, *amigo,* this you can take to the bank."

"You're going to need major cubes to move this monster," I said to Gordo.

"It *came* with major cubes, man. More than six liters' worth. Twin fours, duals, high compression . . . I'll bet it could *move,* back in the day. But there's no way we'd ever find a drop-in lying around. I been studying on it, and I figure, the way to go, we get us a custom-rebuilt Hemi. *Plenty* room under there for the Elephant; and that way, we got something real special, you with me?"

"Perfect!" I agreed, offering him a palm to slap. "There's no replacement for displacement."

I hung around for another hour or so, listening to Flacco. How he was not only going to make the hood scoops functional, he was also planning to flare the fenders so the nineteen-inch wheel-and-tire combo would look as if it were factory stock. And then Gordo explained how he was going with a full air-bag suspension, so the monster could get into the weeds for show but be driven on the street without a problem.

Just before I left, I asked them if they had a convertible I could borrow for the night.

"Sure," Flacco said. "You got clean paper, *amigo*? *La Migra* is a motherfucker."

It was their joke that I was running the same risk with INS they were, only paper standing between me and deportation.

"I'll just speak Spanish," I told them.

That cracked Gordo up. "That plan, it is *muy estúpido, hombre*. They hear *your* Spanish, they know you ain't from down south."

"Not like your English," I complimented them.

"Ah, I got a better plan," Flacco said, bitterly. "I ever get dropped, I tell them I'm a fucking *cubano,* okay? Instead of shipping me back across the river, they buy me a house in Miami. *¿Verdad?*"

"Right," I agreed. America doesn't care much about why you came here, just where you came *from*. We take Marielitos with open arms because they're "fleeing repression." But when people try to cross the Rio Grande to get away from death squads and drug armies and bone-crumbling poverty, we ship them off like a NAFTA export.

The real reason Congress excludes Mexicans is that it doesn't want California turning into another Florida. You give wetbacks a chance at political power, the ungrateful bastards will actually *use* it.

"Hell, friend, no offense, okay?" Smilin' Jack told me the next day. "But I'm trying to run a comics business here, not a message drop."

"Sure, I understand. But, like you said, you're a businessman, right?"

"Right . . ." he said, guardedly.

"And a business like this, one thing you always do, you take extra-good care of your best customers, right? I mean, let's say they wanted to meet one of the artists who draw these comics, and you knew the artist was going to be in your store, well, you'd be sure and let the customer know, right?"

He nodded like he was going along. But then he blew me off with, "One, Madison isn't going to be dropping in to do a signing anytime soon that I know of. Two, you're not exactly what I would describe as a good customer."

"What's a good customer?" I asked him. The store was empty, but I needed more than just his casual attention. I had to keep him engaged until he saw the light.

"A good customer is, first of all, a *regular,*" he said, as if he could conjure one up by describing the prototype. "We keep a hold for all our regulars."

"What's a hold?"

"Well, it's, like, the customer tells us what comics he wants. And every month, or whenever their favorites are published, we pull what they want from our shipment and we hold it for them until they come in."

"What's the big deal about that?"

"Well, for one thing, we're taking a risk."

"What risk?"

He tapped his fingers on the counter, waiting patiently to educate me. "We have to *buy* the merchandise we sell. I mean, we pay *cash* for it. Then we own it. So we can sell it for whatever we want. But if we *don't* sell it, we eat it. That wasn't so bad, once. When sales were slamming."

"So what happened?" I asked, picking up from his tone that those days were gone.

"The elevator cable snapped before the car got to the top floor," he said. "Some people were smart enough to get off in time. And they made a *ton* of money. But most weren't. It was wrong, anyway."

"I'm not sure I follow you."

"Comics are about the . . . Well, it's like music, okay? Melody and lyrics? Comics are about art and story. Not about how 'collectible' they are. It all went to hell when folks started buying comics like they were stocks—more like stock *options,* actually. Most people, they never even *read* them, just bagged and boxed them, and waited for them to go up in value."

"But now . . . ?"

"Now that's not happening. Oh, don't get me wrong. You find me an early enough *Superman* or *Batman,* nice clean copy—with this stuff, condition is everything—and I'll make you some *serious* cash. Quick. And it's not just Golden Age material, either. The early Marvels, they're good, too. But no way the *current* stuff is collectible. Remember the death of Superman?"

"I must have missed it."

"Yeah, well, it was one of the biggest events in comics history. You had all *kinds* of people lining up to buy copies—with all the variants, too—for whatever the dealers wanted. But how is something ever going to be collectible when you sell millions of copies to start with?"

"I don't know."

"It's *not,*" he said, with don't-argue-with-me finality. "And it's never going to be."

"But didn't they *always* print millions of copies? When I was a kid, they only cost a—"

"Printed? Sure. Survived? Not even a handful. Comics were

printed on low-grade paper, stapled together. They weren't designed to be collected. Most kids rolled them up and stuffed them in their back pockets. And nobody really stored them properly. Back then, we didn't know anything about the effects of light, or temperature, or moisture. Nobody cared."

"But you said that it's going to make a comeback."

"I did. And I believe it," he said, reverently. "But the natural market for comics is people who *read* them. And that's a pretty small, steady group—college kids, mostly. The new generation is more interested in computer gaming."

I walked over to a floor-to-ceiling rack next to the counter. "Is there much of a market for this stuff?" I asked him, holding up a comic with a picture of two women stripped and shackled on the cover.

"Yeah!" He chuckled sadly. "Sure is. In fact, it wasn't for porno, I don't know how most comics operations would survive at all, anymore."

"Pretty expensive, too," I said, looking over the racks.

"It is. But the people who like that stuff, it doesn't bother them."

"You don't sell it to kids?"

"*Hell* no! This stuff isn't exactly *Playboy,* friend. It's really hardcore. I'm as much free-speech as the next guy, but nobody underage even gets to *browse* that stuff, much less buy it."

"Any of your customers have this kind of stuff in their hold?"

"They might," he said, suspicion lacing his voice. "Why do you ask?"

"Well, I was looking at those prices. I bet a guy could easily run up a tab of a couple hundred a month."

"Before, that was common. Now, if we had a customer with a hold that size, he'd be a goddamn treasure, I can tell you that."

I nodded, as if I was thinking it over. "Not all the comics are done by big publishers. You said that before, when I was in here."

"That's right. There's *lots* of people trying to publish their own. Not many as successful as Madison, but there's always new players every month. They come and they go."

"And *some* of those comics—a few of them, anyway—they could end up being collectible down the road, right?"

"It's possible. I wouldn't bet the farm on it."

"Not the farm, maybe," I said, reaching into my pocket, "but what if you pulled two hundred bucks a month worth of those new comics for me? Or maybe a little less, and use the rest to put them in those protective bags. In a couple of years, I'd have a real collection."

"You would. But so what? There's no guarantee I could pick any winners. Or that there'd even *be* any winners to pick."

"I'm a gambler," I told him.

"A professional gambler?" he asked, like he'd heard of them but never met one in the flesh.

"Yeah. Let's say you pull the comics for me every month. And let's say I pay you six months in front, just so you know you're not going to all that trouble for nothing. And so there's no risk."

"That would be—"

"Twelve hundred, right?"

"Well . . . no."

"Is my math wrong?"

"No. No, it's not that. It's just that . . . Well, our best customers get special discounts; they don't pay retail."

"So I'd actually be getting more for my money, then?"

"Yeah. I can't say exactly *how* much more—it kind of varies."

"Sold," I told him, handing over the bills.

"I'll get you a receipt."

"Nah, that's not necessary," I told him, keeping my voice light to take the sting out of what I was going to say. "I know where to find you."

"We'll be here," he promised. "I took a long-term lease on this spot when things were . . . different."

"Great. Now, as a valued customer, I wonder if you wouldn't mind . . . ?"

The convertible Gordo and Flacco lent me was a bone-stock Mustang. It had been sitting around in the shop waiting on a custom paint job. I drove it through the strolls with its top down. The radio dealt out the new Son Seals cut, "My Life," which was getting a lot of air play:

I've been so cheated
Until I was just defeated
But still I went and repeated
All of my mistakes. . . .

I didn't see the Subaru flit by until right near the end of my tour. And I didn't have any better luck with the girls.

"Tonight is satisfactory for you?" Gem asked.

"What does that mean?"

"To meet. As you asked."

"Oh yeah. Your cop."

"He is not *my* cop," she said sharply. "Sometimes I do not understand where you—"

"That's what *you* called him, Gem."

"I did not," she said positively, hands on hips.

"What's the big—?"

"You are wrong," she said, turning her back the way she does when she's angry.

"I'm sure," I told her, keeping my apology deliberately hollow. "What time?"

"It must be after one in the morning. When . . . Detective Hong is off-duty."

"All right."

"He is a very meticulous police officer. If he were to meet you while on duty, he would have to make a record of it."

"I got it."

"Very well," she said. All Gem's movements are economical. She was raised in the jungle, where blending is safety. So it was no surprise that she kept her hips under control. But when she walked away that time, even the subtle hint of a wiggle she usually allowed was gone.

Nobody spun around on their stools when we entered the bar, but the current shifted just enough to tell me our presence was noted.

The booth was the last one in a row of maybe a dozen. The man waiting there was mixed-race Asian, surprisingly tall when he got up to greet us. His hair was jet black, carefully spiked. His face was too rounded to be Chinese. Samoan? Filipino? Mama would have been able to decode his DNA in ten seconds. I just filed it away with the million other things I didn't know. He wore a slouchy plum-colored silk jacket over a black shirt and tie made of the same material, and a heavy silver ring on his left hand with some sort of symbol cut into the top.

Gem kissed his cheek hello. Even in her four-inch spikes, he had to bend forward to let her reach his face. He did it so smoothly I could tell they'd done it before.

We shook hands. His grip was dry, without pressure. "Henry Hong," he said.

"B. B. Hazard," I answered him.

He waited for Gem to slide into the booth before he sat down across from her.

"Gem says there is something you want to know that I might be able to help you with?" he opened.

"Maybe. Depends if what I'm picking up is on your teletype."

"Could you be a little more specific?" he asked politely, taking a gunmetal cigarette case out of his jacket, opening it to make sure I could see what it was. He offered me one with a slight gesture.

"Thanks," I said.

He lit his smoke from a slim lighter the color of lead, then handed the lighter to me. I fired up, blew some smoke at the ceiling.

"I've been spending a lot of time on the hooker strolls," I began. "Looking for a teenage girl. Runaway."

"Where, specifically?"

"Burnside, MLK, Upper Sandy . . ." I said vaguely, implying even wider coverage.

"All right," he said, validating my choices. "What makes you think she would be hooking?"

"Nothing. In fact, I've got good reason to think she *wouldn't*. But she has to be earning money somewhere, and I wanted to just . . . rule it out, you understand?"

"Yes."

"All right. What I'd do, normally, is spread her photo around with my phone number on the back. Tell the girls there's a reward out for good info."

"Normally?" he asked, mildly.

"Yeah," I replied, ignoring the question he was asking. "But these girls are on the hustle. You want to work with them, you have to make sure they aren't working *you*. So you try and get one of them alone, make your pitch."

He dragged on his cigarette gently. I was letting mine burn out in the ashtray.

"That's where I picked it up," I said. "I'm using a flash car—nice new Caddy, no rental plates, clear glass. Nothing that would spook them; anyone can see inside. But they pretty much approach only in pairs. I've even seen three of them at a time. And the ones who don't come off the curb, they're still watching . . . a lot closer than from idle curiosity."

"No offense," he said softly. "But your face . . . Maybe you're just—"

"It's not that," I told him, so he'd know I wasn't being sensitive. "No way they react to my looks from that distance. Maybe some types of rides would make them edgy. I could see it if I was driving a van, even a station wagon. But I even tried it with a top-down convertible, and it didn't make a bit of difference."

"You try any of the escort services?"

"Why would I do that? I'm looking for street info, not the high-priced spread."

"You said she was underage. . . ."

"Oh. Okay. You got any suggestions?"

He looked over at Gem, boxing me out as if he had wedged a wall between us in the booth. I couldn't see her expression without turning sideways, and I wasn't about to do that. I reached over and ground out what was left of the cigarette I hadn't smoked past the first drag. The cop's eyes were downcast, as if he was thinking something over. Or maybe he was looking at the tiny blue heart tattooed on my right hand, between the knuckles of the last two fingers. A hollow, empty heart. My tribute to Pansy.

Burke's NYPD file shows a lot of scars and marks, but no tattoos. They'd never had a chance to photograph this one.

"What do you think it means?" he finally asked me.

"Girls have been disappearing. Girls who worked the streets. Maybe in Portland, maybe somewhere down I-5; word like that moves with the traffic."

"This is a guess?"

"At best. I haven't seen anything in the papers about a serial killer. . . ."

"There was the guy they caught up north."

"Yeah. And he preyed on prostitutes, too. But that's nothing new—they're the easiest targets."

"They are," he conceded. "But that's all you have—that the hookers are working doubled up? Maybe three-way's the hot ticket out there right now."

"You start a sentence with 'maybe,' anything you say after that has to be true."

Gem kicked my ankle. A lot more sharply than she would have needed to get my attention.

"So what do *you* think?" Hong asked.

"I think you're playing with me," I told him. "There's lots of other reasons I've got for thinking there's a killer on the road, but what difference? Either you already know it, or nothing I can say would convince you."

He put his cigarette case flat on the table, helped himself to another. I passed.

"Could you not say what else you—?" Gem started to say. That time I turned and looked her full in the face. She shut up.

Hong smoked another cigarette in silence. I didn't know what Gem had told him about me, but if he thought waiting was going to make me nervous, he was misinformed.

Finally, he snubbed out the butt, leaned forward, and spoke so softly I had to concentrate to get it all.

"There's thirteen of them known gone. Between Seattle and the California line, nine of them in Oregon. No bodies. No missing-persons reports, either. None of them listed as runaways. All but one have priors."

"And habits?"

"It's a safe bet, but not a sure one. We don't think that's any kind of link."

"Their pimps said they ran off? Or just didn't come back one night?"

"Both. A couple of them claimed they knew where their girls ran off to. They pull girls from each other all the time."

"Or sell them."

"True. But the trafficked girls, you wouldn't expect to see them on the street right away. The pimps would want to stick them indoors, get their money out of them as quick as possible."

"No bodies, right?"

"No bodies," he confirmed. "No *crimes,* as far as we know."

"But the girls, they know different."

"They think so, anyway."

"Much obliged."

"Sure. If you pick up anything, I'd appreciate—"

"Bur— My . . . Uh, B.B. could help you," Gem stumbled out.

Something was very wrong with all this. Gem doesn't make those kinds of mistakes.

"How would that be?" Hong said smoothly, as if trying to spackle over a suddenly appearing crack in a plaster wall.

"B.B. is an expert," Gem told him confidently. Like I wasn't there. "He knows more about this . . . kind of thing than anyone."

"Is that right?" Hong asked me, deliberately neutral.

"I know freaks," I promised him.

"And you scan this as . . . ?"

"I don't. I needed to verify what I picked up on with you before I spent any time on it."

"And *why* would you spend any time on it?"

"If there was something in it for me," I told him, making it clear that was the *only* motivation that worked.

"You're going to catch a killer?"

"No. Not my style," I said.

"What, then?"

"Maybe I could get you some information about how it's being worked."

" 'It'?"

"The disappearances."

"Yes? Well, that would be worth . . . something, I'm sure. What is it you'd be looking for in exchange?"

I reached in my jacket, handed him one of the photos of Rosebud I'd been circulating. He took it, nodded.

"And," I said, quickly, before he got the idea that we had a contract so easy, "the name of that escort service."

"Which . . . ?"

"The one that runs them underage."

"What is *wrong* with you?" Gem snapped, as soon as we got into the Caddy.

"With *me*? I was just doing business."

"You were . . . offensive for no reason."

"I don't think so."

"You do not think you were being offensive? Or you believe you had a reason for being so?"

"You sound like a fucking lawyer."

"You do not wish to answer me?"

"What I fucking 'wish' is that you'd keep your little nose out of where it doesn't belong."

"Is that so? Perhaps you believe my nose does not belong in your house, then?"

"It's *your* house," I reminded her.

"Ah," she said. As if I had finally confessed to something.

For the escort service, I would need a hotel room. The only place I'd ever stayed in Portland was the Governor, when I'd been studio-comped by an old pal. It was an old-fashioned, classy joint, with nice thick walls. And it had a back way in that allowed you to avoid the front desk.

Nobody except the room-service folks had seen me the last time I'd stayed there, and if they remembered me at all, it would be in connection with the studio, so a visiting "escort" wouldn't exactly shock them.

I checked in around four in the afternoon. Between taking a nap, having something to eat, showering, and shaving, I easily killed time until it got dark. Figuring the escort service would have Caller ID, I made sure I used the hotel phone. Asked for a "reference," I gave them the name Hong had told me to use.

All that got me was a conversation, kind of like no-touch dancing. I tossed them every hint I could think of—right down to telling them I wanted a girl any father would be proud of; I bit eagerly when they spoke vaguely about "no discipline problems." After running the valid but untraceable major credit-card number I gave them, they promised me a "perfectly behaved young lady" by eleven.

She was about what I expected—a thin, curveless girl dressed down to look fifteen. She even brought her own silk-lined leather handcuffs and a red lollipop.

It took me about ten minutes of soft talking to convince her that I wasn't a cop, and another half-hour to sell her on the idea that she could make some serious money if she turned up Rosebud.

The hooker looked at the photo, almost blurted out that she'd never seen the girl I was looking for, then went into a slow shuffle about how *maybe* she'd seen her around, she just couldn't be, like, *sure,* you know.

Sure, I knew.

Maybe the hardest game on the planet is convincing a hooker you're not a trick.

The girl-looking hooker left early enough for me to go back on the prowl. So I walked a few blocks to where I'd stashed the Caddy and went back to work.

But the only girls who approached me alone were big-time wasted, strung out, and needy. Risking a ride with a serial killer wasn't much compared with their daily game of sticking dirty needles in collapsed veins. But all they could babble was a mulch of "fuck-suck" and "money-honey." Not much point in asking them if they'd seen Rosebud—they couldn't see the end of their own road.

When the sleek Subaru drifted across my path, I had a flash that maybe *it* was what was spooking all the girls. The wheeled shark sure looked menacing enough. Just the kind of car some halfwit screenwriter who thinks all sociopaths are handsome, charming, and intelligent would write into his fantasy.

But around three I saw it parked. Or stopped anyway, with a couple of girls bent low to get their heads down to the driver's window, their bottoms poised high, always working. I slid past on the right. The Subaru's passenger-side window was up. And tinted almost as dark as the body.

I grabbed the license number. Just in case Gem's friend would do me a little favor. If I ever decided to trust him that much.

"What is it that you want from me, exactly?" Madison's voice, on my cell phone. I guess Smilin' Jack *did* take care of his regulars.

"Just to ask you some questions. About comics . . . I think."

"You . . . think?"

"I have this picture. I mean, it's a drawing. But in ink, whatever you call that. I want to show it to you, ask you a couple of questions about it."

"And this is all because . . . ?"

"Because it's a clue. To that girl I told you I was looking for."

"What makes you think I would know anything of value?"

"I think you know a lot of value," I told her. "I've read all the comics now."

"How nice. But as to this . . . drawing?"

"Oh. Yeah, well . . . I'm not sure."

"Why me, then? Portland's full of experts who could take a look at—"

"It's the connection to you. To your work, I mean."

"Do you think it was *my* drawing?"

"No. It obviously isn't. Not your style at all. But that's not what I meant. Look, Ms. Clell—"

"Madison."

"Madison. Rosebud collected *your* comics. There isn't a sign that she ever collected anything else. So, the way I figure it, if anyone knows what this drawing means, it's you, okay?"

I listened to the cellular's satellite-connect hum for a few long seconds. Then she said, "Okay."

I'd already run across every street-kid thing from New Age to Wicca to skinhead. Pretty extreme range, but one thing in common—music drove all their cultures. Sometimes it just ran in the background, sometimes it was the sun everything orbited around. But it was always there.

I knew my chances of just bumping into Rosebud at random weren't worth much, so I concentrated on making friends. Financial friends. Bouncers at clubs, clerks in bookstores, swastika-inked tribalists, buskers, multi-pierced statement-makers, druggies, day-trip runaways.

Bobby Ray was always ready to talk with me, but he never came up with anything. I knew he was testing—pumping for info, back-checking to see if I told the same story twice—but I didn't know if he was sitting on knowledge or just looking for some.

When you're hunting, you tell different people different things. Or, at least, you drop different hints, let people draw their own conclusions. The bouncers thought I was looking for the kind of underage runaway that could only make trouble for them if they let her inside. But she could make them some real cash if they lifted the rope, and made a call while they had her boxed.

Other people got the idea Rosebud didn't know her sister needed a bone-marrow transplant. The skinheads thought I was up to something privately ugly. I made sure they knew she wasn't Jewish, and that if anyone but me hurt her, I'd hurt them.

One night, I passed by a couple of low-grade humans who thought that wearing stomping boots made them street-fighters. They were busy slapping around a tired old burnt-brain who lived out of garbage cans. I pointed the pistol at them and held the index finger of my left hand to my lips. They moved away quick. I figured, since the burnt-brain spent all his time on the street, he might have seen something. But whatever he saw he couldn't bring out into words.

Every time he saw me after that, he gave me a gathering-spiderwebs-from-the-air kowtow. A fragment from an earlier part of his journey, maybe.

The punk who thought the *snick!* of his switchblade opening would paralyze me must have thought the neat round third-degree burn on his right hand happened by magic. That would be later, in the emergency room, after he'd stopped screaming. If he'd taken a closer look at the cigarette lighter I'd been toying with as we talked, he would have seen they make piezoelectric blowtorches real small nowadays.

I was getting the kind of shadowy reputation that can buy you anything from information to a bullet. But I wasn't getting any closer to Rosebud.

In fact, I couldn't be sure she was anywhere close by. Not one confirmed sighting . . . although plenty of people told me otherwise, thinking they'd see the color of my money before they actually went out looking. The color was all they got to see.

I had one idea, but it was as close to a hole card as I was holding, and I didn't want to play it too soon.

"Any progress?" the lawyer asked me.

"It's not like building a house," I told him. "You can't see it going up. I haven't *found* her."

"Yet?" the father asked.

"It's always 'yet,' " I answered him, not taking my eyes from the lawyer. "Until you get it done."

"Can you at least tell me if she's in Portland?"

"I'll be able to tell you in a couple of weeks, max."

"Why by then, particularly?" the lawyer wanted to know.

I shrugged.

"I've already spent a lot of money," the father reminded me.

"Uh-huh," is all he got back.

"Isn't there any way to get more . . . aggressive about this?" the lawyer said, his academic tone designed to take some of the insinuation out of his words.

"Not much point hurting people for information they don't have," I said, bluntly.

"I'm opposed to violence," the father said.

"Me too," I assured him, catching the lawyer's thin, conspiratorial smirk.

A pro burglar had trained me. I mean a *professional,* not a chronic. To the public, you do the same thing often enough, you're a "professional," no matter if you're a total maladroit at it. The government feels the same way about the people who work for it.

The newspapers will call some congenital defective who sticks up a dozen all-night convenience stores in a month a "professional criminal," but people who actually make a *living* from crime know better.

The old-timers knew how to ghost a house so slick, they could unload the pistol you kept on the night table in case of burglars and put it right back in place between your snores—just in case you woke up while they were sorting through your jewelry like an appraiser on amphetamine.

They prided themselves on never carrying a weapon, never

hurting anyone, and never stealing anything they couldn't turn over quick. Back then, if one of the black-glove freaks who combined house invasion with rape ever dared to call himself a thief, he might get shanked just for disrespecting the profession.

Today, your average burglar is like your average bank robber: an amateur or a junkie. Both, most likely. The take is always small, and the cops don't even bother to dust for prints. They just give you an incident number, so you can lie to your insurance company.

There are still pro jobs being done, but they tend not to get reported to the cops; the victims aren't big fans of law enforcement.

The guy who taught me said that a truly pro touch is when the mark doesn't even know he's been hit. Until, one day, he looks for whatever's been taken, and comes up empty. The pro also told me that daylight jobs are the best, if you can blend into the area where you're working.

I could do better than that, now that I'd code-grabbed the remote for Kevin's garage door.

I watched the mini-bus with the day camp's name stenciled on its side, as it stopped at the corner to collect Daisy. If the schedule held, the mother would be off within an hour or so. She always did the same things. Some leisurely shopping, lunch with friends, then maybe a salon for her hair and nails, maybe a bookstore. Aimless, time-killing stuff, but she appeared devoted to it. She never got home before four in the afternoon the whole week I kept watch.

I'd thought about borrowing Kevin's Volvo for a couple of hours, but I couldn't know if he would use it at lunchtime. Or if his neighbors would make it their business to mention they'd seen a strange car enter his garage. My impression of the neighborhood was that it wasn't upscale enough for the pure-leisure class, and everything Gem had learned so far confirmed that. Best bet was that the houses were mostly dink—double income, no kids—occupied, and even the people that had kids worked during the day.

I had an additional layer of protection. Even if some suspicious citizen called the cops, my story would be that I was an invited guest, and I knew the father would back that up. He might not be happy about it, but he'd keep his mouth shut.

At a quarter to twelve, I was in position on the corner. I'd swapped the Caddy for the nondescript Ford again. If any nosy neighbors had seen it when I came to the house the first time, it would dull the edge of their suspicion.

I rolled just past the driveway, then reversed and backed in, triggering the remote as I rolled. The garage was big enough for three cars. And empty. I tapped the remote again, and I was alone in the darkness.

I made my way through the connecting passage to the house, carrying my equipment in one hand, sensors on full alert. Nothing. Rosebud's room was exactly as I remembered it, curtains open to the light, but no way for any outsider to see in. I used the mini-camera's flash just for fill—it was so faint it wouldn't have spooked a parakeet.

I never thought about trying Daisy's room. Any girl that maintained such an ungodly mess so diligently would know where every single little thing was. And she'd pick up any intrusion quicker than a motion-detector.

I went downstairs, then back up to the adult side of the divided house. The bedroom was apolitical, with that antiseptic, anonymous look that tells you they paid someone to pick out the furnishings. Lots of artifacts from the civilization they'd conquered—brand names on the clothing, jewelry from all the best places, severe-modern furniture. Even the bed linen screamed *Designer!* very tastefully.

If the mother was telling the truth about having no maid, she did a hell of a job. The place was as dust-free as an autopsy table.

Kevin's den was as rabid as the bedroom had been sterile. The walls were papered like a wood fence around a construction site. Everything from a giant symbol of the Symbionese Liberation Army to an old magazine cover where some overdosed-on-privilege twit proclaimed Charles Manson to be a great revolutionary. Giant head shots of Huey Newton and George Jackson side-by-side in unconscious irony.

He covered the international front, too: the Japanese Red Army, the Baader-Meinhof gang, the Red Army Brigades, a "letter to the people from Assata Shakur, s/n JoAnne Chesimard," mailed from Cuba. The whole place was strangely time-warped, as if nothing had happened before or after a ten-year period carved out of the sixties and seventies. Nothing about the IWW. Nothing about the Tamil Tigers.

It didn't have the controlled chaos that flavored Daisy's room, and if a maid was being paid money to keep it clean, she was ripping them off.

But none of it was worth a thing to me.

My last shot was the apartment over the garage: the one his wife said he used as an office. I had saved it for the end, because it was closest to my way out—the same way any good burglar starts with the lowest drawer first. I hadn't seen any stairs leading to it on the outside of the house, so I wasn't surprised when I found the door off the inside of the garage.

The steps had carpeting, but no decorator had picked it out. The door to the office was a joke—I'd loided tougher ones when I was a little kid.

Inside, a drafting table sat in a far corner, its surface cleared, as if awaiting some action. A clever wall unit had been built over lateral file cabinets, the top of which formed a work surface featuring one of those fax-printer-copier combo machines. I hooked a gloved finger into one of the file drawers and pulled experimentally. It came open without resistance. I used a pocket flash to scan the neatly arranged manila folders inside. They were labeled in a draftman's writing, all apparently names of projects he was working on.

I checked my watch. Still had almost twenty minutes of the forty-five I'd allotted myself for the job. Where the hell was the . . . ? Then I spotted it, lying casually on a small black leather couch: an IBM notebook computer.

I used wooden matches to mark its corners, then picked it up and carried it over to the work surface, reciting to myself the instructions Gem had given me.

First, I made sure the machine had a floppy drive installed . . . yes! . . . and checked access to the parallel port. Then I took fourteen different cables, each individually twist-tied, out of my bag and gently tried each one in turn. Hit paydirt with number six, and connected the notebook to the pocket-sized SCSI drive I was carrying.

I inserted what Gem's geek had told her was a DOS boot disk into the computer's floppy drive and powered it up. As soon as its screen showed a progress bar moving slowly to the right, I checked my watch and left the machinery to its own devices.

Kevin didn't keep his secrets in the usual places. Nothing taped to the underside of drawers, no cutout portions of books, none of the pens were hollow. The carpeting was napless enough to be industrial, but the padding under it was so thick it was spongy to the touch. And the ceiling's acoustical tile extended halfway down the walls. Maybe it was a look—interior design isn't one of my specialties.

I expected a DSL connection, or maybe a T1. But he wasn't even running his online stuff through the TV cable; it was a straight dial-up connect.

And another surprise, there was only one phone line, with no switcher, so he'd have to physically unplug the phone to go online. The phone itself was a high-tech Bang & Olufsen, ultra-audio, directly connected to a large reel-to-reel tape recorder. The setup was pure professional—that recorder could roll for hours and stay as quiet as cancer.

There was no number on the phone. I thought about using it to call my own cellular, then doing a star-69 to capture the info. But the setup spooked me, so I left it alone.

A book was lying open next to the copier. *Last Man Standing,* Jack Olsen's monster bestseller. I'd picked it up when it first hit the stores. It was about Geronimo Pratt, an innocent man who had spent a quarter-century in prison, a monument to Hoover's psychosis of the late sixties, before the courts finally kicked him loose. The book was marked up to the max: pages highlighted in half a dozen different colors, with tiny scribbles in some of the margins. I left it as I found it, open to the same page.

A slight bulge in the carpeting pinpointed the floor safe. It didn't look like much, but punching or peeling it would have been as subtle as spray-painting the walls. And I didn't have time to play with the dial; the progress bar on the computer's screen read "100%."

I popped out the floppy disk, powered down the machine, removed the cable, and packed up the portable SCSI drive. The notebook went back exactly where I'd taken it from.

One quick scan to make sure I hadn't left any calling cards, and I was ready to fade, still within my time limit.

Back inside the garage, I started up the Ford. A few seconds' exposure to carbon monoxide was worth the running start it would give me if I needed it. But when I sent the door up, the driveway was empty.

I was gone in seconds.

Gem wasn't at the loft when I returned with my swag. I left the computer stuff and the film canister for her; she knew what to do with them.

The meet with Madison wasn't for three days. I didn't want to play my hole card until after I'd spoken with her. I went back into the streets.

I always carry significant currency when I work. It isn't just for the *mordida* that's so much a part of the kind of business I do. A piece of it is emotional—I feel scared without some cash in my pocket. Only born-rich people are comfortable walking around without money.

In New York, it'd take you years of lurking before people noticed you—unless you were crazy enough to hang around a drug drop or a mob storefront. But in Portland, it didn't take long at all. I didn't know what the whisper-stream had about me, but I knew I was part of its flow from the way people reacted when I rolled up on them. By then, they all knew I was looking for Rosebud. But they didn't know why. Unless they bought my story . . . whichever one I'd told them.

I'd put a notice in the personals column of the *Willamette Week*—an alternative newspaper that was above-ground enough to survive on advertising, mostly from cultural events. If Rosebud saw my ad, she never answered.

There were a few 'zines going around, mostly about the local live-sounds scene. I tracked one of them back to its editor, a nice kid with a color printer and a passionate love of industrial music. He said he'd never heard of Rosebud, didn't recognize her picture.

He didn't look like he got out of the house enough to be that smooth a liar, so I figured he was playing it straight. I asked him what it would cost to run a box ad. He told me he didn't do stuff like that; his "operation" was "noncommercial." But he did hook me up with another 'zine, this one devoted to what they called thugcore music. "Hardcore's like bubblegum to us, man," the kid in charge told me.

He listened as I explained that Rosebud wasn't tattooed or pierced, hadn't shaved her head, and didn't spend a lot of time in mosh pits. But when I told him that she played acoustic guitar, he told me to keep my money.

There's another music scene that doesn't get air play—unless you count the shortwave psycho-shows. NSBM—National Socialist Black Metal—a bizarre brew of confused mysticism and real clear race hate. You can't find it over-the-counter, but it does a big enough business on the Internet that it's already being ripped off . . . bootlegged, big-time.

From the picture I'd been putting together of Rosebud, I couldn't see her anywhere near that crap. So I passed on the thugcore kid's offer to get me some names.

I didn't like it that the father was so sure she was still in Portland, so I followed him around for a couple of days. He had a lot of meets in semi-public places—walking along the waterfront, having a snack from a street vendor, in a coffeehouse—with people I didn't recognize. But none of them were within thirty years of the kid's age. Maybe he'd covered his bets, hired some more personnel.

"That's Geof Darrow's work, all right," Madison said, tapping one long fingernail on the sixteen-by-twenty-inch enlargement. I'd had it made from the photo I'd taken of the drawing in Rosebud's room. "It's as distinctive as a fingerprint. There isn't another artist in the world who could do this . . . although plenty try."

"Never heard of him," I said. Which wasn't quite true. My old prison partner, Hercules, had everything Darrow ever drew.

"God. You didn't see *The Matrix*?"

The way she said the words, like it was something sacred, I knew she was talking about a movie.

"No." This time, it was the truth.

"Okay," she said, as if pronouncing judgment. "Anyway, I can tell you something more about this . . . drawing. It *is* a drawing, right?"

"Yeah."

"Wow. I didn't know Geof Darrow even *knew* Charles de Lint."

"Who?"

"See these crows? Well, they're not birds. See where it says 'Maida and Zia'? Those are the crow girls," she pronounced.

"I didn't see that movie, either."

"Look," she sighed, impatient with my cultural deficiencies, "the crow girls are recurring characters in books by Charles de Lint. He's a fabulist."

"A what?"

"A writer of fables. And he's a musician, too."

"A . . . Wait a minute, Madison. Would a teenage girl like his stuff?"

"You're kidding, right? It depends on the girl, of course. But he writes *beautifully*. I adore his work."

"Have you gotten any letters from—"

She got up to leave. I took it for an answer.

The Borders on Third Street was too damn big to stagger through one rack at a time. I was wandering aimlessly when a dark-haired guy came up and asked me if he could help. His face was too professionally unexpressive for him to be a clerk, so I figured him for the manager. I told him what I wanted, and he knew exactly where it was.

I sat down at one of the tables and got myself a tuna sandwich on what Portland thinks is a bakery roll. Then I started to read what the guy had told me was the latest of the dozen Charles de Lint books they had on their shelves.

It was set in one of those mythical cities that you recognize from the road map of your own experience. The style was realistic, but the narrative was full of magick and faeries and mystical connections between people and objects. All driven by a culture that evolved from street kids, intertwined with their music, their poetry, and their at-bottom goodness . . . almost as if the mysticism was in their gestalt, not their spells. I could see why Rosebud felt close to this stuff. And, reading it, I felt closer to her.

But no closer to where she was.

"I bought you a present," I told Gem when she came in late in the afternoon.

"What?" she said. The last time I'd said those same words to her, she'd clapped her hands like a little girl and jumped up and down until I gave it to her.

"Just a book," I said, handing her what I'd bought earlier.

"This is very nice," she said, taking it from me. "I have not read it. Thank you."

I wanted to ask her what the fuck was wrong, but I had a date with a pack of skittish whores.

The soft Pacific Northwest rain didn't sweep the streets clean, but it did cut down on the traffic. I had no luck talking a lone hooker into the Caddy. So, when I spotted the Subaru ahead to my left, looking even more sharklike in the wet night, I tucked in behind and tried my luck there.

The black car ambled along in a gentle series of right-hand turns. If the driver noticed me on his tail, he sure wasn't panicked about it. Fifteen minutes brought us back to the outer rim of the stroll. The Subaru glided to the curb. When I saw the chubby blonde girl climb out the passenger side, tugging her mini-skirt back down over her hips, I knew that either the driver was a regular or his approach was a lot better than mine.

The hooker was heading back up the street to where I was parked. The Subaru was pulling away. Snap decision. I hit the switch for the curbside window as the blonde came up alongside.

"You working?" I asked.

She glanced into the Caddy, a tired-looking woman who'd been promised diamonds and silk and gotten zircons and polyester. I let her have a good look. She glanced up the street to where she'd been headed. Then back to me.

"Some other time, honey," she said.

I got back around three. The loft was empty. The Charles de Lint book was where Gem had put it down when I'd first given it to her.

"Can't you . . . put on some pressure?" Kevin asked me the next day.

"Money's the best pressure," I told him.

"I understand that. You're not saying I should increase the—"

"No. If somebody's holding her, that could always be a factor. But if they were, you'd have heard about it by now."

"How can you be so sure?"

"The two hardest things about a kidnapping have nothing to do with the snatch itself."

"Kidnapping?"

"Look, am I getting confused here? You told the cops Rosebud was missing. They *presume* runaway, her age and all, but they have to be *thinking* something else, right?"

"Something else?"

"She either went away on her own, or not, okay? But, sometimes, it's a bit of both. A boyfriend, maybe tells her he's going to take care of everything. But what he thinks is, *you're* going to be the one doing that."

"I don't—"

"This boyfriend," I went on, like he hadn't said a word, "he figures: you got a nice big house, fancy cars, in that neighborhood and all . . . you got to have serious money," I said, choosing my words carefully. He wasn't the type to be flattered by references to his money, so I put it out there as a mistake some kid could make. Me, I understood just how "working-class" he really was.

I waited for his nod, then went on: "By his standards, anyway. So he tells Rosebud they're going to *fake* a kidnapping. Just to get enough money for them to go—ah, who knows where it is this year? Amsterdam? Paris? Daytona Beach? I don't know. But you get the idea, right?"

"But the note. It said—"

"Yeah. Look: One, the cops never saw that note. Two, *anyone* could have written it—it wasn't even in her handwriting. Three, even if Rosebud *did* write it, she might *still* be with a boyfriend . . . and he springs this ransom thing on her after she's already left. No way she wants to come back and admit her big adventure was a flop. Or maybe she's got some resentments. . . ."

"You don't have any idea of how close we . . . are," he said. "Buddy and I . . . You're going in the wrong direction."

"All right. Like I was saying, the two hardest things about a kidnapping are keeping the person alive and healthy while you negotiate . . . and collecting the ransom without getting caught."

"But you just said—"

"Sometimes, you get a girl who runs away voluntarily. But when she wants to go back . . ."

"I never thought of that."

"There's no reason to think about that. Yet. That is, unless you've heard from—"

"Of course not. If Buddy had called me—"

"Not your daughter. Anyone else who . . . anyone who's telling you something like they might be able to locate her—an opening like that?"

"Nothing," he said, sadly.

"All right."

"Can't you . . . ?"

"What?"

"Sometimes money isn't the answer to everything," he said, not so cryptically.

"If I thought leaning on one of the street kids would help, I'd do it," I told him. "But all that would do is make everyone nervous, keep me from getting close."

"It seems so . . . hopeless now."

"You want me to call it a day?"

"I . . . don't know. Do you think you're getting any closer?"

"Yeah, I do. But I couldn't tell you why, or give you any specifics, so I wouldn't blame you if you thought I was just hustling you for a few more weeks' work."

"Jennifer said she would speak to you," he said, suddenly.

"The girl Rosebud was supposed to be spending the—"

"Yes. I wanted to clear it with her parents first."

"When?"

"This evening."

"Okay. I'll come by—"

"Seven," he said. "And . . . no disrespect, but could you wear your suit?"

"Jenn will be down in a minute," the guy who had introduced himself as her father told me. He was shorter than me, but much wider through the chest and shoulders, with an amiable face and eyes as warm as ball bearings.

"What do you need to talk to her for?" a kid who I figured for her brother asked. He was taller than his father, leaner, with an athlete's grace to his body.

"Michael . . ." the father said, gently. He turned his attention back to me. "The police have already been here," he said, as if that disposed of the matter.

"Yes, sir, I understand," I told him. "I don't know how much you know about investigations—"

"I'm a forensic psychologist," he interrupted.

"Sorry, I didn't know," I told him. *But I know* something *about you, pal. Any Ph.D. who doesn't introduce himself by sticking*

"Doctor" in front of his name doesn't have a self-confidence problem. "What's your specialty?"

"The effects of incarceration on mental health," he said, holding my eyes.

"Fascinating," I said, my voice as flat as his. "Anyway, the core tool is the same, right?"

"I'm not certain I follow you."

"Interviewing. That's it, isn't it? Whether you're doing an evaluation or debriefing a source or questioning a suspect, it all comes down to the interview."

"Well, there are various tests as well as—"

"Sure. No argument. But you'd always *want* an interview if you could get one, wouldn't you?"

"I would," he agreed.

"And interviewing, it's a special talent, fair enough to say? Some of it you can teach, but some of it's a gift . . . combination of instinct and experience."

He nodded silently, a professional's way of telling me to keep talking.

"And, bottom line," I said, "it's not mechanical. One interviewer could get information another wouldn't even ask about."

"That's true. So what you're saying, Mr. . . . Hazard, is it . . . ?"

My turn to nod.

". . . is that you would do a better job than the detectives."

"That's been my experience," I said. "And I'll bet it's been yours, too."

"Sometimes." He chuckled. "Not always."

"Joel, you said he could—" Kevin started to say.

"Your daughter, you let her go out on dates?" the psychologist interrupted Rosebud's father.

"Uh . . . yes."

"So that's the permission piece. But you still want to meet the young man, don't you? Kind of make up your own mind right on the spot?"

"Well . . . yes, sure."

"What I told you was that you could have *somebody* come here and talk to Jenn. You brought this gentleman with you. I wanted to talk to him first. Is that okay with you?"

Kevin didn't say a word. He knew the last sentence hadn't been a question.

"Go get your sister," the psychologist said to his son.

"What did you do time for?" he asked me, as soon as the kid left the room.

He may have been guessing, or he may have smelled it on me. Didn't matter. I sensed that if I didn't give him what he was looking for, his daughter wasn't going to be interviewed.

"Violence for money," I said, trying to cover it all in as few words as possible.

"Where?"

"You got a glass?" I asked, giving him a thumb's-up signal.

Kevin looked confused.

"Your investigator is offering his fingerprints," the psychologist explained to him.

"Is that really—?"

He shrugged. Then barked, "Michael!"

The kid came into the room with what I took to be his older sister, a strikingly pretty girl, who didn't seem aware she was.

"Daddy, why are you *bellowing*?" she said, a smile in her voice.

"I thought you were still upstairs," he said sheepishly.

"Hi, Mr. Carpin," she said to Rosebud's father. "Hello," she said to me. "I'm Jennifer."

"B. B. Hazard," I said, getting to my feet and holding out my hand. She took it, squeezed gently, and pulled away.

"Mr. Hazard wants to talk with you about Rosebud," her father said.

"Yes, Daddy. You told me. We'll talk in my room, okay?"

"I'll be right down here," he said. As clear a threat as I'd heard in years.

Jennifer's room was smaller than Rosebud's, but it looked as if it got a great deal more traffic. She pulled a one-armed panda bear off an old easy chair like a maître d' showing me to my table. I sat down and she jumped into the air, spun around, and landed facing me on the bed.

"How can I help?" she asked. Her father's daughter.

"Well, you can tell me what you know."

"About Rosa?"

"Rosa?"

"Yes. That's the name she liked. Not everybody called her that, but I did."

"You've already told me more than I knew when I came."

"Oh. All right . . ."

"What did they tell *you*?" I asked.

"The police?"

"Or her father."

"Well . . . they seemed to think Rosa had run away. But they weren't sure."

"But you know, don't you, Jennifer?"

"Me?"

"Sure. You and Rosa were very close."

"You didn't say that like it was a question."

"It's not. I know you were."

"How?" she challenged.

"You told her father that Rosa had never come over to spend the weekend with you at all."

"That's right. She hadn't. . . ."

"But you told him *after* she didn't return on Sunday night."

"That's when he asked me."

"I know. But if he *had* asked you, *during* that weekend, you would have told him Rosa was around somewhere. Or in the bathroom. Or at the movies. Whatever you agreed on. Then you'd have called her, given her the heads-up, and she would have called home."

"Why would you say—?"

"She needed you for a running start. Probably figured nobody would ever check—she seems like a very smart young lady, and she would have been planning this for a while. But she had a backup plan in case they did."

"You don't know that."

"You mean I can't *prove* it, don't you, Jennifer? They're not the same thing."

"I'm not saying anything," she said, folding her arms.

"Okay. Tell me about the crow girls, then."

She narrowed her eyes, trying to read mine. Someday, she'd be even better than her father, but right now she wasn't in his league. "What about them?" she finally said.

"Charles de Lint . . ."

"Yes, sure. I mean, everybody knows that. But what are you asking me?"

"How could I read about them?"

"The crow girls? Why, they're in all . . . Wait!" She bounced off the bed, walked over to a short bookcase suspended over her computer terminal, pulled down a book, and handed it to me.

"*Moonlight and Vines,*" I read aloud. A different title from the one I'd gotten at the bookstore.

"There's a separate story just about them—the crow girls—in there."

"Thanks. I'll bring it back to you."

"Okay."

"Well, Jennifer . . . thanks for taking the time to talk with me."

"That's all? I mean, you aren't going to—?"

"No. There's no reason for you to trust me. I was trying to think of a way I could convince you that I'd never do anything to hurt your friend. I just want to find her, make sure she's all right.

If she doesn't want to come back home, I wouldn't try to make her. But I see you're not ready to believe me."

She tried to polygraph my eyes again. Then asked, "Are you going to say anything about—?"

"Your phone relay system? No."

She nodded slowly. "It was just for that weekend," she said quietly. "The number is no good anymore."

"No answer when you called the next week, Jennifer? Or was it disconnected?"

"How did you—? Oh. It was a pay phone. On the street. Whoever answered it told me that."

"And the next time you tried it?"

"The next time, it was a different person. Just someone passing by in the street."

"Thank you."

"I want Rosa to be okay."

"I know. Me too."

"Will you tell me?"

"Tell you . . . what?"

"If you find her. If you find her and she won't go back, would you let me know? First, before you . . . do anything?"

"I promise."

"Be careful," Jennifer's father told me by way of goodbye. His son didn't say anything; he was too busy cracking his knuckles and memorizing my face.

"What was that all about?" Kevin asked me on the way back to where I'd left my car.

"What do you mean?"

"That business with Dr. Dryslan at the end. He almost seemed to be . . . I don't know . . . warning you or something."

"He's a father. Jennifer's his daughter. You know how that goes."

"Yes," he said.

Maybe he convinced himself.

"I must go to work soon," Gem said. She absently twirled a towel into a turban for her just-washed hair, oblivious as always of her own nudity.

"Tonight?"

"I do not mean for one night. *Back* to work. With Flacco and Gordo."

"Ah."

"Yes. In another few days, we must go."

I didn't say anything.

"You have no questions?" she said.

"No."

"Not where I am going? Not when I will return?"

"No."

"Why is that?"

"It's none of my business."

"So . . . where *you* go, what *you* do, when *you* would be back . . . that would be none of *my* business, yes?"

"Yes."

"You are my husband."

"Gem—"

"It is not for you to say; it is for me to say."

"Is that right? How would you like it if some guy came up to you and said, 'Hey, bitch, you're my wife'?"

"It is not what I *say,*" she said calmly. "It is what happened. Between us."

"But you just said—"

"Those are just words."

"This isn't making any sense."

"That is your choice," she said, walking out of the room.

I went back into the night, looking for a working girl working alone. When I finally spotted one, she was wearing orange hot pants, standing hip-shot in invitation.

Right next to the black Subaru parked at the curb.

I figured whoever was in the Subaru had her covered, but I could live with that. I nosed the Caddy alongside her, hit the power window switch with my left hand, and slid my right over the grip of the Beretta.

She stuck her face all the way into the car so that her heavy breasts draped over the sill, made a kissing sound at me.

"Where've you been, baby?"

"Looking for you," I told her. Her hair was raven black, bowed out around her cheekbones and curving back sharply just past her chin. Couldn't see much of her features in that light.

"Well, you found me. Now what do you want to *do* with me?"

"Talk."

"I'm not out here to—"

"Talk for money," I cut in quickly. "Buying your time, same as anyone else. Only you keep your clothes on."

"But not my mouth shut. Sounds like a date to me."

"I don't care what you call—"

"Unlock the back door," she said, suddenly.

I hit the switch, heard the distinctive thunk. She pulled herself out of the window. I heard the brief clacking of her stacked heels as she walked around to the back. The door opened as I turned to look behind me. She leaned in, sprayed the interior with a little pocket flash, then pulled her head out and slammed the door.

I glanced toward the passenger window. Blank. Caught something moving up on my left side. I was about to stomp on out of there when I recognized her.

"I'm going to walk around the front of your car," she said in my left ear. "So you can get a real good look at me in your headlights, okay?"

"Why?"

"So you'll know what you're passing up with all this talking stuff," she said.

She dropped into the Caddy's front bucket seat butt-first, taking her time about it. The orange hot pants were worthy of the name, but the "For Sale" tattoo I knew was underneath them doused any flame before it could flicker. She spun around to face me, crossing her fishnet-wrapped legs.

"Take the first right," she said.

I flicked the lever into gear and pulled off, slow, my eyes on the dark street.

"Two more blocks, then watch for a red house on the left."

"Yours?"

"Sure!" She laughed. "Just the driveway. And that's a rental, understand?"

"Yep. Pretty slick. The cops can sweep the street, but off-road is off-limits. You pay by the night, or by the trick?"

"Why do you ask?"

"If it's by the trick, whoever owns the house has to stay up and keep count."

"You sound like you know the game."

"Not me," I assured her. "Is that it, coming up?"

"Yes. Just . . . what are you doing?"

"I feel more comfortable backing in, all right?"

"The customer's *always* right."

I reversed the Caddy and backed a little way into the driveway, just past the sidewalk. Then I killed the engine. The power door locks would work even without it running.

"Like I said," I told her, "I just want to talk."

"Whatever gets you there, honey."

"It's not like that. I'm a private investigator. I'm looking for someone. A girl. She might be—"

"I know," she interrupted.

"How do you—?"

"We already talked about it, Mr. Hazard," she said, pulling the midnight wig off her head and shaking out a short, tight mass of auburn curls.

"Well, if it isn't the fake Peaches herself."

"Surprised?"

"Yeah," I lied. Age switches aren't that big a deal for some women. Gem did it all the time, for her work. It's easier for Asians-facing-Caucasians, but they aren't the only ones who can pull it off. "You went to a lot of trouble for nothing."

"Nothing?"

"The deal's the same as I told you when you were playing teenager. Or are you playing grownup now?"

"I'm thirty-one," she said, as if that was some kind of credential. "And I've got my own deal."

"Which is?"

"What do you know about wires?" That one came out of left field, but it didn't surprise me as much as her undoing the snaps on her blouse.

"Enough to know you need them in that bra," I told her.

"Very funny," she said. She shrugged out of the blouse and popped the clasp on the front of the black bra. Her heavy breasts gleamed creamy in the darkness. She slipped her arms out of the bra in a smooth fluid motion, and tossed it across the console into my lap. Then she raised her arms above her head. "See any place I could carry a recorder?" she asked me.

"Not from the waist up."

"Help yourself," she said, undoing the top of the hot pants.

"No thanks," I told her.

"You'll take my word for it?"

"It doesn't matter. I'm not going to say anything the police couldn't hear. You already know I'm not a trick. And I already knew you weren't selling it."

"And you knew that exactly *how*?"

"You'd be the first hooker I ever saw who didn't carry something to put money in."

"Maybe I put it in my—"

"No. You don't. Besides that, it's three in the morning. You'd have been out here for hours, but you smell like you just stepped out of a bubble bath."

She was silent for a long minute. "I know some things about you, too," she said, finally.

"Do you?"

"Yes. You do things for money."

"That's why they call it work."

"I don't mean just . . . this. Looking for the girl. Things."

"What 'things' are you talking about?"

"Does it really matter? If the money's right . . ."

"Sure, it matters. I would never do anything illegal."

"Yeah, you're just a model citizen, huh?" she whispered. "Want to give me back my bra?"

I handed it over, my thumb telling me I had been right about the underwire.

"Can I have one of your cigarettes *now*?"

I gave her one. She leaned over the console so I could light it for her. Her perfume reminded me of raw sugarcane.

"Thanks."

I keyed the ignition enough to activate the electronics, zipped her window down.

She leaned back and enjoyed her smoke. Didn't say a word all through it. "That was good," she said, snapping the butt out her window into the darkness. "I haven't had a Kool since the last time I was locked up."

Sure. Nice of her to spell it all out for me. And in such big letters.

"Want me to take you back to where they're waiting for you?" I asked her.

"Where would that be?"

"The Subaru."

"Okay, then; *who* would that be?"

"I'm not following you."

"No. I've been following *you.* For quite a while. In the Subaru. It's mine. There's no one in it now."

I pulled alongside the sleek black car. She opened her door, turned to face me.

"This one's on the house," she said. "The girl's not strolling. I can help you find her if she's anywhere in Portland. You don't believe me, ask around."

"I already did that. And you didn't come up aces . . . Peaches."

She poked a finger into one of the thick bands at the top of her fishnets, took something out, and handed it to me. A poker chip, it felt like. "Ask again," she said.

She got out, slammed the Caddy's door closed with a well-padded hip, and climbed into the Subaru in one smooth motion.

I would have wondered about her leaving her car unlocked in that neighborhood, if I hadn't seen the shadows shift in the front seat when we'd pulled up.

I'd imagined all kinds of exotic things for the little disk I'd been carrying around in my shirt pocket for a couple of hours. Embedded microchips, the female half of a set, maybe some mystical symbols to a code I'd be expected to crack . . .

But when I finally took a look at it under the lamp over my chair, it turned out to be a plain white plastic disk with milled edges, lettered in black. Just "Ann O. Dyne," with "Pain Management" underneath, like it was a specialty of the house. On the flip side: "cell/page/cyber," with separate numbers for each.

I rolled the poker-chip business card between my fingers, trying to get something from it beyond the words. I knew a hundred ways to say S&M, but "pain management" was a new one on me. If that's what it was . . . and I didn't think so.

I might have asked Gem, but she wasn't around.

The kid was small and slender, lady-killer handsome, with blond hair, big liquid brown eyes, and a gentle smile. He circled the table slowly and deliberately, eyeing the scattered balls like an *I Ching* hexagram he was decoding. "You're done," he said to a tall, scrawny guy in his twenties.

"You going to jump it in?" the scrawny guy sneered. "I don't think so."

I took a look. From where I was sitting, I could see the cue ball frozen to the short rail at the foot of the table. The green six ball was hanging on the pocket, but the black eight blocked the shot. The scrawny guy was right; the balls were too close together to jump the cue into the six.

"Massé," the kid said.

"Right!"

"You don't think so?" a man asked, echoing the scrawny guy's words.

I turned to look at the speaker, a well-put-together man in his thirties with a shaved head, black-rimmed glasses, and a bright, shallow smile. He sat calmly against the wall, his arms crossed over his chest.

"No, I *don't* fucking think so," the scrawny guy responded.

"How sure are you about that?" the man challenged.

"Real sure."

"A hundred bucks sure?"

"Oh yeah," the scrawny guy assured him, affirming the side bet.

The man with the shaved head got up slowly, took a pair of

fifties out of his pocket as if he'd been carrying them around just for such an occasion. He put them on the table at the other end from where the kid faced the shot. The scrawny guy came up with his ante. Everybody moved back to give the kid room.

He took one more look. Chalked his cue absently. A couple of teenage girls giggled together, sharing a secret. The kid stepped to the table, held his cue almost perpendicular to the green felt surface. He gripped it overhand as he stroked a couple of times to get the rhythm, then snapped it down and back as smooth as a punch press. The cue ball made a quick semicircle around the eight, gently nudged the six ball home, then reversed at the long rail to give the kid perfect position on the seven ball.

"Big A!" his backer congratulated him, offering a palm to slap.

The scrawny guy nodded his head, as if finally understanding something that had been explained to him many times.

The kid ran the seven, eight, and nine without drawing a breath. The scrawny guy didn't stay for the finale.

The two teenage girls argued over who was going to rack the balls. I sat down next to the backer. "You taking on all comers?" I asked him.

"Someday we will," the backer said. "Not today."

"Why not today?"

"Big A's not ready. Another couple of years, yeah."

"He looks ready to me."

"He's got the stroke," the backer said. "And he's got the eye. But he's still learning the game. And stamina's an issue, too—some of the pro games can go for hours, day after day."

"That's the plan, to turn him pro?"

"It is. He's not old enough to play in tournaments yet. By the time he is, we'll be ready."

"You're Clipper, right?"

"Uh-huh. And you're . . . ?"

"B.B."

"Oh yeah. I've heard about you."

"Then you know what I'm looking for."

"Runaway. At least, that's what people say."

"For once, then, word on the street's true."

"I'm a businessman," he said. "Not a social worker."

"Sure. That's what I want, to do business."

"You think *I* know where—?"

"No. But I've been here for a while, and I noticed a few things."

"Like what?"

"Like how your boy works with a house cue, very slick. And the way he pulls girls like a rock star."

"He does," Clipper said, proudly.

"So I figured I could maybe talk to him, show him this picture I've got of the—"

"Lots of people out here looking for runaways," he interrupted.

"What's your point?"

"I don't know you, that's my point."

"Fair enough. But I'm not asking you to turn the girl over. Or even to tell me where she is. Just to get a message to her."

"What's in it for me?"

"Money."

"I've got enough money, pal."

"All right, then. How about if I show you a crack in your boy's game?"

"What kind of crack?"

"He's still a kid."

"So?"

"So let's him and me play. Nine ball, like he's been doing. A ten-spot per game. And I side-bet *you* a hundred I get him out of his rhythm before I drop the same amount."

He leaned back in his chair and gave me a long look. "Big A doesn't intimidate," he said quietly. "Not with me around."

"That's not my style. What do you say?"

I refused to lag for break. It was his table; I figured I'd have a better chance with a coin toss.

"Rack them *tight,*" I told the chubby little girl in a *Hard Looks* T-shirt. She nodded, tongue protruding in concentration.

Instead of breaking from the far end and stroking low to stop the cue ball near the center, I came off the side rail slightly off-center, striking high. It was a sucker move—good chance I'd leave myself snookered even if I pocketed a ball. But it was the best way to swing for the fences.

The cue ball attacked the rack, driving deep, compressing the balls until the yellow-and-white-striped nine popped out like a mouse out of a hole and squirted into the left-hand corner.

The kid just chuckled.

For the next game, I went to a more professional break. This time, I pocketed the seven in the corner and the one in the side, leaving myself clear on the two at the other end. I dropped it home. Then passed up a fairly easy line on the three in favor of a long combo to the nine. It didn't drop.

The kid chuckled again. Too quickly. I'd left him a no-look at the three. He went two rails for the hit, but he couldn't pocket anything.

My turn. I lined up on the three, whacked it hard with enough draw to come all the way back down the table, and almost kissed the nine ball in.

"Stroooke!" one of the young guys watching barked.

The kid nodded his head, on to my game now. He ran the table, pulling us even.

For the next hour, it went like that. I went slap-and-slam, kiss-and-combo, almost always playing the nine ball, no matter what was open. The kid played straight pool—one at a time, methodical. He should have been way ahead. He wasn't.

And I was having a lot more fun.

Another hour. The kid started to take some chances. He had a beautiful stroke, but he hadn't trained for extreme English on the ball. He was a little more accurate; I was a lot more radical. And the watching crowd was into radical.

After a while, the kid started to put more muscle into his breaks. A mistake—his game was finesse, not power. Twice, he scratched, leaving me easy. I vultured those racks . . . then broke even harder than I had before.

By two in the morning, the kid was tired. And playing more cowboy all the time. He was working the crowd, showing off, beating me at my own game . . . almost.

He was sixty bucks ahead when Clipper said, "Let's get something to eat."

"I'd like to play you again," the kid told me. We were sitting in a diner, working on a nighthawk's breakfast.

"He *already* played you, Big A," Clipper told him.

"Yeah. But I—"

"*Played* you, understand?"

"What?" the kid demanded, annoyed.

"You're a lot better than me," I said. "You should have wiped me out." I was flat-out lying—the margin was actually pretty thin. But when you're hustling, ego is the first thing you shed. "You know why you didn't?"

"Sure," he said, high-confidence, proudly reciting what he'd been taught. "A slop player can beat a pro any one time. That's why nine ball is such a perfect sucker's game. Luck can change the result. *Sometimes.* It's the pool version of gin rummy. But over the long run, I'd always get your money."

"Not the way you played," I told him.

His fair complexion made the angry flush clear, even in the diner's dim light. "My game—"

"You didn't *play* your game, Big A," Clipper said, gently. "That's what Mr. . . ."

"Hazard."

". . . Hazard is trying to tell you, son. You got caught up in the crowd. Remember how you learned? Nine ball is nothing but one-rack rotation, right?"

"Yeah. I know. I was just—"

"I know what you were doing," I told him.

"What?"

"You were having fun."

"Huh?"

"People do things different when they do them for fun. The way you play, it's *work,* right?"

"Sure. Me and Clipper—"

"I know. Thing is, it *was* fun, wasn't it? Combos, kisses, heavy draw, billiard shots . . . slamming through on the break . . . ?"

"Yeah," he said, flashing a smile.

"And we were playing for chump change, so you could relax, let the crowd get into it?"

"Maybe . . ." he admitted, grinning now.

"Only thing is, you *can't* do that, Big A," Clipper told him firmly. "You can't do your work for fun. It changes your game. Those little things, they creep in around the corners when you're not looking. Next thing you know, your edge is gone. Remember how many times we talked about *focus*?"

The kid just nodded, solemn-faced now.

"It's not your fault," Clipper told him. "This guy"—nodding at me—"he conned you into it."

"He won't do it again," the kid said. He turned to me. "Were you a pro, once?"

"I was a gambler."

"What's the difference?"

"A gambler plays all the time. A pro makes a living at it."

"Heh!" The kid chuckled. "*We* make a living. Well, maybe not yet, we don't. But we will, right, Clipper?"

"Guaranteed."

"What do *you* think?" he asked me.

I knew what he wanted. "In two, three years, if you stay inside yourself, if you practice only on pro-standard tables, if you listen to your father here . . . you'll make your mark on the circuit."

"How did you know Clipper was my father?" the kid demanded. "We're not—"

"My family's the same kind as yours," I said.

Big A and Clipper looked at each other, then nodded a silent amen.

"Well?" I asked Clipper, while the kid was in the restroom.

"Fair enough," he said. "You said you'd show me a crack. And you did."

"It's not a deep one. And it's not permanent, either."

"You're right. You got a picture of the girl?"

I showed him what I had. He didn't react . . . but I wouldn't have expected him to, even if Rosebud's face rang a bell.

"Here's my card," I said. "All I want is for you to ask her to give me a call. Twenty-four/seven."

"She doesn't know you?"

"No."

"So why would she want to call?"

"Because I have a message for her. From her father. All she has to do is listen to it, then she can do whatever she wants; fair enough?"

"It's not up to me."

"I know."

"We'll ask around. If she *does* call you, don't waste your time with a trace—it'll be from right here," he said, unhooking a cell phone from his belt and holding it up.

"The kid . . ."

". . . Big A."

"Big A. He'll maybe know . . ."

"If he does, we'll ask her. Don't worry. Me and Big A, our word is gold."

"You're not just teaching him pool, huh?"

"I'm teaching him everything I know," Clipper said.

Another thing Clipper knew was the address of a safehouse for kids trying to get off the street, or out of The Life. I knew the phone number; I'd seen it posted all over town. But the address was something else again.

I thought about trying it right away. Sometimes people on night duty get lonely, and they're easier to talk to. But safehouse antennas extend higher when darkness comes, and I decided to take my shot in the daytime.

I thought about going home. But nobody would be there. And it wasn't my home.

I had another idea, but it stumbled into the generation gap. When I was a kid on the streets, one place you could always find open in the middle of the night was a church. Not all of them, but there would always be a couple.

Not the ones I tried.

When Pansy had been with me, we sometimes watched the sun come up together. Facing the day. Now I watched it come up alone. And went to sleep.

It was a little after three in the afternoon when I rang the bell on the side of the three-story blue clapboard house. A woman, maybe in her twenties, answered, her body language making it clear that I wasn't going to be invited in.

I gave her the same spiel I was handing out all over the streets. She nodded, not saying anything. I handed her a photo of Rosebud. She took it without even glancing at it. I thanked her for her time and left.

Her act was a little too cool and removed. And I didn't have anything resembling a lead. So I was back that night.

Like so many other safehouses, they were hyper about their doors and windows, but didn't pay much attention to anything past their immediate perimeter. Patience eventually dealt me the parking spot I needed. From the Ford's front seat, I could triangle on both the front and side doors. They had incoming all night long. None of the girls looked anything like Rosebud. Nobody left after ten. Maybe a house rule?

I got out, walked around the block to where I could do a visual on the house, looking for openings. I did the risk-gain math. There wasn't a scrap of evidence that Rosebud was there. And the place had to have *some* security.

Maybe some other time.

One of Portland's real fine Mediterranean restaurants, Touché, has a poolroom upstairs. The tables are just props—nobody would play a serious game there, much less for serious money. But I'd heard the place drew a lot of college girls, so I thought it was worth a once-over.

The sound system was good, if a bit strong. The mix was eclectic—probably Napstered and burned onto CDs—but whoever put it together knew what they were doing. When the tracks switched to doo-wop, I almost felt at home.

"Please Say You Want Me" came on, the kid singing lead working a deeper vein than Frankie Lymon had ever mined. I overheard one of the women hanging out ask, "Who's *that*?" I didn't say anything. But then one of the upscale lounge lizards told her, "That's the Students. Mid-fifties stuff."

I turned slightly, saying, "No, that was the Schoolboys. The Students were the guys who did 'I'm So Young.'"

The lounge lizard muttered something about me being old enough, I'd probably heard them in person.

Maybe not, I thought to myself, *but I sure as hell am* getting *old, opening my fool mouth in public like that.*

My hole card wasn't exactly the ace of trumps, but holding it back any longer wasn't going to raise its value. So, the next morning, I shaved carefully, used the flesh-color stuff Michelle had given me on the bullet scar under my right cheekbone, and put on a pair of nonprescription glasses with a faint gray tint. It didn't turn me into Mr. Rogers, but with the light canvas sports coat over a white T-shirt and a pair of stonewashed jeans, I could pass as a local at first glance.

Flacco and Gordo had lent me an egg-yolk-yellow Camaro. In Portland, it would be a lot less conspicuous than the Ford. I hadn't driven one of the new ones before, and I was surprised at how damn *big* it was—the front end seemed to stretch on forever. Even at around-town speeds, it rode stiff.

I found a perfect spot on a rise overlooking the campgrounds. Too far away to pick out individuals, but close enough to see the group activities.

I fitted the rubber-covered little 8× monocular to my eye, focused it down, and breathed shallow until I got it steady enough to scan.

They were playing softball. The left-fielder looked a lot like Daisy, but I couldn't be sure from the angle I had. When the inning was over, I followed her all the way to the bench. Yes.

Daisy didn't seem especially interested in the game. She just sat there pensively, while her teammates shouted and waved their arms and jumped up and down at the slightest sign of activity from each batter.

I played the scope over the area, looking for a likely spot. It had to be a dead-drop system they were using. There'd been no phone in Daisy's room, and it didn't seem like the kid was ever home alone anyway. This was the one place she went to every day. One place where her parents were never around. And the supervision didn't seem all that intense.

A low, crumbling stone wall decoratively separated the playing fields from a rambling one-story structure. I took that to be the place where they had the indoor activities. Beyond the outfield was a thick stand of mature trees. The grounds were unfenced—easy enough to come by at night and leave a note to be picked up the next day.

They were playing slow-pitch, but the tall girl on the mound made a high parabolic arc out of each serve, and most of the batters whiffed. Not Daisy. She waited patiently for the ball to drop, stepped into it, and drove it hard through the right side of the infield. When the outfielder was a bit slow in coming to the ball, Daisy took a wide turn at first and steamed into second standing up. Her teammates on the sidelines seemed a lot more excited about her hit than she was.

The next batter popped up to shallow left. Daisy never hesitated, charging so hard she was around third and heading home by the time the fielder dropped the ball. The run triggered a wild celebration. I could see the coach—a teenage girl in shorts and a bright-green sweatshirt with some kind of logo on it—saying something to Daisy. It didn't look like congratulations. Probably telling Daisy she shouldn't have taken off—what if the fielder *hadn't* dropped the ball? Daisy wasn't arguing, but she didn't look real interested.

They changed sides again, and Daisy went back to her position in the outfield. I watched her for signs of anxiety, but she didn't glance around, didn't fidget—just concentrated on each batter as they came up. I couldn't tell how far along in the game they were, and I didn't like sitting out there in the open. I backed the Camaro out and made a slow circle of the grounds until I found a good spot maybe a quarter-mile away.

I parked, locked up, and started walking. The woods were deeper than they'd looked from the other side, but it was no problem finding my way back with the noise of the game to guide me. I marked my way with quick spurts of red paint from the little spray can I carried. Being a strict environmentalist, I didn't deface any of the trees, just the NO TRESPASSING signs.

When I found a direct sight line to Daisy, I sat down with my back against a tree and did what I do best.

"Daisy!" I heard someone shout.

She ignored the noise, trotting toward the woods, in no special hurry. Wherever she was headed was past where I was waiting, because she practically stomped on me as she went by.

"Hey!" she yelped.

"Easy, Daisy. You know who I am."

She pulled up short, hands behind her back, watching me warily but not making a sound. Maybe she didn't want to alert the camp counselors to where she was. I kept my hands loose in my lap, projecting waves of calm out to her.

"What are you . . . ? I mean, how come . . . ?"

"I was waiting for you, Daisy. I wanted to talk to you."

"Why didn't you just come to the house?"

"The same reason Rosebud doesn't write to you there."

Her eyes flashed at the word "write," fear and fire each taking a turn. If she'd been a little older, a little more used to deception, she would have kept those eyes on me. But a quick glance to her left told me my hunch about a dead drop had been right.

"I'm not after the letters, Daisy."

"I have to go back."

"Sure."

But she didn't move, rooted by the letter she hadn't read yet. It was her link to her sister, and she wasn't going to let that chain snap without a fight.

"Daisy, listen to me. If I wanted to, I could have hidden myself and waited for you to pick up whatever Rosebud left for you, right? You never would have seen me until it was too late."

"You better leave her alone," the child said, drawing herself up to her full height, small fists clenched.

"I am," I said softly. "I am leaving her alone. I'm not going to try and bring her back. If I wanted to do that, I would have spent the night here in the woods, and just grabbed her when she came to drop off your note. I didn't do that, either, right? All I want to do is talk to her, make sure she's okay."

"She's fine."

"I'm sure she is. I just want her to tell me herself. Once."

"No."

"Not in person. Not like we are here, you and me. Just on the phone. Give her this card," I said, slowly taking it out of the breast pocket of my jacket. "It's got my phone number on it. She can call me anytime. Anytime at all."

"And you won't try to—?"

"I won't try *anything,* Daisy. I promise."

"Daisy!" The shout was a lot closer now.

"I have to—"

"I know," I said, getting to my feet. "I'm going to walk over that way," pointing to where I'd stashed the car. "I'm leaving the card here, okay?"

I turned my back on her and moved off. She didn't say anything, but I heard her crashing through the woods, in a hurry now.

On the drive back, I wondered why I hadn't done what I'd told Daisy I could have—just waited in those dark woods last night and grabbed Rosebud when she showed.

Nothing came to me.

"Anything going on?" I asked.

"All quiet," Mama said.

"Word's still that I'm—"

"Yes. All same. You working? In that place?"

"Yeah. Sort of."

She made a sound somewhere between a sigh and a snort.

"It's not a big job," I assured her. "Won't take much longer."

"You need Max, maybe?"

"No. It's not that kind of—"

"Yes. Okay. Fine."

"What's wrong, Mama?"

"Wrong? Nothing wrong here. Very quiet, like I say, okay?"

"Sure."

"Woman still with you?"

"I . . ."

"Woman say marry you, yes? But me, *I* say: must have permission. You remember, right?"

"Yeah."

"Woman still with you?" she asked again.

"I think so."

"Ah!" Mama said. "Better you come home."

"I have to—"

"When job finish, come home."

"We'll see, Mama. I—"

The disconnect click cut me off. That's how I felt: cut off. My family was still watching out for me. They'd even risked going back to my place for my few treasures. Like the pair of postage stamps that had been canceled inside Biafra during the tiny slice of time when it had functioned as a country. They'd been given to me one ugly night inside the war zone. By an old chief I'd shared the last of my freeze-dried food with. He had nothing else of value to give me, he said. And that, if I managed to survive, the stamps would always remind me of a country that had not.

They'd taken all of Pansy's stuff, too. Not because I wanted it—I couldn't even look at it—but because they'd never let the cops have anything that had been part of my heart.

That's my family. That's the kind of people they are.

And that's why I couldn't go back. Not yet.

"I think you're right . . . about her still being around, close by," I told Kevin the next day. "But all of that info's secondhand at best. I can't vouch for any of it. And I can't tell you I'm any closer to her."

"It's been—"

"I know. I've been out there every day and every night. There's . . . traces of her in a lot of places, but that's all they are—traces, not trail-markers."

"Do you think if you had more time . . . ?"

"This kind of work, you can go for months drawing blanks, then stumble over what you're looking for. Or it could turn up in a few hours. I seeded the ground heavy and—"

"What does that mean, 'seeded the ground'?"

"I've gone to a lot of places where Rosebud might have been, or where she might show up eventually. I talked to some people who might have seen her, might even know her . . . or that she might run into sooner or later if she's out there. It's a thick, deep forest she's in, but it's not a big one. The trails crisscross; the same people travel them. I left word. I planted some money, and I promised a lot more. The word's out. Some have even come to me offering to sell, and—"

"You followed up, didn't you? These people, they probably have no loyalty. For enough money, they'd—"

"The only following up I did was to offer hard cash for hard information. I don't care what's missing—a kilo, a kitten, or a kid—hustlers are going to crawl out from under rocks. I could spend a lot of your money on scams if I wasn't careful. If any of them have the goods, they'll have to deal straight up."

"Why should they trust *you*?"

"Let's say you had . . . uh, let's say you had a photograph of your great-great-grandmother, okay? It's the only one in existence; the only connection you have to your ancestors. You keep this photo in a nice frame in your living room. A junkie burglarizes your house, steals a bunch of the usual crap. And he snatches the photo, too.

"So you hire me to get the photo back. Say I find a middleman, someone who can deal with the junkie, all right? I'm willing to spend real coin for the photo, but only for *that* photo. What's he going to do? It's precious to *you,* but it isn't worth squat to anyone else. He's got no bargaining power.

"You understand what I'm telling you? Your daughter's not *worth* anything to anybody but you. Nobody's holding her prisoner. This doesn't read like a snatch. Not even her cooperating with some boyfriend to hold you up for money . . . even though the odds favor it."

"Why would you say something like that?"

"In kidnappings when the subject is more than twelve years old, about three-quarters of the perpetrators are known to the victim."

"I never heard—"

"That's the latest FBI breakdown," I told him. "That's why they collect criminal-justice data in America . . . so someone can get a grant to analyze it. Then they publish it. And write another proposal for more funding."

"Oh."

"Yeah. But, look, if it *was* like that, you would have gotten a ransom demand, way before now. So what's that leave? She's out there. Somewhere. People have seen her; they must have. Maybe someone even knows where she's staying. That's information. Information is worth money. But only to the person who *wants* it, like I explained.

"You with me? When it comes to info about Rosebud, I'm like you'd be with your great-great-grandmother's photo—the only buyer in town. Whoever knows, they may not *want* to trust me, but what choice do they have?"

"I understand. But if you don't stay on the case . . . ?"

"See this card?" I said, handing him one of the hundreds I'd spread all over town. "That number, it rings right here." I tapped the cell phone's holster. "I'm not disconnecting it. If it rings tonight, or tomorrow, or two weeks from now, I'll answer it. You don't need to keep me on the books just for that."

"Do you have any other leads you could follow?"

"Leads? Sure. How good they are, I don't have a clue. They may all be dead ends. Or out-and-out bullshit."

"The authorities—"

"I talked to them, too," I said. It was true enough; Gem's boyfriend qualified. "They've got other things on their minds."

"I don't understand." His complexion shifted. Just a touch, but I'd hit one of his trip wires.

I kept my face flat, said: "A major case they're working. It's got nothing to do with your daughter. But they've got a manpower shortage."

"That's what the cops always say," he said bitterly. "It's just a ploy to get more money. They've always got all the manpower they need when the media's on their case."

"Sure. Anyway, you can take this to the bank: they're not working this one real hard."

"I know."

"If we had any reason to believe she was across a state line—"

"She's not," he said, too quickly.

"How do you know?"

"You have any children, Mr. Hazard?"

"No," I said, wondering if his lawyer had told him different.

"Then I couldn't explain it in any way you'd understand. I love my daughter. We're . . . connected. And I know she's close by."

"Well, it wouldn't have to be strictly the truth, would it? The Mann Act is something the feds take pretty seriously. . . ."

"What's that?"

"It's the old 'white slavery' law. Transporting someone across a state line for purposes of engaging in prostitution. They wouldn't use it on a pimp driving his stable from Portland to Seattle; but if the girl was underage, or if she was taken against her will . . ."

"No."

"Huh?"

"Buddy's a very intelligent, very resourceful young woman. I don't believe for a moment she was . . . taken like you're talking about. In any event, you can't just *lie* to the authorities. Sooner or later, they find out."

"But if it puts more horsepower on the street, who cares?"

"No," he said, again. "It's not what I want to do. I don't think it would be in Buddy's best interests."

"You're the boss," I lied.

"Can you stay with it?"

"I can. But . . ."

"I understand. I have a . . . I don't know, a feeling. Call it a father's instinct. I feel you're going to find her. And bring her home. You must have some . . . things you haven't tried yet."

"Yeah. But if I go there, I'm going to need more from you."

"More . . . what? Money?"

"In a way, yes. Not money you'd pay to me, but money you'd have on hand."

"For a ransom? How much would I—?"

"Not for ransom. For bail."

"You think Buddy may be in—?"

"No. Not her, me. If I . . . do some of the things I haven't tried yet, I could get popped. I can't stay in jail, understand. I'd need to be bailed out, and *quick*."

"My lawyer . . ."

"Sure. He can get me in front of a judge fast, if he's got the right connections. But I'd still need a bondsman. And *he'd* need to know the surety's in place."

"How much would I have to—?"

"I guess it's ten percent here, same way it is everywhere else. So ten K for a bond is the same as a hundred K in cash."

"If I put up a bond, you'd show up for court?"

"If they took me down for anything you *could* bond me out on, I would, sure."

"All right. I'll set it up with Toby."

We shook hands on it, liar to liar.

"You know a woman who calls herself Ann O. Dyne?" I asked Hong that night.

"Is this your idea of trading?" he asked, leaning forward, watching me like a specimen.

"It could be. I don't know yet."

"From where I sit, it's been a one-way street up to now."

"You don't like where you sit, get up and walk."

"Is that the kind of talk that impresses Gem, tough guy?"

"I wouldn't know. I never tried it on her."

"Don't," he said, his voice crackling around the edges.

I lit a cigarette, left it to burn down in the ashtray, letting my eyes get lost in the smoke.

"What's your interest in this Dyne woman?" he finally asked, his tone telling me he knew her. Or something about her, anyway.

"I don't know if I have any . . . yet. See, I'm a stranger here. I've got no rep, and I've got no way of checking out anyone else's. She said she might be able to help me with finding the kid I'm looking for. I don't want to waste any time or energy on her if she doesn't have the connects out there to maybe deliver, that's all."

"You spoke to her?"

"I did."

"Describe her, then."

"That's not so easy to do. I've seen her look two different ages, right down to the outfits. She likes wigs, so she probably likes colored contacts, too. I'm guessing she's somewhere in her thirties. White woman. A little under medium height. Extravagant build. Kind of an educated voice. Drives a black Subaru SvX. Spends a lot of time cruising the hooker strolls, but she's not a working girl."

"No," Hong said. "She's a missionary."

"A . . . what? You mean like a Mormon?"

"Not that. It's not about religion for her. She tries to pull girls out of The Life."

"She must be a big favorite of the local pimps."

"This is Portland, not Vegas. The average pimp here is just a boyfriend who's too lazy to work. Don't get me wrong—we've got some real beauties here, too. But I never heard of any of them getting physical with Ann."

"Has she got her own protection?"

"I don't know. There's rumors about her, but—"

"What rumors?"

"That she deals in black-market drugs. She was arrested for possession, once. But the charge didn't stick."

"Aren't all drugs black-market?"

"I'm not talking about smack or crystal, here. I mean drugs like AZT and Betaseron."

"What kind of market could there be for that stuff? You can get it with a scrip."

"Not that stuff, exactly. *Like* it. Experimental stuff."

"For people with AIDS?"

"Or Parkinson's, or brain cancer, or any one of a dozen different things. Drugs only available in Europe, drugs that the FDA hasn't approved yet—if you're dying, you don't want to wait for the bureaucracy to catch up with your problem."

"So why work the prostie strolls? How much money could you make there?"

"That's what I mean about her being a missionary. There's something else going on, but nobody's real sure what it is."

"Not a police priority, is that what you're saying?"

"Why should it be?" he challenged. "Between Ecstasy and heroin, our children are being eaten alive. And crank is running wild all over the state. Never mind the rapes and robberies and murders. And the stolen cars, the burglaries, and the shootings. You've been in a war, right?"

I nodded. I didn't like his certainty about that, but I liked the idea of asking him where it came from even less.

"Then you know what triage is. That's what cops do. Not just here, everywhere. Malcolm was right: the squeaky hinge *does* get the oil."

"You said this Ann girl, she spends a lot of time on the street, right?"

"I didn't say that. You did. But it's true, as far as we know."

"You ever question her about the disappearing hookers?"

"Why? You think she—?"

"No. Whoever's doing it, they have a partner. And she doesn't seem to," I said, not mentioning those moving shadows in her car.

"And you know that . . . how?"

"When the night-girl population is already spooked, there's two ways to approach them. One is to pose as a cop, the way Bianchi did. The other is to come on as a couple, looking for a bi-girl to rent. Sometimes the female half of the team makes the approach alone, pulls the girl, and brings her back to where the guy's waiting. Sometimes they work it together, depending on how well they can pass for yuppies out for some fun."

"You think it's a team?" he asked, looking interested for the first time since I'd sat down.

"Yeah. Yeah, I do. It's the only way they could have taken this many without being caught. The man drives, the woman gets out and makes the deal. Then the woman climbs in the back seat, lets the hooker in front. They've got her boxed then. No way out. It could be a gun, could be chloroform, could be a needle . . . there's a hundred ways. Or, if the girl goes for the fake and comes back to their house, they play a little bondage . . . only the last rope goes around her neck."

"We've been looking for a drifter," he said quietly.

"I don't think so," I said. "Respectfully, I think it's a pair. And working close to home. Brady and Hindley did little kids that way years ago. Bernardo and Homolka worked the same thing, only with teenagers, up in Canada. All those maggots had something else in common, too."

"What?"

"They made tapes. Brady and Hindley used audio; Bernardo and Homolka, video. But they all take trophies," I told him, thinking about the word games the oh-so-sophisticated like to play with terms like "snuff films." No question freaks film people being killed. But if they don't make them "for commercial purposes," they don't qualify, so snuff films remain an "urban legend." How cute and clever.

"And that's important, why?" he asked.

"Because it means they've got a place to stash them. Not a furnished room or a cheap motel. Probably not even an apartment. A house, my best guess."

"You think we release serial killers on parole here?"

"I think you do it all the time. You and every other prison system. Only, on the books, you're not releasing a serial killer. It's a rapist. Or a rapist that pleaded to burglary. You understand what I'm saying; don't act like you don't, Hong. You look close at some of the unsolved pattern-crimes, you'll see they had a . . . break in the action. That was while the perp was Inside. But dropped for something *besides* the killings. He does his time. He's a good inmate. And the Board cuts him loose. Am I wrong?"

"Angkat said you were—"

"Who?" I asked him, knowing the answer, but wanting to see what he said.

"That's what I call Gem," he said, eyes challenging me to keep driving down the same road I'd turned onto.

"Uh-huh," I said.

When he saw I wasn't going to say anything else, he picked up where he'd dropped it. "She said you were some kind of expert on these things."

"These things?"

"Predators."

"I know them," I acknowledged.

"You know *them*? Or you know what they do?"

"Both."

"You're a criminologist?"

"About as much as you're Chinese."

"I'm half Chinese," he said, seriously. "My mother is Samoan."

"Exactly."

"Where are you going, Mr. . . .?"

"Not where you are, pal. You didn't forget my name. Not the one I gave you, anyway. And you know a lot more about me than you're acting."

"Why do you say that?"

"Because you and Gem—"

"We're not—"

"Done. I know."

"That isn't what I was going to say. Our . . . whatever was between us, it's not your business."

"And my name, that's not yours. But it didn't stop you from asking around, right?"

"I didn't need to ask around to know you've done time."

"Sherlock's got nothing on you, huh?"

"Relax," he said, shifting his body posture to match his words. "That was just my way of saying that I think you know what you're talking about."

"No. It was your way of saying that you think you're protecting Gem. Am I getting closer?"

"I don't *think* I'm protecting her," he said, his face tightening. "If anyone hurt her, it would be a mistake."

"What are we having here, a fucking meaningful moment?" I sneered at him. "You telling me if I break your little girl's heart you'll beat me up or something?"

"Angkat's heart is her own," he said, softly, not playing around anymore. "I don't know why you're here, or what you're doing. You say you're looking for a runaway girl. Maybe you are. But I don't see a man like you being a good Samaritan . . . even for money."

"A 'man like me,' money's what I work for."

"So all this information—what you gave me, about the way the hookers could be disappearing, and all you're promising—that's for . . . ?"

"Barter. Like I said it was."

"And what you want, what you want *now*, is whatever we have on this 'Ann O. Dyne' woman?"

"Yeah."

"You already have it," he said.

He stubbed out his cigarette and our conversation with the same gesture.

Back at the loft, there was no message from Gem. We hadn't agreed on that, either. She'd wanted me to sign on to her computer so she could e-mail me. I don't trust anything I don't understand—and a lot of things I do—so I'd told her it wouldn't work for me; she could just ring me on the cellular.

Gem said she didn't like talking on cell phones: anyone could pluck the conversation out of the air. I told her I didn't think e-mail was so fucking private, either. And, besides, she didn't have to say anything that could cause a problem on the phone, right?

She didn't answer me then. And hadn't called.

Me, I hadn't turned on that damn computer, either.

I fingered the poker-chip business card, wishing I had a tip sheet to consult before I placed the bet. Finally, I stuck it in my pocket. I took a look around the loft, decided I didn't feel like sleeping, and went back into the street.

Nosing the Caddy around corners, I felt overwhelmed by what I *didn't* know. I finally had the street grid down pretty good, but not much else.

Wherever I've gone, the games are always the same. That part's easy. Knowing the players, that's where the investment comes in.

I could feel the whisper-stream burbling out the twin exhaust pipes of the Caddy, building rumor as I trolled. If you work like an anthropologist, it might take you centuries to know a town.

But if you profile heavy enough, the knowledge comes to you. Buried knowledge. If you want the full truth out of all the silt people pour over you, you'd better have a very fine strainer and a lot of patience.

Fringe-dwellers do a lot of business in strip clubs; something about the flashing flesh makes them feel safe. Or important. Some of the suckers can't tell the difference. I'd known of girls younger than Rosebud turned out and siliconed up by club managers who kept them in bondage until they worked off the price of the implants, but I couldn't see her going that route. I didn't expect to find her in a biker bar, either. Or an after-hours joint. And a young girl on the Jesus-loves-you flophouse circuit would stick out like a truthful telemarketer.

You couldn't even sell your blood so easy, anymore. Ask any derelict. The AIDS scare had dried up the market for untested blood and put the Dracula vans that once roamed every big city's skid row out of business.

I let the Caddy have its head, my mind busy doing the math. If Rosebud wasn't on the streets in Portland, she was either someplace else, or nowhere else. I'm a good bloodhound, but I'm no cadaver-dog—that dead drop had me convinced she was alive. And in Portland.

All right. In Portland, then. If she was surviving without working the streets in some way, there were two possibilities. Either she was shacked up—the best way, actually: agoraphobics don't worry about Wanted posters—or culted up. Cults don't let the new ones out during indoctrination.

I didn't like either of those. My best reads on Rosebud came from her little sister, Daisy, and her friend Jenn. But even those who didn't know her so well agreed that Rosebud was one strong-willed young lady. I couldn't see her as either needy or dependent enough to go any of the stay-inside routes.

Besides, there'd been little flashes once in a while from my showing the picture around town. Clipper, the pool player's manager, had the kind of face that didn't give anything away. But he seemed like a guy who would pay his debts, and that line was still out, baited. Daisy hadn't admitted getting letters from her sister, but she hadn't denied it, and that fit for me.

Madison was kind of the same way. Maybe she *had* gotten a letter from Rosebud. Maybe Rosebud had reached out to Jenn after that first weekend. I thought I'd connected enough with Bobby Ray so he'd at least pass along my message if he saw her. Odom had eyes and ears out there, and he wanted to get paid.

My business card was sitting in after-hours joints, strip clubs, poolrooms . . . stuck to bulletin boards, sides of buildings, plastered on top of posters for musical acts. I even went Nike one better—kids were walking all around the city with ROSEBUD: CALL B.B.! and my cell phone number stickered onto their backpacks and jackets. I paid five bucks a day for them to be walking billboards.

And then there was Ann.

What there wasn't was any message from Gem when I returned . . . not home, I guess . . . to her place. I knew where she was. Where she said she was, anyway. I could have called. I guess I said that wrong. When I tried to, I couldn't do it. Couldn't punch the damn numbers into the keypad, for some reason. I had every good excuse in the world to call her—Gem's geek was handling whatever code-breaking was required for me to read what was on Kevin's laptop. But I knew she would tell me the minute he was done.

I wondered if she'd tell me the minute we were.

I kept thinking about Hong.

And about going back home.

"If you're looking for Ann, press 'one,' " said the computer-chip voice.

I did that.

"Thank you. Your number is not one recognized by this system. After the tone, please say your name, then press 'two.'"

"Hazard. B. B. Hazard," I told the machinery. And pressed the button.

"Thank you. Please wait while I connect your call."

The music-on-hold was Tracy Chapman's "Give Me One Reason." I flashed on the poster on Rosebud's wall, waiting.

"Where are you?"

"Ninth and Burnside," I told her.

"I told you she's not strolling."

"You told me a lot of things," I said.

"Fair enough. You know how to get to the river?"

"It's a big river."

"Don't be cute. It doesn't go with your looks. You got something to write with?"

"Yeah."

"Okay, take this down." She gave me directions to a spot on the other side of the Fremont Bridge, in North Portland, between the river and the Albina Yard of the Union Pacific tracks. I didn't know there was anything there other than empty space, but she said I'd find it easy enough.

Turned out to be a warehouse district, with an upscale bar positioned like a sentinel right where I turned off Interstate Avenue. There was no activity at the warehouses—I guessed they stopped running the trains after a certain time at night.

About five cross-streets down, I spotted one of those old silver

Airstream trailers. It had one whole side open under a bright-yellow awning—looked like a food-concession booth at a carnival, only much longer. Over to one side, a bunch of cut-down fifty-five-gallon oil drums with the unmistakable rich smell of barbecue wafting off in all directions. Magic Sam's "What Have I Done Wrong?" poured out of invisible speakers, like they were playing my walk-out music for a fight.

It looked like someone had raided the table-and-chairs section of a Goodwill warehouse and scattered the pickings all around the trailer at random: wood, plastic, and everything in between, all sizes and shapes. All they had in common was that nothing matched. Christmas lights were strung above, interspersed with blue bug-zappers. The whole scene looked like something you'd find any summer night on captured-for-the-moment vacant lots in cities from Detroit to Dallas. When a cook's got a rep for *real* barbecue, there's no need for a permanent location. That's what they mean by a "following."

The only discordant note was the cars. Instead of a bunch of bondo'ed American iron, they were all *seriously* high-end. I spotted at least three Rollers, a Ferrari F50, a half-dozen miscellaneous Porsches, a few limos, and a pimped-out gold Hummer—all as neatly parked as if a valet had handled the chore. There was even a huge black custom Featherlite motorcoach, slide-outs fully extended.

Ann's Subaru looked like a poor relation . . . but not one you wanted to fuck with.

I stopped a couple of blocks away from the trailer, killed the engine. A Filipino with a high pompadour and a glistening white jacket materialized out of the dark. He didn't look like anybody's houseboy.

"Twenty to park here," he said.

I handed him a bill.

"*We* park the cars," he said.

"How do I find you when I want to leave?" I asked him.

"Just go anywhere *near* the cars, mister. One of us'll find you in ten seconds."

Meaning the twenty bucks wasn't for parking, it was for protection. Fair enough. I climbed out of the Caddy. If the Filipino was sneering at my low-class ride, it didn't reach his face. I didn't see a bulge anywhere on his starched white jacket, but a knife doesn't usually make one.

I walked over to the Airstream, waited my turn on line, ordered a pulled-pork sandwich with a side of coleslaw and the biggest lemonade they had. That swallowed the best part of another twenty.

I took my food and headed over to the sitting area. Spotted what looked like a discarded canasta table with folding legs surrounded by three ripped-cushion chrome-and-vinyl kitchen chairs. Took me only a second to realize that there was no wall to keep my back to, so I sat down and started to work on the sandwich. Didn't surprise me at all when it turned out to be delicious.

Chicago kept coming to Portland through the speakers. Luther Allison's "The Skies Are Crying." Eddie Boyd's "3rd Degree." Susan Tedeschi's "It Hurt So Bad."

Just as I was beginning to regret I hadn't ordered two sandwiches when I'd had the chance, she dropped into the chair right across from me. This time, she was a brunette, long hair piled on top of her head, held together by a purple scrunchie the same shade as her cotton pullover. The scrunchie was a nice touch, drawing the eye away from the wig.

"Israel makes the best barbecue in the world," she said.

It was too dark to see her eyes, so I focused hard on the pale oval of her face, expecting some lame joke about Jews and pork . . . at best.

She caught my look and blew it off with, "He's about a hundred years old. . . . Israel. Funny name for a black guy, huh? All anyone knows is that he's from Cleveland. He sets up in different places all the time. Word gets out, people come from all over. Then he just disappears again."

"Like you."

"Just because you don't know where to look doesn't mean someone's disappeared."

"Back to that, huh?"

"Why else would you be here? It's not *me* you're interested in."

"I'm interested in what you have. What you *say* you have."

"You think because I like . . . outfits, I'm not for real?"

"This is all blah-blah. You know what 'prove in' means?"

"Sure. Do *you*?"

I leaned forward, looking for her eyes. "The way I figure it, I already have. I don't know you. But you know me. Or, at least, enough about me to want to trade for something I've got. Or something you want me to do. If I'm wrong, just say so, and we'll be done, right now."

She didn't say anything. I went back to my sandwich. Time passed. The night was full of sounds, none of them threatening. I washed the last little bit of perfect BBQ down with a hit of the tangy lemonade.

Still nothing from the woman. Maybe she was showing off her patience, the way she'd shown off other assets the first time we'd met. I wasn't going to sit there and trade thousand-yard stares with her all night. I moved the white waxed paper my sandwich had come in to the side, folded the cardboard tray that had housed the coleslaw into an ashtray, and lit a cigarette.

"When this is gone, so am I," I told her, taking a deep drag.

She took a breath. "Never mind the dramatics," she said. "Come over to my car with me and I'll tell you the deal."

A different Filipino brought her Subaru around. She slipped him something; both of us got in. The dashboard and console for the floor shift were both covered in carbon fiber. I couldn't see any surface that would reflect light . . . and wondered about that shadow I'd seen shifting in her car when I'd last dropped her off.

She drove a few hundred yards toward the river, found a big

patch of gravel, parked. It was prairie-desolate out there; nothing but a few of the deserted-looking warehouses within a couple of hundred yards. No way for anyone to come up on us without being spotted. Another demonstration?

The woman hit a switch and both our side windows slid down. She turned off the ignition.

"This way, you can smoke."

I didn't say anything.

"What do you know about pain?" she asked softly.

"More than I want to," I said, voice flat, deliberately distancing myself from where I thought she was headed.

"*Other* people's pain."

"That, too."

"I hate it," she said. Quietly, the way a nun talks when she tells you about getting the call.

"Pain?"

"Yes," she said sharply, as if I had been sarcastic. "Pain. That's what I am. A painkiller."

"I'm not following you."

"Listen, and you will. I'm not talking about headaches. Or arthritis, or . . ." She took a deep breath, let it out. Made sure she had my eyes. "I mean bone-deep, searing, *unbearable* pain. Like when cancer really gets a grip. When you're near the end from AIDS. When . . . when you'd rather be dead than suffer every single minute. And you know what a lot of those people get? Speeches. 'You make your own pain. It's in your mind. Just take yourself to a peaceful place. . . .' Or they get what someone *else* thinks is the right dose of drugs, as if pain were something you could measure in milligrams."

"Or that they can't have more dope, because they'll turn into addicts," I said.

"Yes! That's the worst of all. Somebody's *dying*, what possible difference could it make if they *were* a damn drug addict? That's the legacy of Nancy-fucking-Reagan, a country where we're so psycho about 'drug addicts' that we sentence millions to be tortured to death. Doctors are so freaked about the DEA, they won't write the scrips. People are in absolute *agony,* and what they get is sanctimonious babbling about the 'war on drugs.'"

"Unless they've got money."

"Sure. If you have enough money, you can get what you need. But how many people have enough money?"

"I don't know. Can't be many."

"That's right," she said, her voice vibrating with barely suppressed rage. "Not many. Listen to this," she said, pulling a long, thin white strip of paper from behind the sun visor. I could see it was covered with tiny words. She cleared her throat and switched to a schoolgirl's recital voice:

" 'In treating the terminally ill patient the benefit of pain relief *may* outweigh the possibility of drug dependence. The chance of drug dependence is substantially reduced when the patient is placed on scheduled narcotic programs instead of 'pain to relief of pain' cycle typical of a PRN regimen.' Do you understand that?" she challenged.

"Yeah, I think so. What they're saying is, instead of giving you a shot when the pain gets too much to bear, they should be giving you regular doses all along, to keep it at bay."

"Of *course*! Pain is the enemy. You have to get on top of it and *stay* on top of it. You don't wait until it's got its hands around your throat before you start to fight back. And if they dispense drugs the way it says here, the *right* way, there's even less of a chance of making a goddamned 'addict' out of somebody who's dying."

"Where did you get that?"

"How about *this*?" she said, ignoring my question, and read aloud again: " 'During the first two to three days of *effective* pain relief, the patient may sleep for many hours. This can be misinterpreted as the effect of excessive analgesic dosing rather than the first sign of relief in a pain-exhausted patient.' "

"What about it?"

"Oh? You understand that, too?" she challenged.

"Sure," I said, "it's not rocket science. You're wasted from the pain. It eats you inside, so you can't even sleep. You *finally* get a hit of something that knocks the pain back a few feet, you *can* sleep. So you do. Deep. And a lot. They don't want some chump thinking you're sleeping so long because what they gave you was an 'overdose' and cutting back on the painkillers, right?"

"Right," she said, sounding tired. "You asked me where I got this. It's right on the physician's instructions for Sweet Roxanne."

"Sweet . . . ?"

"Roxanol. Morphine sulfate. It's about the best painkiller out there. Except for maybe methadone."

"Methadone? I thought that was for—"

"Dope fiends? Sure. But, like *all* opiates, synthetic or not, its true purpose is to kill pain. That's why it was developed—by the Third Reich, after their route to the poppy fields was cut off, and they couldn't manufacture morphine."

"So why don't they just give methadone to the people with the worst pain?"

"Why?" she snarled, her voice so loaded with fury I thought it would shatter from the strain. "Because, see, it's very difficult to *detox* from methadone. And we don't want anyone to become a terrible 'drug addict,' now, do we?"

"What difference would it make if they were—?"

"Dying? None, obviously. Or even if they *would* die from the pain if they *didn't* get regular relief from it. Stupid, mean-spirited, nasty little . . . The moralists don't *get* it. The only way a painkiller can really get you high is if there's no pain left to kill."

"No physical pain," I said, letting the words sit between us.

She gave me a long, searching look. "No physical pain," she finally agreed.

She was quiet for a long time after that. Me, too. I knew there was more, and I needed to show her I could wait for whatever it was. I lit a cigarette, held it out the window, watched the smoke drift off into the night, went with it.

"Have you ever watched someone die?" she asked suddenly, snapping me back from where I'd drifted off to.

"Yeah," I told her.

"Someone close to you?"

"Yes."

"Take them long?"

"Not . . . not like you mean."

"Is that so? How do I 'mean,' then?"

"You mean like from an illness."

"Yes."

"No."

"I don't under—"

"I had friends go down slow, but not in front of me. I didn't watch it. I didn't even know about it until after it was over. I saw . . . In battle, I saw death."

"But people close to you, you watched them go?"

"I said I did."

"Can you imagine if it took—?"

"That's enough," I cut her off. "I can imagine anything. I don't want to. It's a cheap trick. You don't need it. I'm already sold."

"I'm sorry. I didn't mean to—"

"Just tell your story," I said. I wasn't going anywhere near watching Belle die. Or Pansy. Both from bullets they took for me. I still had their love. And wherever they were, they had proof of my love for them. In my vengeance.

"It's not my story," she said.

"Yeah, it is. No way you're this . . . intense over some abstract principle. Besides, you dispense the stuff, right?"

"Yes," she said, proudly. "That's what I do. It's no secret. But I've never been caught with the goods. Not enough to make it stick, anyway."

"Maybe nobody's all that interested."

"Maybe nobody local. But the feds—that's all they live for. Drugs. Sacred, holy drugs. Drug *czars*. Drug *budgets*. Drug *squads*. Drug *forfeitures*. Drug money—they all live on it."

"Sure. We lost the bullshit 'war on drugs' a long time ago, and now we're all POWs to it. But what's any of this have to do with—?"

"They need it all," she went on, as if I hadn't spoken. "Oxy-C, OxyContin; the Fentanyl patch; Vicodin . . . you name it."

"Who's 'they'?"

"People in pain. *Everybody* knows *someone* who's been there. A friend, a relative, a . . . loved one. It happens *all* over. But everybody it's happening to, they think they're the only ones."

Like the Children of the Secret, I thought. *Alone in their pain, they never know that it's not anything in* them *that made it happen. Freaks made it happen. There's freaks all over. And when you get down to the bone, where the truth is, one person's pain is always about another person's power.*

"There's no immunity from terminal pain," Ann said. "And when people are going to cross over," she said, "they deserve to go softly. That ghoul with his horrible suicide machine, he wouldn't have any takers if people could get true pain relief."

"And if Nancy had bone cancer, she wouldn't worry about turning into an addict."

"But you, you don't care?"

"You know what I think about 'care'? I think there's only so much of it to go around inside everyone. The more different things you 'care' about, the less you can 'care' about any one of them, you see what I'm saying?"

"No."

"The people who want to *stop* women from having abortions, that's the *only* thing they 'care' about. But the people who want women to be *able* to have abortions, they 'care' about a whole lot of stuff—clean air, pure water, logging, cigarette smoking, racism, gun control, animal rights, affirmative action, freedom of speech—"

"I get it."

"I don't think you do. Fanatics always have more impact than dabblers. When it comes to getting something done, whether it's breaking a brick with your hand or overthrowing a government, *focus* is the best weapon of all. People on a jihad are willing to do things most people aren't, see?"

"Yes, I see. I don't apologize for what I am. So what's your point?"

"My point is that I'm sorry about people dying in pain. But it isn't the thing I care most about in the world."

"And that would be . . . ?"

"My family."

"And if one of your family was dying in pain?"

"I'd get them the drugs," I told her. "No matter what I had to do. Or who I had to do it to."

She went quiet again. I waited, again. Time passed.

"So, if someone in your family needed them, how would you get the drugs?" she finally asked.

"Buy them. Everything's for sale, if you know where to look."

"And you do?"

"For heroin? Who *doesn't*?"

"Not heroin. The stuff I told you about."

"They keep it in hospitals. People work in hospitals."

"You have no idea how strict the—"

"It just means it would cost more, that's all. If you can get drugs in prison—and, believe me, you can—you can get them anywhere."

"And if, just let's say, nobody would sell you any . . ."

"It wouldn't stop me."

"You'd steal them, then?"

"For my family? If any of them needed a *heart,* I'd get them one, never mind some damn pills."

"That *sounds* good."

"I'm not trying to convince you of anything. You asked me a question; I answered you."

"Yeah. You did. Some people say you were a mercenary."

"Some people say Elvis lost weight recently."

She went quiet again. I went back to where I'd been.

"How bad do you want that girl?" She broke the silence. "The one you've been looking for."

"Bad enough to finance a suitcase of the stuff *you* want so bad."

"Not enough."

"There's a budget," I said. "And it's got a ceiling."

"Not cash," she said softly. "A trade."

"I don't have any drugs. And you don't have the girl."

"You can help me *get* drugs. And I can help you get the girl."

"You said that before."

"I know I did. I was telling you the truth. Some of it, anyway."

"Sure. Okay, turn her up and we'll talk."

"I don't think so. But I *will* show you enough to make you believe me."

"Look, I already told you about 'caring.' Don't knock yourself out trying to make a believer out of me."

"You don't have to believe anything. Just tell me what you have so far—whatever you're willing to, that is. I can work from nothing . . . or nearly nothing . . . but it would go a lot faster if you'd . . ."

"Here's what I know," I said. And gave her an edited version of the truth.

She listened carefully, nodding her head at various points, but not taking any notes. When I was done, she said, "I'm going to take you back now. Tomorrow, be around. It doesn't matter where. Three o'clock. Call me. I'll pick you up. And take you a lot closer to the girl than you've been since you started, see if I don't."

When I let myself back into the loft, Gem was there.

"Were you successful?" she greeted me, as if I'd been out trying to sell encyclopedias door-to-door.

"I might have gotten closer. Or I might be getting hustled. I can't be sure yet."

"How have you eaten?"

"Fine."

"Yes? Very well, then."

She approached me. Tentatively, as if not sure of her reception. As I stepped to meet her, I could see her eyes were closed. I kissed her lips, lightly. Her arms went around my neck.

"I was afraid," she whispered.

"Of what?"

"That you would be gone."

"It's not that dangerous a—"

"Not dead. Gone. Gone away from me."

"I—"

"I know you will go. I was afraid you would just . . . vanish. Without saying anything to me."

"I wouldn't do that."

She stepped back slightly, her hands still clasped behind my neck. "Yes you would. If you thought it was . . . if you . . . if it made sense to you, that is what you would do."

"Why would it make—?"

"Stop it, Burke. You are not a good dancer. Come back into the bedroom with me. I want to show you something I bought."

It turned out to be a simple ottoman, just a solid rectangular lump of black leather with some kind of pattern in red on its top.

"What is it? An antique?" I asked her.

"It is old, but that is not its beauty. You do not like it?"

"I don't *dis*like it or anything. It doesn't race my motor, that's all."

"Be patient," she said, tugging her jeans down over her hips. When she was nude, she positioned herself over the ottoman on her hands and knees.

"Walk around it," she said, throatily. "Look at it from all angles. Perhaps you will appreciate what I have brought you then."

I never made the complete circuit.

"Are Flacco and Gordo back, too?" I asked her the next morning.

"*Sí,*" she said, mockingly.

"What's that all about?"

"They speak better English than you do." She chuckled. "I don't know why men play those games. *Machismo.* It sounds so much stronger in Spanish, yes?"

"Hey, *I'm* not the one who tries to speak Spanish, miss. I tried that once—it almost cost me my life."

"Truly?"

"Oh yeah. Square business."

"Tell me?" Gem play-begged, kneeling next to where I was sitting.

"You want to hear about how stupid I was?"

"Oh yes!" she said, smiling.

I leaned back in the chair, tangling my hand in her long black hair. "You know I was in the war in Biafra . . . ?"

"Of course."

"Well, by the time I showed up, the rebels were pretty much surrounded. They'd lost their only seaport, and very little food was getting in. There were only two routes for it: overland through Gabon, or by night flight from São Tomé, a little Portuguese colony island just off the coast.

"The island was like any small town. Only smaller. They didn't get tourists. There wasn't but one reason to be there: every visitor was there for the war."

Gem shifted position slightly, just to let me know she was paying close attention.

"I was trying to make my connections to catch a ride on one of the merc planes, figuring out who to approach," I went on. "So I spent a lot of time just hanging out. Anyway, in this bar, I met a guy . . . Evaristo, I remember his name was. He was being friendly, showed me how the nut-bowl trick worked. . . ."

"What was that?"

"When you bought a drink, the guy behind the stick would ask if you wanted the 'nuts.' He said it in English, but I didn't know what he was talking about, so I always passed. This 'bar,' it was right on the beach. White sand, so pure it looked new. The place was made out of wood, and it was left open on one side. No doors, no windows, no wall, no nothing. When they closed, I guess they just took the stock home with them.

"One day, Evaristo is in there with me when the bartender asks me about the nuts. Evaristo nods his head at me, like he was saying, 'Yeah, go for it.' So I did. The bartender hands me a covered wooden bowl full of . . . well, nuts, I guess. And seeds, and all kinds of things I wasn't going to put in my mouth. Evaristo, he grabs the bowl, closes the cover, and shakes it. Sounded like the way a dried gourd rattles, you know?

"In two minutes, the place was full of birds. *Amazing* birds, like I'd never seen in my life. I guess they were parrots of some kind. Huge things. Colors I never even knew existed. Evaristo opened the bowl, scattered the nuts all over this wooden plank they used as a bar. The birds hopped up there like they were used to it. I mean, they were close enough for me to touch, and it didn't bother them at all. I'd never imagined such fabulous things, and there they were, right on top of me.

"I was just a kid then. Nineteen. It was one of the coolest things I'd ever seen. I bought Evaristo a drink, to thank him and all. And we got to talking. It wasn't a whole *lot* of talking, because he didn't speak much English. I knew the island was under Portuguese control, but it sure *sounded* like Spanish to me. Evaristo, he showed me a picture of his wife. *'¿Muy blanco, eh?'* he says. I tell him, yeah, she sure is.

"He smiles, and I figure I got enough street Spanish to get by; maybe we could talk. Like I said, I was a kid.

"After that, I saw him all the time. He drove a taxi, but I couldn't see where he had much business.

"This was when Portugal was still a major colonial power in Angola . . . and having trouble holding on. That's why they were big players in Biafra—pretty hard to fly bombers from Lisbon all the way down to southern Africa. If the rebels had won in Nigeria, the Portuguese who backed them would have had themselves a perfect launching pad.

"But São Tomé itself was unstable. I kept hearing talk about some 'independence movement,' but I never actually saw any signs of one . . . not even so much as a piece of graffiti.

"One day, we're in the bar, talking, and Evaristo points to me, says 'Biafra?' And I think, Here's my chance to make a plane connect, so I tell him, *'Sí,'* like I'm a real native. Then he goes, *'¿Soldado?'* and I say, 'No.' He tries *'Jornalista?'* and I shake my head again. Then he moves me up the ladder even more. *'¿Médico?'* But I have to shrug him off again.

"He makes a '*What,* then?' gesture. I figure now's the time to tell him I'm on this humanitarian mission, so I try to figure out what the word for 'social worker' would be . . . and I come up with *'socialista.'* "

"Burke! You *didn't!*"

"Yeah, I did. And Evaristo, all the blood goes out of his face. He looks around, makes a *'Shut the fuck up!'* gesture at me.

"I didn't think anything of it until a few hours later, back in my room. When I heard the slides being racked."

“Slides?”

“On the machine guns.”

“Oh!” Gem gasped, like it was the most terrifying thing she'd ever heard in her life. Women.

“*La polícia* wanted to talk to me,” I told her. “I guess I fit the Outside Agitator profile.”

“What happened?”

“Well, I *couldn't* speak Portuguese. And, after that, I wasn't about to try. After a couple of hours, they took me to a priest. He translated. Or maybe he didn't. I never knew what he told them, but, finally, they left.

“The *padre* told me I better do the same. Right then. Don't go back to my room, don't do *anything*. Just get to the airstrip and catch the first thing smoking.”

“You did that?”

“Yep. Evaristo, he was waiting outside, with the motor running. The plane was on the strip, propellers already spinning. The back was open. I just jumped on, like hopping a freight. One of the mercs looked me over, asked me, was I from the Company? I said I was, and that was it.”

“You were so lucky,” Gem said, her palms together in a prayerful gesture.

“More than I even knew at the time, honeygirl. They made two runs every night. The late run was the best—darker, less chance of getting hit by enemy fire going in. But I didn't have any choice. The one I took was the early run.”

“Why was that so—?”

“That night, the late run went down.”

“Ah,” she said, accepting. That was the real Gem. A child who had developed fatalism to keep the fear from stopping her little heart. Grown now. But with the same core.

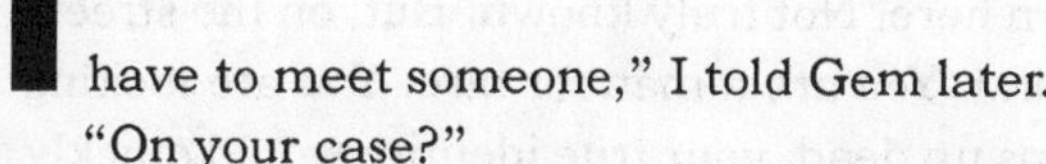

“I have to meet someone,” I told Gem later.

“On your case?”

"Supposedly. I've been digging—well, maybe not digging, little girl, scratching around the edges, more like—for a while now, and there isn't a whole hell of a lot I found that I'd take to the bank."

"You believe she is here, though?"

"Yeah. I do."

"Because . . . ?"

"She's in touch with her little sister. Leaves her notes."

"She could be using a—"

"Sure. And if she is going through a cutout, I've got a candidate for that, too," I told her, seeing Jenn's calm, strong face in my mind. "But, the big thing, I'm sure she's alive."

"You had doubts, then?"

"Sure. The streets eat their young. Vampires at one end, vultures at the other. And I thought maybe her father . . ."

"What?"

"That he killed her. And hired me as a red herring for the cops. But I don't think that anymore. I think *he* believes she's out there. Close. He's been feeling me out."

"For . . . ?"

"He's just touching the edges. Nothing that would incriminate him even if I was wired," I said, flashing on the elaborate phone-recording system in his private den. "But he's real interested in my capacity for . . . violence."

"Some wealthy people seem to be excited by such things."

"I know. It doesn't feel like that to me. Ah, maybe a little bit . . . But I think he's really asking if I'd cap his daughter, if it comes to that."

"I don't understand."

"Neither do I, miss. It's almost as if he wants the *option,* you know? A 'just in case' kind of thing."

Gem got up and stalked over to the kitchen table, her movements agitated. "Burke, this is not a good thing for you to do."

"What makes you say that?"

"You are not known here. Not truly known. But, on the streets now, it is getting around. You are a man for hire. You are looking for this girl. If she turns up dead, your true identity would quickly become known. And once the police learn of your . . . background, it would be bad. Very bad."

"Detective Hong tell you that?"

"What?" she snapped, her voice sharp. "Is *that* your interest, then? Not what I know, but how I know it?"

"Not mine," I lied. "But this 'man for hire' stuff on the streets . . . *you* didn't pick that up. These streets, they're not your territory. So I figured maybe your—"

"My *what*?" She chopped off my sentence. "My . . . boyfriend? My secret lover? Is that what you really want to know?"

"That's your business," I told her.

Gem turned her back and walked out of the room, not a trace of wiggle in her hips.

I went out to meet Ann.

I called her from the car, went through the voice-mail routine, got her on the line. She told me where to park.

Ten minutes after I pulled in, the Subaru rolled up. It sat next to the Caddy, idling. I couldn't see into the car: the window glass was too heavily tinted.

As if reading my thoughts, the passenger-side window whispered down. Ann was in the driver's seat. She made a "Come on!" gesture.

I climbed into the Subaru's bucket seat and we moved off.

I didn't ask where we were going. It turned out to be a black-windowed storefront on a narrow side street. It looked like a porno outlet that hadn't gotten around to painting the "XXX" on the windows yet. When I followed Ann inside, I saw that the place was actually a triple-wide, extending out on either side into what looked like a blank wall from the street. It was a used-book store of some kind, with floor-to-ceiling shelves made up out of whatever some after-hours scavenger had found lying around on a construction site.

And it was full of kids. All kinds of kids, dressed all kinds of ways. A boy who looked about eighteen, and straight off a farm in Iowa, stood next to a girl whose age I couldn't guess under all the Goth makeup. If they even noticed each other, they gave no sign. Cheerleaders mingled with the multi-pierced. If there was a shade of human color not represented, it was one I'd never seen. Some of the kids pawed through stacks of books, others sat in battered chairs or flopped down on the floor. Nobody was smoking, or drinking coffee.

In a far corner, a pale, skinny young guy with long hair was bent all the way over a battered twelve-string, strumming so softly I couldn't pick up the notes.

I was scanning for Rosebud, focusing hard on each girl's face, putting it on the left-hand side of the screen in my head, comparing it with Rosebud's photo on the right. I had gone through about a dozen when I felt Ann pulling on my coat sleeve.

I followed her lead . . . over to where a heavyset mixed-blood Indian woman in a red caftan sat behind a counter.

"Hello, Choma," Ann said to her.

"Ann," the woman said back. I could see the shutters open and close in her black camera eyes.

"This is a friend of mine. B. B. Hazard."

"Yes?"

"He's looking for Borderland."

"We don't use the Dewey Decimal System here."

"I know," Ann said patiently. "That's why I brought my friend over to ask you."

"Does he speak?"

"Yes," I told her. "I was trying to be polite."

"What does a hunter want with a book?" she asked.

I didn't waste time denying what she already knew. "There might be something in it of value to me."

"Might be?"

"I didn't know Borderland *was* a book. Not until a few seconds ago."

"Ah. It is an expression you heard?"

"Yes."

"So it is *you* who made the connection?" the Indian woman asked, head swiveling to Ann.

"It's no secret," Ann said, shrugging.

"Not to some. It was to him," the woman said.

"He is not a danger to any of your—"

"He is a hunter."

"I do other things," I said gently.

"Yes. I am certain you do. I was saying not what you do, only what you are."

I bowed slightly, the way Mama taught me a million years ago. Done properly, the gesture crosses cultures, conveying respect without submission.

She focused hard on my good eye. Finally, she nodded, said: "Ask Berto. . . . Ann knows him, he's right over there. Ask Berto where he's got the Charles de Lint books."

"Thank you," I said, keeping my face blank as the synapses fired in my mind, looking for the connection. Crow girls? Was that it?

The Indian woman gave me a look that said, "You better be telling me the truth," and turned away just enough to be a dismissal.

Berto turned out to be a Latino kid—I guessed Panama, but it *was* a guess—maybe sixteen years old. As soon as Ann said "Borderland" to him, he led us over to a whole wall of paperbacks, and deftly plucked a copy of *Life on the Border* from a high shelf. It showed a young man and a girl dressed in a combination of street gear and club clothes, leaning against a telephone pole in front of an ancient Cadillac sedan with a taxi light on top and bullet scars all over its doors. It said the author was Terri Windling, and I was beginning to think the kid had confused the title when I saw Charles de Lint's name up top, next to the title.

"How much?" I asked the kid.

He gave Ann a glance, his eyebrows raised in a question.

"Give him twenty," she said to me.

I did it. The kid didn't offer me a courtesy shopping bag. Or a receipt.

"Is that a rare-book store?" I asked Ann, examining my prize on the front seat of her Subaru.

"Not especially. They have some hard-to-get stuff there, but it's not exactly antiquarian."

"This one cost five bucks new. And it's ten years old."

"What's your point?"

"Twenty bucks seemed a little steep."

"They work on a sliding scale there. Kids pay whatever they can afford, like on the honor system. When . . . someone your age comes in, they try to get whatever the traffic will bear."

"And that keeps . . . people my age out of there for the most part."

"That, too," she said, smiling. "Is the book going to help you?"

"I don't know yet."

"All right. You know where to find me."

"That's it? That's all you got?"

"No, Mr. . . . Hazard, that's what you call yourself, yes? . . . I've got a lot more. But you might as well see what this is worth first."

"Fair enough. Whatever's in this book, it might give me a clue or two, but it isn't worth—"

"Here you are," she said, as she slid the Subaru alongside where I'd left my car. "Things don't have 'worth.' That's a nonsense concept. Things are worth what people are willing to pay for them. You think a hit of street heroin is 'worth' what they're getting for it?"

"That again."

"Yes. That again. I told you—"

"Thanks for the book," I interrupted. "I'll let you know."

As I was climbing out of the car, she said, "Madison might be a lot more willing to talk to you if she thought you and I were working together . . . ," letting the words trail out behind her as she pulled away.

"What is that you are reading?" Gem asked me that night.

I held up the paperback so she could see the cover. "It's a book about kids. Runaways. And this place called Bordertown that they all run *to.* It's a place that runs on music and magic."

"A fantasy?"

"More like a fable. About the kind of community kids wanted to build in the Haight-Ashbury days. Maybe the kind of community they saw in their heads if they dropped enough acid, I don't know. It's not one of those post-apocalyptic jobs—this is kind of a parallel universe. I mean, this Borderland, it's not perfect. There's a kind of racism—or species-ism, maybe—there's two different species, and a third that comes from mixing. People have to have jobs or they have to scrounge. There's a goods-and-services economy, just like here. But the kids are building something out of their own needs. Something real different from what's out here for them now."

"Why is this important?" Gem had been a child in a place where dreams kill as surely as bullets, only with a lot more pain.

"The note . . . the one Rosebud left. It said she was going to find 'the Borderlands.' Not Border*town,* like in this book. And not Borderland, singular. It says here there was a book of that title, by these same people. I think it means she's looking for this kind of life. And there's another connect, too. The crow girls . . . in that picture on her wall . . . they're from a Charles de Lint book. And Charles de Lint, he's one of the writers—I guess maybe one of the architects—of this Borderland thing. At first I thought the crow girls were supposed to be

Rosebud and Daisy, but after I read it a couple of times, I don't think so."

Gem let her impassive face ask the question for her.

"The crow girls are . . . contemporaries. Not just sisters. They're about the same age. Different personalities, but . . . a lot alike."

"Who do you think the other one is, then?"

"I'm going to try and find out. Maybe tomorrow."

"Your daughter lent me a book," I told the psychologist on the phone that night. "I'd like to come by and return it."

"You mean you want to talk with her again."

"Yes, sir."

He covered the mouthpiece with his hand, but I could still hear him yelling for his daughter. A few minutes passed. No music-on-hold.

"It's too late tonight," he said when he got back on. "Come tomorrow. Seven-thirty."

"Thank you."

"Mr. Hazard?"

"Yes?"

"Come alone."

"Sure."

"Alone," he repeated. "That means by yourself. Unarmed. With no recording devices. Do you understand?"

"Completely."

He hung up on me.

"You know what would be exciting?" Gem whispered to me around midnight.

"What?"

"To suck your cock while you read those books."

"Why would that be so—?"

"Just read your books," she said softly. "Keep reading them."

I showered and shaved, put on a chambray shirt with a plain black knit tie under a cream-colored leather jacket. Looked at myself in the mirror and realized it was all for nothing—dressing me up was like tying a red ribbon around the handle of an ice pick.

As soon as I pulled into their driveway, I stashed the Beretta and its holster under the front seat. I even unclipped my carbon-black Böker sleeve-knife and left it on the dash.

The father-and-son tag team greeted me at the door. The father's gaze was professionally flat. The son was having a little trouble with hostility management.

"Thank you for having me," I said formally.

"You're not a guest," the kid said.

"Michael . . ." his father muttered, moving his arm to the side to show me where he wanted me to go.

We all sat down. "We're not a family with secrets," the man said. "But that doesn't mean we're a family without privacy. Do you understand?"

"I . . . think so. Whatever I say to Jennifer, it's between her and me?"

"Up to a point," he warned. "I promise you, Jenn's a very smart young woman. She doesn't *have* to tell me anything, but she's *free* to, got it?"

"Yes."

"Then I'll get her," he said, getting up.

"You play ball?" I asked the son, looking for an opening.

"You mean like football?"

"No. I mean . . . you look like an athlete to me; I was just making conversation."

"You didn't come here to talk to me."

"Not specifically. But you seem to have some . . . negative feelings about me. And I thought, if we talked, maybe I could find out why."

"So why didn't you just ask me, straight out?"

"Because I'm an idiot," I told him. "I should have seen you're the kind of man that appreciates a direct approach."

A grin flashed across his face. "My dad's an athlete," he said. "He was a wrestler."

"He looks it."

"Yeah. Now he plays basketball to keep in shape. From what the guys he plays with say, though, he's still a wrestler."

I chuckled at that, envious of the man who had such a son.

"Michael mention soccer to you?" his father said, coming back into the room.

"Not a word. You play that, too?"

"Me? Huh! Michael's all-state. Striker. Tournament MVP in the—"

"Pop!" the kid protested.

"He's got about a hundred scholarship offers," his sister added, beaming at him.

"Aaargh!" the kid grunted, his face flaming.

Father and daughter sat down together. My envy went up another notch.

"Dad says you want to talk to me?" Jennifer said.

"That, and to return the book you lent me."

"Thank you," she said, taking the book I handed her. "Well?"

"I thought you'd rather . . ."

"I want my father to be here, this time," she said firmly.

Michael shifted his stance, making it clear I'd have to deal with all of them.

"Sure," I said. "Jennifer, I'm trying to figure this out. Rosa left her home for some reason. Some *good* reason, I'm thinking. She didn't go far. She's close by. And in touch, too."

Two spots of color appeared in Jennifer's cheeks.

"I don't think you know all the answers," I went on smoothly, "but I think you know some of them."

"Let's say I do," she said, her mouth a straight line. "Why would I trust you with such . . . information?"

"That's why I'm here," I told her. "To try and convince you. I think I already did . . . a little bit anyway . . . or you would never have lent me that book."

"I . . ."

"Or was it a test? To see if I could make anything out of it?"

"Not a . . . test. But I did want to see if you were really interested."

"In finding Rosa?"

"No. *In* Rosa. In Rosa herself. As a person. Not just a job her . . . father gave you."

"You don't trust her father?"

She was silent for a few seconds. Then her brother came out with, "That's right, we don't."

I watched a look pass between the two of them, tapped into the current, saw it for what it was. The kid didn't give a rat's ass about Rosebud's father and knew even less—he was just backing up his sister.

"You think because her father is paying me—"

"Would you be looking for her if he wasn't?" Jenn asked, rhetorically.

"No. I wouldn't have known anything about any of this," I said. "But now, after all this poking around, *now* I would, yes. And I meant what I said, Jennifer. I'm not dragging her back home, period. I just want to talk to her, listen to what she has to say. If she doesn't want to go back, I'm not going to make her."

The girl turned, looked at her father, said, "Dad?" He took the handoff as smooth as if they'd practiced the trick for years.

"If Rose's father's intentions are so legitimate, why go to a man like you?"

"Like me?"

"What word didn't you understand, Mr. . . . Hazard? There are plenty of PIs in this town."

"I'm employed by his lawyer, Toby—"

"Right. I'm not saying what you're doing is illegal. But why would Kevin go off the books?"

"He tried a PI firm. They didn't get anywhere."

"Maybe because of what they weren't willing to do."

"Maybe," I said, shrugging. "Who's your problem with, here?"

"You," Michael threw in, his face tightening like he was going to make a move. "You're bothering my sister, and—"

"And we're dealing with it, Michael," his father said, gently. "Nobody is going to bother Jenn, okay?"

The kid nodded, not entirely convinced.

"Here's the problem," the father said. "I don't know you. I doubt Kevin knows you."

"He doesn't," I said. Thinking this guy wouldn't make the same mistakes an amateur like Kevin would, judge by appearances. I knew a guy in prison once. Ferret-faced, with a weak, trembly chin, and watery, frightened eyes. He was a stone life-taker. And I had the strong sense that Joel knew the same truths I did.

"So . . . what's your word worth?" he asked. "That's what it comes down to, you understand that?"

"I do."

"And . . . ?"

"I haven't got any references. None that would mean anything to you."

"Try me."

"I can't do that, either."

His pale eyes took my pulse. "Tell us what you can," he finally said.

"I've been to prison," I said. "But I always went in alone. Where I live, your word is your life. Good or bad. If you promise to do something . . . anything . . . you have to do it. Otherwise, your protection's gone."

"I don't understand that," the girl said.

"He means if you threaten someone you have to make good on the threat," her father said.

I nodded to show he had it right. "That's one side of it, sure. Not the only one. But . . . all right, here it is. I've done all kinds of things in my life. Some I think you'd approve of, others I know you wouldn't. That's okay, I don't expect you to be my friends. Here's what I *never* did: I never went out to hurt a kid. Or use one. Or turn one up for people who wanted to do any of that."

"Is that because—?" Jenn started to say.

"Yes," I cut her off. I didn't want the empathetic pain that had suddenly flashed in her deep, dark eyes. "I was a runaway myself when I was a kid. Much younger than Rosa is now. More than once. And I would have rather died than go back to where I ran from. I give you my word that I will never bring her back if she doesn't want to go."

"I don't know how to tell," Jennifer said, honesty and fear mingling in her voice.

"I do," her father said. "But I also believe in insurance. And I think it's time to take you up on your earlier offer, Mr. . . . Hazard." He turned to his son, "Michael, would you get me that little hand mirror your mother has on her dresser, please?"

After I'd rolled my thumbprint onto the freshly Windexed mirror, the father said, "Ask your questions."

I nodded my agreement to the deal we'd never spoken out loud—he wasn't going to show the thumbprint to anyone in law enforcement unless I broke my word. Turning to Jennifer, I asked, "Which one are you, Maida or Zia?"

"Oh!" Her blush turned her beautiful face into a work of art.

I waited, patiently, deliberately not pinning her with my eyes.

"Zia," she finally said. "I thought you'd think . . ."

"That it was she and Daisy, yes?"

"Yes. They're so close, those two. But . . . I should have known. Daisy is very . . . grown-up for her age, I think. But Rosa's her *big* sister, you know?"

"Yes."

"I knew she was going to run," Jennifer admitted.

I stole a glance at her father. If he was surprised at the revelation, I wouldn't want to play poker with him.

"And it's you who plants the letters for Daisy?" I asked her.

"Yes. But Rosa plants them for *me*."

"I don't follow."

"I don't *see* Rosa. She calls, she tells me where there's a letter. I pick it up, and I leave it for Daisy."

"You haven't seen Rosa since she split?"

"No."

"Did she tell you why she left, Jennifer?"

"Do you know about Borderland?"

"Just what I read."

"That's all any of us know."

"So the note, the one Rosa left, it was legitimate?"

"I don't know about any—"

"It said she was going to find the Borderlands."

"Oh. Yes, that was what she said to me, too."

"Jennifer, do you have any way to leave a note for *her*?"

"No. No, I don't. I asked her . . . but she said it was too risky."

"But she *does* call you, right?"

"Yes. When she wants me to—"

"Okay. I've got an idea," I said. "Something that could work, and ease your own minds about me. How about if you ask her to meet with me, wherever she wants, but you and your father come along?"

"What about me?" Michael said, belligerence all over his voice.

"Oh, Michael, she doesn't know you," Jennifer told him.

"Not for her," the kid explained patiently. "For him," he said, pointing a finger at me.

"We're not there yet," his father cautioned.

"I'm . . . scared for Rosa," Jennifer said.

"Because . . . ?" I tried to lead her.

"Because this wasn't supposed to last so long. If you know about . . . Borderland, you know it isn't an actual place. It's more like a . . ." She groped with it for a few seconds, then said, ". . . collective state of mind."

Her father beamed at her.

"That means more than one person, right, Jennifer?"

"I'm not sure I understand. . . ."

"A *collective* state of mind. Rosa, she'd have to find others who felt the same way she did, to make that work."

"Yes," the girl said, more confident now. "She said she *knew* they were out there. I think she had an idea where she'd be going. Not to any one place, exactly. Or even with particular people. But . . . kind of where she'd *find* them, do you see?"

"I think so," I told her. "You said this was making you scared . . . ?"

"Rosa wasn't looking for a *place*. Or even for people. She was looking for some answers."

"To what?"

"I don't know," the girl said, her voice too full of truth to doubt. "She would never talk about it. But it was something big. Something very important."

"She wasn't . . . pregnant, maybe?" I asked, taking a stab.

"No," she said, almost snorting the word.

"You'd know?" I probed gently.

"Yes. I would know. Maida and Zia, just like you said. She told me *everything*. Except . . ."

Another hour's conversation didn't get me any closer. The father walked me out to my car. "What's your take on Kevin?" he asked me, way too casual.

"I don't know the words you do," I said, stalling.

"I get the impression that you do. But say it however you want."

"He's a wrong number. A fucking three-dollar bill."

"What makes you—?"

"Just instinct."

He gave me a long, slow look. "I don't think so," he said.

I shrugged.

He shifted his weight, rolled his shoulders slightly, like he was getting ready to try a standing takedown. But he didn't say anything.

My move. "If *you* didn't think so, you wouldn't let your daughter talk to me," I told him.

Then it was his turn to shrug. After a few seconds, a grin popped out on his face. "Jenn knows what she's doing."

"And *she* doesn't trust—"

"Don't go there," he warned. "You've got your reasons. I've got mine. I'd like to protect Rose, but my own is where I draw the line, you with me?"

"Yeah."

"Let's be sure," he said, softly. "I like Rose. I really do. But I'd cut her loose in a second if I thought she was going to cause harm to Jenn."

"I get it."

"And you," he said, moving very close to me, "if I thought *you* were going to hurt my child . . ."

I had a little information, a few possible promises . . . and not much else. My watch said it wasn't even eleven. I didn't want to go back to Gem's. Didn't feel like patrolling, either. Wherever Rosebud was, she wasn't on the street—by then, I was pretty sure of that.

I decided to go see if Hong was at the joint where he hung out. Maybe he knew something about Ann he hadn't told me.

Gem had pointed out Hong's car the first time we'd met: a candy-apple Acura, slammed, with big tires and checkerboard graphics along the flanks. It was sitting in the parking lot.

I went through the door, poked my nose around the corner, spotted him in his booth. A girl was with him. They were sitting close together, side by side. Gem.

"You were asleep when I got in last night," Gem said the next morning. "I was surprised—usually you are out so late. I did not want to wake you."

"Thanks."

"We must go away again. Soon."

I knew she didn't mean me. Gem, Flacco, and Gordo, they were professional border-crossers. I don't know what they ran, but I know they were good at it. I met them through Mama. She didn't know them personally, but an old friend, a Cambodian woman who ran a network similar to hers, had vouched heavy, her own rep on the line.

"All right," is all I said.

"Before we leave, I will try to get you the information you want."

"About Rosebud?" I asked her, surprised.

"No. But the . . . person who gave you the equipment to

get into her father's computer, he should have results for me soon."

"Ah."

"You do not sound enthusiastic, Burke."

"It was a long shot."

"What is not?" she said, sadness in her voice.

I did the math. The kind you do all the time in prison. Not counting the days—that's okay for a county-time slap, but it'll make you crazy if you've got years to go on a felony bit. The *balancing* math. Like when you're short—getting out soon. What you want to do is stay down, out of the way, not do anything that would mess up your go-home. But word gets around the tier like flash fire. And some guys who wouldn't have tried you when you still had heavy time to serve suddenly get brave. So you have to dance. Stay hard enough to keep the wolves off you, but not do the same kinds of things you did to send that message when you first came in.

Inside, if you're *with* people, everything's easier. Same out here. That was part of the math. I didn't have people in Portland. Flacco and Gordo were good hands, but they were pros; bringing them into anything without money at the end wasn't something you could do. Besides, they were with Gem, not with me.

I missed my own.

Ann's whole ante was promises. Sure, she'd made the Borderland connect for me, but I would have stumbled across it anyway, sooner or later. Especially with . . .

Yeah, I had a lot more cards in my hand. Higher ones, too. Jennifer would help, now that her father had okayed it. She was the lifeline between Rosebud and Daisy, and the older sister wasn't going to walk away from *that*. Maybe I couldn't get inside Rosebud's head, but I knew her well enough to put my chips on that number.

I had other things working. Bobby Ray. Clipper and Big A. Maybe even Madison. To some extent, I think they all bought it that I wasn't Rosebud's enemy. If they crossed paths with her, I was pretty sure they'd at least tell her how to find me.

I had money working for me, too. Talked to a lot of people like Odom, made it clear there was a bounty. Any of *them* stumbled over her, they'd call, quick.

As I learned Portland, the town got smaller. Maybe I was years away from the web of contacts and connections Ann had put together, and maybe I'd never have the credibility her mission brought her, but all that added up to was . . . she *might* have a chance to find the girl. And she wanted a lot in return.

I totaled it up. Not worth the risk.

I was in an upscale poolroom, watching Big A work a sucker. The kid was using a custom cue this time, but handling it like it was a status symbol, not a tool. Beautiful.

Clipper was giving me a rundown on the game when the phone in my jacket vibrated. I stepped off a few paces, opened it up, said, "Hazard."

"It's me." Ann's voice, some undercurrent to it I couldn't catch.

I held back—no point telling her I wasn't going for her deal if she was about to give me a locate. Said, "So?"

"Just tell me where you are now. I'll come there."

Not on the phone? Maybe she had . . . I told her the name of the poolroom. I was in the middle of giving her the address when the connection went dead.

She didn't need anyone to announce her; the change in audio-pitch and the craned necks took care of that. She was wearing a black skirt about the size of a big handkerchief, and a red tank top that didn't even make a pretense of containing her breasts. Red spike heels with little black anklets. And a flowing mass of blond curls. By the time she'd reached where I was standing, she'd paralyzed every man in the joint.

"Hi, cutie," she said to Big A, giving him a little kiss on the cheek. The kid's face flamed from the effort of trying to be cool about it.

"Hey, Ann," Clipper greeted her.

"Making any money?" she asked him.

"A little bit."

She shot a hip, turned to look at me over her shoulder. "We have to talk," she said.

"Talk's fine," I told her. "But I don't hold press conferences."

"Then let's go," she said, taking my arm.

"Your car," she told me, as soon as we hit the sidewalk.

I pushed the button on the key fob to unlock the Cadillac. I could have charged admission to watch her climb into the front seat.

"What's this all about?" I asked her.

"Not here."

"I'm not talking about whatever you've got to tell me. I mean the whole display."

"Display?" She half-smiled, taking a breath deep enough to make the tank-top fabric scream for mercy.

"Not . . . you. That's factory stock. I mean making sure everybody in that joint knows we've got something going."

"Oh. That was for protection."

"Mine or yours?"

"Both. Turn left up ahead."

I followed her directions for a few minutes without saying another word. Parked where she told me to.

"Come on," she said, getting out of the car.

I followed her up a driveway next to a three-story stone building. She unlocked a side door and climbed the stairs. The skirt climbed her bottom. She didn't have to tell me to follow her.

At the top of the last landing, she produced a key and opened a plain dirty-beige door with no nameplate.

"This isn't mine," she said, stepping inside.

It didn't look like anybody's. Generic hotel furniture, even down to the Muzak-in-oil painting on the wall.

"Sit," she said.

I took the seasick-green armchair. She pulled off the blond wig, shook out her own short auburn hair, pulled the tank top over her head, and tossed it on the mustard-yellow couch. Then she yanked the skirt up to her waist and fiddled with it for a second, and it came free in her hands. When she put one foot on a straight chair to pull off her shoe and the anklet, I could see she was wearing a simple black thong. Finished with her footwear, she walked over to a closet and starting rummaging around.

What looked like a couple of cafeteria tables were against the far wall, covered in stacks of paper. I took a casual look: *The Lancet, Scientific American,* the *Washington Post Health* . . .

Ann came out of the closet with an armful of clothing. Without a word, she fitted herself into a black sports bra with straps that crossed over the back, then pulled on a baggy pair of white shorts and a white T-shirt. Barefoot, she came over to where I was sitting and perched herself on the end of the couch.

"That's better," she said.

"Speak for yourself," I told her.

"Ah, you're a silver-tongued devil, aren't you?" she said, smiling.

"That's me. All the moves."

"Listen," she said, dropping her voice. "Things have changed."

"You know where she is?" I asked, stepping on what looked to be a long story.

"No."

"You got any solid leads?"

"No."

"You got *anything* new since the last time we talked?"

"No."

"Okay. Look, you're a girl who likes her games, I guess. And that's fine. For that, you bring enough to the table, no question. But for what I need, no. I thought about it. But you know what? I don't trade promises for performance. I appreciate what you did at the bookstore, but we can't do a deal, you and me."

"Don't be so sure, B.B. You think I brought you here just so I could tell you I don't have anything new?"

"No. I guess I—"

"—thought I was going to sex you into signing on? Grow up. A man who'll steal for pussy will talk for it, too. If I'd scanned you as anything but a professional, I wouldn't ever have talked to you."

"All right. You tell me, then."

"What I said before . . . about protection? I think you and me, we're going to *have* to team up. And it would help you if people in the street think we're together."

"You don't have anything to—"

"Yeah. I do. You've spent some time, thrown around some money—even impressed a few people. But you're not plugged in."

"And you are. And so what? You're no closer to her than—"

"Not to the girl, no. But closer to the truth. And here it is, Mr. Hazard. You're not the only one hunting her."

I never try to Teflon a threat off my expression. Instead, I turn it into smoke, make my face a lattice, let it pass right through me. So I didn't flat-eye her, or stay expressionless. I raised my eyebrows slightly and twisted my mouth just enough to show what I thought of street rumors.

"Two men," she said, watching me closely. "White. Late thirties, early forties. Short hair, government suits. And they're offering something better than what you put out there."

"Which is?"

"Get Out Of Jail Free cards."

"They're promising . . . what? Immunity? A break on sentencing? A stay-away off some operation that's running?"

"They're saying they can 'take care' of things. Not being specific. But they're making the rounds."

"You know this exactly . . . how?"

"One of the people they talked to is someone . . . someone it's important to me to keep tabs on."

"This is getting more complicated with the telling."

"No. No, it isn't. Don't bother baiting me; I'm already telling you what I know. The man, the name he goes by is Kruger."

"Kruger? Is that supposed to be German?"

"It's short for Krugerrand. He's a pimp. Word is, he got the name a long time ago, when he put all his money into gold, got rich when inflation hit."

"Doesn't sound like any pimp I ever heard of."

"He's smarter than most, I'll give him that. But the story may be all nonsense. Stuff gets distorted on the street, you know that."

"Yeah. Stuff like two white men—"

"These two men, they went to see Kruger, that much I know for sure."

"How?"

"There's a nightclub where he hangs out. He likes to do business with his ladies draped around him."

"And one of them talks to you?"

"More than one. And he knows it."

"Is that a problem for you?"

"He's a pimp," she said, as if that explained everything. "To a pimp, it's all game. Everything anybody does; ever. All game. He knows what I do—what people *say* I do, anyway—but he's not buying it. He thinks I'm all about something else."

"What?"

"He thinks I'm trying to pull his girls. And not just his. The way he has it scoped, I'm a dyke with a plan."

"You wouldn't be the first—"

"Lesbian pimp? Of course not. Some dominas make their subs . . . Ah, never mind. Kruger's not the only one who thinks that's my play. But he's the only one with enough power to be a problem."

"Anyone with money could be a—"

"Sure," she said, cutting me off. "I'm not talking about money. Kruger's connected."

"How high?"

"I don't know. Nobody does. But," she said, holding up her hand like a traffic cop to stop whatever she thought I was going to say, "it's not just street talk. For sure, he's got an in with the blue boys."

"So anybody putting pressure on him would be—"

"Yes. That's about the size of it."

I leaned back in the chair. Closed my eyes, trying to see it. Ann moved closer. Soundlessly, but I could feel the air displace next to me. And smell her sugarcane perfume.

"Sounds right to me," I said after a while. "The suits are G-men. And the local law put them onto this guy Kruger."

"But why would the feds care about a runaway?" she said softly, much closer to me than I'd thought.

"Maybe the Mann Act. The state line's, what, ten minutes north of here? Kruger run underage girls?"

"Not a chance. He's an old pro."

"Yeah . . ." I spooled it out slowly, thinking it through. "If

Kruger's tight with the local rollers, there's only two reasons for it: he's handing out cash, or he's piping info. Either way, I can't see them touting the *federales* on him so quick."

"You want to ask?"

"The suits?"

"No," she said, her lips against my ear. "Kruger."

The hooker was a tall brunette, wearing a transparent wrap over what looked like a lime-green two-piece bathing suit.

"Oh!" she said when Ann's window slid down.

"Just keep working," Ann told her.

The hooker got the message, stuck her head inside the window so it was inches from Ann. Anyone watching from the outside would see her hips, figure she was negotiating.

"Tell Kruger I want to see him," Ann said.

"Who's this?" the girl asked, looking over at me. "Your man?"

"The other way around," Ann said.

"You're *working*?"

"Sort of. Mr. Hazard over there, he's the one in charge."

"And it's him wants to see Kruger?"

"That's right, Chantal."

"I'll tell him."

"You got your chalk?"

"I . . . I ran out."

"You stupid cunt," Ann said sharply. "I feel like slapping your dumb mouth."

Chantal licked her lips. Said, "Yum yum."

"Ah . . ." Ann said, disgustedly. "What color is yours?"

"Pink. Well, fuchsia, actually. But that bitch Shasta's been using it, too."

Ann was rummaging around in her huge purse. "Here," she said, handing over a small box of chalk. "This is fuchsia, okay?"

"Okay, honey." Chantal grinned at her.

"Oh, get your skinny ass out of here."

Chantal gave Ann a loud, smacking kiss, turned, and swivel-hipped her way down the block.

"What was that all about?" I asked Ann as I pulled back into traffic.

"You heard."

"I don't mean about this Kruger guy. The chalk."

"Oh. Every girl's supposed to carry chalk. When they see *another* girl get in a car and go off, they write the license number down. On the curb, on the side of a building, it doesn't matter. If the girl doesn't come back, maybe it'd help find whoever . . . whoever's responsible."

"But if they each have their own color, the cops could . . ."

"The cops don't have a clue," she said, almost defiantly. "It's about *self*-protection. This way, there'd be a specific witness, instead of some 'word on the street' crap. *We'd* be the ones in control, not the cops. They wouldn't be hassling any girl who came forward, not at all—she'd be their lead witness. One maniac out there threatens everyone. We don't get him dropped, he *stays* out there."

"You actually convinced working girls to do this?"

"Why not? You've been around the track for more than a few laps. You should know better than to think they're all morons."

"Sure. It's just . . . hard to think of hookers so . . . organized."

"They're really not," Ann said, sadly. "I mean, sure, I've got some of them doing the chalk thing. A good number of them, actually. But it's not like you can always rely on them. Girls in the same stable, they call themselves wives-in-law, but they're more likely to hate each other than to think of themselves as sisters."

"So why bother?"

"They do what they do for . . . a lot of reasons."

"Another form of pain management."

"Yes! I . . . Oh, you're making fun of me, is that it?"

"No," I said, turning my face to hold her eyes.

"You're sure?" Hong asked me.

"Yeah. I saw it with my own eyes. They run a strike-line through the license plate when the girl comes back to the stroll."

"Chalk, huh? That wouldn't last too long, kind of weather we get around here."

"The idea wasn't to make a permanent record."

"And each girl has her own color?"

"No. That's just what . . . what they were told. There aren't enough different colors to go around. Just a way of making them feel a little special, maybe."

"Working girls don't cooperate with us, unless . . ."

"Unless you've got a case on them, sure. This isn't about the cops, it's about them. They're cooperating with themselves."

"You think this is something they've been doing all along?"

"I don't know. But *they* know someone's out there, picking them off. This . . . I don't know, maybe it makes them feel a little more secure."

"If what you say is true—"

"Let's take a ride," I said.

"Where to?" he asked, buckling himself in behind the thick-rimmed Momo wheel.

"You decide. If I pick a spot, you'll think it's a setup."

"I . . . Okay."

He drove in silence. I ran my eyes over the interior. It was all custom—black anodized aluminum dash with extra dials, black numbers on white faces, with red needles. Even what I guessed was a boost gauge mounted on the A-pillar. When he hit the gas, the turbo whine convinced me I was right.

"I don't see a switch for the bottle," I said.

"No nitrous," Hong answered, knowing where I was going. "Twin turbos. The front's all intercooler and heat exchanger."

"So nothing until you tach up to, what, five grand?"

"A little more than that," he admitted.

"And no torque."

"Maybe not. But I've got a glove box full of eleven-second time slips."

"Yeah? You must give the Detroit boys fits."

"Some of them. You don't fancy the rice-burners, right?"

"I'm from a different generation," I told him. "No substitute for cubic inches."

"There's a lot of that still going around," he said, smiling.

In the next hour or so, we watched maybe a dozen pickups. And counted seven separate times when chalk-holding hookers recorded the plates. "Pretty damn good average," Hong admitted.

"Worth something?"

"Could be. What did you have in mind?"

"Kruger."

"I'm not on the pussy posse," he said, proudly. "I work Homicide."

"I know. I'm not looking for anything on him. Just checking out something I *heard* about him."

"Which is?"

"That he's wired."

"An informant?"

"That's one way to use the word. The other way is . . . connected."

"What are you saying?" he said, voice going soft with threat. "That he's got cops in his pocket?"

"I'm not *saying* anything. I'm *asking*, remember?"

Hong pulled to the curb. "No smoking in the car," he said. Then he unbuckled his seatbelt and got out. I followed.

He took out his gunmetal case, offered me one. I took it. He lit us both from his lighter.

"Kruger's a very careful man," he said, finally. "He's got heavy game, but that's what it is—game. He doesn't run them underage, doesn't play with coat hangers. . . . If a girl wants to go, he doesn't try and hold her. But he's got a real organization. Lawyers on retainer, owns a bunch of apartments where he puts up the girls. He's smart enough to let them keep some money, go shopping, you know. He pays for medicals, won't have anyone on waste drugs."

"Waste drugs?"

"Crack. High-octane speed—you know, like dust. I don't mean he's anti-drug, just that he's got his rules. Snow, E, recreational stuff—it's all part of The Life. And they all want to style. His stuff is always the best, on all levels. It's a prestige thing to be one of his girls. And he's okay with anything that lets them keep working."

"So, as pimps go . . ."

"It's not like that. We'd have a hell of a time making a case against him. The man is clever. And he's been at it a long time. Most pimps, they give us something besides a pandering charge to work with—assault, that's the most common. Kruger, he's absolutely nonviolent when it comes to the girls."

"But he's got muscle working for him?"

"Nothing serious. More like bodyguards than to do any work on anyone, you understand?"

"I do. But, even with all that . . ."

"He's been . . . helpful, I won't deny that," Hong said. "In his business, he hears things. And he's been known to pass stuff along. Compare that to our chances of ever nailing him on anything big. . . ."

"Makes sense."

"Yeah. The only way Kruger's exposed is with the IRS. But that's not us; that'd be the feds."

"You got anything *way* upscale?" I asked Gordo the next morning.

"Like a Rolls? In that league?"

"Yeah."

"We got . . ." he said slowly, looking around the big garage, "I don't know, *hombre*. Stuff flashes; don't mean it costs, right?"

"Right."

"We got the Cigarette," Flacco offered.

"The what?" I asked him.

"Cigarette, *amigo*. Like the boat."

"That's flash all right," I agreed. "But I don't think, where I'm going, they got a dock."

"No, no. I don't mean the boat. I mean the people who *make* the boat. 'Cigarette,' it's like a brand name. They take certain cars, work them over, then they put their own name on it."

"Like AMG does with Mercs?"

"*¡Sí!* You got it."

"What do they work on?"

"Suburbans."

"Like *Chevy* Suburbans? Those giant SUVs?"

"*Lots* of aftermarket tuners rework the big ones, man," Flacco said, and ticked off names on his fingers, "Ultrasmith, Becker, Stillen . . . Suburbans, Excursions . . . turn them into mini-limos. Come here, take a look at this baby."

The Suburban's black paint was so deep it looked like the whole thing had been dipped in oil. A faint pair of red stripes swept from the front wheel well to the rear quarter panel, where a white oval with a big red "1" in the middle sat proudly. I stepped closer. The beast sat on what had to be twenty-inch star-pattern wheels, the better to display the red Brembo calipers lurking underneath. It squatted low, its air of menace enhanced by the lack of chrome and the xenon headlights.

"Check out the threads," Gordo said, opening the front door.

The interior was wall-to-wall gray . . . leather everywhere but the floor. The instruments in the dash and on the console were white-faced, with red numerals. It did look a little like the cockpit of a fast boat.

"Got kicker speakers, flat-screen DVD set into the back of the headrests, GPS . . . anything you could want," Gordo said.

"Can it get out of its own way?" I asked, more to make conversation than anything else. For what I wanted, it could be as fast as an anchored rowboat.

"For *damn* sure," Gordo promised. "Sucker's huffed. Got headers, and a chip, too, I think. Cruise all day at a buck and a quarter."

"It'd be perfect," I said.

"Listen, *compadre,*" Flacco said, pulling me aside. "Me and Gordo, we've been thinking. . . ."

"Yeah?"

"You've been borrowing a lot of different rides. . . ."

"I know. And if anyone's beefed, I can—"

"It's not about that. None of our business, what you do. You bring the rides back same shape as you took them out, a little mileage on the odometer, nobody's going to care."

"Then . . . ?"

"Bullet holes, that'd be another story."

"I'm not doing that kind of work."

"You carrying, though."

"Just a habit."

"*Bueno.* You know what this ride cost?"

"Seventy-five?" I guessed.

"Double that, plus."

"I'm not bringing it to a gunfight, Gordo."

"Here's what I think, man. What I think, Flacco and me, we should be careful about letting rides like this one go out without some insurance, you understand?"

"Yeah," I said.

Flacco was standing next to his partner by then. He saw the look on my face. "*¿No comprende, eh?* What you think we're asking for, man?"

"Just a . . . deposit, I guess you'd call it."

"Nah, you don't get it. What we're asking is, how about we come along?"

"Pretty swank," Ann said, as I walked her toward the Cigarette.

"I even got us a driver for the night," I told her, so she wouldn't spook when I opened the back door for her.

"And got all dressed up, too," she tossed back, making an approval-face at my dove-gray alpaca suit. Michelle had made me buy it before I went hunting for the man who'd changed my face with a bullet. It had cost a fortune, but everything she'd said about it was right. Maybe it didn't transform my appearance, but it sure answered any questions about my financial standing.

Flacco was behind the wheel, Gordo in the front passenger seat. Neither of them said a word, looking straight ahead. As soon as they heard the door close, they took off, slow and smooth. The big SUV rode like a taut limo.

"Do you think—?" Ann started to ask, before I cut her off with a finger against her lips.

She nodded that she understood. Flacco and Gordo had end-played me perfectly. Anytime a man offers to back your play, you're cornered. So we went through this whole elaborate game where I'd tell Ann they were just hired for the night and they'd pretend they were really worried about me . . . instead of Gem.

When Gem hadn't even asked me where I was going, I knew I was right. I didn't blame them for it. They were with her, not with me. She wouldn't ask them to spy on me—besides anything else, it would be a real loss of face. But if they decided to ride along on their own, well . . .

Flacco docked the Cigarette like it *was* a boat, backing it into a narrow slot between two other cars only a few yards from the front door of the joint. Once in, he moved forward so we could open the back door, making it clear that he'd be ready to leave as soon as we were, and that we wouldn't have to look for him when we came out.

I jumped down, held out a hand for Ann. She wasn't wearing a streetwalking outfit, but her burnt-orange sheath was slit so deep on one side that it opened almost to her waist as she stepped down. A beret of the same color sat jauntily on top of long straight black hair that fell to her shoulders.

If there was a doorman at the club, he stayed invisible. Two-fifteen in the morning; the place was moderately full, most of the attention on an angular brunette in a classy blue dress. She was singing "Cry Me a River" into a microphone that looked like it was out of the forties. The mike had to be a prop—the sound system was Now and Today all the way, draping itself over and around the crowd without a hint as to speaker location.

The waitresses all wore French-maid uniforms with only a moderate amount of cleavage. This wasn't a joint for jerkoffs or gawkers—players were expected to bring their own.

I ordered a bourbon-and-branch, told her not to mix them. Ann asked for a glass of white wine.

"You like her?" she asked me, making a little gesture with her head in the direction of the singer.

"She's no Judy Henske."

"Who *is*?"

"You know her?" I said, surprised. Judy's river runs real deep, but it doesn't run wide.

"I know her work. I caught her in L.A. Twice. She's . . . amazing. What's your favorite?"

" 'Till the Real Thing Comes Along,' " I told her.

"Amen," Ann said, holding up her glass.

The girl in the blue dress finished her set, walked off with a wave, glowing in the applause.

"Pretty slick, huh?" Ann said.

"What is?"

"That girl, she's one of Kruger's."

"A hooker?"

"A 'performer' is what he'd say. All his girls are stars. They want to be actresses, Kruger gets a video made, sends it on the rounds of studios. They want to be singers, he's got a place for them to perform. And he's got an agent, a legit one, handles their careers."

"It's a scam, though, right?"

"It is and it isn't. That's the secret of how he stays on top. Is that girl who just got off the stage going to get a recording contract? I don't think so. But this town is *loaded* with great musicians who never get studio time, just work the clubs, building a following. And everybody knows that, so . . . is it really a scam? She *is* working."

"And the movie girls? Where do they end up? In porno?"

"Some do," she said, seriously. "There's all kinds of porn, some of it real high-end. Kruger wouldn't go near the ugly stuff. Wouldn't let any of his girls do it, either."

"You sound as if you admire him."

"I admire anyone who knows how to work a system. That's what I'm trying to do."

"With the pain-management thing?"

"Yes. But now's not the time to talk about it." She turned to the hovering waitress, handed over one of her poker-chip business cards and a folded bill. "Would you please tell Kruger that my man would like to buy him a drink?" she said, smiling sweetly.

The girl in the blue dress was just starting another set when the waitress came over, bent down, and whispered something in Ann's ear.

"Let's go," she said to me.

I followed her as she made her way between tables, heading for a horseshoe-shaped booth in the far corner. When she stopped, we were standing before a man seated at the apex of the booth, a line of girls stretching out on either side. He was a mixed-breed of some kind. Small head, dark-complected face with fine features and very thin lips under a narrow, perfectly etched mustache. Dark hair worn very close to his scalp, tightly waved. He was draped in several shades of off-white silk: sports coat, shirt, and tie. A two-finger ring on his right hand held a diamond too big to be fake.

"Well, Miss Ann," he said, just a trace of Louisiana in his voice.

One of the black girls on his left laughed at the crack. I kept my face flat, as if I hadn't gotten it.

"Kruger," is all Ann said.

He made a little gesture with his diamond. Every woman to his right stood up and walked away.

Ann slid in first. I had to look past her shoulder to see Kruger, who turned his back on the girls to his left and squared up to face us.

"So?" he said, smiling just enough to show a razor-slash of white.

"This is Mr. Hazard," she said. "He wants to talk to you."

"Why didn't you simply come yourself?" he asked me.

"You don't know me," I said. "I'm nobody. You're an important man. It wouldn't be respectful to just roll up on you, unannounced."

He measured my eyes to see if I was juking him.

"What is it that you do, Mr. Hazard?"

"I find people."

"Yes. Well, you found me. And . . . ?"

"I'm looking for a girl. A teenage girl. Runaway. She's—"

"Oh, Miss Ann here will tell you, I wouldn't have anything to do with—"

"I know," I cut him off. "The thing is, I'm not the only one who's looking. A couple of the other people looking, they came to you."

"Is that so?"

"Yes. And it's them I'm interested in."

He shifted his small head slightly. Said, "I didn't think you liked men, Miss Ann."

"Some men," she answered him, levelly.

"You've got game," he said. Approvingly, as if he was complimenting a kid on the basketball court.

"I'm straight-edge," she told him.

"I don't think so, Miss Ann. You're *all* curves, girl."

Ann twisted her mouth enough to acknowledge the barbed stroke, said, "Something for something."

"What have you got?" he asked me.

"I wouldn't insult you with money. . . ." I let my voice trail away, in case he wanted to disabuse me of that notion, but he just sat there, waiting. "I'm out and about. A lot. I hear things. I could run across something that might be valuable to you. If I did, I'd just bring it. No bargaining, no back-and-forth, I'd just turn it over."

"You must be . . . an unusual man, I'll grant you that. I've never seen Miss Ann here with a man before. Are you and she close?"

"Is that what we can trade for? The rundown?"

"Hah!" he snorted delicately. "That was just idle curiosity, Mr. Hazard. What is your first name?"

"B.B.," I said.

"As in King?"

"No relation."

"Maybe it stands for Big Boy," a blonde on his left said, giggling.

Kruger turned slightly in her direction. He didn't say anything. The other girls got up.

"I . . ." the blonde girl appealed.

Dead silence.

She slid out of the booth and walked away.

Kruger leaned forward slightly. "It's always difficult to determine what something is worth to someone else. A man like you, if a fly landed on the table, you'd probably ignore it. But if someone paid you, you'd slap your hand on that same table and crush it. The fly isn't worth anything, do you follow me? But your time is."

"Sure."

"My time is valuable as well. And right now I'm afraid I can't spare any of it. I've been quite preoccupied with this problem I've been having."

"Yeah?"

"I am unsure as to the . . . dimensions of this problem, to be frank. But one aspect of it stands out rather clearly. He calls himself Blaze," Kruger said, shifting his glance to Ann.

She nodded at Kruger. Dropped her hand to the inside of my thigh, squeezed hard enough to get my attention, said, "Some other time, then," and twitched her hip against me to tell me to get up.

I held out my hand. Kruger made a "Why not?" face and shook it.

Flacco and Gordo dropped us off on a quiet block in the Northwest. The Cigarette purred off into the night. We got into Ann's Subaru.

"I've got to go change," she said. "I'll tell you all about it there."

She hung the burnt-orange sheath carefully on a padded hanger, put the black wig on a Styrofoam head, and sat across from me. She crossed her legs as casually as if she'd been fully dressed.

"You can smoke, if you want," she said.

I made a "Thank you" expression, fired one up, and put it in a heavy crystal ashtray.

The smoke rose between us.

"You're not an impatient man," she finally said.

"It never changes anything."

"Yes, it does!" she whispered harshly. "Me, *I'm* impatient. Tired of waiting for the government to do the right thing. You know my name. Do you know what it means?"

"Yeah, I know what 'anodyne' means," I said. "I just *look* stupid."

"I didn't mean to offend you."

"I don't think you could. We're just talking about a different kind of patience. You ever been on a flight where the take-off's been delayed? You know, you sit out on the tarmac for an hour or two, you know damn well you're going to miss your connection, and the pilot comes on the PA system in that fake down-home accent they all use and says, 'Thank you for your patience.'

"Some people get real angry at that. I don't. That's the kind of patience I have. When I got no choice, I wait. When it's smarter to wait, I wait. But it's not a religious thing. I don't think people should wait for what's theirs."

"Like civil rights?"

"Or revenge."

"I'm done waiting," she said. "There's a new drug, Ultracept-7. It's only been out a few months. Another form of morphine sulfate, but this one's supposed to be the most potent of all."

"I never heard of it."

"Why would you? But you've heard of Paxil, right? And Zyrtec, yes?"

"Yes."

"Anyone who's ever watched TV has. Some drugs get advertised very heavily. Because there's a big market for them. Anti-anxiety, impotence, allergies, baldness—lots of competition for *those* dollars. But pain? There's *no* competition. Not much point convincing you to ask your doctor for a certain *kind* of medicine when it's the *dosage* that's your real problem."

"This new stuff . . ." I put out there, to try and stop a rant-in-progress.

"It's sensational," she said. "Maybe ten *times* as potent as anything out there now. A tiny bit goes a real long way. But that's not what's so great about it. What's so great about it is that I know where there's going to be a lot of it . . . a *whole* lot of it."

"And that's what you want."

"That's what I want. It's got a much longer shelf life—much deeper expiration dates—than anything else out there. I get enough of it, it could last for years. Enough time for things to change, maybe."

"I already told you—"

"I know. And here's what Kruger was really telling *you*. There's a crew, nobody knows how big, moving on working girls."

"Trying to pull them?"

"No. They're not pimps. They sell insurance. Operating insurance."

"What tolls are they charging?"

"Nickel-and-dime. Literally. They must be crazy. Even if they got every girl in Portland to pay, at twenty bucks a night, how much could they be making?"

"I don't know. But what*ever* they make from a lame hustle like that, it's all gravy."

"It's not a hustle," she said. "The one who calls himself Blaze? He cut two different girls. He's got a white knife. Supposed to be so sharp the girls didn't even know they were cut until blood started spurting all over the place."

"He cut them for not coming up with twenty bucks?"

"Yes. And he may have done more. He told one girl he was going to fire her up, for real. Showed her a spray bottle, said it was full of gasoline. Said that's where he got his name. Scared her out of her mind."

"How come the local pimps don't—?"

"I don't know what it's like where you come from, but it isn't an organized thing here. Not many stables. A lot of girls freelancing. And for most of them, their pimp is their boyfriend. Probably even another addict like they are. Nobody's exactly patrolling the streets looking for punks with knives."

"So why does Kruger care? They cut one of his girls?"

"No. At least, not that I ever heard about. But nobody can be sure these guys can tell who's who, and it's got everyone nervous. It'd be good for his profile if he did something about it, anyway. His game is that he looks out for *all* the working girls."

"You know anything else about this Blaze guy?"

"White. Young guy, but not a kid. Tattoos on his hands. Nobody got a close enough look to see any more than that."

"His car?"

"No."

"How long has this been going on?"

"Not even a week."

"And two girls cut already?"

"At least."

"There isn't much chance of catching a guy who operates like that. Nobody can watch all the girls all the time."

"I know how to do it," she said. "Let me show you something."

I was sitting at the kitchen table in Ann's hideout, a street map of Portland spread out in front of me. Ann's hand rested casually on my shoulder. Every time she leaned forward to point out something, her breast casually brushed my cheek. The whole thing would have been a lot more casual if she'd had any clothes on.

"One girl was here," she said, tapping a street corner with a burnt-orange fingernail. "The other was . . . here. And he confronted other ones here, here, and . . . here. You see it?"

"A triangle."

"Right. And not a big one."

"He doesn't *have* to be operating from inside the triangle. But it makes the most sense."

"Because he doesn't have a car?"

"I don't know about that. But . . . yeah, that could be it. If those tattoos are jailhouse, it probably is."

"Why would an ex-con be more likely to—?"

"Pro bank robbers don't do Bonnie and Clyde crap anymore. It's still hit-and-run, but you don't run far. Best way is to have a place to hole up real close to the bank. Just put a little distance between you and the job, then go to ground. And *stay* there. Disappear. The longer the law looks, the farther away they think you got. Sounds like the way this guy is playing it, too."

"He would have learned that in prison?"

"Sure."

"It doesn't seem . . . I mean, it's like a trade secret, right? Why would anyone give away information like that?"

"Couple of reasons. In prison, talking is one of the major activities. And you want to be as high up on the status ladder as you can get. There's always old cons doing the book who'll—"

"Doing the book?"

"Life. Some older guys, they like the idea of being mentors, pass along what they've learned, teach the techniques. And not just the pros. The freaks do it, too."

"Freaks?"

"Rapists, child molesters, giggle-at-the-flames arsonists . . ."

"What 'techniques' could *they* have?"

"Why do you think so many ex-con rapists use condoms? So they won't leave a DNA trail. Or why so many ex-con child molesters marry single mothers? Or why—"

"I get it," she said, repulsion bathing her voice.

"This guy learned about shaking down street whores from somewhere. And about having a place close by to duck into. But whoever told him about ceramic knives left something out."

"What's a ceramic knife?"

"What he's using. They're not made from steel, they're made from glass . . . like the obsidian knives the Aztecs used a long time ago. Glass takes a much sharper edge than any metal could. Ceramic knives come in black, too, but steel doesn't come in white, see? So, if the word's right about a white knife . . ."

"It is," she said, confidently.

"Okay, then that's how we play it. Thing is, ceramic knives aren't just *made* of glass, they can also *break* like glass. They're great for kitchens, but you wouldn't want to fight with one."

"He's not doing any fighting."

"That's right. They're for slashing, not stabbing. But it's what he carries. And if he *has* to use it against someone who's got a blade of his own, he's going to come up short . . . unless he's *very* good with it. That's the problem with prison knowledge—there's no way to really check it out until you make it back to the bricks. Inside, everybody's fascinated with knives. A good knife-fighter can get to be a legend in there," I said, thinking of Jester the matador, a million years ago. "And a good shank-maker can get rich. So maybe somebody was talking about how ceramic knives are the sharpest thing going. This guy was listening. And when he got out, that's the first thing he bought."

"Or maybe he . . ."

"What?"

"Maybe he wasn't talking with knife-fighters at all. Maybe the prisoners he was talking with, like you said before, their experience was in terrifying people."

"Or torturing them, yeah. There's a school of martial arts that concentrates on fighting with edged weapons. Filipino, I think. Or maybe Indonesian. But they teach offense *and* defense. Meaning, the other guy's got one, too, see? It's for a culture where they don't have a lot of guns. Prison's like that, but Portland's sure as hell not. You probably nailed it, girl. He wasn't learning from pros, he was learning from freaks. I'll bet that's why he went with white. He *wants* people to remember him."

"Do you think I'm right about the other thing, too? That he has a place inside the triangle?"

"I do. It scans like a guy just out of the joint, looking to build up a little stake before he tries something bigger. But there's a few things I'd need to know."

"What?"

"Housing inside that triangle. Is it expensive?"

"Nothing's *all* that cheap in Portland, especially with all the gentrification going on. Neighborhoods that used to be skid row are fashionable now. But right in here," she said, tapping the spot on the map, "there's a couple of buildings tabbed for renovation. You know what *that* means."

"Yep. Okay, you said the knifeman was with a crew, nobody knows exactly how big. Where'd you get that?"

"There's at *least* one more. A black guy. Even younger than the guy with the knife. He's collected from some of the girls."

"Any more than him?"

"Not that I know about."

"All right. But even if they're holed up close, in one of the squats, that doesn't solve it. I can't go door-to-door without tipping them. And I can't Rambo a whole building by myself."

"But if you *followed* him . . ."

"Sure. But what's the odds of me being in the exact spot where he—?"

"Pretty good," she said, putting both arms around my neck and pulling herself against me, "if you have the right bait."

It took us the better part of the next day to get the four different cars in place. If Flacco and Gordo were getting a little tired of playing rent-free Hertz for me, they kept it off their faces. But since they pretty much kept everything off their faces, I didn't have a clue.

By the time we were done, we had the yellow Camaro, the black Corvette, a blue Ford F150 pickup, and a clapped-out eighties-era Pontiac in red primer all within a two mile radius of where Ann was going to make her stand.

"You sure you want to do this?" I asked Flacco.

"Why not?" He shrugged. "What's the risk?"

"It's not that. It's . . ."

"What?" Gordo tossed in. "What's up with you, *hombre*? This is just business, right?"

"I don't know," I told them, honestly. "I'm getting paid. But the guy who's paying me, he isn't paying for *this,* understand?"

"You double-backing on him?"

"I might," I said. "If he turns out to be what I think he is."

"I still don't see what's the problem," Flacco said.

"Look . . . I don't feel right about . . . this. You guys, you're doing things for me out of friendship, right? But I'm getting paid. I'd feel better if I was—"

I caught Gordo's look, nodded, and swiveled my head to bring Flacco into it, too. "See what I mean?" I said to them both. "You're insulted if I offer you money, but . . ."

"We like you, *amigo,*" Flacco said, his voice soft. "But this isn't about you, okay?"

"Then what—?"

"It's about Gem, *¿comprende?*"

"No," I said, flatly, squaring up to face him. Glad to finally be getting it on.

"She didn't ask us to do anything," Flacco said, hands extended on either side of his face, palms out, as if ready to ward off a blow. "But we know how you and her . . . and . . . we're *with* her, you see where I'm going?"

"Yeah. But *I* don't even know how it is between me and Gem. So you shouldn't be—"

"That's not our business," Gordo said, quickly.

"But you just told me—"

"Gem, she wouldn't want nothing to happen to you. We don't know what you're doing. From what you say—what you say *now*—maybe *she* don't know what you're doing, either. Don't matter to us. You know how it is with women. You don't have to be with them for them to be with you."

I didn't say anything, listening to the quiet of the big garage, trying to decode what they were telling me.

"You know a guy . . . a cop, named Hong?" I asked them.

If anything, their faces went even flatter than usual. When neither of them said a word for a long minute, I tossed them a half-salute and walked out.

I made the first run just before eleven that night, driving the Corvette. Ann was standing in front of a vacant lot, about a third of the way down the block from the corner where some working girls were showing their stuff. Her location would make sense to the watcher that we hoped was on the set: close enough to the action, but not right in the middle of it. Just about right for a new girl who didn't have a pimp with enough muscle to clear a prime spot for her.

She was wearing neon-lime hot pants, chunky stacked heels with ankle straps, and a not-up-to-the-job black halter top. Her hair was short, straight, and black. She looked luscious . . . but already too used to stay that way for much longer. Perfect.

She played it perfect, too. Let the Corvette cruise by the girls on the corner, then stepped out and waved like she was greeting a friend. I pulled over. She poked her head in the window.

"Any sign of him?" I asked her.

"Nothing."

"Okay. Get in. If he *is* out there, let's give him something to see."

I brought her back about twenty minutes later. She jumped out quick, still trying to stuff her breasts back into the halter top as I left rubber pulling away.

At the corner, I passed the Camaro, Flacco behind the wheel. Making sure Ann wouldn't be spending any time out there alone.

And by the time Flacco came back, I was ready with the pickup.

"Anything?" I asked, as soon as she climbed in.

"No. But he's there."

"How do you know?"

"I got the high-sign from one of the girls on the corner. He's been around tonight. Collecting. I figure I've been doing so much business he hasn't had a chance to move on me yet."

"We're going to do one more. You remember?"

"Yes," she said impatiently. "Black Corvette, yellow Camaro, blue pickup—all done. Next up's a rusty old Pontiac."

"Good. Now, don't be—"

"Just re*lax,* B.B. I'm not getting in any strange cars."

"And if he does make his move . . ."

"I just turn it over, and watch where he goes, if I can. I don't try and follow him," she recited, sighing deeply to show she didn't need another rehearsal.

"Okay."

"At least it's easier to do it in a truck." She chuckled.

"Ann . . ."

"Just *stop* it, all right? I'm fine. I know what I'm doing. He's not going to do anything if I turn over the money."

"And you think Kruger will really pay off? Tell me what he knows?"

"If you get it done? Sure. That's his rep. He's had it a long time. And he wants to keep it."

I pulled over where she told me. Saw several other cars full of the same cargo. But this was no Lovers' Lane; it was the checkout line in a sex supermarket, and I wasn't worried about disturbos interrupting the action. Ann made herself comfortable on the front seat, her head in my lap. From the outside, it would look like the real thing.

"Are you going to do it?" she asked, softly.

"What? This isn't a—"

"Not *this,*" she said harshly, giving my cock a squeeze. "Help me get the Ultracept."

"I told you before. I don't know if—"

"I don't have much more time."

"Then maybe you'd better go ahead without me."

"Didn't anything I showed you mean anything?"

"You've got me confused with one of the good guys," I told her.

"No, I don't. How does a hundred thousand dollars—in cash—sound to you?"

"Like nice words."

"Not just words."

"Uh-huh."

"Never mind. Just take me back and let's get this part done. Then we'll . . . then *you'll* see."

I met Gordo where we'd arranged. Flacco and I changed places. I took the passenger seat of the 'Vette, he got behind the wheel of the pickup and moved off. Gordo drove me around to the back of the vacant lot, kept the peek while I pulled on a black hooded sweatshirt. I was already wearing black jersey pants, black running shoes, and black socks. A thin pair of black calfskin gloves covered my hands. I pulled a navy watch cap so low down on my head that only my eyes showed . . . then I slashed some light-eating black grease below them, and pulled the hood up. The Beretta went into my waistband, concealed by the sweat-shirt. I fitted a heavy rubber wristband over the black leather slapjack, and I was ready.

Gordo looked me over, nodded approval, and vanished. He'd be close by, in case I had to exit fast.

I'd been over the waste ground a couple of times in daylight, and had a sense of where things were. I found a deep pool of pitch-black near a pile of rubble that was an open invitation to rats, and settled in.

From where I knelt, I could see the old Pontiac pull up. Watched Ann climb in. I knew I'd have some time to wait, so I concentrated on my breathing, letting the ground come up inside of me, settling my heartbeat, trying to become one with the rubble I was lurking in.

By the time I'd achieved that state, I knew we weren't alone.

It took me a few minutes to focus him out of the shadows. Tall and slender, wearing a denim jacket with some kind of glitter design sewn along the sleeves, light-colored slacks that billowed around the knees, then narrowed to the top of shiny boots that looked like plastic alligator, at least from the thirty yards or so that separated us.

He wasn't so much lurking as lounging, his stance as lame as his outfit. Whoever schooled him forgot to mention that predators don't pose. There's always bigger ones around. Or smarter ones.

He stuck something in his mouth and fired it up. From how long it took him to get it going, I figured it for a blunt. Pathetic little punk. Then I thought about the white knife, and let the ice come in.

All he did for the next fifteen minutes was watch the street, drag on his maryjane stogie, and fidget like a guy who thought he was going to get stood up. He was about as inconspicuous as a macaw on a glacier.

The Pontiac rolled to the curb. Ann got out, taking her time, as if she was scanning the street for new customers. When nothing showed, she stepped into the lot, walked behind an abandoned sofa, pulled the hot pants down to her thighs, and squatted below my sight line.

I couldn't tell if she was relieving herself, or just making it look real. The watcher thought it was real—he hung back until she straightened up and pulled her pants back on. When he made his move, I made mine, cutting across his path, hanging just over his right shoulder so I'd be ready to follow him as soon as he split.

I didn't want to get close enough to spook him. Couldn't hear what either of them said, but I could see him brace her. Saw the white knife that earned him his rep. Watched Ann open her tiny little purse and take something out, hand it to him.

I saw him turn to leave. That should have been it, then—just follow him to his crib and take care of business. But he changed the game when he reached out and grabbed Ann by the arm. I saw the white knife slash, heard her make a grunting sound and go down to one knee. I was already moving by then, heard him say, "Fucking cunt! Don't ever forget me!" as he backhanded her across the face.

Ann saw me coming, waved her hand frantically. He took it as a "No more!" gesture. I took it that she wanted me to stay with the plan. He made up my mind for me when he wheeled and headed back toward where he'd come from.

As I merged with the shadows, I caught a glimpse of Ann sticking a small packet in her teeth, tearing it open with one hand, then smearing it all over her arm. Alcohol swab? I couldn't wait to see—the knifeman was moving now. Not exactly running, but making good time. And plenty of noise. Following him was no trick.

Ann's guess about his hideout was on the money. He made his way through an alley to the side of an abandoned building. The door was barely hanging on the hinges. But when he swung it open, I could see a metal gate inside. His key opened the padlock. He stepped inside, about to vanish.

"Show me your hands, punk. *Empty!*" I said softly, the Beretta a couple of feet from the back of his head.

He whirled to face me. "I . . ."

"Now!" I almost whispered, cocking the piece.

His hands came up. Slow and open.

"You made a mistake," I said, moving toward him, using the cushion of air between us to force him back inside the building. We were in a long, unlit hallway. All I could make out behind him was a set of stairs.

"Look, man. You got the wrong—"

"I don't think so. They told me, look for a jailhouse turnout who carries a little white knife. And that's you, right?"

"I'm not no—"

"Yeah, you are. That's why you hate women so bad. And the white knife, that's like your trademark, huh?"

"That was your woman? I didn't know—"

"My woman? I look like a fucking pimp to you, pussy?"

"No, man. I didn't mean—"

"Where's your partner?"

"My . . . I don't have no—"

"I don't care what you call him, punk. The nigger you've been working with."

"Look, you don't get—"

"Yeah. I do," I said, reading his face. "I do *now.* He's not your partner, he's your jockey, right?"

"Cocksucker!" he snarled, dropping his right shoulder to swing. I chopped the Beretta viciously into the exposed left side of his neck. He slumped against the wall, making a mewling sound, left hand hanging loosely at his side. I brought my knee up in a feint. He went for it, tried to cup his balls with his good hand. By then, the slapjack was in my left hand. I crushed his right cheekbone with it.

I pocketed the slapjack, then turned him over. It was hard to do with only one hand, especially with him vomiting, but I managed it without letting go of the Beretta. When I saw there was nothing left to him, I went back to work with the slapjack, elbows and knees, all the while whispering promises about how much worse this could get, until he passed out.

Kruger hadn't asked for a body. And he hadn't offered enough to trade for one, either. My job was done.

I started to get up and fade away when I flashed on Ann. In that vacant lot. The white knife . . .

A good needle-artist could change the tattoos on his hands. But no surgeon was going to reattach the first two joints of both his index fingers. I took them with me.

The maggot wasn't going to bleed to death, even in that abandoned building—I used the little blowtorch to cauterize the nice clean amputations his pretty white knife had made.

By the time I got back to the vacant lot, Ann was gone.

"She took off in her own ride. The Subaru," Gordo told me. "I asked her if she wanted to go to the hospital, but she told me she had it under control. I didn't know what to—"

"You handled it perfect, Gordo. Let's get out of here."

"You have to do the motherfucker?"

I unwrapped the black handkerchief, showed Gordo the two index fingers.

"Should have taken his fucking *cojones*. He cut that girl for no—"

"He didn't have any to take. Besides, the other one's still out there."

"Yeah? You think that *gusano* could describe you?"

"Not a chance," I said confidently. "His eyes were closed." But even as I spoke, I knew he'd gotten a real good look at Ann. And if I was right about the black guy being the jockey . . .

"Where you want to toss the fingers, *hombre*?" Gordo asked.

"Anyplace there's rats," I told him.

"Never in all my life been no place where there ain't," he said, pointing the Corvette toward the waterfront.

"You okay?" I said into the cell phone, relieved that she'd answered at all.

"Fine. It was a clean cut. Shallow. He was just like any other trick, doing whatever he has to do to get off."

"Look, knife wounds can be—"

"It's fine, okay? I swabbed it out, put on some antibiotic paste, gave myself a tetanus shot, and butterflied it closed. It was strictly subcue, didn't get near the muscle. I'll be fine."

"You did that all yourself? You didn't go to the—?"

"Don't be dense," she said curtly. "And don't talk so much on the phone."

"Okay. When do we get to see—?"

"Meet me at my . . . at the place I use."

"When?"

"Now."

"Can you drop me at—?"

"No, *hombre*. Here's what's up. I call Flacco, he comes to where we park, we leave you the 'Vette. You come back whenever you come back."

"Why not just—?"

"Don't be putting us in a cross, *amigo,*" he said, his voice full of that special sadness that works best in Spanish. "Gem asks us—and—you know what?—I don't think she's *gonna* ask us, but, if she does—we tell her the truth, understand? We don't *want* to know where you meet anybody. Especially that woman."

"It's just a—"

"Don't matter what it is. What you *think* it is, anyway. We had your back tonight, yes?"

"Yes. And I'm—"

"You don't got to be nothing, man. Like we told you; it's for Gem, bottom line. Get it?"

"Yeah. Thanks, Gordo."

"De nada."

As I guided the Corvette to where Ann said she'd be, I turned to one of the blues programs you can find on KBOO at odd hours. Slim Harpo's "What's Going On?" growled its way out of the speakers. The way I was going, I might make that one my Portland theme song.

The radio kept it going. Butterfield's "Our Love Is Drifting." Then Bo Diddley's "Before You Accuse Me." As if the DJ knew I was listening.

But before I could call Hong the other mule, what I had to figure out was . . . if it was really my stall.

Ann was waiting on me, her left biceps wrapped in a startlingly white bandage.

"Pretty sexy-looking, huh?" she greeted me.

Considering the bandage was all she was wearing, I decided not to guess what game she was playing and just nodded.

"What happened?" she asked, following me to the armchair.

"I took your signal, shadowed him back to where he was holed up. He went for his knife," I lied, planting my self-defense seed just in case. "He ended up getting hurt."

"Bad?"

"Yeah."

"Dead?"

"No."

"Think he'll go to the cops?"

"Not a chance."

"And he's done putting the muscle on the girls?"

"He's done with muscle, period."

"So we can go to Kruger now."

"We'd better give it a few days. No reason Kruger should take anyone's word for anything. Besides," I said, watching her closely, "that other one—the black guy—he's still out there."

"But he never cut—"

"Listen to me, Ann. I was there, okay?"

"So was I."

"Not the same way I was. And you don't come from the same place I do. The white guy, he *liked* doing what he did. But, the way I see it, the black guy, the whole shakedown thing was his idea. And he had a bigger plan in mind than these penny-ante payoffs."

"What are you saying?"

"That it may not be over. And if it's not, we've got nothing to trade to Kruger."

"Damn! All this for . . ."

"Maybe not. But for the next few days, I think we have to play it out."

"How?"

"You go back on the stroll. Or at least be visible. And I'll be right with you. Only not."

"Not . . . what?"

"Visible."

"Like my bodyguard?"

"Not like tonight. If I even see him, I'm going to drop him."

"But you don't know what he looks like. And neither do I. Those descriptions, they aren't worth the . . ."

"If it's like I think, it won't matter," I told her, keeping my voice level.

"I don't—"

I reached over, grabbed the fleshy pad at the inside of her thigh, squeezed it hard, pulling her closer to me.

"You're—"

"I know I am," I said. "But you *are* going to listen. And you *are* going to fucking 'care,' understand?"

"Yes! Now let me—"

I released my grip.

"You want to kiss it and make it better?" she half-snarled, flexing her thigh.

"You really *are* a stupid bitch, aren't you? *Fuck* you, listen or don't. The way I see it, the black guy *can't* let this one go. He's got a lot invested. Plus, he has to show his punk he's stronger, understand?"

"No."

"Stop pouting and pay attention. The black guy wasn't the lackey; he was the leader. He's been watching the street for a while. *He* probably knows you're no hooker. *He* probably knows your car. And *he's* probably going to try to take you out."

"Kill me?"

"At the very least, hurt you. Real, real bad."

She dropped into my lap. A bruise was blossoming on the inside of her thigh. It took me a minute to realize she was crying.

Gem wasn't around when I got back to the loft. I realized how I felt about that when I let out the breath I was holding.

It didn't take me long to throw everything I needed into my duffel. I found one of her cross-ruled pads; wrote:

> I've got something I have to do. Don't know when I'll be back, maybe in a few days. Don't worry. I'll call you if I can.

I spent a minute trying to think of how to close it. Came up with nothing. So that's how I signed it, too.

The penthouse topped a high-rise in downtown Portland. The woman who let us in looked to be in her early forties—impossible to tell when they've got unlimited money and are willing to spend it on their looks. The living room was overpowered by a condo-sized aquarium, densely packed with brilliantly colored fish. I didn't recognize anything inside it except for what looked like a pair of miniature gray sharks near the bottom.

"It probably started with gays smuggling AZT," the woman said. "That wasn't even for pain, necessarily. But the pain of knowing there's something out there that *could* maybe save you—or give you more of your life—and you can't *have* it, that's . . ."

"You're sure about the Ultracept?" Ann interrupted.

The rich lady didn't seem to mind. "Absolutely sure. Men just love to boast, don't they?" she said, talking to Ann while giving me a piece-of-meat look. "It's not information they'd guard zealously, like some hot stock tip. One thing about those dot-com parties, honey, they're much more egalitarian than the kind you'd find at a country club. They're all so very into *mind,* you know? Nerdy little biochemists who wouldn't get listened to at a backyard cookout behind one of their tract houses, well, they get a *lot* of attention from people who just *come* at the prospect of a new IPO."

"I'll need some—"

"Whatever." The rich lady waved her away. "Is this the man you're going to use?" she asked.

"No," Ann said smoothly.

"He doesn't talk much. Is he yours?"

I didn't rise to the bait.

"He's not anybody's," Ann told her.

The football game filled the big-screen TV that dominated the glassed-in back porch of the little house set into the side of a hill. I figured it for European pro; it was too early for pre-season NFL.

"Hi, Pop," Ann greeted the massive man in the recliner. She bent down to give him a kiss on the cheek. "Who's winning?"

"Not the fans, that's for damn sure," the old man snorted.

"Pop used to play," Ann told me.

"Is that right?"

"That's right," he answered. "Played for NYU when it was a national power." Seeing my slightly raised eyebrows, he went on, "That was before your time, of course. But you could look it up. Hell, I played against Vince Lombardi; that was the caliber of the opposition back then."

"The game's changed since—"

"*Changed?* It's not the same game, son. We didn't play with all those pads. And the helmets we had, they wouldn't turn a good slap. You played both ways then, offense and defense. None of this 'special teams' crap, either."

"And no steroids," Ann put in.

"That's right, gal," he said, smiling approvingly. "Annie knows more about the game than ninety-nine percent of the wannabe faggots who lose the rent money every week."

"People bet their emotions," I told him, on more familiar ground now.

"They do; that's a fact," the old man said. "Especially with pro ball. Doesn't make a lot of sense to me. What's the point betting on men who don't give a damn themselves?"

"You mean the big salaries?"

"I mean the *guaranteed* salaries. When I played pro, it was a pretty harsh deal. Fifty bucks if you won. And five if you lost."

"Was that a lot of—?"

"In 1936? That was still the shadow of the Depression. Fifty bucks, that was more than most men could hope to make in a month, and you could earn it in a couple of hard hours."

"Who'd you play for?"

"Ah, teams you wouldn't recognize. Not the big leagues. *My* dad did that," he said proudly. "He played for the Canton Bulldogs, before the NFL. With me, it was all semi-pro. I was just a kid then. I did time with the City Island Skippers. . . . You know where City Island is?"

"Sure. In The Bronx."

"Ah! You from the City?"

"Born and raised."

"Good! Best place in the world . . . if you're young and strong."

"Doesn't hurt to be rich and white, either."

"That doesn't hurt anywhere, son. I played with the Paterson Panthers, too. Same time as I was playing college ball. Way it worked, you played college on Saturdays, pro on Sundays."

"Did the coaches know about it?"

His laugh was deep and harsh. "Know about it? Who the hell do you think took us to the games on Sunday? And got paid to do it?"

"I thought they were insane-strict with amateurs back then."

"Yeah, if your name was Jim Thorpe, the racist hypocrites. The same ones who wouldn't let Marty Glickman run in the Olympics, mark my words. Nah, they all knew. And they all looked the other way."

"Did you play pro ball after college?"

"Never finished college," he said, pride and sadness mixed in his voice. "Once that piece of shit Hitler made his move, well, I was bound and determined to make mine."

"Pop was a war hero," Ann said, standing next to him, hand on his soldier, as if daring me to dispute it.

"Shut up, gal," he said, grinning. "I wasn't a hero, son. Got a few medals, but they gave those out like cigarettes to bar girls, if you were in on any of the big ones. I started at Normandy and made it all the way up with my unit—what was left of it by then.

But I'll tell you this: wasn't for guys like me, guys your age, you'd be in a slave-labor camp or gassed by now. You're a Gypsy, right?"

"Right," I said. No point in telling this fiercely proud old man that I didn't have a clue as to what I was. And even less pride in it.

He had small eyes, light blue, set deep into a broad face. I watched his eyes watching me. "You were a soldier yourself, weren't you?" he asked.

"Not me."

"You've got the look. Maybe you were one of those mercenaries . . . ?"

"I was in Africa. During a war. But I wasn't serving—"

"I don't hold with that," he said, plenty of power still in his barrel chest. "When I went in, I could speak a little high-school French. So they put me in charge of a Senegalese gun crew. Bravest fighting men I ever saw in my life. Didn't have much use for the damn mortars, I'll tell you that. Couldn't *wait* to get nose-to-nose with the krauts. One volley, and they pulled those big damn knives and *charged.* I don't hold with a white man killing people who aren't bothering him. Far as I'm concerned, Custer got what he fucking deserved."

"Pop . . ." Ann said, putting a hand on his arm.

"Ah, she's always worried about my blood pressure, aren't you, gal?"

"I just don't want you to get all excited over nothing. B.B. wasn't a mercenary, that's all he was trying to tell you."

"B.B.?" he asked me.

"That's what it says on the birth certificate," I told him, truthfully.

The old man sat in silence for a minute. Then he turned to Ann and looked a silent question at her, his glance including me in a way I didn't understand.

"We're going to do it, Pop," she told him, her eyes shining.

The old man took a deep breath. "I watched her go," he said, his once-concrete body shuddering at the memory. "That fucking

Fentanyl patch, that was supposed to take all her pain. Well, it *didn't.* And my wife, she was the strongest woman—the strongest *person*—I ever knew. She wasn't afraid of a thing on this earth. All she ever cared about, right down to the end, was what was going to happen to *me* after she was gone. She was . . . she was *screaming,* and they wouldn't give her any more medication, the slimy little . . . I got my hands on one of them once. Shook him like a goddamned rag doll until his eyeballs clicked. So they gave *me* a shot. Told me I was lucky they didn't put me in jail. Watching Sherry like she was, I thought my heart was going to snap right in my chest. And then Annie came. With the right stuff. And when my Sherry went out, she went with a smile on her face. You understand what I'm telling you, son?"

"Yes."

"I hope you do. I hope you're not fooled by this damn cane I have to use to get around with now. Whatever my little Annie wants, she's got, long as I'm alive. And when I'm gone, she gets—"

"Shut up, Pop," Ann said, punching him on the arm hard enough to make a lesser man wince.

The old man just chuckled. "You sure I can't come along?"

"No, Pop. But you're in the plan, I promise."

"Honey, think about it, all right? I can drive. I can pull a trigger. Maybe not like I could, but good enough. What difference would jail make to me now? Be about the same as here, way I see it. They'd have a TV there, I could watch the games. You'd still come and visit. Food's food. And ever since my Sherry left, I don't care nothing about . . ."

"Jail's not like that," I told him. "Not anymore." Gently, so he'd know I wasn't being disrespectful.

He gave me a long, hard look. Nodded. "I see Sherry every night, before I go to bed," the old man said softly. "She's smiling. At peace. I know she's waiting for me."

Ann was silent for the first half-hour of the drive back. "You never asked me," she said, suddenly. "About Pop."

"What's to ask?"

"If he's my real father, or . . ."

"He's your real father," I told her. "Biology's got nothing to do with things like that."

"You have . . . ?"

"Family, too? Yeah. Back home."

"You miss them?"

"You going to miss *him* when he's gone?"

The mobile home hadn't been mobile for decades. It lurched on its cracked concrete slab as if held in place by the endless guy-wires running from it to the ground. Maybe it had been painted green, once. Now it was impossible to tell. Driving up the rutted dirt road, obeying the signs that said "5 Miles Per Hour!!!" in self-defense, I had mentally placed the trailer about midway up the prestige scale in that particular park. The whole place looked like an insane breeding farm for kids, dogs, and satellite dishes.

Ann said, "We're right up the road," into her cell phone.

When we approached the door, it opened before she could knock.

"About time!" a tall, wasp-waisted woman with shoulder-length, improbably red hair yelled at Ann, grabbing her in a hug hard enough for me to hear the air pop out.

"I told you we'd be here," Ann said, as soon as she could get her breath.

"This him?" the redhead asked.

"B. B. Hazard, meet SueEllen Hathaway."

"Hmmm . . ." she said. "What'd you look like before you had your face rearranged?"

"I was so good-looking, women used to give me presents."

"Is that right?" she said, flashing a grin. Her teeth were way too perfect for a trailer-park diet.

"Yeah. But the clinic always had a cure for it."

"I'll just bet," she said, laughing. Then, over her shoulder to Ann: "And, honey, that's SueEllen Fennell now."

"You went back to your maiden name?" Ann asked her.

"Always do, child. Always come back here, too. This address makes it a lot easier for my lawyers to squeeze the max out of my exes."

"Don't they make you sign a pre-nup?" I asked her.

The redhead fired a killer smile at me, instantly shifted to a sexy pout, put her hands behind her back, bowed her head, thrust her hips a little forward, said, "Oh, baby, you don't *love* me at all, do you? Not one little bit, you don't! You just like what I . . . do for you. Like I'm some mangy whore, after your money. I mean, who's in charge, Daddy? All this," she whispered, cupping my balls like she was testing them for weight, "or those nasty little lawyers? Don't they work for *you,* sweetheart?"

I laughed. Couldn't help myself.

"It's not *funny,*" she said, still mock-pouting. She turned and walked off. The back pockets on her jeans danced. I could see where a rich old man wouldn't have a chance.

Ann plopped down on a sagging bile-yellow couch, patted the spot next to her. I took a seat. The redhead perched on the arm of a chair, crossing her ridiculously long legs. She was wearing white spike heels . . . like putting whipped cream on coconut cake.

We'd been touring around for days, and I thought I had it figured out by then. "Who was it for you?" I asked her.

"My brother," she said, no hesitation. "My little brother Rex. They named him right. He was a king. My mother wasn't worth crap, and my father made *her* look like a goddess. I took care of Rex from the time he was born. Anything he ever needed, anything he ever wanted, I got it for him. I was his big sister, and I could do anything. I did all *kinds* of things to be able to do that. Never bothered me. Rex was my precious.

"When he got sick, I could see it in his eyes. 'Big Sister, you got to fix this for me.' And, Christ knows, I tried. I looked for the Devil to sell him my soul. But he wasn't around. Or maybe he figured mine wasn't worth it, I don't know. Rex was always a delicate little boy. He wasn't much for standing pain. When it came, he . . . I died a thousand times every time he . . . hurt. His pain was so real to me, I could feel its . . . texture, like a piece of cloth against my skin.

"And the pain, it took everything from him. It . . . degraded him. He had no dignity. They wouldn't give him what he needed. Kept telling me what the 'dose' was supposed to be—like he was a fucking gas tank and they were reading a gauge to know when he was full!

"Well, Big Sister, she knows how to play *that.* I got him what he needed, right to the end. 'You always watch out for me, SueEllen,' that's what he said, just before he left. And I been snake-mean ever since. It just sucked all the honey out of my heart. Before it . . . happened, I never thought about much. I was a party girl. Just having fun. And taking care of Rex. After he went, I got to thinking. How many other boys there were, dying like that. No dignity. So I looked around until I found Ann."

"Without all the money you put up, we'd never have been able to—"

"Oh no you don't, missy," the redhead snapped at her. "I am in on this. That is what you *promised.* I want to do it with my own hands this time."

"I said—"

"I don't *care* what you said. If you just came for financing, you came to the wrong place, this time. You want my money, you got to take my body, too. How's that for a twist?" she laughed, looking at me.

I gave her a neutral half-smile, kept my mouth shut.

The redhead kept her green eyes on me. "Ann thinks she's been around. And she has. But not around men. Me, I have.

Plenty. And I'm not dumb enough to think every ex-con's a tough guy."

"I didn't say I was—"

"Which?"

"Either."

"Oh, you been in prison, baby. Or someplace bad. What I want to know is, did it make *you* bad?"

"Some say I was born bad."

"And SueEllen Fennell says nobody's born bad. That's one of those Christian lies. Nothing but a damn fund-raiser. Answer my question."

"Ask Ann," I told her. "I'm going for a walk."

The trailer park wasn't designed for tourists. I found the DMZ between the whites and the Mexicans—a ditch filled with something liquid. I sat down on the bank, in a spot from where I could keep an eye on SueEllen's trailer, slitted my eyes against the sun, and breathed shallow. After a while, my mind drifted to where it always goes when I need to figure something out.

When I came around, my watch said it was almost an hour later. And the math I'd been doing kept coming out to the same total, no matter how many times I added it up.

"Some of those 'gatekeeper' nurses, they'd be happier working at Dachau," the emaciated man in the wheelchair told me. "When they see you coming, they look for the pain in your eyes. It gets them excited, the dirty little degenerates."

"Douglas . . ." Ann said.

"But you know what *really* gets them off?" he said to me. "When they get to tell you 'no.' "

The small house was modest, but in pristine condition, its fresh coat of blue paint with white trim set off against a masterful landscaping job that used boulders for sculpture. The 'Vette's big tires crunched on the pebbled driveway. In the carport, an ancient pink Firebird squatted next to an immaculate Harley hard-tail chopper, its gleaming chrome fighting iridescent green lacquer for attention.

The man who answered the door was big, powerfully built, with dark, intelligent eyes. He looked past Ann to me. "I told Dawn we were coming," Ann said.

He nodded, stepped aside.

The living room was dominated by a rose-colored futon couch. And the striking strawberry-blonde who sat on it. She was a pretty woman, but you could see she'd once been gorgeous. And way too young to have aged so much.

Ann went over to her. They exchanged a gentle hug and a kiss. The man who'd opened the door took up a position behind the couch.

"Tell him, Dawn," Ann said.

The woman's gaze was clear and direct, azure eyes dancing with anger. But her voice was soft and calm, almost soothing.

"I've got MS," she said. "When I was first diagnosed, I set out to find out everything I could about it. Kind of 'know your enemy.' Back then, the medical establishment would go into this 'Pain is not usually a significant factor in MS' routine every time patients complained. Now, finally, it looks like they figured it out. . . ."

"Or decided to finally give a fuck!" the man standing behind her said.

Dawn reached back with her right hand as he was reaching down with his. Their hands met as if connected by an invisible wire. "Yes," she said. "And *now* the Multiple Sclerosis Society is admitting that as many as seventy percent of folks with MS have what they call 'clinically significant pain' at some point, with around forty-eight percent of us suffering from it *chronically.*"

"You couldn't get painkillers for *MS*?" I asked her, surprised despite everything I'd been hearing.

"Well, you could *always* get *drugs,*" she sneered. "Even in the bad old days, neurologists liked handing them out—stuff like Xanax and Valium. *Not* because our muscle cramps and flexor spasms were 'real,' you understand. Since the pain was 'all in our heads,' they figured the tranqs would calm us down and make the problems in our brains and in our spines magically disappear. And since they *did* acknowledge that the deep fatigue was 'real,' you could always get stimulants."

"But aren't all those just as addictive as painkillers?" I asked her.

"Addictive?" She laughed. "Oh, *hell* yes. I had one neuro prescribing eighty to a hundred milligrams of Valium a *day* for me. She told me not to worry, there was no chance of becoming addicted. Needless to say, she was full of it. She just wanted her patients calm and placid, so they wouldn't complain or take up too much of her time. Medicaid wasn't paying her to give a damn, just to keep us quiet."

Her left arm twitched. Her mouth was calm, but I saw the stab in her eyes. She took a deep breath through her nose, pushed it into her stomach, then her chest, and finally into her throat. Let it out, slow. A yoga practitioner, then. People in pain try every path out of that jungle.

"Let me tell you," she went on, "detoxing from the Valium was a megaton worse than jonesing off cocaine. They used to say *that* was nonaddictive, too. But when I was young, I was into all kinds of street drugs, even freebasing. And I got off all of them myself. No programs, no nothing. But that Valium . . . damn!

"And all the stims they hand out for fatigue, they have pretty serious side effects . . . *plus* a potential for permanent damage I'm not willing to accept. The hell with the neuros. These days, I treat the fatigue with good strong coffee and naps."

"What about the pain?"

"All I get for that is the medical marijuana—it's the only 'illegal' drug I've used since I got pregnant, and Tam's eighteen now. And in college," she said, proudly. "But even that doesn't always work."

"And that slimy Supreme Court just struck down the law that *allows* medical marijuana," Ann said, fiercely. "They won't let people even—"

"Shhh, honey," Dawn said to her. "Look," she said earnestly, turning to me, leaning forward slightly, her man's big hand on her shoulder, "the thing about neurologically based chronic pain is, it doesn't work like 'normal' pain. Pot isn't enough. It relaxes the muscles just great, but does nothing at all for 'nerve burn.' It's like a really bad sunburn, only all over your whole body. I can even feel it *inside*—like if you could get a sunburn on your large intestine, or something.

"And the thing about *that* is, when it gets bad enough, it makes you . . . I don't know . . . something less than human. When you can't sleep, can't sit up, can't move, can't get any kind of relief, just lay there and cry, curled up in a ball. It got to the point where I was willing to do just about . . . anything to make it stop, even for a few minutes."

"The only people who really understand pain are the ones who *have* it," her man said, making it clear he was ready to help a few doctors learn. "When Dawn scratched her cornea, that lowlife punk in the white coat acted like she did it on purpose, just to score a few stinking Vicodins. You think I couldn't find better stuff in ten minutes? You think I don't know where the tweek labs are? If Dawn hadn't . . ."

He didn't finish. Didn't have to.

"What's with the Grand Tour?" I asked Ann on the drive back toward Portland.

"I'm not sure what you mean."

"All these people, the ones you're making sure I meet. They're all in on whatever scheme you've got going. What do I need to see them for?"

"I thought, maybe if you knew that it wasn't just about cancer . . . if you knew the . . . caliber of the people we've got involved, and why they're doing it, you'd—"

"What? Enlist in the cause? This was supposed to be a trade, remember?"

"I told you, I'm ready to take you back to Kruger any—"

"And I told *you,* I don't think it's over. And if I want to get anything out of him, I need to make sure it is."

"That's the real reason you've been with me every second, then. Not because you really wanted to meet the others."

"You like saying things like 'real reason,' don't you? Like you're just pure virgin goodness and, me, I'm a man for hire. You're right about the last part, anyway. Only thing is, I'm not a *stupid* man for hire. Reason you brought me around to all those people is so they'd get a good long look at me, right? Just in case something goes wrong . . ."

"What could go—?"

"I think you've got a lot of information, and maybe even some halfass plan, but you're not sure yet. Besides, I think maybe you've got desire confused with skill."

"What are you talking about?"

"I knew a girl once. Janelle. She was loyal to the core. The kind of girl who'd never drop a dime. But she was so dumb, she might let one *slip,* you understand?"

"Yes," she said, keeping her anger at bay because she wanted something. Or maybe she was smart enough to realize I wasn't talking about her.

"We've been doing this running around for almost a week," I told her. "I met a lot of people. More than one who could do anything I could do. Dawn's man, he's a good example. So here's what *I* think, lady. *I* think I'm the perfect man for your job. Because the people you've got, they're all *good* people. In your mind, anyway. You don't mind them doing some stealing, maybe.

But violence, that's not their thing, as far as you're concerned. And that's all that counts, what *you* think. No plan is perfect. If things go wrong, if somebody has to be hurt—"

"Like that . . . man with the white knife."

"Yeah. Like him. I'm perfect for it, the way you got it scoped. If I have to take a fall, well, I've been down before. And you know I wouldn't take anybody else with me."

"You think I set up the whole—?"

"Yeah. Yeah, I do. I mean, sure, it's true: there *was* a freak doing shakedown. And Kruger *was* burned about it. And maybe there even *are* a couple of men looking for Rosebud, too. But I think this was all about me proving in. Again."

"What are you talking about?"

"A test. *Another* test."

"That's not true! I need your help, I told you that. And I wanted to show you that we could . . . I mean, SueEllen alone, she's good for the money I promised you. But I never thought it would come to—"

"I see how careful you are about risking your own people. You had it your way, *none* of them would be in on it."

"They're not criminals. All they want is to—"

"Sure. I've heard it. Heard a *lot* of it, these past few days. So it's just you and me, right, bitch? Joan of Arc and the expendable fucking ex-con."

She did a lousy job of trying to slap me as we were rounding a long curve, but a pretty good job of almost running us off the road. I kept my right hand and forearm in a blocking position in case she wanted to take another shot, but she seemed done.

"You bastard," she said, quietly.

"I was in a war, once," I said, softly. "There were two kinds of people you never wanted to go into the bush with: morons and martyrs. Understand?"

"Yes!"

"These drugs you want to hijack—you get caught doing it, they'll never get into the right hands. So that only leaves three possibilities."

"What?" she snapped.

"Either you want to get caught, go out in a blaze of glory, get a lot of media attention about your great sacrifice . . . like that. Or you don't really *have* a plan; just a lot of information."

"You said there were three."

"Yeah. Or you plan to use me as bait: send me down a blind tunnel, tip the cops, then make your own move while I've got them tied up for a while."

"I don't even know what you're talking about. How could you tie up a bunch of cops?"

"I don't mean with ropes. I mean . . . I mean, I'm not going back to prison. So it might take them a long time to bring me in. And it wouldn't be cheap at their end. And I think you know all that."

"Maybe you give me too much credit."

"Maybe. Only I don't think so. I think people spend so much time looking at your chest they never figure out how smart you are."

"And you, you're, like, immune?" she said, bitterly.

"Not immune. I just don't get D-cup blindness."

"Good," she said. "Fuck your*self*."

The light was gone by the time we got back to Portland. Ann had changed in a gas-station restroom, so when she popped out of the Subaru she looked ready for work. I was slouched in the passenger seat, making it look like she was working unleashed, no pimp. We couldn't be sure what information the knifeman had given his boss. We couldn't even be sure he'd given any information at all. There hadn't been anything in the papers, but that didn't necessarily mean he'd even survived. So we stayed with the script.

Ann took a few tentative steps on the cheap spike heels, wiggling her bottom like she was practicing her moves. She headed for the same patch in the vacant lot where it had all started. I settled in to wait.

When it happened, I almost didn't pick him up. A black kid, looked maybe nineteen, smooth brown-skin face, neatly trimmed natural. He was wearing a way-oversize black-and-white flannel shirt with sleeves so long they covered his hands, moving in a bouncy, prancing strut, covering ground like he owned it. Typical gangsta-boy moves, about as menacing as Martha Stewart.

But I was working, so I hit the switch and the window slid down in sync with the kid rolling up on Ann's left side. That's when I saw the chrome muzzle protruding from the tip of his right sleeve. He was maybe fifteen feet away and closing when he brought the gun up in the trigger-boy's Hollywood flat-sided grip.

By then, my left forearm was along the windowsill, with the Beretta resting on top. I had three into him before Ann heard the sound of the shots.

"Get in here!" I yelled at her.

She ran toward the car, stumbled to her knees, got up quickly, snatching one of the spike heels off the ground, and half-hopped her way around to the driver's side. I was already next to the kid's body, relieved despite myself to see the faint light from down the block reflect on the flashy chrome semi-auto in his hand—it was the real thing, all right.

I knew, from the standard mumbo-jumbo every shooter gets when he can't afford anything better than Legal Aid, that "self-defense" also includes "defense of others." But if I shot the kid again once he was down, I couldn't ever use that one in court. I balanced it in my head for split seconds. The people who'd ambushed me back in New York hadn't made sure of their kill, and paid heavy for it later. But I couldn't see a sign he could make it even if someone around there *had* 911'ed the action. He spasmed once. Then he crossed over.

I was back inside in a flash, and Ann had us gone from the scene in less than that.

Her hands were steady on the wheel as she slid the Subaru around corners, not giving the impression of great speed, but really covering ground. My hands were trembling a little, so I left them in my pockets.

"What happened?" she asked.

"That was the other one."

"He was going to—?"

"Kill you? Yeah. That's what the fucking gun was for."

"B.B., take it easy, okay? I'm all right. He didn't—"

"This piece—the one I used—it has to go. Quick. We get stopped with it in the car, I'm done."

"But you were just protecting me!" she said, as if reading my mind back when I stood over the kid's body.

"That's a law-school thing. Maybe even a courtroom thing. But with my record, even if I eventually walked, I'd be no-bailed for months, maybe years. And by then, people would know who I am."

"Who you *really* are, you mean."

"That's right. Now, just go where I tell you."

"¿Q*ué pasa?"* Gordo asked me, as if walking into the garage at one in the morning was the most normal thing in the world.

"I need to borrow some tools."

"What for, man? You ain't no mechanic. Just bring whatever you got in here and we'll—"

"It's not a car. And it doesn't need fixing; it needs destroying. Better you don't see what it is, okay?"

He gave me a long look. "This . . . thing, it's, like, metal, right?"

"Sure."

"Not another . . . ?"

"No."

"¿Cuánto?"

"Just the one," I told him.

"I know this guy," he said. "He's got his own junkyard. Works a car-crusher there."

"It has to be now, Gordo."

"*Sí.* Just go and get it, *compadre*. Take me ten, fifteen minutes. Take you hours. I do it perfect. You do it, maybe not so good. Just go and get it."

The unrecognizable pile of metallic filings and shavings and chips made a gentle rattling sound when Gordo shook the clear plastic box that held them. "Like a maraca, huh?" He laughed.

I pointed to Gordo and Flacco, separately. Bowed slightly. Said, *"Obligado."* And walked out of the garage.

Ann was still in the front seat of her Subaru, but now she was dressed casual, in a pale-blue pullover and jeans.

"Where to?" she asked me.

"You've got all kinds of medical stuff, right?"

"Sure."

"Got sulfuric acid?" I asked.

In the shadows of one of the bridges, just before a steel-gray dawn broke, I poured all that was left of the pistol out of a big glass jar into the Columbia River. We'd kept the news on the radio, but either the kid's body was still in that vacant lot, or he hadn't been important enough to crack the airwaves.

I went back to the apartment Ann used as a hideout. She said she wanted a shower. I wanted about four of them, but I told her to go first.

The next thing I remembered was waking up. It was late afternoon. I'd never had that shower, but I was stripped, laying across the bed, a soft, warm blanket across my back.

Ann.

I could say I was half asleep. I could say she started it. I could say I was still heavy-blooded with the killing in that vacant lot. And it would all be true.

But not the truth.

She ended up on her back, her face in my neck, not even trying to match her own counterthrusts with mine, just *getting there.* It didn't matter who I was, maybe—she never called my name. When I felt her teeth part on my neck, I slipped my shoulder so she lost her grip. She reached out with one hand, grabbed a pillow, stuffed the end of it into her mouth, and bucked under me until she let go.

By the time I finished, she was already going slack. I felt as if I'd lost a sprint.

"Do you want a smoke?" she asked me, later.

"Huh?"

"A cigarette. Some people like to smoke after . . ."

"You read that in a book?"

"Look," she said, propping herself up on one elbow, "I'm not a hooker, you already figured that out. But I'm not a virgin, either."

"It doesn't matter."

"Which?"

"Either."

"Did I do something wrong?"

"No," I told her. "Not you."

Later, when I was in the shower, my back to the spray, she parted the curtain and climbed into the tub, facing me. "This is the perfect place," she said into my ear.

I didn't say anything.

"I never tried to swallow before. I don't know if I can. And if I can't, it'll all just wash right off. . . ."

When she carefully got down on her knees, I wasn't half asleep. Turned out she couldn't swallow it all. And that she was right about it not mattering.

But not the way she meant it.

When I got back to the loft, it was empty. But my note was missing. In its place, a piece of heavy red paper, folded origami-style to make a cradle for a single fortune cookie. Chinese inside Japanese—Gem's idea of a joke? She once told me how the Vietnamese soldiers finally stopped the Cambodian mass-murderers, who supposedly took their ideology from the Chinese, who still hated the Japanese. . . . I remembered how she laughed bitterly when anyone used terms like "pan-Asian" to her face. I picked up the fortune cookie. It was weightless in my palm. I made a tight fist, crushed it to dust.

A tiny piece of paper was left when I opened my hand. Hand-lettered, in all caps:

FOR A MAN WHO WALKS CARELESSLY

THE PAST MAY BECOME THE FUTURE

It wasn't like Gem to be cryptic. Mysterious, sure; but not mystical. This read like one of those sayings that took meaning only from interpretation . . . like the Bible. It sounded like a caution. But, for some reason I couldn't pin down, it felt like a threat.

I stayed around long enough to take another shower, shave, change my clothes. I didn't know what to do with all the laundry I'd accumulated during the past few days, but somehow I knew, if I handled it myself, that would be the end of everything with Gem.

If it wasn't already.

Kruger didn't put us through any elaborate ceremony this time. No sooner had we walked in the club than one of his girls came over and ushered us to his table.

When Ann started to slide into the booth like she had before, Kruger shook his head no. At the same time, he rapped twice on the tabletop with his two-finger ring. All the girls in the booth with him got up as if they'd been jerked by puppeteers.

Kruger rolled his head on his neck, like a fighter getting ready to come out for the first round. But it had nothing to do with getting out the kinks. His eyes swept the place, making sure everyone got the message: we wanted to be alone.

"You do good work," he said.

"I keep my word," I answered. Not acknowledging, reminding.

"Names help you, or you just want what they said?"

"Everything for everything."

"Yes. Only I never *asked* for 'everything,' remember?"

"I don't remember you asking for *anything*."

He eye-measured me for a few seconds. Nodded to himself, as if confirming his own diagnosis. "G-men. Partners. Longtime, from the way they were with each other, you know what I mean?"

"Yeah."

"Chambliss and Underhill. Salt and pepper."

"Not new boys?"

"Not close. These guys had a lot of miles on their clocks. Very soft-shoe."

"And they wanted?"

"What you figured. This girl. The runaway. Rosebud Carpin. They had photos. Good ones, recent."

"And they thought you had her?"

"No, man. Even the feds know I don't go near that kind of thing. What they wanted was . . . what you wanted. Keep an eye out; pull their coat if I got a line on her."

"Just that?"

"Well, they sort of implied they'd be real grateful if I could put some . . . personnel on the matter as well."

"How'd they come on? Muscle or grease?"

"Wasn't a single threat between the two of them, man. Just how much they'd, you know, *appreciate* it if I could be of assistance. Like I told you, all soft-shoe. Nice little shuffle. 'Even the most astute businessman can find himself in delicate situations occasionally, sir, especially with agencies such as the IRS. I am quite confident you would find it to your advantage to have certain, shall we say, *references,* should such a situation effectuate.' "

He had a gift for imitation; I felt like I was listening to the G-men themselves. "You took them seriously, right?"

"As a punctured lung," he said solemnly. "And I've *got* people looking. Okay, that square us?"

"No," I said, watching his eyes.

"I'm not following you, Mr. Hazard. I already told you everything they—"

"What would square us," I said, very soft, "is if you were to call *me* first. Not a *lot* first, just a little head start, understand? You get information, you sit on it just long enough to call me, then you go ahead and do what you have to do."

"But if she's not there when they go looking, how much of a favor did I really do them, then?"

"They're pros. They'll know she *was* wherever you said she

was, just jumped out a little before they closed in, that's all. They'll be grateful." I paused a long few seconds. "I'll be, too. Everybody wins."

He took a little sip from a tall glass with some colorless liquid and ice in it. Maybe water. Maybe vodka. Couldn't tell from any expression on his face.

"A little while ago," he said, "a young man was brought into the ER. Got in some weird accident. Chopped off the tips of a couple of his fingers. Must have happened when he fell down that flight of steps, busted his face all to pieces. He's never going to walk without a limp, either."

"Yeah?"

"Yeah. They didn't buy his story in the ER, especially when they ran a blood tox and found he'd been blasted with some primo horse before he got dropped off. Whoever shot him up knew exactly what they were doing—he was feeling no pain, but he was coherent enough to stay with his story. So the ER called the cops. But this guy, he wasn't saying anything. Ex-con, you know what they can be like."

"I've heard."

"What *I* heard was that his street name was something like . . . Blaze, I think. Looked like someone tried to put out his fire."

"Or just made it hard for him to strike any matches himself."

"There's that," he acknowledged, saluting me with his glass of whatever. "Anyway, whoever was shaking down the night girls, that all stopped."

"And that's good, right?"

"It is. Should be sweet out there now. Only . . ."

"What?"

"Only there was a shooting right on one of the strolls. Pretty unusual. I mean, around here, you can't buy dope and pussy on the same corner. It's just not done, you understand? If it wasn't about dope, had to be gangbangers. The guy who got smoked, he was a black dude, so the cops, I guess they're satisfied."

"Why tell me?"

"Just making conversation. This black guy, he looked young, the way I'm told. Only, turns out he was thirty-four. Too old to be banging. And he sure wasn't an OG. Not local, either—they had to get their info from his prints."

"Doesn't sound like he was Joe Citizen, either."

"True. Very true. Anyway, the cops aren't as dumb as they act. Some of them, anyway. Whoever took this boy off the count, they knew what they were doing. Heavy caliber. Close range. Nothing *like* a drive-by. And nobody saw a thing. Must have been a professional hit man. You know, the kind who'd know enough to make the gun disappear after he used it."

"Who cares?"

"Sure. Anyway, Mr. Hazard, let me ask you something, all right? You know the difference between a crazy man and a professional?"

"There's lots of differences."

"Not really. The big difference is, the crazy man, he doesn't have a sane *reason* for what he does. It may be a sane thing he's *doing,* you understand. But where he comes up short is on the reason, you following me?"

"Sure. Like what the papers call a 'senseless crime.' "

"Exactly. So—what I want to know from you . . . You want a phone call from me, maybe. I mean, if I hear anything."

"That's right."

"Don't be impatient, now. Here's what I want to know: Are you saying, if I did you this favor, maybe you'd do one for me? Professionally. Or are you saying, if I don't, maybe you'd do something *to* me? Like a crazy man would."

"You know what's funny about senseless crimes?" I asked him, mild-voiced.

"What's that?" he said, shifting his posture slightly.

"They only have to make sense to the people doing them."

I never looked back. Ann caught up to me just as I got to the door of the club. No one gave us a glance on the way out.

"What happened?" she asked when we were a couple of blocks away.

"Nothing. And that's what all this was worth. Nothing."

"Kruger didn't—?"

"I think he told me what he knows. I even think he told me the truth. But it doesn't add up to anything I can use. Doesn't put me any closer."

"Are you mad at me?"

"No. It wasn't your fault. I've bet on the wrong horse before."

"What do we do now?"

"There's no 'we,' Ann. Just me," I said, an acid rain of sadness falling inside me as I realized just how purely fucking true that was.

Whatever nothing I am in this world, I'm even less of it without my family.

She dropped me off where I had the 'Vette stashed, still arguing about me helping her with her crazy plans. I had her tuned out way before I got out of her car.

I sat in the driver's seat, alone.

If I wanted a new piece, I'd have to see Gem.

I didn't want to see her.

No, I did want to see her. I just didn't want her to see me.

Hong's Acura was parked in its usual spot. I stepped inside, prepared to see him sitting with Gem. Prepared to fade if I did.

What I wasn't prepared for was to see them dancing. Slow

and close. Santo and Johnny's "Sleepwalk" coming out of the jukebox.

I went back to being with myself.

I was cradling the cell phone, deciding whether to call Mama, when it chirped for "incoming."

"What?" It was almost two in the morning.

"You know who this is?" Jenn's father asked.

"Yes."

"Come on over," is all he said before he snipped the connection.

They were all in the living room. Joel in his chair, Jenn perched confidently on the couch, Mike standing with his hands behind his back.

"Would you like some coffee?" a woman asked, stepping into the room like it was midday. She was short and trim, dark-haired, with a face I could tell was usually pretty . . . but now it was all focused on her children. She had cave-mother eyes.

"No, thank you," I said, politely.

"I'd like some," Michael said.

I knew she was his mother by the look she gave him.

"Jenn has something she wants to talk over with you," Joel said. "And she said she'd feel more comfortable if we were all together when she did. That all right with you?"

"Of course," I said, side-stepping the warning.

"Rosa called me," Jenn said, no preamble.

I just watched her, waiting.

"It's up to you, honey," her father finally said.

"She wants . . ." Jenn started, then stopped herself.

I went back to waiting.

"What Rosa wants, it's . . . complicated. And I'm not sure it would even be legal."

"I'm not a lawyer," I told her, aiming the words at her father, who'd translate them immediately.

"Rosa's . . . tired of all this," Jenn said. "She wants it all to stop."

"All she has to do is—"

"She's not coming home," Jenn said, no-argument flat. "That's not what she wants. She wants to . . . make her own life."

"You mean, like an emancipated minor?" I asked, remembering what I'd said to Rosebud's father. It seemed like months ago.

"What's that?"

"It would mean she was an adult, for all legal purposes," Joel answered her.

"Could that truly be? Even though she's only—?"

"That would depend," her father cautioned her.

"Oh. Well, maybe that's *sort* of it. But, even if she was . . . emancipated, that wouldn't be enough. She wants something else. Something much more important."

"Daisy," I said.

"Yes! How could you—?"

"I know about big sisters," I said, thinking of SueEllen. And my own sister, Michelle. And how I wished . . .

"But *could* that be?" Jenn asked, breaking into my thoughts. "I mean, could she really—?"

"I don't know," I told her. "Your dad's right. It all depends. I'll have to talk with Rosa to see what she's got."

"Got?"

"I didn't say that properly. I mean, what *information* she's got. Because the only way to work something like that out would be if her parents consented—"

"They'd never!"

"You can't be sure, Jenn," her father said. "Perhaps if Mr. Hazard were to talk to them—"

"*After* I talk with Rosa," I interrupted, not wanting to spell out to Jennifer that I'd need some heavy bargaining chips, but needing Joel to get that message.

"But you think you . . . *maybe* could . . . get her father to . . . ?"

"Maybe. Here's what I can tell you for sure, Jennifer. If I talk to Rosa, no matter how it comes out, I won't tell her father where she is. And I won't try to bring her in myself."

"Really? You swear?"

"Yes. I won't even tell him I saw her."

"I don't see any Bible around," Michael said. His hands were still behind his back, but the cords in his neck were standing out.

"Your brother's right," I told Jennifer. "And I think I know how I can fix it. But to do that, I need to talk to your father. Alone."

She gave Joel a glance. He nodded. "Let's go out in the backyard," he said to me. "Be nice to be outside when it's not raining, for once."

"You can smoke out here," he said, taking a seat on a redwood bench that circled a good-sized table made out of the same stuff.

"I don't smoke," I told him, setting the stage.

"When did you quit?"

"A long time ago. Smoking . . . *looking* like I'm smoking . . . is just another way of making sure people don't know me as good as they think they do."

"And that's important to you?"

"I couldn't do my work without it," I said. "But sometimes I need people to trust me. Like now. If they don't know me, there's only one way to get that to happen."

"Which is?"

"You're worried that I might be lying. Might be working for Kevin so hard I'd say . . . *do* anything to get my hands on his daughter. I could sit here, tell you my whole life story. And if you believed it, maybe you'd believe *me*. Maybe not. Your whole life, it's about making guesses, right? Educated guesses, sure. But . . . you said you were a forensic psychologist. I know what that means. At some point, you have to stand up—in court, before a parole board, maybe before Congress, for all I know—and say something that's a guess. Only, coming from you, from a professional, it's got to be a *good* guess. That's what people pay you for, am I right?"

"If you mean I get paid for professional opinions, yes."

"But they're still guesses, doc. *Good* guesses, I'm sure. But . . ."

"But they're all judgment calls, to some extent, yes."

"And you've made some judgment calls about me. Otherwise, I'd never get within a hundred yards of your daughter, much less invited into your home."

"Some judgments," he acknowledged, making it clear he wasn't finished adding up the score.

"If you had time to know me—or if I had the kind of references you could check—maybe there'd be another way. But there's not. There's no time. So I'm going to give you something else."

"What?"

"A hammer. One you can drop on me anytime you think I lied to your daughter about what I'm up to with Rosebud."

"You're being oblique. And it's late. . . ."

"Check the ER admissions for the past couple of weeks, doc. I know you can do that. You'll find some guy was brought in, all pounded to hell. Big deal. But this guy, somebody chopped off the tips of his fingers. His two *index* fingers."

"And you know this because . . . ?"

"Because I did it," I told him, keeping my voice matter-of-fact.

"All right," he said, not reacting. "And why—?"

"Listen to me, doc. Why I did it doesn't matter. This guy, he refused to talk to the cops. His boss, the one who was running him, he wouldn't have wanted that. But now this boss, he's not around. And this guy, he might be scared enough to say some things."

"Things about you?"

"No. People remember their nightmares, but not the monsters in them. Not unless they know them from real life. He'd never seen me before. The only people who actually *know* who did that miserable little freak are me . . . and you," I lied, smoothly.

"But," he said, leaning back slightly, "if you're not giving me the facts, what good would it do me to go to the police? They wouldn't have enough to hold you."

I leaned into the space between us. "They would when my prints fell, doc," I said. "And you already have those."

He seemed comfortable with the silence surrounding us. But it was no test of *my* patience. Dark and quiet. Safe. I could have stayed there for weeks.

"You think you know, don't you?" he finally asked me.

"Know what?"

"Whatever drove Rose out of her house. Whatever's going on with her and her father."

"Yeah."

He took a deep breath. Let it out. Held my eyes. "It's not *always* that," he said.

"I have what you want," Gem greeted me as I walked in the door. "What you *wanted,* anyway."

"Speak English," I answered her. I don't like it when people get ugly sideways; it always hurts less when they strip away the disguises and come straight ahead.

"The information from that computer you . . . investigated," she said, ocean eyes innocent. "Remember, I told you it would take some time?"

"Yeah," I said, sitting down at the kitchen table. "I remember."

"There was a lot to decipher," she said. Catching my look, she went on quickly: "I don't mean it was in code, or anything like that. There was just a huge volume of information. Apparently, your . . . target is a man who never erases *anything* from his hard drive. My . . . The person I used said that it hadn't even been defragged in probably years."

"Did he use it for e-mail, too?"

"Yes. And browsing. Very unsophisticated. He used a dial-up, and went to the Web direct through his ISP."

"Any Daddy-Daughter stuff?"

"Daddy-Daughter?"

"Incest. He visit any incest sites? Or kiddie stuff?"

"No," she said, her voice measured.

"Corporal punishment, spanking—"

"Sex spanking?"

"Yeah. Most of those sites make it clear they don't play with kids, but some of them . . ."

"No. Nothing like that. He did seem to have an interest in bondage, but only in pretty mild stuff."

"No asphyx-sex?"

"Nothing even close. But he did have a number of images downloaded. Always of men . . . restrained in some form or fashion."

"You think he's gay?"

"No. A trace-back showed that he got the images from dominatrix sites. As I said, very light. If he wanted heavier, it's out there. And if he got as far as he did, he could have gone the rest of the way."

"Is that the only thing he browsed for?"

"Oh no. It wasn't even the majority, not by a long shot. He was very interested in politics and crime, especially where they intersected."

"Yeah, he's a major-league lefty, I know," I said, thinking of the Geronimo Pratt book he'd marked up so much.

"It would seem so."

"You don't sound very enthusiastic."

"Not about . . . that. As I said, Mr. Carpin was something of a slob with his computer. So, if there *was* anything . . . bizarre about his tastes, I believe the trail would still be there."

"Maybe he had more than one computer. Or he's smarter than you're giving him credit for."

"I don't think either one," she said, holding up a thick stack of paper. "Because his banking records are all here."

"Damn! You sure?"

"I cannot be certain he does not have *other* banking records," she said tartly. "But his personal checking account, his savings account, his 401(k)—it is all here."

"Did he—?"

"He paid all his bills by personal check, as near as I can determine," she interrupted, reading my mind. "I have spent several days going over them. Here, take a look."

I got up, moved to where she was sitting, her body covered in paper from the waist down.

"You said there was a phone in his office . . . ?" she asked.

"Yeah. Real fancy one, too. Top-of-the-line. And a lot of recording equipment connected to it, too."

"But there is no bill for it," she said, a faint smile playing on her lips.

"How do you know that?"

"Because he logs all his bills. He uses one of the accounting programs that come pre-loaded on many computers. There are four telephone lines—that is, lines with individual numbers—coming into his house. Each with numerous extensions. But the line in his office has *no* extensions. What you saw was the only connection. And Qwest bills him only for *three* of the numbers."

"Maybe he's got a different carrier for—"

"Not unless he is paying that bill in cash," she said. "And, given the way he conducts his affairs, that seems highly unlikely."

"But . . . wait a minute, Gem. His little accounting program wouldn't show bills he's *not* paying, right?"

"This is true."

"So how do you know how many lines go into—?"

"My friend has access to more than just *this* man's computer."

"Oh."

"Yes. But that is not what I found to be most interesting. Look at these figures," she said, pointing with a French-tipped nail.

"What does that mean?" I asked, looking at a piece of paper with $>10^6$ written at the top.

"It's just shorthand for more than a million," she said, impatiently. "But it is not the totals that are important. Look: see where he shows deposits. . . ."

What I saw was a long string of numbers, none less than five grand, a lot of them in the mid-five-figures.

"So?"

"So, first of all, these deposits are *separate* from his paycheck at the architectural firm. I don't mean they are *deposited* separately—he seems to habitually commingle all his deposits without the slightest concern—I mean they represent an entirely different source of income."

"Maybe he was consulting out. Or even working a few jobs off the books."

"This would be some consulting job, Burke. The income stream goes back at least twenty years."

"Christ. Who was writing the checks?"

"The checks?"

"The ones he deposited."

"I don't think I've been clear enough yet." She chuckled. "A number of the checks are drawn on fictitious corporations—"

"Your computer pal again?"

"Yes," she acknowledged, then went on as if I hadn't spoken, "but the majority of the deposits were in cash."

"Even the ones . . . ?"

"Over ten thousand dollars, yes."

"Son of a bitch," I said.

"It's not possible he's that fucking stupid," I told Gem later. "Even a low-grade moron knows IRS would be on him like Jesse Jackson on a photo op with those kind of money drops. The banks *have* to report every single one. Unless he's—"

"Everything's with a local bank. Same branch for years. If he's got an offshore account, it's not on the computer you . . . looked at."

"Why didn't he just break them up?" I said, half aloud. "Anything under ten large, the banks don't have to notify the *federales.*"

"Seemingly he did not care," Gem said. "Most of the money came right out again."

"For what?"

"For . . . everything. He has over a dozen mutual-fund accounts. He owns about half a million dollars' worth of Oregon municipal bonds. His personal car apparently requires specialized upkeep, quite frequently. His wife's vehicle is brand-new, purchased outright. And she has had *very* extensive plastic surgery, on several occasions. There is no mortgage on his home. On vacations, they travel first-class. In summary, his entire family lives well beyond the means of his salary."

"So that's *another* way they'd know."

"Who do you mean?"

"IRS. Even without the cash deposits, he has to declare the income from the mutual funds. Hell, they declare it *for* him. Nobody's that nuts."

"Burke. Burke!"

"What?" I asked, shaking my head to clear it.

"You've been . . . that place you go . . . for a long time. Almost three hours. I cannot watch you any longer."

"Was I—?"

"You weren't *doing* anything," she said, anger clear in her voice. "But I was afraid you'd . . . fall or something. And hurt yourself. I have been sitting here, watching you. But I am so tired, I am afraid I would fall asleep myself and you would . . . I don't know . . ."

"I'm okay, Gem. Go to sleep."

"Are you very tired yourself?"

"I . . . don't think so. Not now."

"Then would you carry me?" she said, soft-voiced.

In my life, I've slept next to a lot of women who'd been through hardcore trauma when they were kids. Some of them when I was just a kid myself—when you're on the run, you look for the closest thing to a litter you can find. And I had sex with some of those women, but that isn't what I'm talking about. One thing you get used to, sleeping with a woman who's been through a lot, is how they startle so easy. The ones who don't dope themselves up so they can sleep at all.

But Gem always amazed me. When she was a child, every time she closed her eyes there was the chance of waking up to death—if the class-cleansers Pol Pot had unleashed were merciful enough to make it quick. But she always slept as deep and as trusting as if she'd been raised by wolves.

She'd tried to explain it to me, once. Something about casting her lot and . . . whatever happens. Not quite fatalism. Something about choices. Even if you're on the roof of a burning building, it's still up to you to decide which direction to jump off.

Gem had never been anything but good to me. I couldn't figure out why I didn't feel guilty about Ann.

Once, that was what I wanted. No conscience. How I envied the sociopaths around me. Without moral and ethical baggage weighing them down, without the boundaries that restrain the rest of the world, they're the most efficient human beings on earth. You can kill them, but you can't hurt them.

I was a kid then. What I wanted more than anything was not to be afraid all the time. So I tried to go in the other direction—not to be afraid *ever.*

I never got there. Wesley did. And what he got was dead. By his own hand, when there was nothing left to play for.

I still remember what he told me about fear. "I'm not afraid of anything," he said back then. "And it's not worth it."

What happened to me was I . . . split. There's a part of me that would pass every test for "sociopath." I meet all the criteria . . . when it comes to strangers. I can watch people die and not give a damn. I can *make* them dead, if it comes to that. Nothing goes off inside me—I don't feel a thing.

Stealing, lying, cheating . . . it's not just something I *can* do, it's *what* I do. I'm a man for hire. And, with a few exceptions, there isn't much you can't pay me to do.

But there's another piece of me. The part that's with my family. The family I chose; the family that chose me. I feel everything that hurts them, or makes them sad. I wouldn't just kill for them; I'd die for them. They're all I have. They're everything I have. And what they give me is . . . that piece of myself that's clean.

Not the part that worships revenge; I came stock from the factory with that.

I mean the part that told Joel the truth when I said I'd never give Rosebud up.

I looked at Gem sleeping next to me. Wondering if she'd already let me go.

"What shall you do now?" Gem asked me the next morning.

"I have to go to the library."

"Because . . . ?"

"Because, when I was . . . thinking last night, I got an answer. Maybe not the right one, but . . . something I have to check out, anyway."

"In the library?"

"A newspaper morgue would be better. Or even the AP wire. I'm looking for a—"

"—pattern?" Gem asked, maybe remembering my search for the humans who had tried to kill me. A search that took me all the way back to my childhood stretch in an institution for the insane. To a crazy, god-faced genius who makes a living finding patterns in chaos. And spends his life in a futile quest for the answer all Children of the Secret seek: Why did they do that to me?

Lune had unraveled the failed murder plot's tapestry for me. And I'd made a noose out of the threads.

"Yeah," I told Gem. "If I'm right, it won't be that hard to pick up. Just take a long time."

"I could help."

"You've already helped. A ton. And I know you want to . . ."

"What?" she asked, sharply.

"I don't know," I finished lamely. "Go back home."

"Burke, it is you who wants to go back home."

"This place, it isn't for me."

"I know."

"But *I* don't know how things are back home anymore. I don't know how I'd . . . make a living. I was working off a . . . reputation, I guess. But the street thinks I'm dead. Been gone for a while. I wouldn't want people thinking I'm a goddamned ghost. I've been through that one already—when that maniac I told you about decided to bring Wesley back."

"Home is not a place."

"That sounds better than it plays, little girl. My family, they're *rooted* there, understand? That's where they're . . . safe. Where they know how things work. There's things you just can't . . . relocate, I guess."

"So—what, then? You go back and . . ."

". . . and maybe put them *all* in a jackpot. Don't you get it,

Gem? Word gets out that I'm . . . back, I guess, and who knows what that kicks off? My family, they'd be right in the middle of it."

"That would be their choice."

"No. You *don't* get it. They wouldn't see it that way. If I was in it, they'd be in it. I'm the one who has to decide. Nibble around the edges, maybe. Test the waters. . . ."

"So why have you not, then?"

"I want to finish this thing here."

"The missing girl?"

"Yeah."

"And that is all?" she asked, her dark, fathoms-deep eyes empty of accusation.

"That's right."

She got up, left the room. In a few minutes, I heard the shower going.

"If you are going to search newspapers," she said later, "there is a database."

"Like NEXIS?"

"Yes. Or one could check Reuters and the AP and even various international services easily enough."

"You mean with the computer?"

"With the Internet, yes."

"It's probably not that simple."

"I am not simple, either," she said, a trace of annoyance showing in her voice.

The cell phone in my pocket made its noise. Gem stalked off. Maybe to give me some privacy, maybe to underscore how little I was pleasing her.

"What?" I answered.

"It's Madison. Ann vouched for you. And I have the proverbial good news and bad news."

"Can you say it on the phone?"

"Sure. The person you were asking about got in touch."

"And . . . ?"

"And she says someone she trusts is going to set up a meeting between you and her."

"What's the bad news?"

"The bad news is, you were right. There *was* a connection between my work and what she was looking for. But it doesn't have anything to do with her. Not with her*self,* see?"

"Not exactly."

"That's the bad news. I can't tell you what she told me. I promised not to. But it is very, *very* serious."

"You wouldn't have called me if you couldn't tell me *something,*" I said.

"Do you know what 'empathy' means?" she asked.

"It's when you feel someone else's pain."

"Close enough. *That's* her problem. And that's all I can tell you," Madison said.

I was just starting to ask her another question when she hung up.

"I need to get in the street," I told Gem.

"I understand. Do you not want me to—?"

"I do want you to help. I apologize if I gave you any other impression."

"You are very formal to a woman who has you inside her."

"I . . . That doesn't have anything to do with—"

"You act like a very stupid man sometimes, Burke. You know I was not talking about your cock. Or you *should* know."

"I'm just screwing this up, Gem," I told her, feeling hollow.

"Then do what you *know* how to do."

"I . . ."

"You know how to hunt. That's what you do. What you are. I will get my pad. I will write down what you tell me. And then, while you are doing whatever it is you . . . must, I will get the information you want. Yes?"

"Yes," I said, not wondering where the guilt had gone to anymore. Not with it sitting on my shoulder like a fucking anvil.

The way Madison had related the information told me her conversation with Rosebud hadn't been over the phone. The girl was close by; I was sure of it.

Anyway, I knew enough about her now. Rosebud wouldn't ever get too far away from Daisy.

And she *had* said she was going to talk to me.

I just didn't know what I was going to do when she stopped talking.

"I'm not doing it," I told Ann.

"Why?" she demanded, hands on her hips.

"I don't need you anymore. There's no chance of a payoff. I'm in contact with the girl—through other people—and she's going to come in."

"Just like that?"

"I never said I would—"

"The money isn't enough?"

"A hundred grand, against the hundred years I'd have to do if I got popped? No."

"But that's not the real reason, is it?"

"No. I already told you the real reason."

"That you think I want you for a fall guy."

"Or you've got a martyr complex."

"The opposite," she said. "I lose these"—flicking a hand across her breasts dismissively—"I might as well have had plastic surgery. Nobody who knew me here would ever recognize me. Once this is done, so am I."

"How could that be? No matter how big the score, it can't be enough to take care of all the—"

"I'm not giving up the struggle. I'm just going after it in a different way, once this last job is done. It's not as if we're alone. Some places—VA hospitals, for example—they know how to deal with pain. And they *do* it. There's also—"

"VA hospitals?"

"Don't look so surprised. The VA hospital system probably knows more about pain management than any other place on earth. Some of them, like the one in Albuquerque, they're like . . . beacons in the night, for us. And Sloan-Kettering has been lobbying for changes in these stupid DEA laws that won't allow them to administer enough—"

"Politics?"

"That's right, politics. That's where the change is going to be made. But I said politics, not politicians. You think there'd be any difference, no matter who was in office?"

"Me? I think the last two guys who ran for president were a pair of mutants."

"What does that mean?"

"It means they'd been line-bred for generations, like the way you'd do a bird dog or a racehorse. They never had any other purpose, right from birth. Problem is, you breed a dog to fetch birds, he might do it perfect, but he couldn't *shoot* the birds, see?"

"No."

"Politicians are bred to run *for* office, not to run the office once they get it. That, they don't have a clue about."

"That's *right*!" she said, her voice juicy with promise. "They're all whores."

"I don't think that's fair to whores," I told her. "All they do is fuck for money. Most of them would draw the line at the stuff the average politician takes in stride."

"You think all politicians are sick?"

"Like mentally ill? No. What they are is litmus paper. They turn color depending on what's poured over them. You think *any* of them actually have a position on *anything*? George Wallace first ran for office with the backing of the NAACP. After he lost, he vowed he'd never get out-niggered again. The only ones who truly have a position are the fascists. *They're* for real . . . which is why they'll never get elected. And neither will that narcissist Nader. Some 'green' party he's running—all he accomplished was to vampire enough dumbass liberal votes to elect a guy who'd sell the Grand Canyon to a toxic-waste dump operator."

"You're right. Which is why I'm going into a new line of work."

"What's that?"

"Fund-raising," she said, with a truly wicked grin. "You know how it says, 'God bless the child who's got his own'? Well, people dying in pain in America don't have their own. But we can *buy* some for them."

"That's a better plan," I agreed. "If the gun people can do it . . ."

"Yes! I know. We've *all* been thinking about this for quite a while. Things *have* to change. Even when there's a huge market for a drug—like the so-called 'abortion pill'—it took forever to get FDA approval. Not because of science—remember, this is something they'd tested on *humans,* and for *years*—but because the politicians were afraid of the anti-choice lobby. With pain medication, it's a thousand times worse. The only market for new painkillers is for the 'nonaddictive' type. But the very *reason* for taking pain medication dictates that you become dependent on it. If it keeps you from being tortured, why *shouldn't* you be dependent on it?"

I stepped away from her a little. Obsessives make me nervous. Maybe that's why I scare people, sometimes. About some things.

"I'm not arguing with you," I said, gently.

But it was too late to derail her train. "Do you know why dealers started cutting heroin with quinine?" she said, her voice shaking. "The U.S. government taught them. The military used to mix quinine into the morphine styrettes soldiers carried into battle in the Pacific Theater, because of the malaria threat. Nothing too good for our fighting men . . . until they come back home. The government doesn't care. And neither do the drug companies. The only real R and D going on is for the illegal stuff, anyway. Like Ecstasy. You get a real quick turnaround on the research—instant profits—plus, you don't have to pay the human guinea pigs; they pay you."

"I know," I said. Thinking about the morphine pump they'd hooked me to while I was recovering from the bullets meant to kill me. That magic pump that fired a little bit of painkiller into my veins every time I squeezed it. But I could only squeeze it six times an hour. And every time I did, the hospital's billing computer went *ka-ching!* That machine hadn't been developed to kill pain; it had been designed by an accountant.

"But don't you *get* it, B.B.? The DEA *creates* the market for new ways to get high. The pious, hypocritical—"

"I get it, Ann. But what good is one big score—even a humongous one—against that?"

"We need that shipment," she said, adamantly. "We need something to sustain the ground effort, while the rest of us pull back and put the pressure elsewhere."

"I can't help you."

"Yes, you can," she said. "And I'll show you why."

I piloted the Corvette to Ann's instructions. If she was trying to confuse me, she did a great job. I wouldn't have been more lost if I'd been blindfolded. We pulled up to what looked like the bank of a river, but we were facing the wrong way for it to be the one that runs through Portland.

"Milwaukie," she said, as if that explained everything.

"What do we do now?" I asked her.

"Wait. It won't be long. Besides, it's dark out."

"So?"

"So haven't you ever heard it's much sexier to fuck outdoors?"

"No."

"No, you haven't heard it? Or no, you don't believe it?"

"I've heard it. When it comes to sex, there's people who get turned on by everything from latex to liverwurst. But, me, I'm a big fan of privacy."

"That's part of the fun," she said softly, giving her lips a quick flick with the tip of her tongue. "That someone *might* come along."

"Save it. When I was a kid, that was the only way it *ever* happened."

"Outdoors?"

"Standing up in an alley. On a ratty couch in a basement with no door. On a rooftop; in the park when the weather was right . . ."

"Sounds like you had a lot of experience."

"Experience? With sex, sure. With sex where you felt safe, like someone wasn't going to run up on you any minute—not until I was much older."

"I never tried it," she whispered. "You sure you don't want to show me?"

"I'm sure."

"You don't *feel* sure," she said, giving me a rough squeeze.

"You didn't ask me how I felt. You asked me what I wanted. And I told you."

"You think, if we . . . if it happens again, you'll be stuck? That you'll have to go through with it?"

"No. And stop with the word games. There's nothing for me to 'go through' *with.* I never made any deals."

"You implied . . ."

"If you'd turned her up before I could do it on my own, I would have traded, like I said. But you didn't."

"Wait and see," she said, folding her arms under her breasts. Then lifting them a little, just to show me what I had passed up.

"Time to go," she said, about fifteen minutes later.

"Go where?"

"I'll show you. We just had to park so . . . some people could be sure we weren't followed."

"So we never *were* going to be alone, huh?"

"*You* wouldn't have known."

"I get it."

"No, you don't. But this isn't about that now. Just drive."

The area behind the warehouse looked deserted. Except for the bright-red Dodge Durango.

"Flash your brights a couple of times," Ann said. "Then pull in right next to him."

I J-turned so that I could back in. As I was reversing, I saw two figures get out. By the time I was parked, they were sitting on the lowered tailgate of the Dodge.

Clipper and Big A.

"Hey, handsome," Ann greeted Big A, giving him a kiss on the cheek, half big sister, half "Someday soon."

"What's up?" Clipper asked her, as if he was sitting in a coffeeshop and she'd just walked by.

"I don't know," Ann told him.

I took a step back, grabbed Clipper's eyes, and took off my jacket. "All you had to do was ask," I said to her.

"It was more fun my way," she mock-giggled.

Big A ducked his head so I wouldn't see him blush.

"What were you worried about?" I asked Clipper. "A piece, or a wire?"

"Guns scare me," he said, calmly.

"We'll be right back," I told him. Then I reached over and

grabbed the back of Ann's neck. I would have used her hair, but I knew the wig would come off in my hand. "Come on," I said.

She came along meekly enough until we got to the corner of the building. I had to put on a little pressure to get her to make the turn, out of sight of Clipper and Big A.

"Do it," I said.

"Do . . . what?"

"Search me. Do a good job. I don't know what all this is about, but I want you to be able to tell Clipper that I'm not carrying."

She ran her hands over me. Tentatively, not sure what she was doing, but covering all the ground. It didn't surprise me that she missed the sleeve knife.

"Can I . . . ?"

"Whatever you want," I said. "Just get it done."

She unsnapped my jeans. Pulled the zipper down. She tugged at the waistband just enough to get her hands inside. Spent more time there than she had to.

"All right," she finally said.

We walked back around to where Clipper and Big A were sitting.

"He's empty," Ann said. "Now let me tell you what's happening. B.B. doesn't want to help us out with our . . . project anymore."

If Clipper had a problem with "our," he kept it off his face.

"And the reason he doesn't," she went on, "is because he thinks he's found what he's looking for."

"Is that right?" Clipper asked me.

"Some of it. I never *did* want to 'help out.' It was supposed to be a trade. You know what I was looking for. If Ann turned it up, then that would have been different."

"That 'it' you're talking about is a human being."

"Hey, that's a good one. *Very* sensitive. You ever been a guest on *Oprah?*"

Big A started to get up. Clipper put out a hand to restrain him even as Ann started to step between us.

"You think she's coming back soon?" Clipper asked.

"What I think is that she's going to meet with me. Coming back, that's her decision. All I ever wanted was the meet."

"When do you think it's going to happen?"

"Any day now."

"I don't think so. More than a week. Maybe even two."

"And you'd know that . . . how?"

"Because she's with us," Big A said, pride strong in his voice. "She's been with us all along."

"Sure."

"I kind of thought you might react like that," Clipper said. "So I did something I hate doing. But I didn't see any other way."

"You ever just talk straight out?" I asked him.

"Sometimes," he said, nodding as if he was agreeing with something.

"Want to take a walk, cutie?" Ann asked Big A.

"I'm staying here with—"

"Go ahead, Big A," Clipper said to him. "I don't want Ann to hear what I've got to say . . . and I don't want her wandering around back there alone, okay?"

"Okay," the kid said, accepting the wisdom.

We watched them walk away. When they were out of sight, Clipper reached in his pocket. "Recognize this?" he asked me. "It's a micro-cassette recorder. The fidelity's pretty good. Just touch the button right . . . there."

I did that, then put the little machine down on the tailgate, so I'd have both hands free.

The voices came out of the tiny speaker thin and metallic, but clear enough so there wasn't any doubt.

"Jenn, are you *sure*?"

"Yes," Jennifer said, her voice patient and gentle. **"But I wouldn't want you to trust only that. Daddy talked to him. A lot. And he found out some things about him, too."**

"Like what?"

"Daddy wouldn't say, Rosa. But Daddy said he'd *never* make you go back if you didn't want to go."

"Does he know what I really—?"

"Pretty much. Not *everything,* but almost. Daddy thinks, maybe, he could even help you get . . . the rest of it, too."

"For real?"

"Yes!"

"Oh, Jenn! That would be so . . . I can't believe it."

"Are you sure you don't want to tell me what your—?"

"No! I can't talk about that."

"All right," Jenn soothed her. "That's all right." A long pause, then, "I saw Daisy."

"How is she?"

"A little fireball, like always."

"She *is.*" Rosebud chuckled. "She's always been like that."

"I know."

"Jenn?"

"What?"

"You'll never know. You'll never know what it means to me that you're so . . . so *loyal.* So loyal and true."

"You'd do the same for—"

"That's not the point!" Rosebud said, harshness in her tone. "Plenty of people are good and loyal. But that's not always a two-way street."

"Do you want to—?"

"You're just like your father," Rosebud laughed. "No, Jenn. I do *not* want to talk about it, okay?"

"Okay."

"Jenn, you know what?"

"What, Rosa?"

"I'm . . . still not sure. And I don't want to meet with this . . . man until I am. I need more time."

"How much more?"

"A week. Maybe a little more. I have to . . . check some things. Then I'll be ready."

"Okay. You know where to—"

"Yes. I love you, Jenn."

Then the sound of a phone being hung up.

"Voice-activated," Clipper said.

"Uh-huh. This a wiretap?"

"No. On *my* line. In *my* house. Or where I'm staying now, anyway."

"With Rosebud?"

"That's right."

"And what you're saying is, if I do this . . . project, you'll bring me to her, even if she decides she doesn't want to go through with it?"

"Yes."

"You'd sell her just like that?"

Clipper stood up so suddenly we almost bumped. His voice was low and hard, urgent. "Look, I don't need lectures on ethics from mercenaries. One, it's all about the greater good. And, two, she *can't* stay like she is. I don't know what's wrong. Not exactly, anyway. But she can't keep this up. I was going to call her friend Jenn myself, if Rose didn't decide to come in on her own. And since you seem to have passed muster with *her* . . ."

"I get it."

"Yeah? Well, if you *want* it, now you know what you have to do."

The rich lady's penthouse looked like it had all been redecorated since the last time we'd been there. Probably one of her hobbies. I walked over to the huge aquarium. About half the fish were missing now. And the little sharks looked bigger.

"Nice joint you're running here," I said.

"That's the way of the world," she shot back, sounding annoyed. "In microcosm. Don't you agree?"

"Sure. People with money put things in cages. Then they watch them eat each other up."

"That isn't what I meant."

"Oh, that's right. I forgot. You're one of the *good* people."

"B.B.!" Ann hissed at me.

"Hey, fuck the two of you," I said. "You know why *I'm* doing this, okay? You want a good attitude thrown in, you're out of luck."

The rich woman stood up. Walked over close to me. "I like you," she said, huskily. "What do you think about that?"

"What I think is that I don't like you."

"Because of an . . . *aquarium*?"

"That's right."

She turned and walked away. "You picked yourself a real beauty," she said to Ann.

"Were you deliberately *trying* to get her to drop out?" she asked in the elevator on our way down.

"She'd never drop out," I told her. "It's like her . . . thing, right?"

"You're disgusting."

"And you're purity personified. You and Clipper and everyone helping you. Me, I'm just a hijacker who's getting hijacked himself."

"Everyone's got a handle, B.B. I told you where mine was. Why are you so angry I found yours?"

"I have a lot of data for you," Gem said that night. "But it's raw. And it could take you a lot of time to sort it. Can you narrow down the criteria for me, just a little bit?"

"Sure."

"Burke, what is wrong? You sound so . . . angry."

"Not at you."

"At who, then?"

"At me, little girl. Wesley warned me. A long time ago."

"What did he—?"

"He told me," I said, cutting her off, "that anyone who knows how I am about . . . some things, it's like a bull's-eye painted on my back."

"You mean . . . children?"

"It's not about kids. I don't even like kids. It's those fucking freaks who feed on them. . . ."

"Burke, stop!"

"What?"

"When you start to talk like that, it frightens me."

"Why? I haven't even raised my voice. I'm in control."

"It is so cold in here now," Gem said, shuddering. "And you, you are . . . not in control. Not at all."

"You sure you can do it?" I asked SueEllen. "You're the key. He doesn't come along, we can't—"

"Honey, we got a *lot* of information. Everything you said you wanted. But there's no way we're going to know in front if that man likes women. Don't believe everything you see in beer commercials."

"Fair enough. Besides that, can you—?"

"Oh, spit it out, mister. I can do *anything* for those damn drugs. And I will, okay?"

"Okay."

"We have about a six-hour window. Maybe a little more, depending on what time we get on the road. But once it's docked, the whole thing has to be empty *and* gone, fast."

"That's covered," Clipper said, emotionless. It was the first time I'd ever seen him without Big A.

"And you're *sure* about the information?" I asked Ann, for maybe the third time. "If any little piece of it's off, so is the deal."

"Yes," she said, patiently, "I'm sure. It's not as if they ever take precautions with this stuff. It might as well be a load of TV sets, the way they set up security."

"I'll handle my end," the old man said.

"Pop, you know all you're supposed to do is—"

"Create a little diversion for the County Mounties. Don't worry about me, gal. It's going to be fun."

Ann shook her head sorrowfully. "If anything happens to you . . ."

"I asked Sherry," the old man said.

"That is what you want me for now? To be your alibi?" Gem said, sneering the last word. "That is not how you treated me before. . . ."

"This is different."

"So you say, master. I hear and obey."

"Gem, you don't want to do it, just—"

"Just . . . what? Get out of your life completely?"

"I'm not saying that."

"You are not saying *anything,* Burke. And you have not for a long time."

"When this is over . . ."

"Ah."

I took a deep breath. Let it out shallow and slow. "Are you going to do it?"

"You are a fool," she said.

Hong watched me approach his table like I was a bad biopsy result. "What are you looking for this time?" he asked, when I sat down.

"I'm not sure I get your meaning."

"You're not sure you *like* my meaning. Your little 'trades' seem to have a way of causing more problems than they solve."

"Yeah?"

"Yeah. For example, Kruger's stock has gone way up in the past couple of weeks. Any idea why that would be?"

"Not me."

"Right. Not you. Only there was this gutter-punk who'd been shaking down hookers. And now he's out of business."

"What's bad about that?"

"By itself, nothing. In fact, we didn't really put the whole thing together until we showed him some pictures."

My face didn't reveal anything—I was confident of that. But if Hong had my sheet, I was . . .

"Not what you're thinking," he said. "Not a mug shot. A morgue shot."

"I'm not with you."

"Oh, I *know* you're not. If there's anything I'm sure of in this whole mess, it's that you're not with *me*."

"And I was supposed to be?"

"Let's stop playing, okay? The punk—you know, the one with the missing fingertips—he wasn't saying a word. But when we showed him a picture of his boss on a slab, he went into a panic. Can't *stop* him from talking now. He'll cop to anything we want, if we promise him PC on the Inside and the Program when he makes the gate."

"What's he got to trade?"

"A lot of crap about his big 'operation' he was fronting. Not much use to us, seeing as how the fucking 'kingpin' is dead. So the only thing he can give us is whoever did the job on him."

"You mean, like an assault?"

"An assault-with-intent, pal. Pounding on him is one thing. But mutilation, that's what we call an 'enhancer' in these parts. Whoever goes down for it is looking at a long bit. And if that person had priors . . . well, you know the deal in Oregon, don't you? He might never see the street again."

"So you know it was a man?"

"Ah, you're a piece of work, Hazard . . . or whatever your name is. Yeah, it was a man. And, no, we don't have a description we could do anything with. Except . . ."

I raised my eyebrows, like I was getting bored with his pregnant pauses and wanted him to get on with it.

"Like I said, this is one *scared* boy. We put a bunch of guys in a lineup, whisper 'Number Three' in his ear, guess which one he'd pick out?"

"Sounds like a defense attorney's dream," I said, still bored.

"It does," he conceded. "But that doesn't change the truth."

"Tell it to O.J."

"You ask me about Kruger. A favor gets done for Kruger. So I figure Kruger must have done a favor for you."

"Kruger didn't do a goddamned thing for me," I said. "And you can take that one to the polygraph."

"Maybe. But now you come here on another visit. What do you want *this* time? And who's going to get themselves dead?"

"More hookers are," I said, taking everything out of my voice but the truth I needed him to hear. "It's not one man. Like I told you before, remember? It's a team."

"Two men? You're trying to tell me that the little degenerate with the missing—"

"No. A man and a woman. You've run every sex offender who's been released in the past, what, five years?"

He nodded, listening now.

"What you want to look for is a man who's been either married or living with a woman for some time. Either he's using her to pull hookers, like she wants to bring the girl home for a three-way, or she's right there in the car with him. Something like that Bernardo case."

"Yeah, you mentioned it before. In Canada, right?"

"Right. The freak made torture videos of some of the girls they captured. When he got popped, the search didn't turn them up. He told his lawyer where they were. The lawyer kept quiet, so his girlfriend got to cop to light time in exchange for her testimony against him. If the cops had found those tapes first, she'd have been buried as deep as he is."

"That might be the scenario, but it doesn't narrow things down much."

"I'm sure it's a man-woman team. Not two men, like the Hillside Stranglings, where those two dirtbags played cop to get girls in their car. It wouldn't work up here."

"I'll buy that. What makes you think it wasn't that guy from Spokane? Robert Lee Yates. He just copped to a whole ton of hooker killings."

"Any of the missing ones on the list?"

"Two."

"Sure! So why would he leave out the others? He made his deal; all the details, plus he showed the cops where a couple of the bodies were buried. Took a life sentence in exchange. What would he have to gain by *not* mentioning some of them? Freak like that, the more kills he can claim, the more letters he's going to get in prison. Better chance some asshole will set up a Web site for him, too."

"Okay. But even if you're right, we've got no starting place to look."

"You might. You already have the lists of men who were released. Go back and check, see which of them ended up marrying a woman who met them through some kind of prison correspondence, or even a prison visiting program."

"That happens a lot."

"Sure. And most of it's straight-up legit. People get together for all kinds of reasons, and some of them are righteous. But what *you're* looking for is any of those women you can't find now."

"I'm not sure I . . ."

"The women, they were the citizens, right? Not the outlaws. So why would *they* go missing?"

"You think . . . ?"

"That the guy you're looking for, he cut her off from her family and friends. That nobody knows where she is. That she's some kind of 'slave' to him by now . . . or she loves the killing, too. And that her family . . . her friends . . . her old job . . . *somebody* would be worried enough about her to have said something. Maybe even gone to the cops, but—"

"If she was an adult, it wouldn't be a missing-person case."

"Yep."

"It's a *real* long shot."

"It is."

"But . . . okay, worth playing. Thanks."

I got up to go.

"Wait. What did you come to see me about?"

"What I just told you."

"That's it?"

"That's it."

"Sit down a minute," Hong said. He lit a cigarette, pushed his gunmetal case over to me.

We smoked in silence for a minute.

"You know what 'Angkat' means in Cambodian?" he finally asked.

"Yeah," I said. "I do. And I know you think you're packing the glass slipper, too."

When I got up to leave then, he didn't say a word.

On my way back, I found the blues program on KINK-FM. Otis Rush was the featured artist. "You Know My Love." I wondered if anybody did.

Gem and I watched a bull-chested raven float down onto the flat top of a mailbox, then calmly drop whatever he'd been carrying in his beak to his personal chopping block and go to work. When he was finished, he left the table. In a few minutes, another raven took his place, with his own score. Word gets around.

"We went for a long drive down the coast," Gem said. "We packed a picnic dinner, because we wanted to sit on the seawall at midnight where we first met. To celebrate our anniversary. We were in that car," she said, nodding toward the Corvette. "I remember setting the trip odometer, because Gordo was curious as to what kind of mileage the car gets, now that he's worked on the engine. We got back to the loft around four in the morning. We made love. Twice. Then I took a bath while you watched TV. I will have the shows taped for you to watch when . . . later. You took a shower while I made us an early breakfast. You had a three-egg omelet, with mushrooms, onions, and roast pork. I had waffles, with ice cream. All the ingredients for these are in the loft. I will prepare the dishes. I will eat some of the food, and make sure the rest is disposed of. If you are there when the police come, then you never left. If you are not, you went out just before they arrived. I do not know where you were going, or when you will be back."

The ocean was an angry slate. The winds were cross-gusting. I watched a hovering gull briefly resist, flapping its wings hard for stability before straightening them out and just going with it, riding the vector.

"Perfect," I said, trying for the same path I'd just witnessed.

"Oh no; it's not," she said sadly. "It is not perfect at all."

Gem dropped me off about a mile from the truck stop. I made my way through an open field, carrying my gear. Found my lurking place, and hunkered down to do what I do best.

It was almost eleven before the semi rolled in. Couldn't miss it; big silver rig with the drug company's logo covering the length of the trailer.

I watched the driver get out and head for the truck stop. He'd left his engine running—they pretty much all do if they aren't going to sleep, and the word was that all his route permitted at this stage was a meal break.

Between SueEllen inside the diner and Ann slutted up somewhere in the shadows, we had him bracketed—provided he hadn't already made a CB appointment with one of the lot lizards. I saw a couple of them strolling halfheartedly, so I figured most of the business was prearranged over the air. The rich lady's info had been perfect, but it didn't drop all the way down to the identity of the individual driver, much less his sex habits.

One time I never want a smoke is when I'm waiting. Too many men are doing time for that. Too many dead, too. I let part of my mind go to a safe place, opened my sensors to full alert. Another mistake amateurs make is to assume watchers don't get watched.

Every time the door swung open from the inside, I was on it. No need for night glasses. They kept the parking lot dark, but the diner was bathed in floodlights, making it look like an oasis in a desert of darkness. I guess that was the idea.

When I saw SueEllen come out, long red hair swinging, her left hand on the right arm of a big guy in a blue windbreaker and matching cap, I knew it was a go—I just didn't know exactly what the mark had gone *for.*

"My husband will whip my ass *big*-time, he ever finds out where I was tonight," SueEllen said, giggling, as they passed by where I'd moved to . . . a pool of shadow between a pair of parked trucks. She made the prospect sound like fun.

"How's he gonna find out?" the guy with her asked. "You said he works nights."

"Well, my girlfriend—remember, the one I told you came with me?—she's got a mouth on her."

"But she's doing the same thing you are, right?"

"Sure, baby. That's right. But she's kind of . . . well, she's not exactly *skinny,* if you get my drift. So maybe she won't get as lucky as I did. Just remember, this has got to be *quick,* okay? Next time you're back this way, you let me know in advance, and I'll . . ."

"You never gave me your number."

"Oh, I *will,* honey. But there's something else I want to give you first. . . ."

"My rig's right over there. You sure you don't want to get a room? They have some nice—"

"No *way,* baby! Every time I see one of those *huge* trucks thunder by, I wonder what it would be like to do it right inside the cab. You said there was a . . . sleeper thing?"

"Sure," he said, proudly. "Wait'll you see how it's all fixed up."

I stepped out of the shadows, the dark stocking mask pulled down, the watch cap concealing my hair. And the sawed-off shotgun riveting his eyes.

"Put your hands up," I said. "*Very* quiet. If there's even a *little* noise from you, there's going to be a *big* fucking noise from this, understand?"

SueEllen and the driver raised their hands.

"You!" I said to SueEllen. "Drop your purse."

She did it.

"Kick it over to me. *Careful,*" I hissed.

She did that, too.

"Now turn around," I said. "Just the bitch," I told the driver, when he started to do the same thing.

"Lady," I said. "Pull your pants down."

"I'm not—"

"Now!" I soft-barked at her. "I'm not fucking around."

The sound of her zipper was clear in the darkness. The truck driver could barely keep himself from turning his head.

"*All* your pants, lady. Down to your ankles."

"You sick motherfucker . . ." SueEllen muttered, even as she was doing what she was told.

"Good. Now take off those boots. And the pants. Quick!"

She did it, making below-audible sounds.

"Travis, you there?" I called softly.

Three distinct raps on the side of the trailer SueEllen was facing answered me.

"Pick up her pants and boots. Find someplace to throw them away. She's not going to be running anywhere real soon without them. And when she finds them, I don't think she's going to the cops, either, are you, lady?"

"No!" SueEllen hissed at me.

"I didn't think so. Your husband might not understand, huh? Now, you," I said to the driver, "open up your cab."

"I don't keep no money in the—"

"Friend, this isn't about money. Me and Travis, we broke out three days ago. We've been hiding out around here ever since. What we need is a ride out, understand? Now, Travis, he says he can drive a big rig. But, me, I got my doubts. So you're going to be the chauffeur, understand?"

"I . . ."

"A *ride,* pal. That's all. We don't need to make this a murder rap. You can't see what I look like, and Travis's going to be behind you . . . in that sleeper . . . all the way. You get us to where we need to go, we jump out, you keep driving. Far as we're concerned, you can tell the cops the truth after that—we'll be over the border."

"The border? I'm not set up for—"

"Yeah, you are, pal. You don't have to make the crossing into Canada. All we need to do is get close. The rest of the way, we go on foot, get it? Now, let's go. Either you be the chauffeur, or we find out if Travis can really drive. Your choice."

I had him open the cab, turn his head to face me as Ann climbed inside and got in back. I let him get in from the passenger side, the scattergun so close he never even thought about doing anything but obeying, me right behind.

We pulled out of the parking lot and headed north.

"Your name's Norman?" I asked the driver, glancing at his license. I'd made him hand over his wallet, but hadn't touched the bills inside. "What do your friends call you? Norm?"

"Hoss, my friends call me Hoss."

"Used to play some ball, huh?"

"In high school," he said modestly. "Defensive end."

"Uh," I said, thinking of Pop, "must have been brutal."

"It wasn't so bad."

"Neither is this, Hoss. I promise you. Just keep this rig rolling, don't be silly with the lights, you know the deal."

"I got you. Don't worry."

"We're not worried. Are we, Travis?"

For answer, Ann stuck the tip of a hunting knife just behind the driver's ear, then flicked the lobe.

He shuddered.

I shared a sympathetic look with him. "That's right, partner. Be glad it's me holding this shotgun and not Travis. He is one stone-crazy psycho motherfucker."

We were gone almost an hour when the CB crackled with the news that any trucker in the area could go pedal-to-metal without worrying about the law. Seems the troopers were all converging on the spot where some drunken lunatic was driving a bulldozer right through some little town. I mean *through* the town. Had the 'dozer all covered up in sheet metal, like a damn tank, one of them said. And the driver was armed. Kept shooting out windows and stuff like that, too.

"Kee-rist!" Hoss said. "Some people."

"That's the truth," I agreed.

The roads were near-empty. A light rain came and went. And the big rig motored right on through, just a tad over the limit. Hoss and I talked about football, women, and prison. . . . He was real interested in prison.

I gentled him down, working the job. When you need people to do as you tell them, you need to induce a little fear. But you have to avoid panic at all costs. If you're going to be with them for a while—like if you're waiting for the banks to open in the morning so they can make that phone call you want—the sooner Stockholm Syndrome sets in, the better. You handle it right and they start to see you as a friend, not a hostage-taker.

Just like I was taught, I thought to myself, thinking about hijackings I'd pulled with my own family. Next to those, this was a cakewalk. I felt my people with me, heard the Prof in my mind: "You want to walk that track, you better know where the third rail is, Schoolboy."

When we got close, I had to give him step-by-step directions, but he handled the semi like a maestro, never missing a beat.

Somewhere in the darkness, a rich woman was watching. A rich woman with a cell phone. When we got within sight of the warehouse, I could see the door was wide open.

Hoss pulled in. Killed the motor.

"Okay, partner," I told him. "Hands on the wheel. I'm going to cuff you there. By daylight, someone will be here to open up."

"But we're not that close to Canada," he said, sounding almost disappointed.

"No. That was kind of a scam, Hoss. We've got friends waiting. Right outside. In a few minutes, we'll be gone. *Ka-poof!* Let's see, it's almost four in the morning. By the time they get you loose, we'll have three hours. More than enough. Come on, now, let's get it done."

He put his hands on the wheel. I worked the cuffs one-handed until I had him locked.

"Look straight ahead," I told him as Ann slithered out of the cab. "You know better than to yell, right? I mean, I don't have to gag you or nothing?"

"No," he said, shaking a little.

"Re*lax,* Hoss. If I wanted you dead, I would have let Travis go to work with his blade as soon as we had you cuffed."

I jumped down from the cab, leaving him alone.

We let a few minutes pass, just to be sure Hoss was going to play his role. Then we let him hear some car doors slam, people moving around. . . .

I popped back into the cab. "Okay, partner, we're ready to split. Your smokes are right here. Be a little tricky, but you can reach them all right. Just flick the butts out the window when you're done. Don't worry, the floor's all been swept—they'll just burn themselves out. I can't offer you much to pass the time. Sorry I had to disable the CB, but you want the radio on? It won't run the battery down that much."

"Yeah. Please."

"All right, Hoss. You've been a man about all this. Now that my boys are here, I'm not broke anymore. I'd like to show my appreciation."

"You don't have to . . ."

"I know. I was thinking, maybe you could use an extra ten grand," I said, bringing closure to the job the way I'd been trained, by cementing the bond. When you make the victim a beneficiary, it may cost you a little cash . . . but it costs the cops a witness. "But I can't just stick it in your wallet," I told him. "The cops look at all that, they might think you were in on this. Maybe I could stash it somewhere in the cab for you?"

He didn't answer, but his expression told me everything I needed to know.

"All right. Now, I *could* just have it mailed to the address on your license," I said, "but, for all I know, your wife . . . Ah, look, never mind. I wasn't trying to insult you. I got ten thousand, right here," I said, holding up the thick wad of hundreds so he could see them. "I can mail it to your address, plain brown wrapper . . . or even mail it someplace else, if you want. Your call, Hoss."

He was quiet for a minute. Then he gave me an address. A different one than was on his license.

"Okay," I said, shaking his cuffed hand to seal the bargain. "Now, how about a cold one?"

"A beer?"

"Sure. The boys brought a cooler-full. Been a few years since I had one, but there's plenty to go around."

"I wouldn't mind that at all."

"Wait here," I told him.

When I got back with an ice-cold bottle of Bud, he was real grateful. I even held it for him as he gulped it down.

He was out in ten minutes.

I walked past what seemed like dozens of people unloading the truck and transferring the cargo to all kinds of different vehicles. A couple of women ran around with handheld bar-code scanners and clipboards. A lot more folks than I'd expected. And a lot more efficient, too.

I found the anonymous little Neon out back, where they'd promised me it would be.

Clipper was standing next to it. "You did a great thing," he told me. "This load, it's going to change the lives of—"

"If the meet doesn't go down, and Rosebud isn't where you say she is, Big A's going to be an orphan," I told him.

I drove myself to downtown Portland. Found a legal spot. Walked for a lot of blocks through the Northwest sector, stopping to throw the Neon's ignition key into a Dumpster.

The streets were crawling with bottom-feeders, looking for carrion. None of them bothered me. Smart fucking move.

I was in bed with my alibi before six.

Sometimes after a job, the fear-jolts that kept me alert while I was working keep dancing around inside me for a while. They have to work their way to the surface, and it looks like I've got the shakes, bad.

Didn't happen this time. I didn't feel anything.

When I woke up, it was mid-afternoon. Gem was standing over the bed, looking down at me.

"Why did you go to see Henry?" she demanded.

"Not for the same reason you do," I said.

I didn't even try to block her slap. In a few minutes, I heard the door slam.

I watched the tapes Gem had made for me. Old movies, off cable. She probably figured I'd seen them before, give me a little edge. I hadn't, so I watched them close.

Then I waited for night. My time, since I'd been a little kid. A scared little kid, just learning to prey.

I needed another pistol. And I didn't want to ask Gem to paper me through again.

As I walked into the kitchen to see if there was anything ready-made to eat, I saw several perfectly aligned stacks of paper on the table. Gem's work. From the computer runs, using the newly narrowed criteria she'd asked me for. I picked up a stack, being careful not to mess up the others, and brought it over to the easy chair.

By the time it was prowler's-dark out, I knew I'd been right.

"I'm done," I told Ann, holding the cellular a little bit away from my ear. "I told you where to leave . . . what you owe me."

"I know," she said. "That's not what this is about. There's something I want to give you."

"Already had it. Thanks anyway."

"It won't work, B.B. That icy act isn't getting over. And I'm not playing. I have something I know you need. I'm leaving. You can meet me and get what I've got before I go, or you can just buzz me off, it's your choice."

"I'll meet you," I said, playing out the string.

"Good," she said. And gave me a street corner and a time.

The Subaru glided to the curb. Before I could open the passenger door, Ann bounced out, dressed in a gray sweatshirt that went almost to her knees. "You drive," she said.

I got behind the wheel. "It's got real good traction," she told me. "Hard to spin the tires even in the wet. Try it."

I mashed the throttle. Even on the slick streets, the Subaru felt solid under me. Ann gave me directions as I drove. The steering was nicely weighted, the brake pedal a little mushy for my taste, but the binders worked really fine.

"I never drove one before," I told her. "Are they all like this?"

"Almost. This is a '97, the last year they made them. I had it all redone, to get it looking like I wanted. They changed a few other things—gas shocks, bigger brakes, wheels, and tires. Even 'freed up' the engine, whatever *that* is."

"I wonder why they didn't sell a million of these."

"I don't know. Maybe the kind of people who buy Subarus didn't want all the luxury stuff. And the people who buy luxury stuff didn't want Subarus . . . ?"

"And what do *you* want?" I finally asked her.

"Just to tell you a few things. Things you need to know."

"Like what?"

"Like the driver—Hoss—is fine. He woke up in Battleground—that's in Washington, north of Vancouver. The company doesn't think he was in on it, not at all. The cops cleared him completely. They figure it was a professional job all right, but that the hijackers thought they were getting something else. Like taking down an armored car and finding it empty. They had a pretty fine laugh over it."

"Good."

"It may interest you to know that Hoss described you as a black man."

"No. I figured he'd turn out to be a class act."

"Yeah. Only SueEllen isn't saying the same thing about you."

"What's her problem?"

"You know what her problem is, B.B. Did you have to make her . . . do that?"

"I had to do *something* to make Hoss cooperate without thinking he was going to get murdered at the end of the run. The way I did it, he saw I wasn't going to be killing people just to keep them quiet. And if SueEllen *really* had to run around looking for her pants in the dark, that would have given us plenty of time to get in the wind, especially with the back roads you had mapped out. It was simple and quick. Hoss never would have bought it if I told 'Travis' to tie her up and leave her somewhere. And it would have scared him a lot more than I wanted him to be."

"Well, if I was you, I wouldn't be stopping by SueEllen's trailer anytime soon."

"I don't want to see any of you, ever again."

"Except Clipper."

"Not him, either."

"So that last threat you made to him—"

"That wasn't a threat. We had a deal. I kept my end. I was just telling him he better keep his."

"It sure sounded like a threat to me."

"Cherish the thought," I told her.

"Here we are," she said, a few minutes later. "Pull in there."

I'd recognized the signs for the last few minutes. We were in that same place, on the riverfront in Milwaukie. I backed the Subaru in.

"What's wrong?" she asked.

"I don't like it here. Too much foliage. Anyone could just come up on you and—"

"Then let's get out, talk outside. How's that?"

"Okay," I said, wanting to hear the rest of whatever she had.

We climbed out. Ann put both palms on the Subaru's front fender and hopped up, posing the way she had when we'd first met.

"What else?" I asked her.

"One, the girl *is* with Clipper and Big A. She's been there almost from the beginning."

"If he turns her over like he—"

"B.B., just listen, all right? I think her father did something to her."

"I know he did."

"But she still loves him."

"Sure. I know. That's not so unusual."

"You act like you know all about this."

"It's no act. What else?"

"This car," she said, handing me a scrap of paper, "picked up street girls. A bunch of times."

"So?"

"So . . . I don't know what your whole game is, B.B. I'm not sure why you want the girl . . . the runaway so bad. I don't know who you're really working for, or even what you do. But I know you want . . . something. I saw . . . I mean, I know the way you . . . when that freak cut me. I get this strange idea that maybe you're looking for a killer. The one picking off all the street girls."

"Lots of people get ideas. Don't make more out of me than I am."

"Uh-huh. Okay, here's what I have. You don't want it, throw it away. That piece of paper I gave you? It's a license number. The car picks up girls. And it's a woman who does the asking. A man driving, but a woman making the deal; understand?"

"Yes. But all the girls they picked up, they came back, right?"

"Not all of them. One didn't. She went by Merlot. . . ."

"Like the wine?"

"Yes. And, the way it was figured, she was holding out on her pimp and made a break one night. It happens."

"So the only thing you have is that it was a man-and-woman team—"

"That's *not* all. The license plate . . ."

"What?"

"It showed up a few times. On different cars."

"Oh."

"Yes. Maybe that's nothing by itself, but . . ."

"You're not wrong, Ann."

"So it *is* worth something."

"It could be, anyway."

"This *certainly* is," she said, holding up an envelope.

"Pretty small envelope for a hundred grand."

"That's in the trunk," she said. "In a Delta Airlines bag. Just like you said: all hundreds, used, random serial numbers. This," she told me, waving the envelope, "is the title to the Subaru. I signed it over. You can register it any way you want, but it's yours now."

"I . . ."

"Take it, B.B. I know you don't have a car."

"How could you—?"

"Either you're fabulously wealthy and you've got a whole stable of vehicles . . . which I don't *think* so . . . or you borrow cars all the time. Anyway, where I'm going, I won't be able to use it."

"Why?" I asked, despite myself.

"I told you. It's *all* going to change from here on out. I don't want anything tying me to Ann O. Dyne. She was always a myth. Now she's going to disappear."

"All right."

"Aren't you going to check your money?"

"I know it's there," I said. And knew I was right even as I spoke.

"You ever think about . . . ?"

"What?"

"Making a change, too. Starting a new life. Starting over."

"I can't start over," I told her. "I'm not a myth. I'm me. Forever."

"But people can . . ."

"No, they can't, girl. Not all of them, anyway. Not me, for sure."

"I'll know you if I see you again," she said, getting to her feet. "But you won't know me. Without these," she chuckled, reaching down and hauling the sweatshirt up over her head, "probably nobody would."

"I'd know your eyes," I told her.

She stepped close. "You probably would. You looked there, often enough. Tell me something, B.B. When you were a kid, when you . . . did it outside, how did you do it?"

I took her shoulders, gently turned her around so she was facing away from me. Then I put my hands on her waist and cranked my thumbs forward until she was bending over, her hands on the fender of the Subaru. "Like this," I whispered in her ear. "That way, we could keep watch while we were . . ."

Later, she told me to just take off. By myself. Whoever was waiting on her was close by.

She stood on her toes, gave me a goodbye kiss. "You can find your own way back," she said.

I wondered if that was true.

"What do you want for all this?" Hong asked me, fingering the slip of paper Ann had given me.

"Your throwdown piece," I told him.

"You think this is New York?"

"I think cops are cops."

"Well, I don't carry one," he said, huffily.

"All right."

"You have a drop?" he asked.

The next morning, under the loose cinder block in the corner of the garage Gordo and Flacco used, I found a brand-new Browning Hi Power 9-millimeter. The Mark III, with the non-glare finish, still in the original sealed carton. And two boxes of shells.

Not exactly the most powerful man-stopper on the planet, but a beautiful, expensive weapon. And maybe Hong was trying to send me a message by not going with the same caliber of slug the autopsy team would have pulled out of the black guy who'd tried to smoke Ann in that vacant lot.

I night-swept with the Subaru a few times, the tinted windows clouding anyone's view of who was doing the driving. Maybe it would buy Ann a little more of a head start if people thought she was still around.

I hadn't changed anything about the Subaru, but I'd done one thing to make it mine. The license-plate number Ann had given me was taped to its dash.

"Now." Joel's voice, on the cellular. My watch said it was six-thirty in the morning.

"Where?"

"Just come here. I'll take you."

Joel's car was a green BMW Z3 with a tan canvas top, one of the early ones. He drove aggressively, keeping the little car in its lower gears until the tach asked for mercy. He braked late for corners, occasionally kicking the tail out, but always catching it smoothly. By the time he got to where I recognized a few landmarks, I knew where we were headed.

"She wants the meet where Daisy picks up her letters?"

"Yes. She said you already know about it, but nobody else does. She feels safe there."

"Is that where she spent the night?"

"She spent the night at my house," Joel said, in a "Want to make something out of it?" tone. "Jenn drove her over while it was still dark."

"So Jenn's with her?"

"Yes."

"And Daisy?"

"No. Rose was quite adamant that Daisy *not* be present."

"She's calling the shots."

"Speaking of shots . . ."

"Yeah?"

"I think you better let me hold your gun."

"Why is that?"

"You've made no attempt to conceal that you're armed. I'm concerned it could frighten Rose."

"You know how to use a gun?"

"I . . . no."

"Then I'm keeping it. It's out in the open because I didn't want to hide anything from you. But it's not to scare Rosebud, it's for her protection."

"You think it's that bad?"

"I know it is," I told him.

Jenn and Rosebud were sitting together on the stone wall. They watched us approach, whispering urgently to each other.

"Maida and Zia," I said, greeting them.

I was expecting a smile, hoping for a giggle. Got neither.

"What do you want to tell me?" Rosebud asked. "You already know I'm not going back."

She looked like she was ready to jump off the stone wall and make a run for it any second. And Joel looked ready to try one of his wrestling moves if I made any attempt to stop her. I had to toss one of my aces on the table, quick.

"Rosebud, if I wanted to bring you back, if I didn't respect what you're doing, I could have just grabbed you and been done with it."

"That's pretty big talk," she said. "You've been looking for me for a long time. Lots of people have."

"Lots of people, yes. Me, no. I always knew where you were, Rosebud. I just went through the motions so I could keep your father from doing something real stupid."

"Where was I, then?" she challenged.

"With Clipper and Big A," I said, quietly. And as I said the words, I finally figured out who'd been making the dead drops for Rosebud.

Her mouth made an O, but no sound came out.

"I know why you went to Madison, too," I said, closing in. "And I have the answer you want."

"Madison wouldn't—"

"She didn't," I said. "I put it all together. From the beginning. I know why Kevin is *really* looking for you, too."

Rosebud turned to Jenn, a look of pain on her face so deep I didn't think another human being could ever touch it. But Jenn gathered her in. They rocked together, both of them crying, Jenn saying "I know," and "Daddy can fix this," and a bunch of other stuff I couldn't follow.

Joel stood beside me, as still as the stone wall. And less movable.

The two girls finally turned to face me, holding hands. I didn't bother to ask Rosebud if it was okay to talk in front of the others.

I told her the truth.

When I was done, she looked at Jenn, who nodded agreement.

"It's right here," she said, handing it over.

"You understand what I'm going to trade it for, Rosebud?"

"Yes. How could he *do* that? How could he be a . . . traitor?"

"And that, if it works," I said, ignoring her questions, "you understand you'll never see him a—?"

"Yes! I have to do this. Daisy needs me. Jenn . . . ?"

"Yes," Jenn said. Adding her vote.

"You take Rose back," Joel told his daughter. "Mr. Hazard and I will go see Kevin. It will all be over soon."

"You're not going with me," I told him on the drive back.

"The hell I'm not."

"Listen to me, doc. You got no idea how much respect I have for you. I see the way your kids look at you; I feel so jealous, I can't put it into words. You're a standup man. But I have to do this one alone."

"Why?"

"Because I made the girl a promise. And I'm going to keep it."

"I'm not follow—"

"How much more do you want me to say? If Kevin goes for the deal, Rosebud will never see him again, right?"

"Right."

"But if he *doesn't* go for the deal, she *still* won't," I said; soft and slow, so he'd understand what I was telling him. "You want to be in on that?"

"I've got her," I told Kevin on the phone.

"Oh God, that's *great!* When can you—?"

"Tomorrow morning, maybe. If you can guarantee your wife and Daisy are out of the—"

"No problem! She's going to drop Daisy at camp and then she'll be—"

"—gone by seven-thirty?"

"Absolutely!"

"See you then. Leave your garage door open. We'll come to your office."

"Okay, okay, sure. Do I have to—?"

I hung up on him.

"What are you going to do?" Gem asked me that night. "Now that you know you were correct about him."

"Depends on him."

"Does that mean . . . ?"

"Yeah."

"Burke . . ."

"I'm doing it, Gem."

"Can you not trust me anymore?"

"Trust? Sure. Hell, I trust *everyone*. If I have to do it, I'll be using this," I said, taking out the pistol Hong had left me. "And if your boyfriend Pearl Harbored me, if this piece is hot, I'm fucked." I didn't bother to mention that I'd test-fired it, just to make sure Hong hadn't given me a bunch of blanks.

She got to her feet, the anger gone from her face. "He is not my . . . boyfriend. I said you were my husband long ago. I meant that."

"But the past can become the future."

"Yes. You understand. But it was not a threat. And it was not about Henry. It was about you. Your past. Your future. I know how you hate it here."

"I don't hate it here. It's kind of nice, actually. Portland's, what, a tenth the size of New York? But it's got more blues bars, and . . ."

"But even that. It is not really *your* music, is it?"

"The blues? Honeygirl, I was born to the—"

"No. I don't mean the . . . feeling. Remember the music you told me all about. Doo-wop, yes?"

"That's right. The Brooklyn Blues, sure."

"New York music."

"I . . . guess it is. When I think of blues, I think of Chicago. Or Detroit. Or even the Delta. But I grew up with *a capella* sounds in the subway tunnels, on the street corners, in the shower rooms of the institutions—it was everywhere."

"And it is not here."

"Ah, it's not much of anywhere, anymore. And the weather's better here. The people are the same, but I'd have to change planets to fix that."

"So it is your family."

"That's it, Gem. My family. I . . . I need to be there with them. Not next door or anything. I don't have to see them every day. But I've got no . . . life here. I'm not a dentist or a lawyer. I can't get an Oregon license for what I do."

"I know all this."

"When I finish with Kevin, I'm going back home," I said.

"I know that, too. I have known for a while. And I shall go with—"

"No. No, Gem. Not yet. I don't know how it's going to be, a man who's supposed to be dead, coming back."

"It does not—"

"It matters to me. And that's not the whole of it. I . . . I don't know if I want to be with . . . anyone."

"I see."

"And I think there are things you need to—"

"Don't put any of this on me, Burke."

"Fair enough."

"I will not wait for you forever. There is always another border for me to cross."

"I don't want you to wait at all."

"Yes, you do," she said.

There was no way to tap Kevin's phone. And even if I could, he had access to too many of them. But I was in his neighborhood at four-thirty the next morning. As I drove by, I spotted Clipper's red Durango and pulled next to it.

"We've been in place since you called last night," he said. "Rotating shifts. Nobody's been to the house. No cars, no cabs, nobody on foot. Nothing."

"Thanks."

"We're all with Rose," Big A said.

"I've got it from here," I told them. "Don't come back."

I was behind the house before five. If anyone else showed up, I'd know. And I'd had Clipper's crew in place half an hour before I'd called Kevin. Not perfect, but the best I could manage.

In Portland, anyway.

I watched the mother's Mercedes sedan pull out at seven-twenty. Good enough. I made my move through the backyards, quick and flitty, now that it was light. Found the Subaru where I'd left it, got in. I made a couple of quick passes before I pulled up just past the driveway and reversed my way into the garage.

He was standing in the open door, one hand on the jamb. I couldn't see that close, but I knew his knuckles would be white.

I got out just as he sent the garage door down. I went behind the Subaru and came toward him.

"Where's—?"

"I've got what you really want," I told him, holding up the leather-bound notebook Rosebud had given me.

He went into shock. More than enough time for me to get the Browning pointed at him. That worked better than smelling salts.

"No!" he shouted. "I can—"

"Keep your voice down," I said. "This is just in case you've got any friends with you."

"I *told* you. I'm alone."

"Let's go into your office."

He turned and started up the stairs, glancing back over his shoulder. Not at the pistol, at the notebook. I could have walked him through the house at gunpoint, made sure he really was alone. But the risk was too great that I'd get jumped from behind if I did that. I'd rather keep the high ground, let them come through Kevin if they wanted me.

"Sit down," I told him, pointing to a chair with its back to one side of the door. I took a seat, too, facing the opening.

"Look, whatever you—"

"I'll tell you what I want. And it'll be very simple for you, Kevin. A man like you, you already made all your choices. A long time ago."

He looked down at the floor. "How did you . . . ?"

"You weren't careful about the money, Kevin. You figured you were working for Uncle Sam, who was going to bother you about unreported income, right?"

"They said—"

"They'll say anything, Kevin. You should know that, better than most."

"But they promised—"

"Sure. Your daughter went missing. And not for any of the usual reasons. You wanted her back. Bad. You wouldn't have come to a man like me if you much cared how it got done, either. But I misjudged you, Kevin. I thought it was all about . . . something else."

"I don't—"

"I thought you'd been fucking your own daughter, Kevin. And that Daisy was next."

He didn't get angry. "I'd never do that," he said, his voice as hollow as his eyes. "I love Buddy. She knows I love her. I never really had a . . . friend. That's why . . . I mean, she *was* my buddy. I would *never* violate her. She knows that."

"You violated her trust. You raised her in your image, not in your truth. So your own daughter thinks you're a traitor."

"No! I'm not. I had no—"

"You had choices, Kevin. You were in the underground. I don't know what went on back then, but I'm guessing you did something pretty heavy. And that the G-men popped you for it."

"I was with the—"

"I don't care," I told him, truthfully. "Maybe you set a bomb to make a statement and it made jelly out of some janitor. Maybe you stood watch outside a bank while a cop got gunned down. Maybe you smuggled a pistol into a prison and people got killed. Maybe . . . What difference does it make? They popped you, and you rolled over on your—what is it that you called them then?—comrades? What's the big deal, anyway? Pretty standard for you people. Didn't Timothy Leary turn in the same people who busted him out of prison?"

"It was a long time ago. You don't understand. That was before Buddy was even—"

"A long time ago, sure. And you were scared. I can understand that. You weren't raised to be a criminal. Turning informant, I'll bet they even convinced you it was the right thing to do."

"It *was.*"

"Yeah. I know. Only, after a while, you got to like it, didn't you?"

"No!"

"Sure you did, Kevin. You've been 'underground' for almost thirty years. Your old network, they can count on you. And you could count on them to spread the word. You were smooth, I give you that. At first, I thought I could just match up the money with the news of one of them getting arrested all out of the blue. You know, one of them that had been underground themselves for all these years. Married. Kids, job, community. A new life. And then it all explodes. Or, sometimes, for no obvious reason, they just 'decide' to come in out of the cold. As if they didn't know the feds were breathing down their necks. But your checkbook didn't prove that one out.

"That's when I snapped to it. You're weren't getting rewards for ratting out your old friends, Kevin. You probably fingered all of *them* a long time ago. No, you were on the payroll. Bringing in new clients all the time. Word-of-mouth is the best advertising of all. That's why all the left-wing stuff; that's why you keep up the image. All camouflage. You would have been fine, except that your daughter, she *believed* it all. She bought your line. Because she loved you. Her daddy could do no wrong."

"Why are you—?"

"You got what you raised, you pathetic motherfucker. A beautiful, intelligent, caring young woman. All she wants to do is change the world, make it a better place. The way her daddy took such risks to do. You told her all your old war stories, didn't you?"

"I . . ."

"Yeah. Well, you did a good job. Such a good job that, when she found out what you were doing, you know what she did?"

"What?" he said, voice breaking.

"She went to an expert in Multiple Personality Disorder. A *real* expert, you understand. Someone who'd been there herself. Because, the way that pure-hearted daughter of yours had it figured, her father could never be a traitor. It *had* to be that you were a multiple. Like an evil twin, you know?"

"Maybe I . . . I mean, part of me always—"

"Save it. Christ, you're a slimy maggot, aren't you? Right to the end."

"What are you going to do?"

"Me? Nothing. It's what *you're* going to do, Kevin."

"I don't under—"

"Shut up. I'll tell you when to talk. How much of this does your wife know?"

"Mo was . . . there with us. At the beginning."

"Yeah. That's the way it scanned to me, too. Good. Makes it easier. What you're going to do is this, Kevin: you're going to sign some papers that make Rosebud an emancipated minor."

"A . . . what?"

"And some more papers," I went on, "that give custody of Daisy to Dr. Dryslan and his wife."

"Daisy?! What are you—?"

"It won't matter to you, Kevin. You're never going to see either of them again. Because I'm going to give you something you never gave the poor bastards who trusted you all these years. A head start."

"Please. Can't you under—?"

"Kevin, it *all* happens. And right now. You're going to sign these papers," I said, taking them out of my inside pocket. "They're all back-dated. Notarized. And tonight, while you're packing, you can tell your wife she signed them, too. Forging *her* signature wasn't much work," I said. Thinking, even as I spoke, about how much I had counted on Gem for all this.

"Packing . . . ?"

"You can take all your money. Even your car, if you're fool enough. But not the house—you're signing that over to Rosebud, so she can sell it and have enough to take care of Daisy until they're both out of school. You can tell your handlers that now it's time to see if the Witness Protection Program *really* works. Or you can try the underground for real; it's up to you. And, Kevin . . ."

"I've still got friends in the—" he muttered.

"They were never your friends," I cut him off. "You think, because they were willing to put a couple of men in the street looking for your daughter, they were *with* you? Don't make it worse. You send your tame G-men after me, somebody may get dead. Might be them. Might be me. But you do that, no matter how it comes out, you are for damn sure dead. Play it wrong now, and every single man, woman, and child you've fucked with your games all these years will know the truth. It's all ready to go. Newspaper ads, the Internet, fax chains, word-of-mouth . . . everything. You'll be hunted down the same way they were . . . only the hunters won't be carrying badges. You wouldn't even be safe in prison.

"But do it right, you can just disappear. People will wonder, but so what? Besides, your wife will want it this way. You'll still have a nice, luxurious life."

"You don't know her. You can't judge—"

"If you're still here tomorrow night, Kevin, it won't be me doing the judging."

"Can you tell Buddy . . . ?"

"What?" I asked him, despite myself.

"Tell her I always loved her," he said, sobbing, trying to manage his own pain the same way he'd manufactured it. "Tell her I understand what she did. Tell her I'm proud of her. Tell her to take care of Daisy. Tell her she did the right thing."

"She still loves you, Kevin. She'd rather you were on the run than dead."

"I'm . . ."

"Kevin, listen good. Me, I don't care if you live or die. I think you know that. But I know a checkout promise when I hear one. Don't do it. If you go to ground—and you sure know how to do *that*—you'll still be able to see Buddy. Not a visit, but you can . . . watch from afar, you understand? Watch over your kid. You do that, I promise I'll tell her what you said. Fair enough?"

"Yes," he said, sniffling.

"Here's your blood diary," I said, tossing it at him. "And, yeah, I've got a few copies. You keep your deal, and no one will ever see them. Understand?"

"Yes."

"Kevin, this is simple. Yes or no. Live or die. Tomorrow night, you be fucking *gone*."

It took four days for me to make sure Kevin had done it all. That he was really gone for good.

Twenty-four hours after that, so was I.

AN EXCERPT FROM

ONLY CHILD

BY ANDREW VACHSS

The men on the door did their job, like always. But they hadn't bothered with the threat displays since that first time.

Mama was at the front, by her register, staying close to the only altar she truly worshipped at. And making sure any stray customers who wandered in got the message that they didn't want to eat there. She and the tureen of soup arrived at my booth at the same time.

"Damn! This is extra good tonight, Mama. You put something different in it?"

"Always something different," she said. "Not good last time?"

"No," I said, laboring. "It was superb the last time. It is never *less* than superb. This time, it was even superior to your usual standard, that's all."

"Huh! So—want more, yes?"

The soup was so hot it burned my mouth. My big mouth.

I was deep into my meal of braised beef and bok choy when Mama dropped it on me. "While you . . . gone, people still call, okay?"

"Okay."

"Not like, all right, okay. Okay, like, you understand, okay?"

"Okay."

Her eyes were black olives. I took the double-barreled scrutiny; looked back, blandly.

"Sometime, people owe money, want to pay. Sometime, want *time* to pay, okay?"

"Sure."

"Sometime," she went on, ignoring me, "want work done, okay?"

"Yeah. What did you tell them?"

"Mr. Burke not here, okay? You call back, okay?" she parroted in her best Chinese-laundry voice.

"You had a long time to be saying that."

"So sorry," she said, in the same voice. "You maybe try again, okay?"

"I get it. But most of the people I deal with, they'd want whatever they wanted right then."

"Too bad, so sad," Mama said, her voice a perfect imitation of her granddaughter Flower. "Oh well."

"So, after a while, the whispers die down. And people stop calling. Is that what you're telling me?"

"New people, stop call. Old people, not same. You understand?"

I nodded to tell her I did. Sure. Made perfect sense. My name had been in the street a long time. Someone coming up on it for the first time, if they needed what I was known for, they'd give a call, take a shot. If they kept getting sloughed by Mama, they'd give it up, go elsewhere. But *old* customers, they'd keep trying.

Like old enemies.

"Sometime, *big* job," Mama said.

I nodded again, not questioning how she could tell all that from a few words whispered into a pay phone—Mama could smell a dollar bill in a slaughterhouse.

"So! Big job, old customer, get different story, okay?"

"What story?"

"Story like I tell you before, okay? Burke not here. *Long* time. Not in country. Special thing. But somebody else do job."

"Who'd you send them to?" I asked, frankly curious.

"No, no. Not send away. Tell to wait. Can't wait? So, okay, I not know anything about Burke business. But *now* job come in, you do; like say before, okay?"

"You mean, be my own . . . brother, or whatever?"

"Not look so much like you," she talked through what I was saying. A train on tracks, rolling. "Little bit, maybe. But same voice. Just like talk to Burke, talk to brother."

"All that for what, Mama?"

"Money," she said, black eyes glowing like a Geiger counter near a rich vein. "Big, big money."

"The snakeheads?"

"Not now," she said. "Snakeheads all the time come. This business, come only once, okay?"

Three nights after my meeting with Mama, I nudged the Plymouth through the still-thick Manhattan traffic, taking my time. This was a quicker contact than I'd expected. When Mama told me who was playing, I'd been sure they'd use foot soldiers to screen me before going face-to-face.

The upper roadway of the Fifty-ninth Street Bridge took me past the luxo highrises on my right as I crossed the river, into another country.

I found the adult-video store wedged into a concrete triangle under the bridge extension on the other side, just before where Queens Boulevard starts its long run through the borough. The store's back was crammed up against a no-star hotel. A long-abandoned gas station made up the third leg of the triangle.

They'd told me I could leave my car at the gas station, but I didn't like that option much. I turned left, up Skillman Avenue, and motored along, watchful. When I saw the white rag dangling from the door handle of an old brown Buick sedan, I flicked the lever into neutral and blipped the throttle.

It was as if the Plymouth's deep-chested snarl had knocked on the Buick's door. I caught a brief glimpse of Asian faces, at least four of them. I pulled up a few lengths, made a U-turn, and waited as the Buick maneuvered out of its spot. Soon as it left, I parallel-parked into the space they'd vacated. I settled in carefully, cranking the wheel full-lock to make sure I could blast straight out if it came to that. I wasn't worried about the decrepit station wagon parked in front of me—it would stay there until the boys in the Chinatown war wagon came back to collect it sometime tomorrow.

I still had a forty-five-minute cushion, so I did a last-minute check to make sure I had everything I needed for the meet. Which was nothing.

Then I took a walk. Up Skillman to Thirty-sixth Street, then a right to Queens Boulevard, across from the old Aviation High School. I glanced at my watch. Still early. I strolled back down toward the triangle, relaxed.

And thinking about Mama. "It don't take no crystal ball, son," the Prof had concluded. "Mama don't want the whole pot. She must have got word, her one chip ain't making this trip."

Maybe. And maybe all the money this meet promised made it worth her while to wait.

At least I was done with trekking out to Long Island all the damn time.

The porno shop was fortified as if some sleazy alchemist inside had turned gash into gold. Gun-turret windows in a slab-faced cinderblock front, the flatness broken only by a pale-blue door behind a set of bars that wouldn't have looked out of place in San Quentin. Red neon, twisted into the usual promises, glowed reptile-cold.

A pair of cross-angled cameras in weatherproof boxes were mounted at the top of the door, as subtle as a handgun pressed against your temple. I pushed the buzzer, waited, my back to the street.

The door was opened by a tall, skinny guy with a hollow-cheeked face. The forehead above the orange sunglasses he wore was an acne graveyard. In the sullen light from overhead, his crooked teeth looked like an ad for nicotine.

I stared into his mirrored lenses until he stepped aside.

The interior decorator's palette had been limited to gray and yellow. A few old posters on the walls, some half-empty video racks, one wall of limp magazines. Not a DVD in sight. No private booths, no lingerie shows. The joint was as erotic as a used condom floating on an oil slick.

The cadaverous-looking guy went back to whatever he'd been doing. I browsed through the racks, playing the role. Ignoring the two other men in the place, but not before I absorbed that they were both wearing the latest in *Sopranos*-chic.

Time passed. No new customers. I didn't look at my watch. I'd gotten there on time, and I was working flat-rate.

Finally, they glided up, one on my left, the other somewhere behind me. I kept my focus on the greasy pictures, letting the sense impressions flood in. Textures and colors. Sharp tang of too much cologne. They never touched me, just air-cushion-herded me toward the back of the store.

Nothing too fancy in the back, just a long rack on rollers, with a door behind it. A door with no knob. A hand came into my field of vision. Two-knuckle rap. A panel slid up in the door, revealing a Plexiglas window. Maybe fifteen seconds passed. The panel slid down. The door opened. I stepped inside.

The only thing in sight was a flight of stairs, going down. "Uh-huh," a voice behind me said.

At the bottom of the stairs, a man in a white lab coat pointed at a long bare workbench. I walked over there.

One of the men stepped close. He was a muscular guy, a couple of inches shorter than me, with longish, heavily gelled black hair. He made eye contact: communicating, not challenging. I opened the channel, waited for his next move.

He held one finger to his lips, making sure I got it. Then he unbuttoned the overtailored jacket to his onyx suit, carefully took it off, and draped it on the workbench. I took off my own jacket with a little less ceremony, placed it on the bench the same way he'd done.

By the time we finished, we were facing each other in our shorts and socks. Without his shoes, he was much shorter than he'd been before. His body was nicely cut and defined, but I had better scars.

The guy in the white lab coat started working on my clothes with some kind of wand.

The guy facing me held his finger to his lips again. I didn't change expression.

It didn't take long.

Then we got dressed.

The next door was much more elaborate; no way you would see it unless you knew it was there. It looked as if the stone wall of the basement had just retracted into itself. I followed the guy in the onyx jacket into a long, narrow room with a low ceiling. Each of the three walls I could see had a separate door, undisguised. In the far corner, two men were seated in padded armchairs. A third chair stood empty, facing them. I walked over until I was standing in front of the empty chair.

"You're Burke," the man to my left said. He was Italian, mid-thirties, darkly handsome, saved from pretty only by a nose that hadn't been perfectly set the last time it had been broken.

I just nodded. It hadn't been a question.

"I'm Giovanni," he said. "And this is Felix."

The man to my right was Latino, maybe a decade older than the Italian. Or maybe a generation; it was hard to tell much in that light. He was lighter-skinned than the Italian, with the face of royalty. Ruthless royalty.

"Sorry about all the . . . precautions," the Italian said. "You understand."

I nodded again.

"Sit down, please," the Latino said.

I caught the briefest flicker in the eyes of the Italian. He wasn't a man who liked being one-upped, not even when it came to class and courtesy. He made a tiny gesture with his right hand. A man came forward, put a fresh pack of cigarettes—same brand as the half-empty pack I'd carried in with me—and a heavy gold lighter on the low table in front of me. A large amber glass ashtray was sitting there, sparkling clean.

"You'll get all your stuff back when you leave," the Italian said. "You want a watch to wear in the meantime?"

"I'm fine, thanks."

"I heard a lot about you," he said. "From a lot of people. For a long time."

"About my brother, you mean."

"Your brother, yeah. But the Chinese lady, she said you were the same."

"Like how?"

"Like you could do the same stuff. The *exact* same stuff. Dealing with you, it would be just like dealing with him. Is that right?"

"Exactly right."

"I have heard much about you as well," the Latino said, offering his hand for me to shake.

I gave him a light-pressure grip. He turned his palm up, holding my hand a second longer than he had to. Long enough to verify the tattoo. "I am sorry for your loss," he said. "To lose one so close to you . . ."

"Thank you," I said, my eyes empty. *Is he playing it straight, buying the "Burke's brother" thing? Or being cute . . . telling me he knows about Pansy?*

"Reason you're here is," the Italian said, "me and Felix, we've got a problem. A problem for both of us, maybe. Or maybe not. That's where you come in."

"I'll tell you where I *don't* come in," I said. "That's between the two of you."

The Latino smiled. "We do not want you to take sides, señor. We want your . . . advice. Your counsel. And, perhaps, your skills."

"Why me?" I asked them both.

"You'll see," the Italian said. "You're a natural for it. And you're getting five large just to listen—like we agreed, right?

• • •